The Grand Turk File

John C Waite

Suspense, intrigue and terror in the Caribbean

The opening of The Grand Turk File, a leisurely description of the Turk and Caicos islands, the setting of the primary action of this novel, lets you know right away that you are in the hands of a competent and confident writer. It does not, however, suggest that you might need to fasten your seatbelt for the wild ride to come, but that might be a good idea. Grand Turk is most definitely a thriller. However, exacting characterization, careful pacing, and good writing make this book much richer than the average thriller.

Self Publishing Reviews

John C. Waite
825 Bayshore Drive
Pensacola FL 32507

https://www.amazon.com/author/johnwaite

www.johncwaite.com

Prologue

From the air, the islands surrounding the Caicos Bank--Grand Caicos, South Caicos, and several smaller cays--seem to merge with the bank itself. So clear is the water that in the lee of the islands where no surf breaks upon the coarse sand, it's difficult to tell where beach and water meet. Conch cruise coral and limestone-sand bottoms, and the banks' reefs crawl with spiny lobster. The rich, clean waters nourish a vast variety of life, and some of the best deep water SCUBA diving in the world is available near Grand Turk, the administrative center of the provincial Turks and Caicos.

The Turks and Caicos nestle within the long archipelago that sweeps from Miami across the Bahamas and Caribbean, halfway between Florida and Puerto Rico. The Caicos form the northern lip of the Caicos Bank with Grand Turk and its lesser cays well to windward.

The islands have little fresh water and little agriculture. Salt ponds, at one time the basis for Grand Turk's only industry, provided quaint names for such establishments as the Saltraker Inn on Grand Turk, and for Salt Cay as well.

For decades, islanders opened small dams to flood shallow ponds. Then damming the ponds, they waited for the equatorial sun to do its work. The sea water evaporated quickly leaving salt crusts behind. But the salt ponds fell victim in the '60s to more efficient means of supplying the world's table salt and today the shallow lagoons lay open to the sea and untended.

Even tourism, the economic mainstay of many Bahamian islands, makes little impact. Tourist accommodations are scarce and expensive. Grand Turk supports a thriving recreational diving conclave but boasts few hotels. And on Provo (Provincial, one of the Caicos), American ultra-rich have established vacation estates that siphon away business from such historic houses as the Meridian Club and the Third Turtle. For a time, Turks & Caicos officialdom all but gave away long-term leases on prime property, stipulating only that homes must be erected on the property within eighteen months, in the hopes of enticing vacation oriented Americans. But the cost of building, where the only natural material available is limestone, prohibited average people from taking advantage of so generous an offer. Thus, names like Vanderbilt and Rockefeller are often topics for happy hour conversation around Provo bars.

But when Jusquevera Segrado de Arreallano wrote his name on the Saltraker Inn ledger on one of the few truly cool days almost no one noticed. It would have meant nothing to most on Grand Turk, except for one expatriate Jamaican. Although the name was held in esteem in some enclaves in Columbia, and with a few, who would relate the name in whispers, no one in the U.S. would find it familiar. Certainly no one in the New Orleans police department was aware of the name.

No one was aware, that is, until a drug snitch included it in a note to a narcotics detective to whom he owed a favor. The snitch, who hung out with a particular couple of street "ho's" heard them making plans to entertain at the behest of one de Arreallano some out-of-town guests; Bahamians who had set up the meeting through a well-known New Orleans pimp.

The name had a certain resonance even when Slats first heard it.

Chapter One

When Slats got the tip, he debated taking it up the chain of command. He did it because he believed that was what Captain Courant would want and the one person in the police hierarchy he had confidence in was Courant.

A confidential informant, code named Skink, had intimated it would be a big bust, but he was mysterious about it. Said it was because what he had heard was mysterious. According to some roustabouts with whom Skink's lady friends occasionally found employment, a South American circus was coming to town.

That, in itself, wasn't particularly unusual. The Ringling Bros circus always drew large crowds when it visited the City that Care Forgot. The fact that this circus was of international origin might be unusual in most places in the U.S., but not in the cosmopolitan New Orleans. In sixty days this Colombian based group would be making its first appearance in The Big Easy.

It wouldn't be using the Super Dome downtown where Ringling Bros usually set up. This circus would be putting a for-real big top up on the Armory Grounds across the River in Gretna, and them moving later to another suburb.

Skink thought it was drugs, probably cocaine, possibly heroin. The score was uncertain. The only thing he was sure of was that a preliminary meeting between an owner of the circus and a well-known local pimp was planned Sunday afternoon at an old apartment house downtown. A lot of money was to be exchanged, and the only thing worth a lot of money these days was coke, or heroin, or meth. Whatever... it was to be worth more than a hundred big ones, that much he knew because his lady friend's roustabout buddy was going to help carry it.

So Capt. Courant listened patiently.

"Skink, huh? He sounds slimy."

Slats had no reply.

"Well, let's head 'em off at the pass."

Courant was fond of old westerns. He had a collection of CDs with every John Wayne western ever made.

"Hit the meeting, if it comes off, and see what you get."

Slats acknowledged with a nod.

"You want me to take a swat team?"

"Don't think you'll need one, but use your best judgment.

Chapter Two

Slats tried to stretch, but the car was too short. Or his legs were too long.

He was hunched over the steering wheel trying to work the kinks out of his back, wishing for some hot coffee and a cigarette. Never mind that he had given up smoking ten years before.

Right now a slurp of Community coffee and a drag on a Pall Mall (God, even one of those Picayunes his Uncle Johnny used to smoke) would be a bit of heaven.

He stared out the windshield.

It had been over a month since the tip, and now the long-expected meeting was to take place. Dominating his view was a white two-story, at least mostly white, shambles of a building about to slide over the curb into Tchopatoulis Street. The ramp to the Greater New Orleans bridge, the Crescent City Connection, in the background added no aesthetics.

The smoky, sweet air of a summer morning not far from the Irish Channel brought back memories of Carnahan's grocery. He could still feel in his nostrils the rank smell of the alley where old produce rotted waiting for the garbage men, its aroma mixed with the odors of alcohol and stale tobacco from Rubio's bar next door, and with the bright wonder of Uncle Johnny's coffee brewing inside the market.

That alley was where Slats had lost his first fight.

Insignificant now, that fight had been the world to him then. His opponent, Boudreaux, had been bigger, heavier, and as Slats learned, just as fast. But Boudreaux was off his turf. He belonged over on the lakefront, not down in the Channel. And he certainly shouldn't have called Uncle Johnny a "Mick."

Slats loved his Uncle Johnny as he thought then only an Irish kid can love. The years since had taught him that such passions, such blood highs, were born as strongly in Cajuns and Creoles, in blacks and high-yellows, in Poles and Serbs, as in the Irish. After the fight, Boudreaux had become a friend, the friend who dubbed him Slats.

Not that he hadn't earned the appellation.

Slats had been a skinny kid. A very skinny kid.

He was so thin that he was able to slip between the slats in the wrought iron fence around the basement at St. Mary's School. It was a girls' school, and behind that fence was the only accessible window to the girls' physical education dressing room. And Slats was the only guy who could breach the barrier. It became his job to report on the girls. What did they look like? What could he see? Was there something awesome between their thighs? How did watching them make him feel?

He was caught, of course.

His punishment was meted out by the Sisters of St. Mary first, and then by his Uncle Johnny. The strapping hurt little compared to the pain brought on by the disdain which his uncle heaped on him. Deep inside Slats knew his uncle was right. Peeping had made him feel guilty.

But it had thrilled him also!

Was it wrong to enjoy being so thrilled?

Slats had outgrown his ability to slip through the fence. But even now he wasn't sure he had outgrown the need for the thrills engendered by surreptitious observation.

Maybe that was part of what he enjoyed about being a detective. He had worked hard to get the job, had spent years as a beat cop cruising the streets downtown and along the channel. He had grabbed every opportunity for schooling and eventually became one of the few college graduates driving an NOPD blue and white.

Observation was always an important part of his job. Usually, he didn't think of it as peeping, but occasionally the sting of his uncle's castigation came back to him. Especially if the investigation involved a woman.

He had once drawn a temporary vice assignment in which he had played "John." He couldn't make the arrest until money had changed hands, and several of the girls had made a real show of stripping for him before asking for payment. Watching the girls had made his heart race and his brow bead with sweat, a reaction he remembered from the times he had knelt on the cool cement as he peered into the girls' locker room window.

One of the prostitutes he had arrested had thrilled him more than he had thought possible. Although very young she exuded pride, a self-assurance that none of the other girls had. She was a dark and beautiful girl. She had a tattoo on her left breast, a symbol of a street sign. He remembered asking her about it.

"Boulevard marks all of his girls that way," she had said.

That was all. She hadn't asked for money. She caressed his hair and started to lead him to the bed.

"Don't you want to get paid," he asked. She didn't reply but stood silently looking at him. He stared back, felt a fiery heat burning in his gut, and heard his uncle's chastising voice.

He quickly identified himself as a police officer, grabbed his clothes and rushed out leaving the door standing open. When he glanced back, she stood nude, framed in the doorway, her head cocked to her left.

He never lost that image. It found its way into his thoughts at the strangest moments; in the midst of a handball game, distracting him as he swung for a kill; often while he completed the daily cop drudge, paperwork. As he sat half drowsing over the last few pages of a nothing workday he would see her staring at him, naked, her head tilted to the left, a quizzical expression lifting the corners of her mouth.

And often as he drifted off to sleep the image became a cornerstone for his dreams. She moved to him, told him to lie down and caressed his shoulders, rubbed deeply along his spine. She rubbed herself against him, the softness of her breasts caressing his skin, her aroma thick about him, almost palpable.

He always awoke before she finished, before he could consummate his fantasy. Every time he awoke erect and perspiring he made a mental note to corner Jerry Marucci, the department psychologist. If he was unbalanced, he wanted to know it!

Didn't he?

But since the fantasy was pleasant, since it harmed no one, since no one, not even his wife, Olivia, was aware of it, his mental notes always erased themselves.

He had been in the car for twelve hours.

He had stretched and shifted, stretched and spread. But it was beginning to catch up with him. The need for sleep began weighing on his arms and legs. The day would be warm and as pleasant as early fall can be in New Orleans. As he relaxed, his fantasy began to intrude. The picture began to form on the headliner of the car. She was beautiful, posed in the doorway.

The hand-held radio in his jacket pocket squawked.

"Slats! Hey, Slats, you asleep?."

The effort to reach the radio made his calf spasm. He pulled the hissing radio from beneath his body, then extended his leg, grabbing his toe and stretching the Charlie horse out of his calf.

"I'm awake now!" he muttered into the radio. "What's happening?"

The voice from the radio was pitched higher than normal, but controlled and soft.

"Big car in the alley, big black car. A Caddy. They're just getting out. Yeah, there's Boulevard. He's carrying a bag, like a big briefcase. And there's a second car, red, T-bird I think. Right against the house. One guy in it.

"Two guys with Boulevard. One's dressed like a fag."

Ivey didn't try to hide his prejudices.

"Okay, Ivey. Where's Johnny?"

"Other side of the building, by the dumpster."

"Give Boulevard three minutes to get inside. No, make it four. The apartment's on the top floor, and Boulevard doesn't move very fast. Then you and Johnny meet me at the staircase."

"Yassa, massa," Ivey chirped from the radio, then the hiss vanished.

Slats checked his watch and eased himself out into the brightening sunshine. He stretched, patted the Beretta 9 MM under his jacket, and walked leisurely to the rickety screen door. It opened with a morose little squeak, and he stepped into a dim hallway.

The hall stretched the length of the old rooming house, a single pane above the rear door adding little illumination to the corridor. Slats patted his weapon again, unbuttoned his jacket, and felt for the .22 backup in his ankle holster. He rubbed his hands together, clenching his fists and flexing his arms, trying to feel each separate muscle. They all ached from the night spent trying to find comfort in the front seat of his car.

The door behind him creaked.

He spun, dropping to one knee, the Beretta suddenly in his hand.

"Whoa, Slats!" Ivey's voice whispered loudly. "You're a hair jumpy, huh dude."

Slats sighed as he stood up and holstered his weapon.

"Just a touch, Ivey," he said. "Just a touch. Where's Johnny?"

Then he saw Johnny's big, square profile outside the screen door. When he joined them, Slats whispered instructions.

"There are three apartments up there. They should all be in the big room up front. But just in case, Johnny you take position near the rear of the hall. Ivey all the way forward by the window, and I'll go through the door. If nothing moves in your areas, get your butts in behind me!"

He waited for acknowledgment, and started up the stairs, hoping no loose boards would announce their arrival.

The upper hall was brighter than the lower, with large swing-out windows front and rear. Three dinghy doors marked the room entries, one near the front window, and two halfway between the landing and the rear window. Slats didn't know if any of the rooms connected, and he thought only briefly about the complications such arrangement might produce.

He watched Ivey position himself under the front window, about ten feet from the door to the large room. Then Slats drew his Beretta and nodded. Ivey and Johnny drew their weapons as well, Ivey a black Colt 45 auto, and Johnny a Colt .357.

Slats walked softly to the door and stood listening for a moment. At least, two, perhaps three voices emanated from the room. One seemed irritated. It squeaked, almost like the screen door. Over it rolled the massive basso-profundo that Slats knew belonged to Boulevard.

Slats examined the door handle. The proprietor of the building had long eschewed maintenance, and the once bright brass showed the effects of years of corrosion and the city's acidic atmosphere. Slats stepped back and slammed his foot into the door alongside the handle. The door popped inward, slamming back against the inner wall.

For a split second, total silence reigned.

In the sight picture over the barrel of his Beretta Slats saw three men, one standing at either end of a large coffee table, and one, Boulevard, between the table and an ancient Queen Ann sofa. It could have been a freeze-frame from an old black and white Sidney Greenstreet movie. The coffee table was covered with stacks of bills, and several bright metallic objects. The whole tableau stood on the side of a threadbare rug, an arm's length from a wall papered in a sooty diamond pattern.

"FREEZE!" Slats yelled. "Police."

And the tableau broke.

The first to move was the man on Slats' right. His right hand snaked under the lapel of a plaid sports jacket so bright that even the stress of the moment couldn't keep Slats from feeling a touch of revulsion. The man was medium-sized, well built, and very fast. Slats swung on him, firing as he moved, and missed. The man leaped almost straight up and fell behind the couch.

Almost instantly the other man jumped toward the open window in the far wall, a large automatic appearing as if by magic in his hand.

But he sprang directly into Slats's sight picture. Slats pulled the trigger twice. The man crumpled in mid-flight and fell hard onto the floor.

"Slats, move!" a voice yelled behind him.

Slats ducked as Johnny's 357-mag blasted away inches from his ear, almost covering the report of the second handgun. Slats saw the sports-coat clad figure rising from behind the sofa, firing.

Slats heard the slug slam into a body behind him, and he looked around to see Johnny crash against the doorjamb.

Instinctively Slats began firing, emptying the clip at the painted sports coat as the figure whipped behind the sofa and launched himself toward Boulevard. Slats looked back to Boulevard. He stood hunched over, and, as Slats watched, blood spurted from his neck.

But the huge man didn't fall.

He reached down and picked up one of the shiny metallic objects from the coffee table. Slats took a step toward him, expecting him to crumple onto the threadbare carpet. But with an uncanny swiftness, Boulevard swung the bright metal in a tight arc and crunched it into the side of Slats' head. Slats felt the blow, but no pain, felt his arm go limp and saw his Beretta clank to the floor.

Slats couldn't believe he'd been hit. Boulevard should be dead!

Slat's legs wobbled, and he sank to his knees, scrabbling at his right ankle with his right hand as he watched Boulevard raise the bright metal over his head. Time telescoped and Boulevard's movement slowed. Slat's fumbling hand found the little .22 backup in its ankle holster, and he began bringing it up as Boulevard's arms began a graceful downward arc, the bright metal clock-like object sparkling in the ray of early morning sun glinting through the window.

Vaguely Slats heard the boom of handguns behind him and saw a flash of a bright color move across the room. The sports-jacket clad figure seemed to grapple momentarily with Boulevard, then crash against the rickety-cash-strewn coffee table before tumbling past, becoming a colorful streak in his peripheral vision.

Slats' arms reached apex before Boulevard could complete his stroke. The little .22 barked twice, and Slats saw tiny holes pop open in the big man's forehead. Boulevard stopped his swing, his hand now open and empty. But Boulevard didn't fall. He stood stock still, staring at Slats.

The time telescope contracted.

Slats stood slowly, watching Boulevard. He heard a crashing sound and a thump, followed by a mumbled "Damn!" behind him. But he couldn't tear his eyes from Boulevard. The big man's throat pumped blood from a hole beneath his left ear, and two tiny flows eased down his forehead from the .22 wounds.

And he was speaking.

"Yes, Mama. We gone do good! We gone be rich, gone get the President...and we gone be rich...the Pres, Mama! He'll neva see it coming."

His eyes stared unseeing at Slats. But he wasn't mumbling. He was speaking clearly, almost forcefully.

"...Mo' money than ever yo seen. Just to get the Pres, honey. Just to get the Pres."

His voice began to fade, and as Slats watched he sank slowly onto the sofa, his head falling forward until his multiple chins settled on his chest and shut off the flow of words.

Slats watched him, knew he was dying, knew he couldn't save him, and wondered at what he had heard.

"Slats!"

It was Ivey's voice over his shoulder. Slats turned and saw his friend pale and bloodied. He was trying to prop Johnny up against the door jamb.

"He's hit bad Slats! Real bad! And that other bastard got away...out the window!"

Slats glanced back, saw one man crumpled on the floor in a spreading pool of blood, another seated, leaning cockeyed against the far wall not far from the broken window.

Slats fumbled in his jacket pocket, keyed his radio, raised dispatch and called for an ambulance. He walked to the window, leaned carefully between the broken shards, and peered downward. There was no one to be seen.

Only the big, black Cadillac remained in the alley.

Chapter Three

It was on Provo that Jusquevera wanted to establish himself.

Having spent much of his youth among the elite, it seemed appropriate to headquarter in the heart of affluence. He could spend relaxing afternoons on a veranda sipping Bacardi and discussing fluctuations in the silver market. Not that Jusquevera understood the world silver market. He knew little about international economics, his education having been interrupted early in his final year at the University in Quito, Ecuador. The change in the Colombian administration that had wrecked his family's business and sent his father briefly to prison had doomed his formal education

It took less than a week on the island to convince him that it wasn't what he sought. Not only did those with whom he wished to mingle, mix little; those whom he did meet took rather a keener interest in him than he had expected. After falling victim to grillings by a pair of New York attorneys with whom he had struck up a casual conversation in the Green Reef Club bar, he had reason to question his decision. The two represented a group planning to open a new multi-ownership vacation condominium on the island. Jusquevera had but mentioned the possibility of setting himself up in business on the island, when the pair descended on him like prosecutors on a hostile witness. If everyone were so territorial, it would mean much more scrutiny than Jusquevera's operations would withstand.

Thus, it was that two months before Slats ill-fated raid, a private Lear jet with Jusquevera as its only passenger had swept down Grand Turk's ten-mile length and circled the airport south of the island's township.

Jusquevera's pilot adored the little jet and his maneuvers sometimes drove Jusquevera to the edge of violent illness.

Today, however, he maintained the dignity the pilot for a major business would accord his employer, and landed the plane gently, with scarcely a thump as the tires touched the pavement. When the plane rolled to a stop at the edge of the parking apron, a beat-up airport service vehicle came to a screeching halt alongside the door. As Jusquevera stepped out, tall, slim and olive dark, carrying an equally slim attaché case, a black face split by a white-toothed grin exploded in greeting.

"G'monin. Need a ride? Wheh yo bags?"

A long black arm snaked out of a crimson shirt that fitted snugly to an almost fleshless body and grabbed the black attaché. Jusquevera maintained his grip and a momentary tug of war ensued.

"Thanks, no! I'll take this," Jusquevera yanked, and the skinny hand relinquished its hold.

Standing there in the morning sunshine next to the jet's open door, Jusquevera looked very much the part he played; an attorney representing an American electronics firm with Caribbean and South American interests. His company wished to construct a small assembly and distribution center for computer components, assuming appropriate agreements could be negotiated. Nothing in his bearing, his tall, angular, aristocratic countenance, or his university cultured voice, betrayed the organization of Colombians who backed his mission with a stolen airplane and drug-market-financing.

His papers showed him to be of fairly recently established Jamaican citizenship. Only he knew that when he spoke of leaving Latin America as a youth to seek his fortune in the Caribbean, he told only part of the truth. No one except his pilot, outside the continental borders of Colombia, knew Jusquevera as head of a tight-knit organization known as El Carib, named after the tribe of Indians who once terrified early explorers of the

Caribbean and coastal South America. As a matter of fact, scarcely anyone anywhere knew of El Carib.

Many of its members were middle-class people working for an administration they hated, shuffling off what funds they could afford from their estates and what they could from the government, to finance their aspirations; dreams that might in their ideology make them saviors of their country. Even a small rent in the organization's sociopolitical cloak could be disastrous to its leadership.

The Venezuelan secret police had once captured documents indicating the existence of El Carib. But since it posed no threat to the government, and, in fact, seemed to influence negatively a neighboring, sometimes inimical government, their knowledge had been filed for reference only. And in the bowels of Washington, DC, pressing proper keys on the right terminal would flash the name on a video display, coupled to a brief description, "thought to be a terrorist organization responsible for several deaths in Colombia."

In neither listing did Jusquevera's name appear.

His full name was Jusquevera Trevino Segreda de Arrellano. From his earliest days, he remembered his father as an international jewelry merchant, respected, even renowned, in Bogota, the city to which he had moved after years spent first as an emerald miner, then as a dealer, in Cartagena.

His father had often been away for months at a time, leaving behind three children and a devoted wife. Jusquevera remembered his mother always with a smile on her face, her cheeks dimpling happily as she chatted to her wards.

She loved being a mother, and while she took her church vows seriously, she dealt with most of life's problems lightly. She raised her children according to her vows, familial and spiritual, and until he left home at seventeen to attend the University of Southern California in an exchange program, Jusquevera had never missed a mass and had spent but a few days away from the tutelage of the Sisters at St. Francis.

Jusquevera remembered a boyhood of plenty, where neither he, his sisters, nor his parents, wanted for anything reasonable. He decided early to follow his father and join him in the business. He spent his first year of university life at UCLA, after an advanced preparatory program, studying marketing and liberal arts, and broadening his horizons. From there he had gone to Quito, Ecuador, to enhance his knowledge of specific areas of international law affecting trade and marketing in Latin America.

Then had come the elections of '66, and Carlos Lleros Restrepo won. Restrepo, later to be honored as one of Columbia's most effective presidents, was not himself to blame. But within weeks, the elder de Arrellano was imprisoned and his business destroyed. De Arrellano himself blamed a political appointee of Restrepo, a high-ranking judge who initiated tax fraud charges against de Arrellano and his semi-private company. Jusquevera blamed Restrepo, the National Front coalition, both the Liberal and Conservative parties, which ruled Colombia for sixteen years, and the entire system which he felt immensely corrupt and corruptible.

Only because the new administration was slow to organize was Jusquevera's mother able to escape the country. She took her personal jewelry, which she sold in Mexico, and set up housekeeping in Mexico City with Jusquevera's sisters. He joined them there.

His mother no longer smiled.

His father's resourcefulness had not died. A cache of funds he had earlier secreted against possible political misfortune bought his freedom, and he joined his family in Mexico six months after his imprisonment, financially depleted, spiritually subdued.

Jusquevera's mother smiled again, although not so readily.

But his father did not. Letters of credit could no longer open doors for him. A well of private backing in Colombia into which de Arrellano himself had poured millions of pesos had virtually dried up. And even those outside Colombia, who his dealings had previously benefited, now shied away from the stigma with which his country's politicos had branded him.

Jusquevera took a job as a bindery worker in a Mexico City publishing plant. His sisters found work as waitresses, and together they maintained life, not well, but adequately, while his father became more and more reliant on cheap alcohol. Jusquevera watched his father's drinking once more drive the smile from his mother's lips and vowed to himself that never would he allow his spirit to be so broken. He stole identification documents from an American paper manufacturer's representative at the publishing plant, quit his job, and told his parents he was returning to Bogota. And he did, traveling mainly on foot, hitching when he could.

When he reached the city, he looked like any of the millions of young itinerants who disappear there annually. For six months he wandered, begging handouts, finding shelter in alleyways and public buildings, watching and listening. He sought his father's former company offices, and found the firm functioning, an unofficial arm of the administration, with its profits disappearing into the pockets of unknown men in the capital.

From behind his mask of dirt and poverty, he managed to talk to those who had once called his father friend. Many of them, he found, were strongly opposed to the way the administration's new leaders had treated de Arrellano, but they would not speak out for fear of their livelihoods, perhaps their lives. He learned from one, Juan Mendez, the name of the judge who had sentenced de Arrellano to prison.

Early on a damp and dreary evening shortly before Christmas, 1979, Jusquevera, a cheap .22 automatic jammed deep in a worn sports coat pocket, made his way up a street of elegant homes, avoiding in his shuffling travel lighted corners and gate lamps. For someone looking as he did, even being seen in such a neighborhood would mean probable arrest. Some thirty minutes after December darkness draped the city, he found the house he sought. He pushed past the gate and mounted the stone steps to stand before an ornately carved door.

He lifted the heavy bronze knocker and let it bang against the brass strike plate.

A dark-haired maid in a long, black dress answered the door, took a quick look at Jusquevera, and ordered him away. When he refused to leave and requested an audience with her master, she all but laughed and refused to admit him even to the foyer. But he insisted, saying he had a message of importance for the man, and she agreed finally to send him to the door, then slammed it in his face. Minutes later it reopened, revealing beneath the foyer lamp a short, portly, gray-haired man, in an obvious bad temper.

In his right hand, he held a linen table napkin.

He was not polite.

"Cual es..." he began.

Jusquevera interrupted him.

"You are the judge?"

"Si! Et tu?"

Jusquevera did not even try to take the gun from his pocket. The .22 caliber slugs ripped through the faded material as he pulled the trigger. The power of the weapon was not sufficient to move the bulky man as the slugs smashed into his chest and belly. He stood as he had when he opened the door, one hand on the door frame, the other holding the linen napkin, watching the disheveled youth on the stoop shoot him, his expressions changing from one of anger and hostility to horror as the bits of lead buried themselves in his hulk. Jusquevera had pulled the trigger six times before the man screamed and staggered back into the foyer. He pulled it twice more as the heavy form collapsed then he yanked the gun from his pocket and threw it at the man. By the time the maid, who had heard the shooting from the dining room where she had been assisting with the evening meal, reached the foyer, Jusquevera had disappeared into the darkness.

The police searched in vain, and the next day's newspapers speculated that an unknown revolutionary group was responsible for the killing. The idea of organized opposition had not imprinted itself on Jusquevera's mind until the stories gave credence to the concept.

Why not? His grudges against the new administration were purely personal, but don't most politics begin with personal grudges? Talking with Mendez and several of his father's contemporaries convinced him that he was right. The new administration had hurt them financially, and they were not antithetical to the idea of striking back. Thus, when at a gathering sponsored by Mendez, Jusquevera accepted responsibility for the death of the judge, he was hailed as a hero and became immediately the center of a movement that, over the ensuing decade, coalesced into El Carib.

For much of the next ten years, Jusquevera, and some of his more ardent devotees lived near the smaller communities along Colombia's Pacific coast. Deep in the sparsely populated forests, their daily lives were pseudo-militaristic. They posed as communes, although there was little in the way of agricultural produce that they could scratch from the rain forest soils.

Those in El Centro, as Jusquevera dubbed the principal unit, lived a frugal life, while operatives reached out into the cities, making discrete contacts, seeking popular support and money. Jusquevera had been disappointed to find among the country's lower classes little idealism and, therefore, a prevailing apathy toward political rebellion. Only among the elite did he find strong tides of political opinion; and those ebbed and flowed according to the whims of the administration.

El Carib never did burgeon into the popular front Jusquevera had dreamed of heading. Instead, it became a small, stealthy group building bank accounts in Europe and elsewhere. The organization, Jusquevera hoped, could eventually run the country. But accomplishing that objective would require subtle machinations instead of active revolution. So Jusquevera and his El Centro planned and carried out numerous operations designed to enlarge the organization's coffers. El Carib blackmailed its way into partial control of one of the larger coffee export companies after supplying the company's president with carefully selected and trained prostitutes, whose expertise included photography. With funds skimmed from the coffee operations, the organization established in the foothills of the Sierra Madre de Santa Marta close to the Caribbean a large farm and processing plant that produced one major crop.

Heroin.

The crop flourished.

On one brief trip into The United States, with stops only in Los Angeles and New York, Jusquevera found buyers who would willingly have purchased three times the farm's annual output. He soon found himself running a thriving, illicit business. Sales earned millions in American dollars. But running the operation required vast amounts of capital, money that went not only for crop cultivation, but for the cultivation of provincial officials, and some administration officers as well.

And on two occasions fire, apparently set by competing farmers, destroyed the crops. El Carib meted out its judicious violence, and the burning stopped. But after more than twenty years, the organization still seemed little nearer its objective. Political control of the country remained in the hands of men who, despite nearly a dozen elections, seemed conceptually identical to their predecessors, and as corrupt.

Although Jusquevera now controlled a relatively wealthy organization, its major resources were not sufficiently fluid to buy the needed power, and he grew increasingly frustrated. Although many of his organization's members now lived the lives of planters and industrialists, and he provided his family still residing in Mexico a comfortable living, he spent most of his time roaming the country seeking the formula for a successful rebellion.

Aging frustrated him further.

He celebrated his forty-fifth birthday alone, on a self-imposed retreat, during which he determined that the intrigues of his life must soon climax.

Thus, it was with a sense of desperation that he had approached El Centro with a plan that appealed to his daring and, to a large extent, others' greed.

Chapter Four

Lt. Col. Charlie Adkins had carried his dreams to McGuire's Irish Pub, one of Pensacola's signatory dining establishments, that evening.

He sat at his favorite table in the back of the dining area near the "L" shaped bar, browsing through the latest issue of "Soldier of Fortune," looking for his war. There are always wars. The Middle East (much too short). South Africa. South America. Indochina. There are always coups; there was enough violent unrest to keep a good soldier busy for several lifetimes.

The only questions were where and when.

Better be soon. I'm looking at fifty-eight; getting a bit old for this!

He started when a hand touched his shoulder, but he didn't look up.

"You look kinda lonesome," she said, her voice melodic above the cacophony of the crowded pub.

"I don't pay for sex," Charlie said without taking his eyes from the pages.

"Neither do I," she replied, slipping into the chair across from him.

Charlie put down his magazine.

And stared.

She was probably the prettiest woman to grace McGuire's that evening. Charlie had seen her face before. Was it on a movie ad? Sophia Loren but encased in leaner, olive-bronze skin, flawless complexion from hairline to cleavage, where ample breasts swelled beneath a lace bodice.

"I seldom sleep with anything less than a full colonel," she said.

Charlie hesitated. He wasn't in uniform. How could she know he was only a Lt. Col.

He had seen her before. On the base. Her name was...

"I'm Maria," she said.

"Yes..." She was a secretary, or receptionist, at some base office.

His composure, which had slipped a bit when he saw her, returned.

She watched him closely. She could sense him regrouping, but she was in no hurry. She knew his lineage. And Maria would match her ancestry against Charlie's any day.

She knew, in fact, everything that was in his personnel file, plus some. Maria worked for Col. Henry "Bulgy" Tichner, the chief of Marine Corps personnel at the Naval Air Station. She was a civilian employee with routine access to all non-secret personnel files.

"I haven't asked you to go to bed. I said you look lonely, might enjoy some company," she said.

Her lips pursed.

He didn't reply.

"I'm a bit lonely too. I think I've been stood up," she said.

"You've never been stood up in your life!" Charlie replied.

"Would you call a waitress. I'd like something to drink."

"I don't even know your name," Charlie said.

"I didn't ask you to buy anything. I pay my own way. And if you don't want company, I'll leave you to your magazine."

Charlie glanced down at the "Soldier of Fortune." A gray and grizzled face stared at him down the barrel of an M-16. He looked back at Maria, her lips full and her eyes welcoming.

He raised his right hand and snapped his fingers. The waitress turned from pushing an assortment of dirty glasses across the bar, shook her blond hair back, picked up a tray, wiped it with her long, green apron, and pushed her way through the crowd standing near the bar.

Maria put her right hand on the waitress's arm as she ordered. At the same moment, her foot touched the inside of Charlie's thigh beneath the table. The contact startled him.

Charlie would never consider that any woman would find him unattractive. Not that he was an exceptionally experienced lover. He wasn't. Still, he remembered no complaints from those occasions when his libido had bidden him perform.

But Charlie had always been the aggressor. Maria's assertive approach made him uneasy, made him feel he wasn't controlling the relationship.

Relationship? He had never jumped from bed to bed but had enjoyed several years each with four lovely women. Whenever the subject of marriage had arisen, however, he found his partner's company less and less appealing. Virtually all had accused him of narcissism.

He watched Maria chatting with the waitress. They were talking about Maria's dress. Charlie examined it, paying particular attention to the cut of the bodice. Although the neckline dipped low between her breasts, Charlie saw no evidence of bikini lines.

Is her skin that color everywhere?

The dark dress flowed over her body, fitted but not tight. It stopped with a hemline just above her knees, where athletically muscled calves led his eyes to delicate feet partially encased in open toe, high-heeled pumps.

He glanced up and found the waitress gone. Maria was watching his face. He stared back at her.

"I'm rather proud of my body," she said, matter-of-factly.

He copied her nonchalance.

"I was wondering why you have no bikini lines?" he replied.

"I sunbathe naked."

An image of this beautiful woman naked on a settee beside the pool, golden in the afternoon sun, sprang unbidden into his mind.

"You're a beautiful woman..." Charlie said.

"You're not bad yourself, soldier," Maria replied, her tone light and flippant.

" ...and very brash!" he continued. " But now that we've finished with the formalities, I'm Charlie..."

She interrupted, her tone almost harsh.

"You are Lt. Col. Charles Adkins, USMC, commanding Marine Corps Training Squadron VCS531," Maria replied.

Charlie stared.

"I work in personnel," she said. "I know everything...almost...about you. Your picture isn't so good looking as you are, but it is you."

Charlie let her revelation sink in.

"And who were you going to meet here tonight?"

"Bulgy," she replied.

"Col. Tichner?"

"He's the only Bulgy I know."

Charlie shuddered.

Col. Tichner's obese frame had towered over Charlie when he was first assigned to the squadron. Charlie had disliked him immediately. And Tichner had been instrumental in keeping Charlie from the Mid East. While many of Charlie's students had lived his dream, driving Harriers and A-10 Warthogs across a desert strewn with tanks, and jeeps, and trucks, Tichner had managed to keep Charlie pinned to a desk, flying paper airplanes and wing-jockeying wet-nosed kids fresh out of T3s into the Harriers.

His trainees went to the Middle East.

Charlie stayed home.

"Nothing I can prove Charlie," Tichner had said. "Just a feeling. You'd probably toss a smarty at an Israeli temple just to widen the war. Besides, I need you here. You can do more good teaching guys to fly than you can flying."

And the CO had echoed Tichner.

So Maria was Tichner's woman!

Suddenly she became even more interesting.

The waitress deposited the drinks with a lack of aplomb she reserved for small tippers, and Maria reached for her purse.

Charlie held up his hand, palm out.

"Oh no!" he said. "We can't have the Colonel's girl buying her own drinks. Put it on my tab."

The waitress nodded, stood for a moment scuffing her foot, then strode away.

"So you know all about me?" Charlie questioned, swirling his drink. Maria lifted her glass with both hands, carefully, to avoid even the hint of a spill.

"Yes."

She leaned forward slowly and the top of her bodice eased away from her body. Charlie had to look. She didn't try to cover. Charlie noticed a purple mark on her left breast. She had a tattoo that looked like a cartoon street sign.

Maria watched his eyes as she spoke.

"You're an engineering graduate, summa cum laude, of Northwestern. You've never failed an exam. Your blood is O-positive. You applied for duty in Nam. A little too late. And you were turned down for a turn in Iraq. "

She leaned back, breaking Charlie's reverie beneath her bodice.

"Your father owns a chain of scientific supply houses. He wanted you to go to Harvard, didn't he?"

How could she know that?

"Your grandparents were from East Germany. You're aggressive. And you probably think I like you."

Charlie lifted his eyes to hers.

"That bit about my grandparents wasn't in my file," he said.

"I have other sources as well."

She paused, reached across the table and flipped the magazine over. She spent a moment examining its cover, then looked away.

"Is this what you want out of this world, Charlie?" she asked.

"Aren't you getting rather personal. Do we know one another well enough to discuss such things?"

She simply stared at him.

"I want a hell of a lot more than I'll ever get in this gay little redneck town!" he blurted.

"What do you want right now?"

"Right now?"

"Do you want me?" she asked

He paused, then answered slowly.

"You're a beautiful woman," he paused, then added. "Now, I don't mind a good looking girl coming on to me. But I don't like her picking at me like I'm a butterfly in her collection."

"You think I want to see you on a mounting board?" she asked.

She leaned in toward him, her breasts flattening against the table.

"What do you want tomorrow Charlie? What do you want ten years from now?"

The intensity in her voice cut like broken glass.

Charlie laughed out loud, raising his arms expansively to each side.

"To rule the world, of course. Anything wrong with that? I haven't gotten much that I want in this life. I wanted to fight in Viet Nam, but everything was winding down about the time I was ready to go. In the first Gulf War, I wanted to go, to drive a Warthog in and chop the Republican Guard to pieces, but your precious boyfriend wouldn't approve the transfer, and the CO agreed with him.

"I want my war, before I get too old, and the rewards that go with it."

She sat up, took a slow drink from her glass, held securely in both hands, and studied him.

"I need to know you better, Charlie," she said. "I know you're smart. I know you made your birds almost ten years ago. And you think you're stuck there, don't you?"

He leaned forward and put his chin in his hands, resting his elbows on the table.

Maria studied him. Neither spoke for several minutes.

"My name is Madere. Maria Madere.

"There's a Hernandez and a Raula in there somewhere. I almost forget sometimes. I was born in Colombia. My parents were well off. My father was a government official, a high muckety-muck in Bogotá." She paused briefly, looked down at the table and began swirling the drink. Her voice grew softer.

"They killed him when I was ten.

"They called it an election. But it wasn't. It was a coup. They declared my father a criminal and shot him.

"My mother and I got away.

"But she died a few months later. I guess she just didn't want to live anymore.

"But I did. I survived. Believe it or not, I stowed away on a container ship and wound up in New Orleans."

She seemed to be shrinking into herself as she talked, staring into her glass and reciting as though reading from the pages of a frightening fairy tale.

"It was half my life ago. Sometimes..." she paused, shrugged.

"Sometimes I feel like I spent a hundred years in the French Quarter." She looked him in the eyes. "I was a hooker! That's how I survived."

Her candor irritated Charlie. He wasn't sure why.

Then she brightened.

"But that was half my life ago. Now I'm this...well."

Charlie was trying to compute the age. Half her life ago?

"Now I have a comfortable bank account, a good job, and a boyfriend colonel who has stood me up."

Charlie stared at her.

"Lady, if that story's true, you're an incredible piece of work."

She smiled and Charlie felt his pulse quicken.

"You're not so bad, yourself, soldier."

"You said that before. But..." Charlie began the puzzle that was building in his mind flowing to his tongue.

"Just how did a Colombian hooker in New Orleans wind up as a civil servant on a US Navy base? What about things like social security cards, credit references, papers that you need to get and keep a job?"

"Enough about me for now," she replied, dismissing his query with a wave. "Later... maybe. I need another drink."

Bulgy's girlfriend! Could revenge be this sweet?

"Not to change the subject, Lady, but...have you eaten lately?"

She did not reply.

"I need something with a bit more savoir than the faire they serve here," Charlie said. "Let's you and I find us a... High-class meal."

"Food's great here," she replied.

"Sure," he replied. "But I'm in the mood for Greek."

"But what about Bulgy?"

"Do you think he deserves you, after keeping you waiting for hours?"

Charlie didn't bother calling the waitress. He walked to the bar and asked the bartender to clear his tab. Maria met him at the door and slipped her elbow under his.

"You car or mine?" she asked.

Charlie hesitated a moment.

"Yours. I'd like to see more of those pretty legs," he replied.

"Don't mind being blunt, do you," she said as she unzipped the shoulder bag and unsnapped a set of keys from its interior.

"You're not so bad yourself, Lady, " he replied.

The lot was full of cars, but Maria walked directly to the third row and stopped at the driver's door of a restored black Pantera.

Charlie whistled softly.

"Uncle must be paying well these days."

Maria didn't reply or even look up. She unlocked the door and stepped away. Charlie pulled the door open as far as the car alongside would allow, looked Maria in the eyes, and bowed.

Maria giggled, curtsied, and sat on the edge of the driver's seat, letting her skirt slide well up her thighs. Charlie's gaze slipped from her face to her legs, then returned to her face.

"Mademoiselle," he said, and stepped back. She turned beneath the wheel, and Charlie closed the door. It shut with a distinctive solidity.

During the fifteen minute ride to the beach, Maria made no attempt to adjust her skirt. Charlie thought he glimpsed in the streetlight flashes of iodine incandescence the tops of sheer hose and garter-belt lace.

Maria watched only the street, driving with a careful precision that belied the quickness of the Pantera. Charlie relished the guttural grumble of its big Ford V-8. He watched Maria's face shade and flash in the intersection lights, and wondered what effect alcohol would have on her.

He remembered his father's admonitions about women when the elder Adkins had tried to talk him into attending Harvard.

"A drunk woman's not much fun ....in...

"Besides," he had said, "A Harvard man can have all the women he wants."

Charlie remembered little of his teen years beyond the constant tension between him and his father.

Except Kent State.

He had been sitting his room in 1970 watching anti-Viet Nam protesters take over the Kent State gymnasium. Suddenly riot-clad National Guard troops appeared. Little popping sounds crackled from the TV. Ice water dripped down Charlie's spine and his scalp tingled.

Images jumbled.

People ran.

Some didn't run.

They fell down.

The popping sounds became gunshots and Charlie realized that he was watching people die.

Watching People Kill!

Virgin nerve synapses fired and every fiber of his body responded.

It was orgasmic!

He watched the troops mete out death, and a fire burned through his gut and erupted into his throat. Spasms shook the loins of his pre-Cambrian brain, and he gave birth to a lifetime goal. He saw himself at the controls of a supersonic jet fighter streaking treetop high across the jungle scattering Viet Cong as a hawk scatters chickens.

But it never happened. Viet Nam was virtually over before he had his wings, and he was indispensable to the training command when the first Gulf War broke out. He had never flown in combat.

Training in the little British VSTOL Harriers had been small consolation. He truly enjoyed flying the little "jump jets," but wanted so much more than just aerobatics.

Maria took the bridges at a pace that might have been prosecutable, but no blue lights flashed. She breezed through the toll plaza, waving at the attendant and pointing to the "Beach Resident Pass" in the window, for Charlie's benefit, not the attendant. She wheeled into the Boy on a Dolphin parking lot and brought the car to a precise stop. Charlie had let her choose the destination. Now he began to regret it. He had never liked the decor or the ostentatiously Greek presentations of food and pastry. But they were shown quickly to a table overlooking the water, which was as dark as the sky, and handed a thick menu.

When the black-garbed waitress arrived, Maria ordered.

"Beefeaters, up, with onion. Bring one for the gentleman too."

She watched Charlie, anticipating his reaction.

"Now that wasn't in my personnel file," he said.

"I told you, I have other sources too."

Charlie started to ask what those sources were. One of his past lovers? But what did it matter? Charlie had nothing in his background to hide.

The only things he kept to himself were almost subconscious: the emotions, the desire, the need to...to ...feelings that etched strange designs on the walls of the room in his mind where he hid those needs.

What does it matter? She can't change those needs, or fulfill them. But she does affect the etchings, doesn't she; the images on the walls are sharper, clearer. He wanted to study the pictures, but her voice intruded, whispering through the emotional door he had left ajar.

"Maybe you should start with some oysters, Charlie," she said, glancing over the top of the leather-cased menu. "I think I'll have some."

Her overt sexuality teased his libido.

I can have her. She wants me, doesn't she? Of course, she does! And there's nothing Bulgy can do about it. He pictured the big man, almost ominous in his dress uniform, his massive belly creating its personal privacy zone. Charlie felt his gut tightening.

"What's he like?" he asked.

"Who?" She continued to study the menu.

"Col. Tichner, ...Bulgy."

She concentrated on the entrees, her index finger sliding up and down the page.

"Bulgy..." she began, absently. "He's...well. He's fat! "

She shut the menu, placed it on the table, rested her elbows on it, and settled her chin on her hands.

Is she mocking me?

"All of the things you hear about fat people, well... that's Bulgy. Fat people are always pictured as jovial, genial, and, well rounded. That's Bulgy. He's all those things. But mainly he's fat. He quakes like a bowl of Jell-O when he laughs. And you should see him when he..." she paused and met Charlie's eyes ..."fucks."

Charlie's breath caught. He didn't want to hear this! Or did he? Her eyes held his. Her scent teased him, even across the table, even among the multitude of aromas that filled the restaurant. How could she allow someone as gross as Tichner to make love to her?

"Poor Bulgy would never get off if I didn't do all the work," she said. She broke the eye contact, leaned back in the chair, and sighed as though she had been describing flower arranging.

"How many men have you had in your life?" Charlie asked, noting an unusually husky quality in his voice.

God, am I as horny as I think I am?

"You mean, how many men have made use of my body?" she asked.

Charlie nodded halfheartedly.

"Too many. Too...too many. But that's over with. It's been over for a long time. These days I favor only special, very special people with. She let the sentence die.

"Bulgy's special. He's done a lot for me. I owe him."

"Are you in love with him?"

God, did I ask that?

"Charlie, I didn't think romantic love was part of your repertoire."

For the second time in the last two hours, Charlie felt lost.

But Maria didn't give him a chance to wallow in his confusion. She leaned forward, reached across the table, took his right hand and pressed it to her cleavage.

"I want some oysters, and a good steak," she said. "And then, Charlie, well... and then I have a proposition for you."

Chapter Five

In due course, Jusquevera arrived on Grand Turk, carrying an attaché case stuffed with American dollars and forged papers. He cleared customs without opening a bag, smiling at the lean black faces behind the counter.

A well-folded bill, adroitly flashed, obtained the services of a clanking mid-70's Chevrolet cab for a quick ride to the Saltraker Inn, which lay a couple of miles north of the airport along a sandy, ocean-skirting road.

The inn itself, plus a half-dozen concrete block rooms tacked on in recent years, all but disappeared into the bougainvillea, shrimp plants, cacti, and other flowering legumes. Concrete walks wended through the thick vegetation around the front of the Inn, past a rotting, wood, salt-rake, to the rear where a cluttered open patio extended into a backyard.

Jusquevera, after depositing luggage in the upstairs room that Jessica Waitland, the inn's owner, had arranged for him, made his way to the patio, where he placed himself gingerly in an over-stuffed chair that had sat through one too many of the island's too-few rainstorms.

All of the furniture on the patio had grown old in someone's attic. Several bent willow chairs surrounded an equally old bent willow coffee table embalmed by liquor stains. A matching gray-stripe settee and sofa seemed to creep from side to side in the light of the sun pouring through the reed slat roof that shaded the patio.

Jusquevera found the small bar at the rear of the patio empty and helped himself to a cold San Miguel from the unlocked cooler. Returning to the chair, he found it occupied by a large black mongrel. He moved to one of the willow and plastic chairs next to the coffee table, placed his attaché case at his side, pulled twice on the beer, leaned back and closed his eyes. What he had to do in the next 24 hours could make or break months of planning.

He let the sounds of the birds and the sea lull him as he reviewed the concept; establish a credible cover, acquire an appropriate site, construct a warehouse-hangar and obtain a plane and a pilot.

The cover he already had, and his first appointment, with the Bureau of Commerce and Development. The upcoming interview would tell him how well his cover would hold up. As far as the site, the airport was mostly open land, with but one hangar already in existence, plus one small service and storage building.

The plane and the pilot had to be quite special. He had researched the numerous options and decided that the British-made Harrier best suited his needs. Acquiring one would be difficult.

But there are ways. Greed is the common denominator. The trick is to find the right numbers with which to divide.

The willow chair on his right creaked. Jusquevera opened his eyes and saw a rotund figure in tan walking shorts and a khaki shirt, stretched tight across a vast expanse of belly, eyeing him. The sun had moved west and south, and the patio was now sheltered in the shadow of the inn. The breeze blew cooler, with the balminess of a Bahamian evening. A chattering and clanking emanated with cooking aromas from the half-open kitchen, the smell of curry spicing the warm fall air. Two younger couples, the women in light cotton dresses and the men in jeans, approached the patio through the overhanging bougainvillea. All four carried drinks and all talked at the same time.

The rotund one on Jusquevera's right spoke.

"Here to dive, sir?" he clipped his words and shoved them together into the patois peculiar to Jamaicans.

Jusquevera sat up, put his feet atop the attaché, sipped at his now stale beer, and replied.

"No. On business, really."

"Jamaican?" the bulky man asked.

"By adoption, not by birth."

"Same. Dutch, you know. But I was raised in Jamaica. Great island. Or at least, it was."

"It was?"

"It was. Until the damn, the stupid government got nervous and started nationalizing everything. It was until they took over my business." The big man leaned back, sipped at an odorous gin and tonic, and continued.

"We were doing pretty well, too. Jewelry, you know. Not that we were rich, but we were doing well. I had even staked out a small Spanish treasure. Mean to go back and salvage it someday.

"And it wasn't like we were some major industry or such. Our little family business could neither help nor threaten the government, but the bureaucrats became paranoid."

Jusquevera nodded. "You had a store?"

"More than just a store. My papa had started it. We sold to stores who sold to tourists throughout the Caribbean. Coral, gold jewelry, pieces of eight, that we made, of course. But we were of the wrong blood, and the paranoid bastards couldn't take that. So here I am."

"What are you doing now?"

"Oh, I teach. I'm the local schoolmarm," he chuckled.

"And that provides you with upkeep?"

"Well, I trade a bit too.

"What?"

"Well," the man leaned his bulk toward Jusquevera and lowered his voice, "Maybe a little smoke, or what have you, now and then. Just to keep the throat cleared a bit," he coughed and took a long sip at the gin.

Jusquevera sorted through the remarks. He stuck his right hand toward the chubby Dutch-Jamaican.

"Jusquevera de Arrellano."

"Pleasure."

The hand that returned the greeting was as chubby as its owner.

"I am Ralph Maarten. Just like in the island, M-double-A-R-T-E-N. I believe you may know my brother."

Jusquevera nodded in acknowledgment.

Francois Maarten, co-owner of the Remy-Maarten Circus, had demonstrated his ingenuity several years earlier after finding his way to Jusquevera on the farm near Santa Marta. He transported large amounts of El Carib's heroin, appropriately packaged in bales of animal feed and in truckloads of sacks that appeared at random inspection to be bagged manure, sold by the circus for fertilizer.

Occasionally small amounts of the product became tainted, and a few customers complained of its peculiar odor and flavor. But such complaints, when they found their way back to Jusquevera, as he and Maarten shared a rum and tonic on the farm-house verandah, merely brought explosive chuckles from the Dutchman.

Distribution and sale of the heroin significantly improved the profit Maarten realized from his primary, and public, enterprise. The operating margin for a circus was so slight that any additional funds were welcomed and put to good use. Thus, when Jusquevera approached him with a proposition that would, in essence, provide Maarten with heroin in exchange for a favor, albeit an intricate one, he was eager to listen. Ralph's presence on the island had been deemed a fortunate circumstance, should Jusquevera need a liaison.

"And you say you are not here to dive?"

"No. I'm representing an American electronics firm. It hopes to establish a small manufacturing and distribution plant here."

Maarten sat up.

"Here? On this island? You must be joking. What would you manufacture here? A SCUBA diving calculator? It would be very expensive to ship in raw materials. Surely you can obtain for your company a better location than Grand Turk."

Jusquevera did not appreciate being put so quickly on the defensive. Would local officials perhaps react as Maarten had just done? Their tete-a-tete might be for show, but some of Maarten's remarks were cutting.

"No, my friend, we aren't going to manufacture a diving calculator, although it does not sound like such a bad product idea. Diving tables I have seen look rather complicated. Perhaps they would be grist for a small electronic mill.

"But the company's plans for the island call for an assembly plant and distribution warehouse. They are already rather heavily into the technical centers of South America, and on some of the larger islands. And..." he crooked a finger at the Dutchman, whose belly sagged across his belt as he leaned toward Jusquevera " Cuba may open up to us soon."

"The company wants to be in the Caribbean basin."

Maarten leaned back, his brow furrowed. His right forefinger rested on his chin.

"So," he said, apparently thinking deeply. "Perhaps your company would have a place for an expert in precious metals and the like. I am quite good at both producing and selling, but there is so little call for that here."

He tossed off the last liquid from his glass, bit into the hunk of lime dredged from amidst the ice cubes, and made a face. "Besides, another six months with those kids and I shall be a raving loony."

"Perhaps." Jusquevera shrugged. "Who knows what might come to pass."

Maarten stared at Jusquevera for a moment, looked about as if searching for attentive ears, and then leaned in conspiratorially. But a parade of black women carrying food interrupted them, and Maarten heaved his bulk from the chair.

"Ah, I see it is time that I took my leave."

"Oh! You do not reside here?"

"No. I merely come by each afternoon to see my favorite tavern keeper."

He lifted his glass toward the bar where Jessica Waitland stood across from a couple who were rolling dice onto a board dotted with small, wooden tiles. His voice boomed across the patio.

"Mistress, please be so kind as to put this on my tab. I shall see to it Friday."

"See that you do," she piped shrilly back. "You have given me not one red cent for a month."

Maarten picked several paperback books from the pile strewn on the table before Jusquevera.

"It's my library also."

He ambled with some unease across the backyard and disappeared behind the lush growth that ringed the patio.

Fifteen other guests had lined up in the half-darkness edging the cement apron between the patio and the house, where a buffet table had been laid. Half-a-dozen tables now sported red-checkered tablecloths, scented candles, the fragrance of which mixed strangely with the bougainvillea, and odd numbers of table settings. Salads and condiments adorned each table, and on the buffet table, large bowls of chicken curry and rice steamed in the night air.

As the guests filled their plates with rice and curry, sprinkling them from a lavish tray of condiments, Jusquevera grew aware of the conversations about him. A pale young New Yorker, by his accent, was describing his exploits with a Nikonis as he faced a Warsaw grouper on a reef ninety feet down. The two women at the table listened attentively while a second man kept dropping expletives into the monolog, in mock awe of his friend's daring.

Every guest at the inn except Jusquevera had been on a dive that day, and the conversation dripped deep water adventure. Jusquevera relished his food, but as quickly as possible he excused himself and retired to his room to avoid the attentions of those to whom his lack of diving expertise would be readily apparent.

The often painted plasterboard walls were warmed by the artwork of islanders, colorful and moving, although about as sophisticated as an eight year old's finger painting. The night breeze puffed white chintz curtains about the window, and billowed the smoke from his cigar, the one cigar a week that he allowed himself, across the room and out over the patio where the tinkle of china and the mumble-drone of voices softened as the night deepened.

Jusquevera should have slept well that night, but shortly after midnight, he awakened to a howling din and raucous braying. The noise died, several minutes after he had awakened, and he drifted off into a fitful slumber only to be aroused by another chorus of howls.

"We've more dogs than people on this island," Jessica told him the following morning at breakfast, served, as had been supper, on the patio. Jusquevera could see that the breakfasters shared the courtyard with several dogs of various sizes and colors; all of which had one commonality; scruffiness. Two were spread out across the striped sofa; the others scattered about on the patio floor, all seemingly asleep.

"Nobody owns them, and everybody owns them. They're like independent citizens, non-taxpaying, of course, as the donkeys."

"Donkeys?"

"Yes. You must have heard them too. There are dozens of donkeys on the island. They aren't wild, really; they just don't have owners, like the dogs. Didn't you hear them last night? They bray at the moon."

"How does anyone get any sleep here?"

"It's amazing what you can get used to if you try," Jessica winked.

In her late forties, and somewhat overweight, she still presented herself attractively.

"Take me, for example. When my husband died ten years ago, I never thought I could get used to running this place by myself. I almost sold out and moved back to New Jersey. But within six months I knew all the stopped up drains, every bit of bad wiring, how to balance the books, who to call to get water. If I'd gone back home, I'd have sat around some quiet apartment and cried myself to death from lonesomeness. Can't be lonely here; too many folks to meet, too much to do."

Jusquevera was no longer listening. The round face before him had rippled and disappeared, replaced by his mother's face thirty years earlier. She clucked at him across the breakfast table to hurry, or he would be late for school. She admonished him to give thanks at the chapel for being fortunate enough among his countrymen to attend school, and to be polite to the priests and nuns who oversaw his education. Her admonishments blossomed from a smiling face, and he was happy.

Something scuffled against his foot, destroying his reverie. One of the mongrels licked a bit of spilled egg from the rough cement. Jusquevera stomped his foot, but the dog only wagged a stub of a tail and continued rasping at the floor with its tongue. Jessica had stopped talking and watched Jusquevera with a questioning expression. He lifted his arm and made a point of examining his watch.

He pushed his chair away from the table and stood, all in one motion.

With a small bow toward his hostess, he excused himself and asked for directions to the Bureau of Commerce and Development.

"Out the front gate and turn right. Just follow the road, and it'll be on your right about the middle of town."

Chapter Six

Jusquevera picked up his attaché, paused at a mirror hung on a post near the bar, then stepped into the tropical sunlight. The surface of the narrow road was hot and dry, and limestone dust quickly shaded the patent sheen on his shoes. Broad, short fences pushed into the street on either side, where there were postage-stamp-size, often unkempt, yards from which grew limestone and stucco cottages.

Nothing in his step or his manner betrayed the tension that welled within as Jusquevera walked the few blocks into the heart of the community. As he approached the settlement, the road veered in a dog-leg to the very edge of the water, where an ancient concrete breakwater held back most of the waves. A few, however, spilled over and puddled in the street. Along this section, the buildings were larger; many two-story, but most in need of extensive bracing or repair. The limestone cottages were replaced by meandering wood and sheet metal or painted stucco. The bright pink, iron-picket-fenced library, dazzling in the morning sun, lent color to an otherwise drab street.

Mostly black faces appeared in doorways of shops with closet-sized inventories. The few tourists, generally wives of avid divers, who liked to travel but hated water, found little to browse through and less to buy. In a long, flat, black and white painted building near the center of the town, its face guarded by two old and rusting cannons, Jusquevera found the Bureau of Commerce and Development, one gray doorway among several other shaded doorways, each with its own large and important looking sign signifying the Bureau of Tourism and the Bureau of Health, among others.

He was seated by a small, chubby officious woman in an unofficious office furnished only with two wooden chairs, a desk, and four shelves of books.

The Minister was running late.

The Minister, in fact, ran thirty minutes late, and when he came in, Jusquevera stood up and towered over the small black man in the white shirt and blue slacks who stood before him, hand outstretched.

"Mr. de Arrellano, my name is Bartholomew Whitehead. I am head of the Bureau of Commerce and Development. They tell me you arrived late yesterday on the little Lear. A very pretty bird, sir. Do you enjoy flying?"

Jusquevera took the extended hand, bowed slightly, caught himself wondering if the Bureau of Commerce and Development had more than one member and replied.

"Mr. Whitehead, thank you for seeing me this morning. Indeed, the plane is a fine piece of equipment. It belongs to the company that I represent. While I enjoy flying, I am no pilot. The company has provided me with a pilot for the duration of this trip."

"Most generous of them. I should like to see the plane sometime while you are here. I am a pilot myself, you know."

"Really? I should be pleased to have you go up with us sometime. I should have plenty of time to show off the plane since I hope to be here for several days."

"Yes. Well, what is the nature of your company's business? I believe your preliminary correspondence said something about bringing in some form of electronics components. You are aware..." he paused and turned toward the rear window which looked out onto a bare brick-walled courtyard. "...but I forget my manners. Would you care for a cup of coffee...or perhaps tea?"

He turned back to Jusquevera, studying him with a friendly but formal expression.

Jusquevera shook his head slightly.

"Thank you, no. What were you saying?"

Whitehead paused a moment then turned back to the courtyard.

"You are aware that we have a rather stiff tariff on most imported goods?"

Jusquevera ignored the question and walked up beside the man who was still staring out.

"I am acting as an agent of Computer Dynamics Corporation, which is now manufacturing an extremely fruitful and sought-after small business computer. The company has sales commitments now throughout the Caribbean and in South America, and while it can fill its initial obligations from existing stocks in the States, it needs to develop a support and maintenance distribution system. Once the original equipment is in place, we will be called upon to provide servers, expansion interfaces, varieties of information and retrieval systems, and numerous other services. The company feels they can best meet the need by shipping prefabricated components for final assembly to a somewhat central area, where labor is available at not outrageous prices, and operating a final distribution plant in conjunction with the assembly plant."

Jusquevera felt that his explanation was sufficiently detailed to be credible, while not providing too many checkable leads.

Whitehead turned from the window and sat at his desk.

"I see. You wish to build a ... a factory here to put together parts of computers ... store them and then ship them out as needed? You speak well. But why here? Why not Puerto Rico, or one of the American islands?"

Jusquevera was ready.

"Sir, you must repeat this to no one. Do I have your word?"

Whitehead looked at him silently a moment, nodded, and leaned back in his chair, lacing his fingers behind his head.

"Go on."

"CDC has been dickering, although without the blessings of the U.S. State Department, with Cuba, where the need for the technology we offer is great, and the financial ability to pay for it abounds in certain circles. The company has reason to believe it may soon be provided the exclusive right to provide the technology, and we wish to be ready, willing, and not too far away, yet sufficiently removed from current commerce bases to be out of mind."

"I see," Whitehead replied, his eyes half closed. His shirt clung damply to his small chest, and a rivulet of perspiration creased his ebony forehead. "Out of mind. Yes, that describes well our island. Can't even get the damn tourists to come here."

He paused, and then squinted up at Jusquevera.

"Then you would wish to employ some of our people, both in the construction of your facility and in the operation of the finished plant?"

"Yes, of course. And when the facility is fully functional, in about six months, it will employ twenty people, most of whom will come from right here."

Whitehead fixed Jusquevera with a wide-eyed stare.

"So few?"

He unclasped his hands and sat up.

"I'm not sure your company would find such an operation here profitable. We would have to levy import tariffs against your parts as they come to the island since they would be used in, in a manner of speaking, local commerce. Employing so few people gives us little reason for granting your company any special allowances."

Whitehead laced his fingers together behind his head and tilted back the chair, to the point Jusquevera expected it to topple the diminutive bureaucrat onto his back.

"Have you any references with you that can establish your company's viability? I would be derelict in my duty if I did not ask for some further assurances."

Jusquevera placed his attaché case on the corner of the desk, the clasps facing Whitehead.

"We foresaw some of your questions. Here are letters of credit from banks in the Virgin Islands, Jamaica, and Ecuador, among others.

"I have the company's charters of operation for several countries, which you may examine, and you will see that they provide us favorable treatment. We do require some assistance other firms might not. For example, we must move materials in and components out so rapidly that we cannot always provide time for inspection of everything that comes through. I think this document," he reached for a thick legal folder on top of the materials in the case "will answer many of your questions."

He lifted the folder and revealed a dozen neatly wrapped stacks of American currency.

Whitehead drew a quick, sharp breath.

He stared at the bills.

Silence simmered like the heat about them.

The sun glanced off the courtyard's brick walls and flooded the room with a rose-tinted glare. Through the door that opened to a foyer, where Whitehead's secretary clicked away on an outdated electric typewriter, came the sound of the surf smashing endlessly against the seawall.

A bead of perspiration trickled down Whitehead's brow.

Jusquevera sat.

He faced Whitehead across the corner of the desk nearest the open attaché case.

Whitehead stared at the money. Finally, and with an effort, he lifted his gaze and turned to face Jusquevera.

"How...how much..is...there?"

"Two-hundred-fifty-thousand-American," Jusquevera said matter-of-factly.

Whitehead returned his gaze to the money. Visibly working to regain his composure, he extended one hand and slowly pushed down the top of the attaché case, then shoved his chair away from the desk and stood. He walked deliberately around the desk and crossed to the door, nodded to his secretary and shut the door quietly.

He walked up behind Jusquevera, and when he spoke his voice had regained its officious fervor.

"I could have you arrested," he said, softly.

"But I have done nothing illegal," Jusquevera replied.

"You tried to bribe a public official," the voice at Jusquevera's back answered.

"I was merely demonstrating the fluidity of the company I represent. After all, does it not require capital to obtain a construction site, something I should like to nail down as quickly as possible."

"Perhaps."

Whitehead walked around Jusquevera to stand at the window looking out onto the empty courtyard.

"Where would you want this site?"

"At the airport. All of our transport will be by air."

"And how long will your construction require?"

"If we can work undisturbed, about three months."

"You place lots of emphasis upon secrecy."

"It's not for the sake of secrecy, sir," Jusquevera replied, his tone conciliatory. "It is simply that the company is working against some rather stringent deadlines, and the dictates of official overseeing could be quite costly."

Whitehead returned to his desk, turned and perched on the corner next to the attaché case. His toes barely touched the floor. He put one hand on the case and looked up at the ceiling. Jusquevera thought he knew what troubled the head of the Bureau of Commerce and Development.

"Mr. Whitehead, pardon me if I'm over-intrusive. But have you any relatives in the Caymans?

"You see, you remind me of an acquaintance of mine. Why just recently he won sweepstakes, an American sweepstakes. But it embarrassed him to come so suddenly into a large sum of money. So he went to one of the more major Cayman banks. He found that he could open an account under a fictitious name, and no one would question him about it. So there he was, his money earning him a good rate of interest, and he was able to withdraw certain sums with no one suspecting that his improved lifestyle was due to fortuitous circumstances

"Yes, sir, a lucky fellow. Are you sure you have no relatives in the Caymans?"

Whitehead was staring at him, his eyebrows pulled down and his forehead knit tightly.

Suddenly his face relaxed. He all but jumped from his perch, snapped the clasps on the attaché and picked it up.

"Sir," he said in his official voice, "if you accompany me, we shall proceed to the airport, and there review possible construction sites."

Once Whitehead accepted the money the rest was easy

A lease on an airport site was quickly signed, and Jusquevera's phone call to Miami set on its way a barge loaded with a prefabricated steel hangar. Within a month, the walls of the building were up, and construction proceeded without the usually watchful eye of the bureaucracy.

Whitehead stopped by on occasion to observe the Turk workmen, under an American contractor's supervision, assembling the prefab. His first appearance at the site had been in a new Cadillac. He talked in the Kittina bar of his expanding wealth, feigning acumen in stocks, attempting to impress a comely waitress, until Jusquevera reminded him that lack of discretion would cost him more than his recently acquired automobile.

With construction progressing well on the hangar and workover facilities, Jusquevera turned his attention to his next task, that of acquiring an airplane and a pilot. For the job, he felt he had an important connection in Ralph Maarten, whose brother was one of the owners of a circus that occasionally toured the southern United States, and a valuable ally in the heroin business.

Jusquevera arranged to meet with Maarten and his brother at the farmhouse at Santa Marta. The little Lear whisked them there in little over two hours. He played host on the farm house verandah. The day was cool, shirt-sleeve comfortable, and the air clearer than usual.

They sat across from one another, a wire-spool table between them. On the table, ice cubes melted in an open bowl, and the scent of lime rose from freshly cut fruit in another. Each poured rum and foaming tonic into the tall glasses. Jusquevera had explained what was needed, and how he would pay for it.

"Can you furnish expense money?"

"Certainly. Can you do it?"

"I believe so."

Francois Maarten picked up the conversation.

"I have an acquaintance in New Orleans who has in the past procured for us. He has never failed to obtain a good price for our product, and he has provided me with some excellent companionship. I believe for a share of the proceeds he has the contacts to find what you need."

Ralph Maarten's clipped English interrupted.

"But I must say I find your request strange. Why do you want such an airplane? I fail to see how it can serve you in your present endeavor. You already have excellent air transportation."

He gestured across the expanse of fields surrounding them, slopping drink over the edge of his glass.

Jusquevera studied the portly man for a moment.

"True," he replied, "but the reasons have nothing to do with you. I believe it best if you function only on a need-to-know basis. And after delivery, it will be best that you forget we discussed such an acquisition."

Francois fidgeted.

"No, my friend. We have done some dangerous business, you and I. But I have always known the odds. I cannot work in the dark."

Jusquevera stared at him, then looked away across the lush fields, sipping at his drink. Maarten could almost feel the fire of the Colombian's emotions, but his face remained expressionless.

When Jusquevera spoke, he chose his words slowly, precisely.

"What if I told you we would use the plane to kidnap the President of The United States."

Francois Maarten choked on his drink.

He coughed, and launched into a string of French expletives. It took his brother several minutes to calm him.

"Surely you cannot be serious! You cannot attack the President of The United States!" Ralph Maarten blurted.

"Why not?"

"But ... why? This is a very dangerous business."

"Yes," Jusquevera replied, pouring more rum into both glasses.

"And that is why you should know little of my plans. The less you know, the less danger you and your interests face. My reasons must remain mine."

He rose, walked to the veranda rail and turned to face the big Dutchman.

"The ship with your circus, has it a Colombian port en route?"

"Uh..yes," Francois sputtered. "It will call in Cartagena."

"Good. And are there other stops before Florida?"

"Two, I think."

"Then you will require much fresh hay and feed. We shall see to your needs."

"Yes!"

The Dutchman's eyes were brighter now. He added rum to his glass.

"We always prefer to have more than necessary. Our prized animals must not go hungry." He raised his glass in a salute to Jusquevera, but his hand shook as he did so, and the drink spilled onto his lap.

"And delivery?" Ralph asked. "Do we fly it here?"

"No!" Jusquevera snapped. "It could be tracked. You will put me in touch with your procurer, and I will give him details of the delivery."

Ralph Maarten felt strangely elated. He leaned back in his chair and propped both feet on the verandah's wooden rail. Dusk was approaching with equatorial rapidity, and the sounds of evening insects permeated the descending curtain of quiet. Maarten sighed and tried to sum up the feelings engendered by the conversation, as well as by pleasant companionship and good rum. The gist of the negotiations left a strange chill in his gut. He shook himself and warmed the chill with another swallow of rum.

"I always enjoy the American tours!" he said. Francois remained silent.

The next day Francois left with Jusquevera aboard the Lear. After depositing Jusquevera on Grand Turk, the Lear took Maarten to Miami, where he placed a call to New Orleans, to a seedy French Quarter bar, where he left a cryptic message for the pimp known as Boulevard. His thoughts as he placed the call were not just of the money that his deal would produce this tour. He thought of the soft, warm women his money would buy, and the rich burgundy he would drink.

Life can be good for those with enterprise.

Chapter Seven

Charlie found it hard to concentrate on the food, his mind toying with Maria's words.

He hurried through what should have been a sumptuous meal and found his frustration growing when Maria took her time, dawdling over her coffee. Finally, she finished and excused herself.

"Be right back," she said and headed for the restrooms.

He summoned the waitress, proffered his Am Ex card and moments later was again holding open the door of the Pantera. Maria grinned at him and slid behind the wheel.

As he slipped in on the passenger side, she turned toward him.

"I hear you have a boat, Charlie. A sailboat?"

"Uh-huh," he replied feeling less than glib. "Another of your sources?"

"Want to show it to me?"

She was smiling.

He wanted to ask what she intended to show him, but said simply "I'd love to."

They drove in silence for the thirty minutes it took for the growling little car to traverse the bay front from Pensacola Beach to the Naval Air Station. Charlie directed her to a parking area above the Navy Yacht Club marina. A light fog shrouded the lot's iodine lamps and lent a ghostly pallor to the bayou. The pier stretched dimly across the darkly lapping waves to a phantom cluster of power and sail craft.

When they stepped onto the dock, a fresh wooden structure with boards just far enough apart to trap a high heel, Maria paused and slipped off her shoes. Charlie's pulse quickened as he watched her. He could feel the warmth of her body as she held his arm to steady herself, reaching down for first the right and then the left shoe. She dropped them on the dock as she followed him, walking gingerly in stocking clad feet.

"There she is."

Charlie pointed down the dock to where a thirty-six foot Cheoy Lee ketch nestled easily into one of the farther slips.

"The Dawn Treader?" she asked

"I was once, as a child, enamored of C.S. Lewis. Did you ever read Narnia?"

She gave him a puzzled look, but didn't answer, and a moment later they were standing at the stern of the trim little vessel. Even in the dim light, the varnished mahogany of the taffrail and the teak trim gleamed; seemed almost to possess its soft light. The stern was a long step away, and the lines too tight to pull her closer.

"I'll go first, " Charlie said, and with an easy bound, he was standing in the cockpit next to the varnished wood wheel.

"Okay, " he said, turning to face Maria. "Jump and I'll keep you from falling in..."

Maria, without hesitation, hiked her skirt high on her thighs and leaped, her foot slipped on the combing, and she crashed into Charlie. They tumbled into the cockpit with him sprawled beneath her.

"Damn! Charlie! Are you all right?" she asked, picking herself up and extending a hand.

"Nothing serious, " he said, taking her hand but handling his weight as he lifted himself. "And you do have great legs."

"Glad you like them, " she replied, starring into his eyes, then glancing at the boat.

"It's very pretty, " she said.

"SHE... She's very pretty!"

"She..." Maria repeated.

Charlie pulled a key from his pocket, used it to remove a small padlock from the cabin hatch, and vanished down the companionway.

"Give me a moment, " he said as he disappeared. Seconds later lights appeared below followed by the music of the Eagles. Charlie reappeared, almost buoyed up the hatch on the chorus of Seven Bridges Road, and he extended his hand.

He led Maria three steps down into the main saloon. The varnished teak sole, and mahogany and teak siding glowed warmly in the soft incandescent light. Maria felt as though the amber woodwork was whispering to her, soulful, ancient runes of hidden glades.

"She's beautiful, Charlie!" she repeated, muting her voice as she would in the base chapel.

"It gets better, " he said.

He dug in a drawer of the tiny galley, struck a match, and carried it to the forward bulkhead. He touched the flame to the wick of a small oil lamp. It caught immediately. As the flame brightened and settled, Charlie flipped off the 12-volts, and the magic deepened.

The aura trapped Maria.

"Oh Charlie!" she breathed. " I'll bet you've seduced lots of women here."

"No one as lovely as you," he said, touching her shoulders and looking into her face. "There's a fire in your eyes."

Then he stepped back and sat on the port settee berth.

"Maria, you're the first woman aboard the 'Treader' in years. " He rubbed the glossy wood. "And she's the only female who's ever been true."

Maria thought there was a touch of self-pity in his words.

"Going to offer me a drink?" she asked.

"Anything you want, as long as its bourbon," he replied, rising and making the short trek (two steps) to the bar nestled in the top of the folded table.

"No ice?" she asked as he offered the high-ball glass with an inch of dark whiskey sloshing in it.

"I don't want to cool you off," he said, grinning. He held his glass out to touch hers, and she smiled back at him, then tossed the whiskey off in an abandoned gesture.

"I do want to talk, Charlie," she said.

"Now?" he asked.

"It can wait awhile, " she said, her voice breathy and soft.

She stood, and began unbuttoning the bodice that had attracted his eyes so often through the course of the evening.

Charlie felt his heart rate nudge upward as he watched.

Maria slipped the dress off her shoulders and let it slide it down her body. Her skin shone like bronze under the lamp's glow. She struggled for a moment with the lacy little bra, her hands working behind her back. Then it was off. Her nipples tipped her breasts with dark rosebuds.

"Watch me, Charlie," she whispered.

He swallowed but couldn't speak.

She turned slowly, giving him a chance to study muscles and sinews that molded her curves. She bent from the waist and stripped her bikini panties down her legs, then turned back to face him, her right hand tracing the line from her breasts to the small, dark triangle at her thighs.

Charlie couldn't help wondering if she had performed so for Bulgy, and recognized the worm of jealously wiggling in his gut. It stilled quickly as Maria took a small step toward him.

She held out her hands, and Charlie stood to embrace her. Although small, her body was hard and muscular in his arms, smooth and lightly perfumed. And beyond the artificial fragrance, he could smell her scent.

Could revenge really be this sweet?

"Make love to me, Charlie!" she whispered.

"Yes, " he said, "Oh, yes!"

He stepped back and began unbuttoning the stiffly starched shirt.

"I'll get it, " she said, reaching for the buttons. Charlie unbuckled his belt, let his slacks fall, then kicked them aside.

"Kiss me, Charlie," she ordered!

But when he put his mouth to hers she pulled back, then sat on the settee, her thighs parted, pulling his face down to her breasts.

"Kiss me everywhere, Charlie!"

Her voice was demanding.

He studied her for a moment; his amour tinged with uncertainty. He wasn't accustomed to such demands. But with his rut high, he bent to his task with a sense of urgency. Minutes later, her voice keening and her body spring-tight, he entered her and she sighed deeply.

"Oh, Charlie!" she whispered.

Their passion gave motion to The Dawn Treader. Neither screamed or yelled, but their guttural exuberance filled the small cabin. They felt the response of the vessel and rode the surf of their passions until the waves crested and tumbled them onto the beaches of their souls.

Then the sounds of softly lapping water replaced the voices of their lusts. They lay briefly exhausted; their arms and legs and bodies entwined, the bunk becoming rapidly too small as they relaxed.

"Oh God!" Charlie whispered.

He levered himself up, lifting his weight from the smaller body beneath, and stared into Maria's eyes. She reached up and brushed a stray lock of hair from his eyes. She stretched upward to kiss him softly on the lips.

"I'm told you fly very well," she said.

"What?" The incongruity of her comment startled him.

"Oh, yes...yes I do," he said, pushing himself back to sit near her feet.

"You do this well too," she said. "Could I have another drink? All this activity made me thirsty."

She sat up but made no move to dress. Taking his cue from her, Charlie moved to the bar and poured two more shots of whiskey, handed her one, then held his glass aloft.

"To a beautiful and intriguing woman, " he said. "There's still fire in your eyes."

Maria lifted her glass, then tossed off the liquor. She rose, crossed the cabin, and reached for her clothes.

She watched him as she stepped back into her panties and slipped on the tiny bra. To Charlie's eye, it went on much easier than it had come off.

"Leaving?" he asked.

"No. At least, not yet. I want to talk a bit. But first, Charlie, I want a cigarette. I'm a bit of a cliché, aren't I?"

She found her purse on the opposite bunk, dug into it and came up with a slim cigarette and a silver lighter. She pushed open the hatch and stood on the first step of the gangway. Her body glistened in the lamplight. The smoke from her cigarette circled her head, then drifted out the hatch to mingle with the fog. She no longer watched Charlie but stared out into the gray darkness.

Charlie got up.

He still breathed deeply, but his heart had returned to its normal rhythm

Great exercise, he thought. I should do more of it.

He put his hand on Maria's shoulder, and despite the smoke pressed his cheek to hers.

"We made some waves," he said. "That was good."

For a moment, Maria said nothing. Then she turned to look at him.

"Yes," she replied, a small nod emphasizing the quiet word.

He held her shoulders and pushed himself away to arm's length.

"Well, thanks for the rousing cheer!"

"Didn't I make enough noise for you while it was going on?" she asked.

"Well," he said. "uh...I didn't notice."

"You are self-centered, aren't you?" she flipped the cigarette butt over the transom, and it hissed into the calm water.

Charlie stepped back and stared at her. He could feel his ears reddening.

Maria watched him. Could she feel his anger? Surely she couldn't see the color of his ears in the lamplight. Charlie bit his tongue lightly.

Then she smiled.

"It...you...were very good Charlie.

"I haven't allowed many men to make love to me in recent years. And when it comes to sex with Bulgy, nothing would ever happen if I let him lead. Thanks, Charlie."

She leaned forward, her breasts almost rolling out of the tiny bra, and kissed him lightly on the lips. His anger vanished. Had it ever been there? And what's that other feeling; just afterglow? The meltdown? Whatever!

"So," he said. "You want to talk?"

He turned and found his briefs and pants, then sat on the bunk still warm from their bodies, to pull them on. She picked up her dress and began dressing as well.

"I've been studying you for a long time, Lt. Col. Adkins," she began. She wasn't looking at Charlie, but concentrating on the details of dressing, smoothing her slip under her dress, straightening the hose that had worked down her legs as they made love.

"Lt. Col. Adkins?"

"I know you're not satisfied with the Corps," she went on, ignoring his query." I think maybe you're ready for something different. Something more of a challenge. Something potentially much more rewarding than being a Lt. Col. in the US Marine Corps."

"And what have you mind?"

She had finished pulling on her dress, and now sat on the bunk across from him, the table between them.

"Freshen my drink, Charlie," she said.

As he picked up the glasses and took the one step to the bar, she reached out and touched him lightly on the back. He jumped.

"You needn't be nervous. If you like what we just had, there can be more. Lots more."

"Now you are making me nervous. I'm not the marrying kind, you know."

"I'm sure," she replied, a little laugh escaping with the words.

He handed her the newly filled glass and waited.

"For background, Lt. Col. Adkins, I'm Colombian, originally. I've been in the States for something more than twenty years."

"You told me."

"Not long ago I was contacted by a man who plans to change things in Colombia. It's not going to be easy, but I'm going to help. "

"Why?"

She frowned for a moment, then smiled.

"Revenge!"

Maria watched Charlie, letting the word sink in.

"Yes, revenge. The people who run the country now, some of them at least, are the same people who killed my father and drove me from my home. I've wanted revenge all my life. Now I have the chance to get it."

"And how do I fit in?"

"We need a couple of things, Charlie. You're one of them.'

"Me?"

"A pilot... no...not just a pilot. A very good pilot."

"You do know how to flatter a guy. First I'm good in bed, sort of..."

"You know you're good Charlie. So do I." She smiled at him. "And when it comes to flying, so does Jusquevera."

"Who?"

"You'll meet him later Charlie. There's one other thing he needs...we need."

He waited.

"One of your planes Charlie. One of those little jump jets!" Charlie stared at her for several seconds, then sat down on the bunk next to her.

"You're serious, aren't you!"

"I've never been more serious in all my life!"

"You want a Harrier?"

"Yes," her reply was matter of fact, something she might say every day. Pick me up some bread and milk on the way home from work, hon. Oh, and please get me a jet fighter too. Don't forget now.

"Do you really think I'm anything but a loyal American fighting man?"

She replied without hesitation.

"Yes."

Charlie stood, glanced down at Maria, lifted his glass and downed its contents. He refilled it and took another sip, then sat across from her.

Chapter Eight

He tried to reconstruct the evening. It had started simply enough.

Depressed!

He had gone to McGuire's to ease his depression and escape the humdrum over a couple of beers and to peruse "Soldier of Fortune." Now, just a couple hours later, he had made love to the most beautiful woman he'd ever known (or was it the other way around), and she was asking him to steal a fighter plane, to throw away his career, and jeopardize his life.

Just another Saturday night?

Maybe he was getting screwed in more ways than one. Maybe Maria was a setup, a decoy designed to test his loyalty, his patriotism. He had heard of sting operations in other branches of the uniformed services. Some had resulted in espionage charges, and more than one proven spy now resided in federal prisons. Even Jason Pollack, who had spied for the officially friendly nation of Israel, might never again know the feel of free soil beneath his feet.

He stared at her.

No, they'd never get a marine uniform on that body. Besides, he could check her out too quickly.

"And what would be in it for me?" he asked.

"A new government will need new leaders. Jusquevera can be very appreciative."

A door swung open in Charlie's mind. Standing in the doorway was General Charlie Adkins, five stars across his epaulets above the dozens of ribbons and medals that adorned his chest.

He shook his head, and the image vanished.

Maria stood.

"You don't have to give me an answer now. Call me tomorrow. The personnel office. It's in the directory.

"I want to go home now Charlie. I'll drive you back to McGuire's."

The trip back to town was quiet. Even Maria's legs, as she drove, couldn't hold his attention. Instead, he kept seeing himself in an office, a general's flags flanking his desk, a view of the city below.

City? What city?

"Will I see you tomorrow?" he asked as he eased himself out of the Pantera.

"Perhaps Charlie. Perhaps." She smiled and drove smoothly out of the parking lot.

He slept little that night. And when he slept Maria commandeered his dreams. She sat on his lap squeezed into the cockpit of A101, his Harrier. They were trying to make love as he bounced the little jet across the beaches. If this plane is rocking, don't bother knocking! But for some reason, there was someone else on the plane too. Impossible, of course. There wasn't room for them. But someone behind him kept calling him.

"General Adkins!"

And when Charlie tried to salute, Maria scolded him.

"Tsk, Tsk, Charlie. Don't salute Uncle. He can't make you feel good the way I can. Salute me Charlie. Salute me!"

And part of Charlie did.

And Charlie crashed!

He saw the beach coming up at him, the sand blinding white.

He awakened with the sun in his eyes, and sweat soaking his pillow.

He rushed through his morning routine, cut himself shaving and cursed the razor. Instead of heading for his office in Building 606, the multi-storied, football field sized, red brick that looked out over Santa Rosa Sound, he headed for Sherman Field.

A101 was hangered, one of a dozen similar fighters awaiting routine maintenance, angled wing tip behind wing tip inside the huge metal cavern.

Charlie walked around to the cockpit ladder and stood to look up, then stroked the aircraft's olive drab flanks. It didn't seem a small airplane standing beside it. But next to an A1A, or an F-16, the Harrier was diminutive indeed. It wasn't the fastest thing in the air. And its firepower was minute compared to a Warthog.

But it was one of the most versatile, maneuverable, responsive little planes in the air. Charlie remembered his first briefings when he qualified for the jump jets. How the British had developed them from prototypes in the early 60's, taking them from underpowered and unstable concepts to well-armed supersonic craft, their Rolls-Royce engines boasting almost five times the thrust produced by the engines in the prototypes.

Charlie patted the plane again.

"You're as pretty as Maria," he said, "almost."

When he got to his office, he poured a cup of coffee and sat on the windowsill overlooking Santa Rosa Sound, the sparkling water cutting the sugar white sand between historic Fort Pickens, which had once imprisoned Geronimo, and the bustling Pensacola NAS. Boats heading for the pass into the Gulf of Mexico dotted the sound.

Trying to think logically about the evening before produced little but confusion, and a chest-constricting desire to see Maria again. He doubted neither her honesty nor her sincerity.

She wanted him to steal an airplane!

She wanted him to help overthrow a government!

That meant a war!

His war!

God, he wanted that!

Didn't he?

He surveyed his office; an office he had occupied now for more than ten years. It had changed little in those years. A plain oak desk, facing the window across an expanse of polished linoleum flooring, flanked by bookshelves and flags. He had added a small color television-video player to the furnishings two years ago and used it to review flight training for particular students.

He poured the dregs of the coffee out the window.

At the stroke of eight o'clock, he picked up the phone and called Maria.

"It's a date," he said when she answered.

"Charlie?"

"Yeah. It's me. Just a bit worse for the wear. When can I see you?"

She paused a moment, and he could hear shuffling sounds. Her voice was muffled.

"I've got some papers for you," she said. "Meet me for lunch at Marchello's. I'll explain then."

Charlie forced himself to concentrate on the stack of flight tests in his basket and struggled to keep flashbacks from the night before from taking over his mind. Occasionally Maria's warmth and aroma flooded him, and he had to get up and pace for several minutes to restore his concentration.

He left the office early and was waiting in the Italian restaurant's bayou side parking lot just off base when Maria's Pantera slipped into a nearby space, its v-8 rumbling softly.

Maria wore a fitted green suit that hugged her body and Charlie felt a distinctive catch in his chest as he took her hand to help her from the car. She greeted him with a touch of her lips that he wanted to linger over, but she wouldn't allow it.

Chapter Nine

The heat stifled him.

Slats wondered why waiting always had to be hot and muggy. He sat at one end of the expansive dark, wooden table. A window was open behind him, and a mid-morning breeze tried half-heartedly to extract heat from the room. Slats felt it, cool against his damp neck. Traffic noise from the boulevard below flowed in with the breeze.

Occupying chairs that virtually filled the space between the table edge and the mahogany wainscoted and paneled walls on either side of the table were three members of the hearing board. They were there to determine whether or not Slats and his squad had acted legally and within departmental guidelines in the shooting that killed Boulevard.

On his right sat Capt. Courant, Slats' supervisor, and Capt. Kraemer, who had conducted the on-the-scene investigation, the results of which the board had been reviewing since the previous afternoon. Slats had sat on the board throughout the sessions, verifying Kraemer's accounts of the scene and answering questions raised by members of the board.

The panel consisted of five members, laymen chosen to establish for public consumption the facts in any shooting incident resulting in death. New boards were chosen at routine intervals and usually, they rubber-stamped the results of the Department's internal investigation.

But Slats' board was different.

He had known that from the moment he had walked into the hearing room. On his board sat Calvin Wasserman, attorney and candidate for a judgeship in the November election. The other panel members listened to Kraemer, nodded occasionally, asked few questions and sat for long periods staring out the window.

But not Wasserman.

He had begun by grilling Kraemer on details.

How far was the table from the door?

How many slugs had Kraemer accounted for?

How much money had been on the table?

And when he addressed Slats, he cross-examined him as he would a hostile witness.

"After all, Lieutenant, you killed three men..."

"No sir, one. Johnny got one. Ivey another. And we're not sure about the fourth man."

"I mean collectively. Together, Lieutenant, your unit killed three men, three black men..." he paused, scanned the faces at the table, and went on "...and for what? Don't we have enough racial tension in this town as it is? You told Kraemer that you were after drugs; heroin, wasn't it? But you didn't find any, did you?"

"No, sir. We found no drugs, except for a few grams of marijuana."

"So why did you kill those men?"

Slats glanced up at the court reporter, bent over her stenographic machine at the far end of the table. He waited for her fingers to stop their play across the keyboard.

"Because they were trying to kill me!"

That exchange set the tone for the hearing.

Now it was nearing noon and three members of the board, plus Slats, Courant, and Kraemer, and the court reporter sat in the steamy little room waiting for Wasserman and the balding little engineer who sat between Wasserman and the door, to return from the bathroom. The traffic rattled and roared along Tulane Avenue, and the blare of a boom box perched on the shoulder of a kid below the window careened about the room.

Cigar smoke, mainly from Capt. Courant's ever burning pencil-thin stogie, collected beneath the high ceiling, where years of such accumulations had stained the oak paneling almost black, and whiffs of smoke whisked out the window on the occasional breeze.

Slats leaned back in his chair, sliding down until his head rested against the hard back. He closed his eyes. His dream; part memory, part fantasy, was waiting; and in it, respite from the heat and strife of the hearing room.

He was in the station house locker room, blushing beneath an opened shirt, staring at a beautiful woman who stood posed in the doorway, the early morning sun flaming through the windows to silhouette her body against the fabric of an already revealing dress. Their briefly exchanged greetings vanished like dust motes drifting from sunbeams into shadows. They stared at one another.

No one witnessed their silent communion.

Had they been seen, Slats would have denied to his deathbed the spark that leaped from his psyche to hers and back, as lightning flies from earth to sky and returns. In the privacy of his mind, he knew he had seen it, and he wondered if she had.

He almost asked, but realized what he was about to say, and simply stopped.

"What?" she asked.

She shifted slightly in the doorway, lifting the toe of her right foot to scratch the back of her left calf absently.

"Nothing," Slats replied.

His composure returning, he went back to his locker, peeled off his shirt and hung it, carefully, and slid a clean white tee shirt from the top shelf. He pulled it on over his head, tucked it into his jeans and zipped his fly, and sat on the bench to slip on the brown loafers nestled beneath it.

When he looked up, she still stood in the doorway, still watching him.

"My name's Maria," she said, with just a trace of an accent. "...and I think you're awfully cute."

The angle of the sun behind her was changing, and Slats could see her better now. He realized that she was younger than he had at first thought. Her poise, her clothes, her make-up, and her dramatic appearance in the doorway had created a goddess where, in fact, a young woman stood.

She must have been no more than eighteen, and she looked very familiar. Could she have been the hooker to whom he had played "John" a few months before? And even the realization of her youth could not completely squelch the aura that surrounded her. It set up a harmonic deep in his being, and he found himself wondering how her body would feel against his.

"You're just a kid," he said.

"You poor old man." Her slight accent thickened the sarcasm. "Why don't you try me sometime and find out what this little kid can teach the big, old man? I'll bet you're all of...what...25?

"Twenty-seven," Slats replied. "What are you doing here, anyway?"

"Waiting for my man to come get me. They picked three other girls and me up about two hours ago. The little room up front is so annoying I decided to walk around a bit; you know, stretch my legs."

Slats got up from the bench. He started toward her, wanting to see deeper into her eyes, maybe touch her arm, listen to whatever story it was she wished to tell.

But a sudden shadow blocked the sun streaming in behind her.

She turned, and Slats saw a massive black man wearing a white linen suit and a white Panama hat. His skin shone ebony against the suit. He carried a cane with a white handkerchief wrapped about the ball in his right hand.

His voice was a rumble from the cavern of his chest.

"Maria, doll child! So here ya are. Hun, it did worry me when Richard called and told me you was in thuh slam."

Massive hands enclosed Maria's waist and lifted her toward the ceiling as a doting father might lift his daughter.

"But don' you worry none. Ol' Boulevard done paid you bail. All's goin' be fine. Les you and me find us some breakfast, what say."

The slamming of a glass-partitioned door cracked the dream frame, and Slats watched it fall apart. He opened his eyes and squinted against the glare from the window.

Why did air conditioners always fail at the worst times?

Wasserman was struggling past the chair near the head of the table, followed by the chubby engineer.

He sat. The engineer followed suit. The board member nearest Slats was snoring slightly, his head thrown back and his mouth wide, a white mustache drooping over his mouth when he inhaled. The dark man on the sleeping man's left reached over and shook a shoulder gently.The sleeper awoke with muttered apologies.

Captain Courant cleared his throat, then spoke softly, looking from one man to the next as he was talking.

"Gentlemen. It's nearing noon. We all have many things to attend to, so let's try and wrap this affair up as quickly as possible, shall we?"

Wasserman leaned forward in his chair, menace in his eyes.

"Captain, you're not suggesting that we sweep this under the rug, are you?"

"Certainly not!"

He looked Wasserman in the eyes. "But we've been over all of Kraemer's material twice now. Don't you think you can reach a conclusion soon?"

"Soon, Captain! Soon." Wasserman replied. "But I do have a couple more questions." He looked first at Slats, then back to Kraemer.

"Captain Kraemer. Just how much money did you find on the table in that room?"

Kraemer picked up a sheaf of typescript from the table and leafed through them. He looked up at Wasserman.

"There was exactly $237,000."

"That's an unusual amount, don't you think? I mean, aren't drug payoffs usually in round figures, like $100,000, or $200,000, or $500,000?"

Kraemer drummed the fingers of his right hand on the table.

"I suppose that's true," he said.

"Is there anything to indicate that some money might have been missing?"

Kraemer sighed.

"That room was a wreck. The money was mostly on the table. It was new bills, mostly hundrerds, some fifties, and twenties. A couple of bundles had been broken. Yes, it is possible some of the money was taken from the room before I got there."

"So we could be missing $63,000, or maybe even $263,000 if there was a half-million-dollar payoff. Is that right, Lieutenant?"

Wasserman leaned over the table toward Slats, his hands before him, fingers laced.

"Wasserman," Courant barked across the table, acid in his voice and fire on his leathery cheeks, "if you are accusing my men of stealing, you'd better have a lot more evidence that I can see in this case."

Courant mimicked Wasserman's posture, then lowered his voice to a tenor whisper.

"If you don't shut up, I'll see that you get roasted in my precincts this fall!" he said. He glanced at the stenographer, whose fingers had ceased their dance over the tiny machine. With a gesture she indicated she hadn't heard the comment, and Courant merely shook his head.

Wasserman's face reddened. His interlaced fingers clenched, and Slats thought he heard his teeth grinding. When he spoke, his voice hissed with suppressed anger.

"Courant, I'm just trying to get a full and complete report on this shooting. I didn't ask for this job, but if the people want it done, I'm going to give it my best." He thought a moment, glancing at the court reporter. He wanted to be sure she had immortalized his words on paper. Her fingers resumed their dance.

"Frankly, this mess stinks to high heaven. Three dead men, two black, one of them this city's biggest pimp for more than a decade! A foreign national shot to death! Almost a quarter-million in new bills on a table in the room where all the gunplay goes on, and nobody can say why it's there.

"And on top of all that, one of the victims gets up and drives away, maybe taking an armload of money with him. If someone else didn't get it!"

He looked back toward Slats.

Courant spoke again, in a voice now minus the anger.

"Wasserman, this board is charged only with determining whether or not the officers involved used their weapons correctly and judiciously. Nothing more. Any theories you have about this case may be expressed through the proper channels.

"Now, is the board ready to write its report?"

Wasserman stared at Courant a moment, then sat back and looked at the other board members. Three nodded assent.

Courant looked at Kraemer and Slats. "Let's go to my office and have some coffee. Let these guys finish."

Five minutes later they sat in Courant's office each holding demitasse cups brimming with strong, pure coffee. Slats preferred a taste of chicory, but he accepted the cup, added a dab of sugar, and sipped. The hot brew melted some of the roughness in his throat.

None of the three had spoken since leaving the hearing room. Slats and Kraemer sat on a small settee facing the coffee table. The table itself was but a plate glass top sitting on three highly polished cypress knees. Facing the table opposite the settee, Courant's easy chair, a great wooden antique, went unoccupied while Courant stood staring through half-closed Venetian blinds into the glare.

Slats felt uncomfortable.

"Captain," he waited for Courant to look at him. "I just wanted to say thanks for the back-up in there."

Courant reached up and pulled the blinds closed. He walked past the desk and its piles of paper stacked in neat rows to the office door. He closed it, then placed himself gingerly in the great chair.

He thought awhile.

"Slats, I hate to admit it, but that S-O-B has some good points. You went in there with a search warrant looking for heroin and all you came out with is crabgrass."

"Now, I know you well enough to know the shootings were without malice, certainly defensive, and part of the job. I also know you well enough to know...or to believe...that you didn't steal any money."

"Johnny's testimony backs up your story. We know who fired the first shot, and the dude who ran could have grabbed the money. But ..." he paused, "...where's the horse? If there was no dope, why was all the money there in the first place, and what's the malarkey about airplane stuff?"

Courant stopped talking as pointedly as he had begun. He sat, the demitasse held daintily between thumb and forefinger, staring at the coat hook on the back of the office door, his expression expectant, as though he thought Slats would provide him with answers to the questions he had just posed.

Slats felt the need to say something.

The questions Courant had asked were the same issues that had plagued him. For the past seven nights his sleep had been shattered a dozen times by a black face that grinned at him and mumbled: "Get the pres, get the pres, get the pres."

Twice he had awakened screaming, startling Olivia so badly that, the second time, she moved into the living room for the remainder of the night.

And his one attempt to make love to his wife, Saturday morning when they could sleep in while the kids watched cartoons on television at Olivia's mother's apartment, next door, disappointed him. Even the little sex games they had developed over their eight years of marriage failed to arouse Slats. He had dealt with other marital shortcomings before but he had never been impotent.

He spent most of the weekend drinking beer and cursing the television programming.

When he had calmed his libido, he and Olivia talked through the case several times, going over and over the same questions, particularly the meaning of Boulevard's ramblings before he died. Slats had told no one but Olivia of the pimp's mutterings. He had originally written them into his reports but deleted them before filing the papers. It seemed obvious that the addition of Boulevard's words turned an already bizarre story into sheer insanity.

Courant sipped noisily at his coffee.

Slats' mind flashed back to the blood-spattered tenement apartment where Boulevard had mumbled his way into oblivion.

Perhaps now would be a good time to remember officially what had happened in those few seconds that only Slats had witnessed? How to work his way into it?

"I can only assume that the money was there to pay off the Dutchman for delivering the horse. The Florida people, the investigators in Miami, think Maarten must have dropped the dope somewhere between Miami and here since we couldn't find it. We took Maarten's trailer apart, but he had stripped it clean before he left. He obviously had no intention of ever going back.

"Captain, the only thing that makes logical sense is that Boulevard and his boys carried the money to pay off the Dutchman. Maarten must have stashed the dope, planning to tell Boulevard how to find it."

Slats couldn't bring himself to reveal his omissions. He shrugged.

Courant sipped at his coffee, leaned back as far as the antique chair could safely support him, and half-grinned at Slats.

"Sure, Lieutenant. With construction that solid, it wouldn't take a hurricane to blow this building away. I could do it like this," he took a deep breath and puffed gently in the direction of Slats and Kraemer, his cheeks billowing with the effort. His breath carried the scent of stale cigars. Slats instinctively wrinkled his nose, and caught himself doing it, but Courant noticed his face.

"Sorry, Lieutenant. But answer me this. You say Boulevard, and his boys carried the money up to the Dutchman to buy dope. But where the hell would Boulevard get a quarter-million dollars, let alone get it in new bills?" His voice sailed half an octave upward.

"And do you think that old pimp would turn loose any money unless he held what it was to buy in his fat black hand?"

Slats shrugged again.

Courant was right. It would have been uncharacteristic.

"And what about the...the airplane parts?" Courant asked.

"I don't know, Captain. Ivey said they were airplane instruments. He's a flyer. He saw them for just a few moments, but...well...he's pretty sure. But I don't know why they were there, or why they disappeared."

"How about this, Lieutenant? The Dutchman was selling airplane parts to Boulevard? Makes about as much sense as vanishing dope, doesn't it?"

"Yes, I suppose it does."

Slats wished he could exchange his coffee for a cold beer, and he could go home and sit in front of his television.

"Hey, don't look so down-in-the-dumps, Jones," Kraemer's voiced boomed in Slat's ear, and a big hand grasped his right shoulder. He had forgotten about the guy the patrols called the 'German jerk-off' and now, somehow, his presence in the room lifted some of the pressures.

"I ran the shooting investigation. The board will clear you. They have no choice. Then you can just put this whole business out of your mind and get back to being a cop again."

It wasn't going to be as easy as Kraemer made it sound.

Not that Slats wasn't confident of a clean bill from the shooting board. He was.

Wasserman had been the only problem, and Courant had effectively disarmed him. But there remained too many whys and not enough wherefores. He would have to answer a lot of his own questions, alleviate his doubts.

Courant's office door rattled.

It was the stenographer.

Courant rose gingerly, crossed to the door and opened it.

"The board finished?" he asked her.

"Yes. I'll have the report for you tomorrow."

"Okay. But tell me what they say in the report."

She hesitated, slipped her glasses on and looked at the slim pile of paper in hand.

"Well, sir, what it boils down to is that the officers used their weapons according to departmental guidelines, that all rounds fired were in the execution of duty, and that the deaths resulting from the shootings were justified by circumstances."

"That should please the chief," Courant said. "Thank you. Please see that we have several extra copies of the report for the files, and for the press."

Slats and Kraemer had stood when Courant opened the door. Courant turned to face them leaving the door standing open.

"Well, Lieutenant," he said, "looks like you can get back to work."

"Yes, sir."

"And Lieutenant..."

"Yes, sir?"

"I still want answers. If you come up with anything interesting, we'll want to know."

He didn't stipulate who "we" might be, but Slats guessed that Courant and the Chief had discussed the case in detail. The Chief was particularly sensitive to racial incidents. After Boulevard's death had been made public, the mood on the streets grew darker. Only the fact that a cop had been shot in the melee staved off a backlash. As it was, several black civic and religious leaders had come forward to decry publicly the slayings.

Chapter Ten

When Slats reached his office, two floors deeper within the granite entombment that housed the principal administrative functionaries, he found Ivey waiting.

"We finally got it, Slats."

"What?"

"A shot at Boulevard's place."

Slats reacted slowly.

"Find anything?"

"Crud, mostly. You've heard 'living in squalor?' Boulevard invented the term."

Slats had tried after the shooting to obtain a warrant to search Boulevard's apartment. But Judge O'Roark balked. He said Slats lacked sufficient cause for the warrant. Since there had been no drugs at the scene of the shooting, there was no substantial evidence that Boulevard was part of a narcotics transaction, he said.

O'Roark was up for retention in the fall election, and Slats attributed his reluctance to the general anti-police sentiment pervading the city. And Boulevard's only living relative, his 300-pound sister, refused the police permission to search the premises, and for four days they had watched her carry from the apartment armloads of household items, clocks, radios, kitchen utensils.

"How'd you get into the place, Ivey?"

"His sister called this morning and said she had everything she wanted. Invited us in. She took every lamp, every pot and pan, every bit of bric-a-brac there was. But she didn't touch his papers; must have known there wasn't any money. All of his clothes were still there, too."

"Well?"

"We found no drugs, no money, nothing remotely illegal."

"Damn!"

Slats had hoped that Boulevard had obtained a sample of whatever it was he was buying and had stashed it at home.

"Sure his sister didn't get it?" he asked.

"She wouldn't know what to do with it. She isn't a dealer, and she'd have a hell of a time trying to sell it with us watching. No. It just wasn't there."

He paused a moment.

"You might find this interesting, though. Did you know Boulevard was into boats? "

"Boats? You're kidding. Boulevard wouldn't have known his aft from a hole in the ground." Ivy grimaced.

"We found these."

Ivey had been holding a tube of rolled papers in his left hand.

"They were on his kitchen table. He had a yardstick across them and had apparently made several plots."

Ivey pushed past Slats to his desk, where he flicked on the gooseneck lamp and unrolled three marine charts of the coastal area south of New Orleans. Two of the charts, detailed sections of an area almost 100 miles southwest of New Orleans, were covered with illegible notes in a large scrawl. In some places, a more defined handwriting appeared on the scrawled notes indicating water depths, and locations of various kinds of oil field structures. On the third chart, in much smaller scale, a line was drawn heading southeast to the chart's margin.

There, in barely legible scribble, Slats made out the words, "THE GRAND TURK, OCTOBER 6."

"Boulevard's never been on a boat in his life, Ivey," Slats said, bending over the little Cajun's shoulder. "I'd bank on it."

"What are these for then?"

"Wish I knew. Where is this?" He pointed his forefinger at a large canal on the top chart.

"That's down near Cocodrie, not far from the Gulf," Ivey replied. "Been fishing down there too many times to count; redfish, specs. Used to be great fishing. Still not too bad, despite all the oil field traffic."

Slats had fished out of Cocodrie in his youth. He remembered the monotonous drive along the Bayou Petite Caillou, crossing smaller branching bayous where people sat beneath moss-draped oak trees watching fishing floats bob in the tidal pull of the brown water. Cocodrie was hardly more than a spot on the map, the end of the road, a jumping-off point for oil field workers, and a supply point for commercial and recreational fishermen. Slats knew it had changed over the years, and now sported several real marinas, and even condominium developments, their presence incongruous in the midst of the marsh and bayous.

"This is ridiculous, Ivey. I doubt that Boulevard even knew that Cocodrie exists. Why would he have these charts?"

Ivey studied Slats for a moment.

"I don't know!

"That's why I brought them back. Too many things about this case don't fit. I figured that something else that didn't fit in probably related to the other things that don't."

Slats stared at him.

"Anybody ever tell you, you have a weird way of expressing yourself?" Slats asked.

Ivey cocked his head and looked over his shoulder at Slats.

"Only wen I talk flat like dey do down duh bayou," he said.

"Look, Slats," his voice returned to normal. He picked up a pencil and used it as a pointer. "Did you notice these circles?"

Slats hadn't seen them.

He moved around Ivey and leaned close. Under the lamp's glare, he saw four concentric circles radiating from the pencil point. Near the circles was a symbol, neatly lettered "tree." Slats looked at the larger chart. The lettering was in a hand identical to the margin notes on the large chart. It was done by fine line pen and appeared fresher than most of the smudged notations elsewhere on the smaller charts. Examining the area more closely, Slats could make out other notations in the same hand, a plot and bearings for a canal leading to the wellhead structure, and hand-entered depth soundings that differed from the depth sounding notations printed originally on the chart.

"That's sure not Boulevard's handwriting," Slats mumbled.

"No. And see how the depth in the canal's all handwritten. That's a well canal, fairly new, probably dredged in the past couple of years. Somebody ran that canal with a fathometer to get those depth readings. And they did it recently."

"Maybe Boulevard planned to go into the oil business? Any theories, Ivey?"

"C'mon guy. Get serious, huh. Look, you're the boss. What's next?"

Slats stuck his left wrist under the lamp. The digital watch face read 4:15. He snapped off the lamp, straightened up, and laid his right hand on Ivey's right shoulder.

"I don't know about you, fella," he said, "but I've had a rough couple of days with the shooting board. I'm going home to a cold beer, a warm wife, and a late movie on the tube. "

He walked around Ivey and retrieved the plaid sports jacket from its hook behind his office door. It was garish. He didn't put it on. Instead, he held it at arm's length and studied it for a moment. The guy who had run from the shooting scene had worn one similar, a jacket that had hidden a shoulder-holstered .45 automatic.

Ivey looked at Slats as though he had just seen him.

"Oh, un...yeah. Well, what was the verdict, Slats? Do we hang at dawn?"

"They found in our favor. They didn't have much choice based on Kraemer's report. But that bastard Wasserman had me going for a while."

Slats couldn't discern whether his news had any effect on the little Cajun. Ivey followed him from the office.

"Okay, buddy," he said, "drink one for me, too. And tell Olive Oyle I'm having wet dreams about her." He headed up the marble-floored corridor towards the locker room.

"You bastard," Slats yelled over his shoulder, "you stop dreaming about my wife."

Chapter Eleven

He took the stairs at the end of the hall two at a time, and when he stepped from the dingy grayness of the building into the bright warmth of the afternoon sun, it pierced the shadows that had blanketed him the past week. Waiting for the bus (he hated driving in the city's traffic and used his car to get to work only when he had too), he decided to take his wife to dinner. They'd go to Tony Angelo's and tell Chuck (what a name for a waiter in one of the country's best Italian restaurants) to "feed us!" Chuck always made good choices. It was one of their favorite excursions.

It would be a warm and mellow fall evening. If he could keep his mind off the case, it would be fun to seduce Olivia; some wine, good food, then maybe popcorn and lovemaking in front of the television, half watching the late movie during occasional intermissions in the lovemaking.

If the kids would visit Granny.

There are advantages to having your mother-in-law as a next door neighbor.

Slats lived in a West Bank apartment complex about thirty minutes by bus from headquarters. He had moved his family into the apartment next door to his mother-in-law a year before, not without trepidation. But it had worked out well. It was less expensive than the French Quarter apartment they had tried to maintain, and it offered better recreational facilities for the boys.

And since Granny doted on the kids, it was natural for them to spend an evening or two a week, and an occasional weekend, with her. Slats and Olivia made good use of their privacy and their relationship, which had begun to falter as Slats career gained momentum.

The apartment was far from what a younger Slats had envisioned in his dreams. It was small, a living room, separate kitchen-family room, two bedrooms, and two baths. It was one of forty similar apartments in a large concourse arrangement, winged about a swimming pool and recreation room. It was run by a dictatorial manager who collected the rent on the first day of each month, but who also answered immediately complaints about leaky faucets, faulty wiring, busted disposals, etc.

On the bus, Slats tried to put the case, and Boulevard's insane mutterings, aside.

But his fantasy took him unexpectedly.

He didn't fight it. He let it take him back through the gates of almost-memory to another life, where he scarcely related his function as a beat officer to his function now. Often he welcomed the unbidden images that sprang to life, as art springs from the eyes of the artist, from sketches blurred by the passage of years; time had begun to dim the boundary between memory and make-believe.

Sometimes he tried to superimpose other pictures over the beginnings of the fantasy, pictures from, say Sunday last, when he and Olivia and the boys had spent the afternoon on the Mark Twain, a scaled-down version of a 19th Century riverboat, meshed among tourists exclaiming over Mississippi River commerce and bayou-side scenery. They made the trip more often than frugal budgeting should allow, and counted it one of their joys. The boys enjoyed it for the sake of the boat ride. Slats and Olivia never tired of meeting tourists and providing bits of factual information to replace the often comic jargon of the brochures they clutched in midwestern-pale hands.

Now and then when the job tired him more than usual, the ride home lulled him to sleep. Then the fantasy, waiting just beyond the threshold of conscious recall, could slip cool fingers into his dreams.

It took the fingernail-on-a-blackboard voice of the not-pretty bus driver, whose name he had not learned in the year he had been riding with her, to arouse him.

"Hey, Lieutenant. Your stop's coming up."

"Huh! Oh, hey, thanks. Don't know where my mind is today."

"Have a good evening."

"Yeah. You too."

The snap back to reality often left him bitchy.

Olivia would read his mood the moment he opened the door.

"Hi," she'd say, peck him on the cheek, and disappear into the kitchen. Half-an-hour later, after a cold beer and ten laps of the pool, he would be a decent human being again. But until then his wife and the boys, forewarned by their mother, avoided him.

But today he arrived at his stop feeling good.

Slats was in good physical condition and that allowed him to keep up with his six-year-olds. He knew several officers his age who couldn't run around the block twice, despite departmental standards. Irv Henson's teenage son was always after Irv to counsel his Boy Scout troop on camping, Irv having been an Army Ranger for ten of his thirty-five years. But Irv preferred to spend his weekends planted in an air-conditioned room before a giant screen television, drinking beer. He looked the part. Only an occasional citation for physical deficiency, which threatened his livelihood, kept Irv from total incapacitation.

Slats bought two roses from a street corner flower vendor, and when he arrived at his apartment door, he rang the bell.

Olivia opened the door, cocked her head to the left so that her blond bangs fell across her right eye.

"Slats. What the...?"

"Comment ca va, Madame?" He brought the flowers from behind his back, "Pour vous."

"Ah, merci," she accepted the flowers and the game, "Merci. Bien. Bien. Et vous?"

He stepped inside the door, grabbed Olivia around the waist and pressed his mouth to hers. She smelled lemony. He squeezed until he heard a slight popping sound from her back. He stepped away and looked at her.

She feigned a grimace, then sniffed at the flowers.

"Nice," she said, then seriously, "I am glad to see you more akin to a human being again. You've been bad weather for more than a week now."

Slats gave her a quick little kiss on the lips and headed for the bedroom to shed his excess clothing.

"Me, too," he said. "I mean I'm glad I feel better. The shooting board backed us up. Now if I could just figure out what the hell was going on, I'd be great."

He re-entered the living room, pulling a striped shirt over his head, then followed Olivia into the kitchen. She was arranging the flowers in a small vase. A fresh lemon meringue pie cooling on the counter near the range scented the apartment. Slats leaned over and took a deep breath.

"I have a proposition to make," he said.

"Oh?"

He reached out and turned her toward him, leaving a hand resting on each side of her waist.

"Yes. I'll take you out for whatever kind of dinner you would care to have if I can have some of that pie, and maybe a few other sweets, during the late show tonight."

Olivia knew her husband's sweet tooth, and his penchant for making love on the floor in front of the television.

She smiled at him.

"You mean I can have supper at the restaurant of my choosing, just for a little piece of pie?"

He pulled her against him. "Just a small piece..." he kissed her.

"Have we got a deal?"

"I'll see if Mama can keep the kids," she said, pulling away.

Olivia's mother agreed readily. She had been searching for an excuse to get out, and she would love to take the kids to see the new Disney animated movie at the mall. Slats knew she wasn't just working hard to get the great grandma award. Having the kids around made her feel things she had thought lost.

Two hours later Slats and Olivia sat at their favorite table, halfway back on the right-hand side, at Tujague's, one of the less pretentious French restaurants in the city. While Slats had his mouth set for Tony Angelo's Italian fare, he was as good as his word and bowed to Olivia's preference. Slat's had nothing against Tujague's, but it wasn't wholly casual. Some of the waiters, old Bavarians in tuxedos, had reputations for being rude, particularly to tourists

From the warm fisherman's loaf, its aroma sinfully delicious, that found its way to the table before the cocktails, to the scalding coffee and petite fours that closed the meal, Slats found nothing that didn't tweak his salivary glands. And the rather rare bottle of Chateau Baret '87 that Slats had discovered handwritten in on his wine list mellowed both the meal and the mood.

As they entered the apartment, Slats strode over and turned on the television.

"How about a piece of that pie?" he asked.

"Coming up," she answered, going into the kitchen. "Want something to wash it down?"

"I'll get that later," he said in a stage whisper that carried into the kitchen.

When she returned to the living room, she found that Slats had pushed the coffee table away from the sofa and was seated on the floor, leaning against the couch, one foot on the coffee table. He looked up at her and patted a small pillow on the floor next to him. The television was on, the volume just audible enough to be understood. On the screen, a tall man with glasses held a pointer to a digital map of The United States, saying something about an early fall frontal system.

"What's on the late show?" she asked, settling on the pillow and placing two small plates, each bearing a bright yellow and white triangle of pie, on the floor at their feet. She tucked her legs into a lotus position and began to eat.

Slats picked up a folded television listing and examined it. He put it down, snickering softly.

"The Bride of Dracula, my sweet," he said, and kissed her on the left side of her neck, nipping gently with is teeth.

"The news will be over in about ten minutes."

Slats consumed his pie in four bites.

"Delicious. Your mama sure knew what she was doing when she had you make that first pie for me."

"The way to a man's heart..." Olivia said, letting the words die. She pushed her empty plate aside.

"Bet I know a shortcut," Slats said. He leaned across, pushing her back against the sofa, and kissed her lips gently. He began unbuttoning the soft white blouse she wore tucked into her suit-cut slacks. Her slight tendency toward chubbiness showed mostly in her legs, and she liked the neat lines of the suit-cut clothing. Not the most stylish, it kept her from feeling bulky. She had shed the jacket to the suit when they entered the apartment, and in less than a minute Slats had the blouse open and her breasts free.

As he kissed his way down her throat, she shook the blouse off her arms and tossed the bra back onto the sofa. She leaned back and stroked his hair as he tongued her left nipple. Her body jerked.

"Sorry," she murmured.

"Ummmm," said the mouth at her breast.

"...while the high tomorrow should be about 86," the television weatherman said. "Now back to Bill."

Slats lifted his head and kissed Olivia's lips slightly. He leaned back against the sofa, his shirt open, the light from the television screen flicking colors across his lightly haired chest.

"You lead a while. I'll follow," he said.

"Is this part of our bargain?" she asked.

"Uh huh."

"Well, I guess a deal's a deal" she replied, leaning across his body and applying her tongue to his left nipple. He twitched at the sensation, then tried to relax. He felt a pressure building in his groin. He opened his eyes to watch her tongue play against his flesh. Lifting his head, he gazed at the television screen, where a green and blue map behind the newscaster looked vaguely familiar. He separated his mind from the tingle in his breast and the pressure in his groin and realized he was looking at a map of the Louisiana coast, strikingly similar to the marine charts he had seen earlier.

It was the sports anchor talking.

"If you're fishing the well-line canals, Cocodrie is the jumping off spot for a treasure of fine fishing. There are thousands of miles of canals that offer excellent habitat for specs and redfish..."

The word stuck in his mind.

Treasure.

The camera was zooming on the map, the canals and bayous coming up fast as though they would explode from the screen. That's it! Those marks on the charts in Boulevard's apartment. They're treasure maps!

The Treasure? What else? Hundreds or thousands of pounds of heroin.

"That's it!" he exclaimed!

The mouth at his nipple lifted to his face.

"Glad you like it, honey. My turn next?"

Slats stared into Olivia's face. He stuttered as he tried to shift his mind back to the moment.

"I've always wanted to leave a man speechless," Olivia said, sliding back and stretching out on the carpet. "Remember now, no rug burns."

Slats gazed at her a moment then reached for the button on her slacks.

"And the Navy has called off its week-old search for Lt. Col. Charlie Adkins."

The camera zoomed past the newsman to the map.

"Adkins disappeared on a routine flight from Pensacola to New Orleans. The Marine Corps pilot and his British-built Harrier jet vanished from flight controllers' screens some fifty miles south of the Louisiana coast. Both Coast Guard and Navy searches have failed to produce any trace of the plane.

"And finally in tonight's news..."

Slats tuned out the newscaster. He tried hard to cut through the mellow fog that had seeped over his mind. The gold fire of lust died.

"Honey?" he asked.

She looked up from her ardor and saw the expression on Slats' face.

"What's wrong, babe?" she asked.

"Well. I'm not sure, but something certainly is."

"Did I hurt you?"

"What? Oh. No! No, it's nothing like that. It's this damn case!"

" I thought I was putting that out of your mind."

"So did I! Until that last report on the news, just now."

"You were listening to the news?"

"Not purposely! But that previous story, about the missing airman. That might just tie in. I don't know. Logically it doesn't make much sense, but..."

He told her about Ivey's finding the charts at Boulevard's apartment and the markings on the maps. He went back over the original shooting, and, as much for himself as for his wife, he questioned why there should be airplane instruments and parts at the shooting scene.

And why had the surviving member of the trio taken the time to grab the parts, instead of just running? He was wounded, and undoubtedly hurting badly.

"Honey, I'm sorry, but I have to make a phone call."

Olivia sat up, gave him a lingering look, kissed his right ear, and said, "Okay. But if I wake up bitchy in the morning, it'll be all your fault."

Slats hadn't waited for an answer. He was already in motion, heading for the wall phone beyond the swinging door into the kitchen. He punched out Ivey's number. It rang five times before a sleepy voice answered.

"Yeah?"

"Ivey. This is Slats. Did you see the evening news?"

"Huh? No. Why?"

Slats outlined the news report he had just heard. Ivey couldn't seem to connect the airplane disappearance to the Boulevard shooting. "C'mon, Ivey. Wake up, man! You still have those charts you were showing me earlier?"

"Sure."

"Well, get over here with them, will you?"

"Okay! Okay! Put some coffee on, okay? See you in a few minutes."

Fifteen minutes later, Ivey sat on the sofa with Slats on his right, and Olivia on his left, poring over the charts. Olivia had just placed three steaming cups of coffee on the table with the charts, along with a copy of a two-week-old newspaper. In the lower right-hand corner of page one was a small story, and a tiny map, describing the disappearance of Lt. Col. Charlie Adkins and his Harrier.

"The Harrier is the one that can go straight up and down, right?" Slats asked.

"More or less. It's a British jet that can take off and land vertically. The Marines have a couple of squadrons of them. Great little birds."

"That's what I thought. Look, this damn little map in the paper is worthless. We need to know the exact location where they believe that this Adkins crashed."

Minutes later he was speaking to the duty officer at the New Orleans US Coast Guard Station.

"Sure, Lieutenant. What you're after is public record. I just find it a bit strange that you'd be calling for it at this time of night," the voice on the phone said.

"Just mark it up to eccentricity," Slats said. "Can you give me some coordinates? I've got charts; I think they cover the area."

It took a few minutes for the night OIC to find the material on Adkins' disappearance.

Slats repeated the coordinates as he received them, and Ivey plotted them on the chart in red ink, making the latest entry clearly distinguishable from the numerous other marks. Slats said thanks, hung up and hurried back to the coffee table.

"What've we got?" he asked.

"I'm not real sure what you want, Slats, but the crash site, at least, what they believe is the crash site, is here,"

Ivey pointed his finger next to a red "X".

"And where are those circles we were looking at this afternoon?"

Ivey moved his arm to remove its shadow from the page. The circles were evident a few inches into the green portion of the chart. Ivey spread his hand along the scale at the side of the page, then stretched it across the space between the "X" and the circles.

"Looks like it's about fifty miles, almost due south of the markings," Ivey said.

"How long would it take a Harrier to cover that distance?"

"You think Adkins didn't crash?"

Slats' answer was high-pitched and edgy. He banged his right fist into his left palm and stepped away from the table. "Damn, I don't know! Maybe this whole mess is just getting too much for me."

He stopped and looked back at Olivia. Ivey looked down at the chart. Slats started for the kitchen. "I need a beer. Want one, Ivey?" Olivia wouldn't drink beer.

"Sure, Slats. Whatever you've got."

Slats returned with two bottles of Abita Amber. He twisted the top from one and set it in front of Ivey, clinking the lid into the ashtray that held down one corner of the chart. The other bottle he had opened in the kitchen. He tilted his head back and took a long swallow of the icy brew.

"I suppose," Ivey started speaking slowly, one hand reaching for the beer while he remained bent studiously over the chart. "I suppose," he repeated, "that a Harrier could get down in that marsh if there were a large enough pad to hold its weight. But I don't know how they would hide it. I mean, the people who own that well must go in there now and then to check it.

"Besides," he looked up at Slats, "why would anyone want to land that plane in the swamps?"

"Ivey, could those airplane parts at the scene when I shot Boulevard, could they have come from that Harrier?"

"What?" Ivey looked from Slats to Olivia. She could almost see his mind churning. "You think Boulevard had something to do with that! Wait a minute now!"

Ivey tilted his head back and closed his eyes. Slats watched his face. Ivey wrinkled his brow. "I've never been in a Harrier. But the stick didn't look ...I mean, ...I don't know.

"I can't say no. I suppose it's possible, sure."

"Thanks, Ivey."

"For what? Look, man, are you trying to tell me Boulevard was buying an airplane?"

"No, no. But I think he might have been selling one. Acting as an agent really. Procurement's always been Boulevard's thing, hasn't it? This time, instead of procuring women, or dope, he procured an airplane."

"But how? And even more to the point, why? If Boulevard procured an airplane for Maarten, well, what the hell was the owner, or part owner, of a French-owned, South American-based circus going to do with a military airplane?"

A picture sprang into Slats' mind. He saw Boulevard sitting, two tiny holes oozing red above his eyes, babbling, "The Pres gone go boom. Oh yeah. You beautiful momma." The audio fuzzed, like a poorly tuned radio. The mind-picture seeped red.

"Slats?" Olivia's voice, a note of worry evident, brought him back to reality. "You all right, babe?"

"Sure, hon. I'm fine." Gooseflesh raised the hair on his arms. "Ivey, how's your boat?"

Ivey looked exasperated.

"My boat? It's ready to go fishing just like always."

Everyone at the precinct knew that Ivey would go fishing at the drop of a hat. His boat, a twenty-four-foot Offshore fisherman, was his pride, and it showed. It stayed beneath the carport next to Ivey's townhouse, always ready to be trailered to the nearest water. His car sat on the drive in the weather.

"Let's hook her up and head for Cocodrie! We might even get in some fishing."

"Babe, it's the middle of the night. Can't this wait until morning?" Olivia asked.

Slats walked around to her.

"Hon, by the time we get everything together and get moving, it'll take us three hours to get there. I want to be on the water by first light."

"That's what I would do if I were going fishing, all right. But we're going looking for a plane? Slats, what will you do if we find it?"

"I'll worry about that when it happens," Slats said, wondering. The whole scenario read like something concocted by Ian Fleming. If they were to find the airplane, which Slats didn't expect to happen, it would prove his reasoning sound. But he wasn't sure he wanted it proven sound. Then Boulevard's final words would be more than just the mumblings of a dying maniac, wouldn't they?

"Slats," Ivey chugged the last of the beer, "I'll hook up the boat. I'll load the fishing gear too, just for the sake of cover, but you still haven't told me why Boulevard would be selling an airplane. I mean, that's a military jet. Was he trying to start a war? "

"I don't know, Ivey. Just before he died..." he stopped. Ivey would believe him, certainly, but would it be wise to expose his suspicions further? "...well. Look, Ivey, if any of this checks out, I'll tell you the rest. Right now, I'd feel like an idiot. Okay?"

Ivey paused, one hand on the door knob.

"Okay, Slats. I hope tomorrow is worth wasting Saturday for."

He pulled the door open and closed it gently behind him. Olivia helped Slats assemble a fishing wardrobe; an old white long-sleeved shirt, stained and faded jeans, sneakers, and a wide-brimmed hat. Almost as an afterthought, he grabbed the blue Ruger magnum his Uncle Johnny had given him ten years earlier as a college graduation gift (BS in criminal justice). The gun was big; a Ruger 454 casull Super Red Hawk. A Dirty Harry weapon, powerful enough to crack an engine block, yet accurate to more than a dozen yards on the range.

He had never been able to convince his uncle his study had more to do with psychology that warfare. But he appreciated the weapon, nevertheless. After logging hours on the range, he made it his weapon of choice in the annual departmental competitions. His scores had earned him a reputation as a sharpshooter.

He slung the Ruger in a holster under his left shoulder. The jeans jacket he pulled over it bulged from the girth of the gun. Ivey took it in at a glance when Slats opened the door at his second ring.

Still standing in the hall, he asked, "Planning to blow some fish out of the water?"

Slats decided he was right. He took off both the gun and the jacket and held the holster in his hand with the jacket covering the weapon. Olivia stuck a brown paper bag in his other hand.

"Couple sandwiches," she said. "Should hold you till breakfast, anyway." He kissed her lightly, and she closed the door after him, whispering "be careful" at his back.

For most of the next three hours, they rode in silence, the boat thumping heavily behind them on the concrete highways south of the city. Slats napped a bit, only to have Boulevard's babbling countenance startle him into wakefulness each time he drowsed.

"Slats!"

He was glad to be wakened. The dreams had sapped his strength for days now. He feared going to sleep to face again and again killing men whose apparent objective in existing was to die at his hand, bloodily, and without reason.

He opened his eyes to a faint daylight.

"Are we here?"

"Almost," Ivey answered, yawning. "End of the road in about two miles."

The highway stopped abruptly at a permanent red and white hash-marked barrier fifty yards from the edge of a bayou that had drowned more than one drunk when the flimsy roadblock failed to halt their speeding cars. Lights blinked from the windows of a large structure raised on pilings to the right of the roadway, and a neatly painted sign near the steps leading to the ten-foot-high porch advertised "T-Boy's Place," ice, cold beer, hi-balls, and milk. Dozens of cars filled an unpaved parking area across from the bar-restaurant-store. Farther down the bayou on the right, a collection of buildings gleamed in the dawn, catching the sky's reflection from the water along docks below the buildings. A lone trawl boat, tied snugly to the dock, silently suffered the indignities bestowed by a well-fed flock of night herons perched on its bow rail.

Ivey wheeled the car around in front of the barrier and backed down the public launching ramp. His boat floated easily off the trailer, and Ivey left Slats holding the anchor rope, slapping at mosquitoes, while he parked the car. Watching him maneuver the trailer in alongside a half-dozen other car-trailer combinations, Slats absently counted the cars in the parking area. There were forty-six cars and pickup trucks, most without trailers.

"Where are all those people?" he asked Ivey on his return.

"Most of those are roustabouts and the like," Ivey answered, scanning the lot. "Old T'boy in the store watches the cars while they're offshore. For a small fee. How about some coffee?"

Slats helped him tie the boat to the pier alongside the launching ramp, and they trudged across the white shell lot to the store. Inside, the front of the building was one large room, with a counter across the back and a door leading to a living area. The counter doubled as a bar, separating beer coolers and a glass front liquor cabinet from public access. Shelves of staple groceries and canned goods lined the walls at both ends of the bar, and six wooden tables and an odd assortment of chairs sat in no particular arrangement about the room. Four men sat at one table near the door, sipping coffee and smoking, watching the smoke drift through the screen door. Two others sat at the bar, facing one another about four feet apart, animated in conversation, their profiles framing between them behind the bar a wrinkled gray countenance that lit up when Ivey walked through the door ahead of Slats.

"Hey, Ivey! Comment ca va, Boy?" A twisted gray arm appeared beside the face and beckoned Ivey and Slats down the bar to a point beyond the argumentative pair. Ivey returned the greeting.

"I'm fine, T'Boy. How've you been?"

"Better on the weekends," T-Boy acknowledged. "Going to get some reds?"

Ivey glanced at Slats.

"Yeah. I haven't caught any fish since last spring. Figured this would be a good weekend to try. How 'bout a couple cups."

The wrinkled gray arms moved quickly, and seconds later two Styrofoam cups, half filled with the oily blackness of dripped dark roast with chicory, steamed before them.

"Still know how to make coffee, eh, T'Boy?" Ivey chided him.

"For my friends, sure," T'Boy rejoined. "Even those who show up only every six months." Although he hadn't spoken to Slats, he kept glancing up at him. He shuffled one step to his right to stand directly across the bar from him. "Sugar...or milk?" he asked.

Slats looked levelly into the deep gray eyes beneath the shock of salt and pepper hair that hung over the creased forehead.

"Just a little sugar. Thanks." A spidery arm reached beneath the counter and planted a slip-top sugar bowl next to the two coffee cups. Slats swished in a half-teaspoonful and tasted. He found the bitter edge of the chicory still harsh. He sipped noisily and felt his face flush above the cup.

"T'Boy, this is my friend and my boss, Liechester Jones. He doesn't appreciate his first name. So we call him Slats."

"Your boss, huh. I didn't know cops had bosses. What do you do, Slats?"

A lot of the bayou flatness fell from his voice as he extended the spidery arm that had fetched the sugar, and opened a small but bony hand above the counter. Slats grasped it. The strength in the diminutive grip surprised him. Somewhere in the twined hands, a knuckle popped.

"Damned old hand," T'Boy said. He looked slightly pained, broke the handshake, and began rubbing his right hand with his left. "It's strong as a mule," he said, with a gesture down the bar to a stainless steel counter and sink, "got to be when you open as many oysters as I do. But I never know when the damn thing's going to give out on me."

He stuck the ailing hand beneath his left armpit and sat on a stool unseen beneath the lip of the counter. He leaned lightly on the counter top, his left elbow on the counter, his chin atop a balled left fist. "You here to fish, Ivey?"

"Sure, T'Boy, why?"

T'Boy was whispering now.

"You guys are narcs, right?"

Ivey attempted to copy T'Boy's almost sinister countenance.

"You know something we should know?"

"The Coast Guard, and the Navy been in and out of here a dozen times in the past couple days. Claim they're looking for a plane crash. We think they're setting up to bust a big dope ring. That's why you're here, huh?"

Ivey glanced at Slats, shrugged and leaned closer to T'Boy.

"Well, fella, I'll tell you..." Ivey began and lapsed into French. Slats' knowledge of the language was rudimentary, and the rapidity of the conversation totally excluded him. He felt affronted by their bilingualism, so he lifted his coffee cup and walked to the door, hoping Ivey wouldn't humor the old man too long. He was anxious to be about his self-appointed task. He stood looking through the screen door, smelling the cigarette smoke from the table of men at his right, listening to the faint whine of mosquitoes trying to make their way through the fine wire mesh.

His gaze settled on the parking lot across from the doorway, and he noticed that from the height of the raised building he could see the tops of all the cars in the lot, some highly polished and shining brilliantly in the slanting sunlight, others little more than rusting lids held tenuously atop hulks that barely moved under their own power. One glinting rooftop tossed the sun's rays askew while the others reflected more or less uniformly the golden fire now burning away the last of the early fall morning mists.

Slats glanced back at the flawed reflection and realized that the car top he was staring at was dented, compressed in the center and flattened an inch or more toward the edges, as though something heavy had fallen on the car. He felt an almost physical jab in the ribs of his memory.

"What the hell?" Slats mumbled to himself, pushing through the swinging screen and letting it slap shut behind him. From the porch, he could not see the car below the doors, but if the roofline had not been compressed, the car might be a Thunderbird.

Had a Thunderbird been parked behind the rooming house?

Tossing his coffee cup over the porch railing, he ran down the stairs.

He bounded across the restaurant's shell lot, stumbled when he hit the concrete of the roadway, and ran full tilt around the first line of cars in the parking area. The car he sought was parked halfway down the second row. He walked slowly around it, trying to picture it sitting behind the tenement where a week before three men had died. There had been a red Thunderbird in the alley that day. Slats stood behind the car and screwed his face up into a painful frown trying to visualize the surveillance photos of the alley. The car had been parked immediately behind, almost against, the tenement's back wall.

Slats stepped up close to the car and examined the top. It was driven down three inches near the center, with creases extending toward each corner. There were traces of red darker than the paint in a smear near the center of the roof. Slats leaned across the top and scraped at one of the smears with his fingernail. It flaked and fell away from the paint.

The car's doors were locked but, peering through the driver's side window, Slats could make out dark stains on the plush velour of the driver's seat.

There was no license plate.

"What's up?"

Slats jumped, slamming his left hand against an old Cadillac parked next to the Thunderbird. He cursed himself for being so easily startled.

"Damnation!" he shook his hand. "Sorry, Ivey. Guess I could use more sleep. I didn't see you come up."

"Obviously. Didn't mean to startle you. What are you doing?"

Nursing his painful hand, Slats stepped away from the line of cars and motioned Ivey over beside him.

"Look at that car carefully," he said, gesturing with his face. "Does it look familiar to you?"

Ivey's face distorted into a puzzled expression that made the little Frenchman seem far older than his thirty-six years. Suddenly his face straightened, and his mouth opened slightly.

"That car was parked behind the house!" he said.

"You sure?"

"It certainly looks like it. I stared at the damn thing long enough sitting in that window up the alley. Boulevard parked right next to it when he drove up. Let me think, now."

He closed his eyes and cupped his left hand to his forehead.

"There were several other cars in the alley too. But this one was right behind the house we were watching." He opened his eyes and looked at Slats, then back at the car.

"What's it doing here?"

"Look at the top."

Ivey looked.

"That bastard who jumped out of the second-story window. He's got more lives than a cat."

"Sure looks that way. We have to be certain. Call the parish sheriff's office and ask them to impound the car. We'll have our boys pick it up later and give it a white glove inspection."

Ivey pulled out his phone and looked at it.

"No signal," he said.

He loped across the lot and up the stairs two-at-a-time to disappear beyond banging screen doors. Slats walked slowly toward the boat launch. He sat on the dock, head down on arms folded across his knees, waiting for Ivey to return. He was almost asleep when he heard footsteps on the dock timbers. Ivey's quick step irritated Slats.

"They going to do it?" Slats asked.

"Yeah. But they're curious as hell. I told them we were going fishing, and we stumbled on a car that was used in a drug operation in the city. They don't believe me, but they'll go along for the ride."

He paused, took a deep breath of the musty swamp air, stretching both arms toward the sky and yawning. "It's a beautiful morning. Want to catch some fish?"

Slats watched him from where he sat.

"They will pick up the car?" he asked again.

"Later this morning. You ready?"

"Yeah. Let's go."

Chapter Twelve

Ivey's well-tuned outboards cranked willingly, and five minutes later they were heading down the bayou at twenty-five knots, the wake of the boat barely disturbing the already roiled surface of the brown water.

Standing next to Ivey at the console of the open fisherman, the breeze flapping his windbreaker about him, Slats felt uncertain. Could Ivey find the right canal? The marshes beyond the bayou banks seemed unchanging, broken only occasionally by brief stands of water oaks and dense shrubbery capping higher ridges at the intersections with other bayous. Here and there shallow bays opened off the main channel, and for a few minutes, their track crossed a chain of bays punctuated by silver and black metal structures atop which burned gas flares.

Ivey gestured at the flares.

"Lots of energy going to waste," he shouted above the roar of his engines, "but they're great places to catch trout at night."

Ivey had the marked-up chart stuck on a clipboard, folded so that their objective appeared near the center of the board. He studied the chart closely as they crossed the last bay in the string. Then he put the helm to starboard and roared away from the marked channel they had followed from Cocodrie.

Five minutes later the shore of the bay rushed up at them and split precisely ahead into a large dredged canal that ran arrow-straight away from the bay.

"This is it," Ivey shouted. He flipped on his fathometer. "It's deeper than most of the canals. Must be some natural flow through here. They usually silt in pretty fast."

On both sides, dredged spoil had been piled up, and the banks thus formed were covered with thick growths of a vast variety of woody and grassy vegetation. Instead of marsh grasses running out into murky shallows the water lapped at heavy black mud. Their wake splashed like dirty wash-water onto the overhanging weeds. The morning sun poured a sticky warmth, and even in the breeze of the moving boat, Slats could feel perspiration dampening his clothing. Both men had already shed their jackets, and Slats would have abandoned his shirt, but for the sunburn that he knew would follow.

Ivey reduced power, slowing the boat. They rounded a long curve and immediately ahead the canal opened into the almost circular cove where a gas line tree rose above an entanglement of pipes and gauges. Ivey threw the engines into idle. They "putt-putted" gently toward the well.

"This is the place, all right," Ivey said, "but I don't see any airplane."

Slats was studying the canal banks.

"Look!"

He pointed toward the bank to starboard. Looking past his outstretched hand, Ivey could see that the vegetation along a fifty-foot section of the bank had been crushed into the mud, and the mud bank itself had been flattened into a gentle incline.

Ivey kicked the boat into gear and nudged them up to the bank. The water was deep to the shoreline. When the bow bumped against the mud, Slats stepped onto the bank and stuck the little Danforth anchor's prongs into the sun-dried humus. Ivey shut off the engines and hopped from the boat.

"What do you think?" Slats asked him.

"It looks like there was a helluva big barge pushed up here. You think they put the plane on that and then towed it away?"

The spoil bank rose from the water's edge sharply, except where it had apparently been crushed by the prow of a barge, to an average height some six feet above the water, before falling away into the sea of marsh and saw-grass that dominated the coastal swamps. Slats and Ivey walked toward the edge of the muddy indention, where they had to struggle up the higher spoil bank.

Slats turned and looked back toward the boat.

"That's what it looks like to me, Ivey. There never was any dope. The Dutchman was paying Boulevard and his..." he paused, "whatever they were, for obtaining an airplane, and not just any plane, a Harrier, to be exact."

He paused again, staring out into the sky.

"Or maybe Maarten sold the dope farther south before he came up here, so he'd have the money to pay for the plane. Whatever. Then this Adkins guy flies over, lands on the barge, and they pull a couple parts off the plane to prove delivery."

"But Slats, wait. There are a couple of big holes here. If somebody wanted an American military plane or a British one as in this case, why didn't they just pay the pilot to fly it out of the States? And who would want a plane like that anyway?

"What about radar, Ivey? You're a pilot. If he had just taken off in a military plane and kept flying south, for example, he'd have been on radar the whole time, right?"

"Yeah. You're right. And they could probably have routed some boys out of South Florida to get him before he put the plane down elsewhere. I was a good flyer, but I guess I wouldn't have been a good thief," Ivey conceded thoughtfully.

"You're a hell of a good cop," Slats said.

"Blow in my ear and I'll follow you anywhere."

A commotion in the sawgrass behind the spoil ridge startled them. They pushed through the jungle-like growth and watched something large and black struggling in the tall grass twenty feet from them. Then it rose into the air, flapping hard.

It was a turkey vulture.

Slats studied the bird as it rapidly gained altitude. Then he looked at Ivey, raised his eyebrows, and started down the spoil ridge.

"Careful," Ivey said, "You'll sink up to your eyeballs! Let me go first."

With Ivey leading, they picked their way the ten feet down the slope and another ten feet across the marsh, where they did sink to their ankles, but no deeper, thanks to Ivey's ability to find the denser humus in the soupy muck.

As they approached the spot from which the vulture had taken flight, there arose a cacophony of scurrying and clicking. Sunk deep in the grass, water pooling about it in foul lagoons, lay the remains of a body, only its clothing holding bone to bone. Bits of the jacket twitched as fiddler crabs ran from the vibrations of approaching feet, then stopped among nearby stalks of marsh grass to await the departure of the intruders so they could return to scouring bone.

The skull lay a few inches farther from the clothing than would have been natural, obviously moved by one of the swamp's carrion eaters. A forefinger-size hole had been punched cleanly through the forehead above the right eye socket, and little remained of the bone that should have composed the back of the head.

The left shoe and its contents were missing. But what held Slats' attention was the jacket.

An obnoxiously bright plaid sports jacket covered the upper torso, and jeans stretched flaccidly down toward the remaining black patent shoe.

Slats saw the jacket in his mind's eye as it flailed about its wearer when he yanked the .45 from its holster. He heard the explosion and the masked thud as the bullet crashed into Johnny Reeves' shoulder, throwing him backward onto Ivey.

"It's him, Ivey! That's the runner."

Ivey didn't reply immediately. He looked pale and seemed to have some difficulty breathing. He turned away from Slats and the stench. He retched weakly.

"God, I'm glad I didn't have any breakfast," he said faintly.

The hot sun and the wind in their faces during the thirty-minute boat ride back to Cocodrie washed the haze from Slats' mind and brought Ivey's color back.

Shouting against the wind and the roar, Slats told Ivey about Boulevard's final words. He described in as much detail as he could reconstruct the aggressiveness in the big pimp's eyes and voice as he died.

"I think there may be a real threat. To national security, maybe to the President," Slats said.

Ivey was skeptical.

"Terrorists?" he asked. "Look, Slats, they can't fly that plane into Washington and bomb the White House, can they? This thing is weird as hell, all right, but I can't believe it's part of a plot against the country. You don't believe that, do you?"

Slats shrugged, but Ivey could read his intensity.

Yes, he did believe it!

The heat and their fatigue, physical and emotional, made the climb up the stairs to "T'boys" an effort for both men. When they pushed the screen doors open, T'boy barked across the room at them.

"Hey, Ivey! Cotch some big 'uns?"

Chapter Thirteen

Slats paced.

Damn he hated waiting!

The marble-floored corridor rang softly beneath his feet. He walked past Capt. Courant's door, stopped, turned, and walked back.

Courant had set the time. Ten minutes ago Slats had knocked, and Courant's voice had cracked through the glass.

"Just a minute, Lieutenant."

So Slats waited, and paced. Hell, being a cop was a lot like being in the Army. Hurry up and wait. Wait for chow in the Army; wait for days on stake-out; wait in line for a promotion. Don't rush the system, or you'll wind up where you started, walking a beat, on a long, perpetually dirty street.

Following the discovery of the body in the marshes below Cocodrie, Slats had spent hours in debate with himself, with Olivia, and with Ivey. The parish sheriff's office had taken custody of the body, then turned it over to the state crime lab. A slug retrieved from the skeleton's shoulder carried rifling that matched Slats' Beretta. There was no doubt that the remains were those of the man who had escaped after Boulevard's death. Beyond that, no identity could be established. But it was clear that Slats had not killed the man. Death had been caused by a large caliber, high-powered bullet that had blown away the back of the man's head.

The car had yielded no clues. It had been stolen several weeks before from a motel in Pensacola, Florida, and its owner was seeking insurance compensation. The owner might never know that a bleeding, dying man had sat behind the wheel, fleeing in a blind panic the scene of a multiple slaying.

Slats played his own devil's advocate, beating down every argument Olivia and Ivey could raise for adding to his report what Boulevard had said before he died, and his interpretation of those words. Even before he began, he knew his arguing was a pretext. He likened his feelings to those he often had when he lay next to

Olivia in the darkness before dawn, waiting for the first tinges of gray in the east.

As surely as he knew in those dark moments that daylight would come, he knew before beginning his debate what he had to do. But the discussion helped him organize the bits and pieces of the puzzle. Although he could assemble only a small portion of it, he could see vague outlines of a much larger picture.

What really showed in that frame? Was there a plot against the President of The United States?

The need for an answer grew into his psyche, like the tap root of a young tree; one that might grow to shade his life from the sunlight forever... the shrinks called it obsession!

Courant's office door opened, catching him a dozen steps down the hall.

"Lt. Jones, please come in and sit down before you wear a groove into the floor."

Only a slight creak in the voice betrayed its owner's age. The almost unlined face and the slim body argued against what the files said about Courant's tenancy on Earth.

Slats marched into the office, adjusting his tie to remove some of the unaccustomed pressure from his Adam's apple. Slats seldom wore a tie. Courant always did. Today it was a thin beige one knotted in a neat overhand. The color matched exactly the narrow-lapel meticulously tailored Versace suit the captain wore to show off his still lithe physique. Rumor had it that the captain's only vice, besides an occasional Jack Daniel's, was young women. But he never bragged, and when he did speak of a woman it was with a courtly discretion.

With the women under his command, he was always formal and businesslike.

Not so with the men in his division.

With them, he was casual, friendly, sometimes paternal. He could be harsh, even a bit cruel if his men did not return the respect which he accorded them. He was one of the few highly ranked officers in the department who had the respect of his officers.

Not that they all liked him.

Some disliked him intensely. Usually, when he was right.

Courant had lasted long on the force, more than thirty years. Intelligence and determination had lifted him to his position, and would have placed him higher, probably chief, some said, had it not been for political considerations. Wealth buys position, and Courant, while comfortable, could not compete with the wealthy.

Sometimes Slats feared the older man; not his place or even how his reports might assist or slow his progress up the promotional ladder. It was the intensity of the steel-sharp eyes that glinted beneath the lean gray brows that bothered Slats.

Courant drew two demitasse coffees from his eternally brewing pot, gestured to the table and placed the cups on its glass top. Slats sat, and Courant settled into his massive antique.

He appeared deep in thought, and Slats wasn't eager to disturb his reverie.

Courant leaned forward, wiped a hand absently over his face, and picked up a pair of glasses from the table. He slipped them on, picked up his cup and sipped gingerly.

When he spoke, his voice was soft and friendly, but his words cut.

"Tell me, Lieutenant, do you believe the President of The United States is in danger? Really?"

"Captain, I didn't say that!"

"I know you didn't say that. But everything you put in this implies that."

He tapped a manila envelope on the table.

"Yes, sir," Slats rested his chin on his left fist.

"Lieutenant, I know what the facts are in this case. I was aware of everything, even without your report, except for what Boulevard said. Or what you think he said."

"Yes, sir, I'm sure."

"Tell me, Lieutenant, why hadn't you said anything about Boulevard's comments before?"

Slats hesitated.

Courant peered at him over the rim of his demitasse; comfortable, waiting, no hint of animosity.

"I wasn't sure I believed what was happening. I mean, I heard him say those things. I have no doubts about what I heard him say. But the whole scene was so weird I didn't think anyone else would believe it. "

The picture crowded back in on Slats: Boulevard on the nondescript red sofa, a dead man at his feet and another draped across a money-strewn coffee table. Slats on his knees, his .22 in his stretched-out hand. Boulevard talking, not mumbling, but speaking plainly, and then his head falling forward in death.

"Lieutenant, it sounds like the insane ramblings of a dying man, ...a dream...or in this case, a nightmare. Or perhaps you were the insane one."

Slats was startled by the implication.

"What? Me? Sir, I..."

"Don't protest too quickly, Lieutenant.

"I've been over your scenario," he again tapped the envelope, "several times. The facts are all right. The same facts were strong enough to support you before the shooting board. And the additional evidence, the car, and the body of the man who fled the scene, indicate that the men you shot were linked to something heavy.

"I still believe that 'something heavy' was drugs."

Courant paused for a sip of coffee.

"We know that there has been a lot of crack on the streets lately, and it must have come in by boat. We know that a lot of illicit material comes in through the bayous. So, the facts that you itemize in your little white paper fit quite well. You are talking about a major drug ring, a ring that you busted, despite the fact that no hard drugs were found at the scene.

"So why talk about a plot against the country?"

"But Boulevard's comments...?"

"Lieutenant, did anyone else hear him say these things?"

Slats thought a moment.

"No sir.

"Captain, what about the plane? Ivey saw the airplane parts."

"One glimpse of something that might have come from an airplane isn't enough to substantiate your theory that Boulevard had an airplane. And if he had, what would he have done with it? Fly in more drugs?

"No, Lieutenant, I'm afraid I can't buy your conclusions. The fabric of your story is woven of gossamer threads. Cold fact tears it to bits."

Courant slipped his glasses off and tapped his front teeth with one ear piece. He seemed to savor the words he had spoken.

Slats knew then he would not convince Courant. But he was certain that Lt. Col. Charlie Adkins and his plane were not buried in the blackness of the Gulf floor.

"Captain, the Navy never found the plane they said went down south of Cocodrie. And there was an awfully big barge in that canal sometime recently."

Courant sipped, listening.

Slats continued.

"Of course, Boulevard couldn't have planned anything that fantastic, but he might have been a go-between.

"I just don't want to shut the door on it yet."

Courant sat watching him. Maybe he was on a positive track. Even though the old man didn't buy his theory, he was interested.

"Captain, I'm not asking for any carte blanche. But this could be crucial."

Courant closed his eyes momentarily and pinched the bridge of his nose.

"I thought you might feel that way, Lieutenant," he said, opening his eyes and leaning back into his chair.

"And while I disagree with you, I'm willing to give you a little more rope. I think you should talk this over with Adrian Falgout."

Falgout was the agent in charge of the local office of the Federal Bureau of Investigation.

"Captain, I don't want to pull the Bureau into this," Slats said.

"The Bureau is already in. Maarten was apparently involved in interstate traffic of illicit materials. I've already discussed the drug angle with Falgout, and I've taken the liberty to send him a copy of your latest report. He'll be available at a mutually convenient time. "

Slats didn't like it.

He knew Falgout slightly and didn't like him.

Falgout had a reputation for ruthlessness and headline grabbing. The guys in the police department pressroom often speculated among themselves on his political ambitions.

"Lieutenant!"

Slats had been staring at his hands.

"Lieutenant, don't look so crestfallen. I am telling you not to go overboard. It has been my experience that the simplest solutions usually fit the best. Occam's razor. Find a simple solution. Maybe Falgout can help."

"I didn't know you were friends, sir."

"Friends?" he paused, frowning. "I don't like the man even a little. But he is smart. And should any of your theories prove correct, the Bureau would take over. Assassination plots are not in our bailiwick."

"But Captain..." Slats began.

"Now get back to work, Lieutenant," Courant said, a hard edge creeping into his voice.

Slats left Courant's office depressed, and the feeling lifted only a little when he stepped off the bus in front of Baptist Hospital. They had transferred Johnny Reeves to Baptist as soon as he was out of danger. At least the view of tree-lined streets from the window in his room would be more conducive to recovery. In the weeks since the shooting Johnny's shoulder had been operated on twice. The first time they had gone in just to sort out the damage.

Then ten days ago they had begun repairing the smashed bone. The relatively slow moving .45 slug had careened off the scapula and torn away large amounts of connective tissue, broken his collarbone and destroyed part of the joint. An inch down and the bullet would have deflected through his chest.

When Slats entered the room, he found Johnny propped up in bed, watching "All My Children" on the too-small television above the foot of his bed. He winced at Slats' greeting.

"I guess I should be glad to be alive, but I'm not sure I am. I never knew there could be this much pain in all the world."

His left arm and his head stuck out of a massive roll of bandages and padding. He was swaddled from the waist up.

Slats put one hand on the big man's uninjured shoulder.

"Anything I can do for you this morning?" he asked.

Johnny took his time about replying. When he did speak, his voice was sullen, remorseful.

"Just get the bastard who did this to me," he muttered.

"That's already taken care of Johnny," Slats replied softly.

Johnny craned his head, wincing with the pain of movement. For the first time in weeks, there was a glint of interest in the big man's eyes.

"No kidding?"

He watched Slat's face.

"Tell me."

Slats recited the story of the trip he and Ivy made to Cocodrie. Johnny expressed some disappointment that Slats had not personally killed the man who had shot him.

"But I'm glad he's dead!"

"I'm not, " Slats replied. "Alive he might have supplied some answers."

Johnny looked puzzled.

"What kind of answers? We busted a drug operation."

"Well, I'm glad someone's sure," he said.

The puzzled expression on Johnny's face melted into exhaustion, and his head slid back against the pillow. He closed his eyes. But when he opened them moments later those same blue eyes were bright and focused.

"Slats, if it wasn't a drug bust, what was it?"

"Well," Slats hesitated.

Could it hurt to have one more person question his sanity? At least, Johnny was a trusted friend.

It took him fifteen minutes to tell the tale, the same scenario he had put on paper for Courant. He wrapped with a blow by blow description of Boulevard's death throes.

"Boy," Johnny whistled softly. "Jim Garrison would turn over in his grave."

Johnny's reference to the notorious New Orleans district attorney of the '60s brought Slats flashbacks of the Kennedy assassination hearings.

"Yeah, " Slats replied. "Courant thinks I've lost it as bad as Garrison did. I'm not far from agreeing with him. But in this case, the President hasn't been assassinated. At least, not yet."

Johnny spoke more softly now, and his eyelids drifted down to half-mast.

"You know, Slats, I've worked with you a long time, and I've never known you to be completely wrong, about anything. That didn't come out quite right, but you know what I mean. You've always had good instincts. I suppose that's why you're the L-T."

Johnny's eyes closed.

Slats watched him a moment, then stood and walked to the window. He watched the traffic and did some quick reflecting. He and Johnny had worked together a long time. They had faced life-threatening situations and had come away from all but the last physically unscathed. They had made many good cases, had lots of convictions, and the commendations to prove their worth.

So why did he now feel so overwhelmed and vulnerable, like a rodeo clown caught out of the barrel.

"Okay, big fellow." Slats said. He turned away from the window.

"Make sure they put that shoulder together right. I can't use a one-armed wing man."

He walked back to the bed and clasped Johnny's good hand in his right.

"I'm going to see Falgout."

Johnny opened his eyes and watched Slats as he went out the door. He said nothing.

Chapter Fourteen

Slats stepped out of the air-conditioned building into the steaming sunshine. The warmth felt good. He had to share with Falgout what he knew, but as far as NOPD went, it was still his case. And Courant had not told him to forget it. He knew the captain didn't entirely buy his scenario, but there were no sanctions on his investigation.

A shift change at the hospital surrounded him in a sea of white, and the nearly empty bus waiting at the stop filled quickly. Slats sat next to a middle-aged woman whose uniform showed the signs of dealing with humanity at its worst. Were those blood stains on the tail of her jacket?

Slats tried not to think about it. He leaned back, ignoring the press of flesh, and closed his eyes. The bus clanked and squeaked. Humanity dinned about him. A warm laziness washed over him and the motion of the bus, the shoosh of the air conditioning, the aroma of confined bodies...

He knew he was falling into the dream, and he didn't try to stop.

He drifted with it...and found himself standing in the doorway of an old bar on Esplanade, not far from the French Quarter. A mild crush of people filled the narrow room and the air pushed toward the door by the overhead fan carried the sickly sweet smell of old alcohol and stale tobacco, perfume, and human musk. The air was as turgid as the flesh inside. It blended with the cooler evening air as it ebbed past Slats, sapping his being as it flowed.

The frustration of being a young, uniformed officer washed over him.

This bar was one of dozens of similar establishments on his beat. In it, humanity teemed, as pervasive and as prolific as the roaches that infested its baseboards and crawl spaces. People grabbed for any pleasure, any relief from lives of tedium; draining it from countless glasses, sucking it from smoke and ash, injecting it, and fornicating with it in damp beds in dark corners.

They pursued happiness so hard that they outran it. They tried to buy it, or steal it, but all too often they simply killed it.

They were legion! How could one cop in a blue uniform press back the tide of rampant mankind?

He couldn't, of course.

He had to deal with people individually. And with their crimes in the same manner. He could attack the problems only on personal levels.

On that level, every drug dealer busted, every user even partially reformed, every prostitute rehabilitated, was a victory.

Or so Slats had believed as a young and ambitious cop. It was what he believed in his soul as he stood in the doorway of that Esplanade bar.

Perched on a stool at the front corner of the bar before it all but vanished into the dark interior was Maria.

Slats stared, again amazed at her beauty. Her white summer dress clung to her, accenting the dark olive skin, her face mobile as she smiled at a young, black, Army officer several stools away. How could any girl so beautiful sell herself? Slats had searched for her since she had left him standing dumbfounded in the squad room, exiting almost regally on the arms of the black pimp Boulevard. From the first he had found it difficult to accept her as a hooker. But she had a record, and when first booked had listed her age as sixteen.

There were no convictions. Apparently Boulevard's legal connections were good, probably paid for as much in flesh as cash. No one at the precinct doubted that she was part of Boulevard's stable, one of more than a dozen girls whom he protected vigilantly. Some said he beat his girls to keep them in line and to guarantee his cut of their take, but none of the women complained.

Slats knew the girl he was watching was very young and had been working the streets of New Orleans for at least two years. He had wondered how many men had used that beautiful body and looked deep into those smiling dark eyes. And he didn't care. He knew that he wanted her.

And he wanted her off the streets.

The first part would be easy. Just pay her fee.

The second part wouldn't be so easy. He couldn't afford to keep her, not on a patrolman's salary. If she didn't want out, she wouldn't get out. He knew hookers who seemed to enjoy their profession.

He would never accomplish anything standing in the doorway.

He walked into the dimness and leaned against the bar between Maria and the Lieutenant. She glared at him a moment. Then recognition.

The soldier stared at his glass, looked at his uniform, then at Slats.

Maria's voice was as confident as her demeanor. Something about her manner suggested more than just street smarts. It wasn't just intelligence or beauty, but bearing and aloofness.

"Well, the man in blue? Want to turn around for me so that I can be sure?"

Slats didn't move.

Maria hesitated only a moment.

"To what do I owe the honor of this visit? Is it business..." she turned to the bar, lifted a gold-tipped cigarette to her lips, lit it.

She smiled.

"Both."

She took a slow drag on the long, thin cigarette.

"Interesting," she replied, her accent sliding the words melodically across her teeth, "since I am also. You see, pleasure is my business."

"I know. I saw you at the station."

"Of course you did."

"It's business because I'm on duty. This is part of my area. But seeing you is a pleasure. It really is."

She cocked her head, and her smile slipped to one side, became quizzical.

"Do you socialize, " she emphasized the word "with all the working girls on your beat?"

"No. " he paused. "Are you always so...brusque?'

"Not with customers. But...you're not a customer."

"And if I were?"

She stared at him for several seconds, then crushed out the cigarette. When her eyes returned to him, her smile was gone.

"I don't want to play games, cop," she started to slide off the stool. "You know what I'm doing here. You want to run me in?" she held out her hands, palms up.

"Hey, no. I'm not playing games! Look, I'll be off in less than an hour. Will you still be here?"

She continued to study his face, but let her arms fall to her sides.

"Will you make it worth my while?"

He nodded.

"I don't come cheap, " she said, then realizing the unintentional entendre, grinned.

"I know. " He paused. "I'll be back in less than an hour. You'll be here?"

She patted the stool.

"Right here."

He turned to leave.

"I was right, you know," Maria said, a hint of laughter in her voice.

He looked back over his shoulder. She was laughing now.

"Great buns, " she said, "even in that uniform."

When Slats got back to the stationhouse, it took less than ten minutes to complete the paperwork for an uneventful day. He took a quick shower, slipped into jeans and a golf shirt and virtually ran out of the station. When he reached the bar, many of the happy hour patrons had departed, and the atmosphere inside lost some of its murkiness. But, Maria wasn't on her stool.

An icicle stabbed into his upper abdomen. Had she given up on him and left on the arms of a trick?

But then he saw her. She was at the far end of the bar, leaning on it with a phone receiver pressed hard to her right ear. One hand sheltered the mouthpiece. Her dress had hiked well up the back of her legs and as Slats walked toward her he traced the contours from her ankles to her thighs. The hemline creased the snakehead clasps of the garter belt fastened to her stockings.

A warm tingle replaced the icy incision in his gut.

Never in his life had he wanted a woman the way he wanted the little hooker who leaned so casually across the bar.

Not that his libido was suffering. At least two other girls in the city would share their beds with him. Independently, of course. Both were girls of whom his parents would approve. Both were good looking, talented women with careers of their own. Each professed to enjoy his lovemaking. And both made him feel good. But neither could generate in his loins the fire that burned there as he watched Maria. Even the anticipation that had boiled in his gut before his first real sexual encounter at the tender age of seventeen hadn't equaled his current rut.

Maria saw him approaching and winked, holding up one finger in a "just-a-sec" signal.

He sat down next to her and despite the still crowded bar, a bartender appeared directly across from him. He stood there, waiting. Until Maria waved him away.

Her phone conversation consisted primarily of listening. Then she was on the stool next to him.

"Just old Boulevard," she said. Her lip curled, but the smile he expected became more of a sneer. "He's got to check on his girls. He's such a big teddy bear."

"You don't like him, do you?" Slats question was really a statement.

Maria's face softened, and the sneer worked its way into a smile.

"Does he hurt you?" he asked.

"No. No... Boulevard never hurts his girls. But look. Man...I don't want to talk about Boulevard. Let's talk about you. What have you got in mind?"

"Let's go to my place," he replied.

"Nearby?"

"Across the river."

"That'll take awhile."

She paused, studying his face again.

"You know, the time I'll be spending with you... I could probably turn several guys."

"And how much would you make?"

"Several hundred..." a black vested apparition appeared and the bartender slid a small stemmed glass across the bar to Maria, a toothpick pierced olive balanced on the rim.

She picked up the toothpick and nibbled at the olive. Then tossed off the drink in a single swallow.

"Look," Slats said. "I'll come up with $350 if you'll come home with me."

She didn't look away, but disappointment tinged her eyes.

"Hey, " he said, "I'm not exactly a rich man."

"Most cops aren't," she replied. But her voice was softer now.

"But, " she continued, "what's wrong with an hour in a place I know just around the corner. Won't cost you half of what you're talking about. And we can still have some fun."

Slats stared at her. He knew he could never be satisfied with a wham-bam-thank-you-mam. He shook his head, hesitantly.

Maria returned his stare without moving, then slid off the stool. He feared she was about to walk out the door, and he could feel his heart beating heavily. But she walked back to the phone and dialed.

He couldn't hear her conversation, but moments later she returned, took his hand and pulled him toward her.

"C'mon. Let's get out of here."

She slipped her arm through his, and they walked elbows locked together down the sidewalk, making most of the block before she broke the silence.

"I must be crazy!" she said. "If Boulevard finds out I'm spending the night off the street, he'll be angry. If he finds out I spent the night with a cop he'll be furious. "

"You said he wouldn't hurt you."

"He doesn't have to hurt me. He just has to quit caring. There're other guys around who'll do the hurting. They love to get hold of Boulevard's ex-girls. You don't know what some of those guys can do,"

Slats did know. He's seen the results of pimp wars. Girls who went from two hundred dollars a trick call girls to twenty-five dollar purveyors of blowjobs, the result of beatings and cuttings administered to punish, or just out of macho egotism.

"But Marianne will cover. She'll tell Boulevard that I'm working a party over in Arabi. He wouldn't go that far to check on me. And your three-fifty will just about cover his part of the take from a good party night."

Slats stared at her.

"But what will you get out of it?"

"Like I said. Guess I'm crazy!"

She hugged his arm.

"It's up to you to prove to me I'm not."

In the car heading across the river to old Algiers, where Slats lived in a three-room walk-up, Maria leaned her head against his shoulder and drowsed. Slats wasn't tall, but his muscular frame dwarfed hers. He felt the warmth of her body through the wispy dress and the awareness sharpened his desire.

At the apartment, she made no attempt to be impressed by his possessions. But she was intrigued by his books. They lined the walls of the living room in makeshift bookcases crafted out of old shipping crates.

"You read a lot," she said as she disappeared into the bathroom. "Got any beer?"

He pulled two Amstels from his fridge, snapped the caps, then hurried into his bedroom and dug into the top drawer of his old dresser where next to his jockey shorts he kept a large piggy bank. Twisting off its head, he pulled out a wad of bills, counted out the three-hundred-fifty, and tucked the rest back.

When he returned to the living room, she was seated on the willow love seat that served as a sofa, her legs tucked under her looking at one of his criminology books. He sat in the chair next to the loveseat, woven willow unpainted like the loveseat, and looked over her shoulder. She had the book open to the chapter on abnormal psyche and was reading a case study dealing with impotent men and their relationships with women.

Maria glanced over at him.

"How can people be so crazy?" she asked.

Slats tried to compose a reply, but couldn't without sounding pedantic and theatrical.

He started to tell her that society, not the individual, defined insanity, but realized he really didn't know what he was talking about.

Instead, he leaned forward and kissed her lips.

She returned the kiss readily, but he thought, coolly. It was probably the same kiss she used on all her johns. Her lips were smooth and dry, her breath slightly smoky.

She leaned back and let her eyes wander over his face.

"I must like you, or I wouldn't be here. But for the life of me, I can't figure out why. I mean, yeah, you're a nice looking guy...but I screw hundreds of good looking guys every month. " she said, and looked away," and some pretty ugly ones too."

"Hundreds?"

Her gaze held his eyes.

"What do you think?" she asked. "Think a trick a night can support me? Well, maybe, but it wouldn't support Boulevard, not in the style to which he has become accustomed. "

She rose and walked toward the window. Her voice stretched thin.

"A couple hundred a month's not difficult...not if you're good. And I'm good."

She turned to look at him.

"Maybe too good."

She seemed to gather herself and the smile returned. She walked toward him, her body taut but moving smoothly. He moved to the love seat and she sat next to him.

He took her hand.

"Why don't you get out of it?"

"I have to eat," she said. "Besides, ..." and she grinned "...sometimes I enjoy myself."

She ran her hand up his chest and began unbuttoning his shirt.

"Hey..." he began...

He felt he should take charge, but as she pushed the shirt from his shoulders and began tonguing his nipples his body tensed and he felt the rush in his groin.

"I want to see you, " he whispered.

"You smell good," she replied. She stood up.

"Watch me now!"

She turned away from him and began a slow undulation, a dancer making her own music. She pulled the thin dress slowly upward. Slats watched fascinated as the hem slipped up her legs, sliding past the garter belt clasps he had seen earlier. But this time, it didn't stop there. It rose over warm tanned flesh between her nylons and green lace that encased her hips. It slid past her waist where the garter belt nestled, and over the smooth skin of her back.

Her hips maintained her slow rhythm as she pulled the dress over her head and loosed her hair. It hung now, free, to her shoulders. She turned slowly, and slats anticipated the sight of her breasts. He smiled back at her as she ran her hands down over the green lace where her pubes darkened the fabric.

Slats sat motionlessly. When she touched him, his skin tingled. She stood before him, swaying slightly, and ran the tips of her fingers across his chest. He reached out, wrapped his arms around her and smothered his face in her tight belly muscles.

She stroked his hair.

"Poor baby, " she murmured. "He's all hot and bothered. Poor baby...want Maria to cool you down?"

She led him into the bedroom, pulled off his jeans, and made him stretch out on his stomach on the bed. A cold splash of alcohol on his bare back startled him, and he started to protest. But her hands kneaded the tense muscles of his back, and he relaxed. She worked her way down his back, manipulating muscles that achingly approved, occasionally drawing a spasm as she probed sensitive areas.

Then she was on the bed straddling his back, and Slats realized that she had shed her remaining clothes.

He glanced up at her over his shoulder. She had an impish grin on her face. Her hand, still damp with alcohol, snaked behind her and between his thighs. Fire traced the path of her fingers as she touched the sensitive skin of his scrotum.

He gasped and bucked, turning beneath the grinning girl who rode him as though he were a saddle bronc, one hand above her head, the other clutching at him behind her back. He twisted onto his back, and they settled on the bed, his erection trapped between her buttocks and pain between his legs giving way to a different kind of fire.

She played with his body for several minutes before she allowed him to enter, and then she rode him until he reached a shuddering orgasm. It was only after he had peaked and was sliding back to normalcy that he realized she too was quaking, her body bowed backward, her hair tickling his legs.

Watching her in the ecstasy of orgasm he felt a rush that he could not categorize. It tied him to her, forged a link fired by the flames of passion, now subsiding in his abdomen, but separate; a link that anchored him in a way he had never known before.

"I think I must be in love with you," he told her as she snuggled moments later in his arms.

"Don't be silly," she whispered, stroking his chest.

They slept.

They awoke as dawn struggled through the foggy West Bank dimness, and made love, this time softly and gently. And again Slats felt the strangely anchoring closeness that he had not known with other lovers.

Then, while Maria busied herself in the bathroom, Slats scrambled eggs and fried bacon. But while Maria accepted gratefully the coffee Slats pushed across the kitchen table toward her, she only nibbled at the food. And while Slats ate, she talked. She told him about Colombia, describing the seasonal beauty of the Andes and fitting in the details of her father's fall from grace in what became a despotic political system. She explained how the squalor of life after her father's disgrace drove her from her beloved country to The United States. She skimmed over the early years of her life in New Orleans, but Slats had seen firsthand the world in which she lived. No one had to draw him a picture of the street life of a hooker.

Her outline of life with Boulevard didn't fit.

She made him sound almost paternal, a father figure who protected and sheltered wayward females. But even in her near praise, he could hear the resentment in her voice. She didn't damn Boulevard, but neither did she espouse any affection for him.

Watching her, pert and freshly scrubbed, Slats couldn't escape her aura: sexuality, vigor, a passion for whatever the new day might bring. How could she be a prostitute? His Catholic upbringing interfered with the emotions that surged inside, emotions that he wanted to cultivate.

Over his coffee cup, as he drew his final sip, he fixed his eyes on hers.

"You don't really like what you do, do you?" he asked.

She looked down at the table, and ran a manicured nail around the edge of the cup, thinking.

"No...most of the time, no."

"Do you hate your pimp?"

Again she hesitated.

"No," she said, " I can't hate Boulevard. He's done a lot for me. He took me away from a couple of bastards who got hold of me just after I got here. They had been screwing me every way possible, taking almost everything I made, beating me if I didn't cough it up...or if they thought it should have been more.

"Boulevard saw them beating on me in a bar one night, and he smashed them up good with that cane he carries. He broke Billy Toilet's leg..."

Slats knew Toilet by reputation. He had been suspected of at least one prostitute murder, but there hadn't been a case to take to court.

"Boulevard doesn't beat me, and he takes a more modest cut...and he does have great connections."

"But,..." Slats began.

Maria pushed away from the table.

"How else can I live?" she asked. "I don't know how to do anything. All I have is this." She shrugged, and the motion enveloped her body.

Her gaze returned to his eyes, and he saw her pride, her ancestral heritage, bubble to the surface.

"But no, I don't like being owned!" she said, her face shining but her eyes cold.

Slats walked over to the stove and poured another cup, then held the pot out toward Maria. She waved it away.

"I'll help," he said, his voice matter-of-fact flat.

She stared at him.

"I mean it, Maria. If you really want out of the life, I'll help you."

She kept her eyes fixed on his face.

"Do you mean that?" she asked.

"I've got some money saved. We can get you off the streets. You can go to school, maybe get you into a business school."

Maria walked to the stove and poured herself more coffee, sipped at it thinking.

"And what," she asked, "do you get in return? Sex... exclusive sex sessions?"

"I'm not looking for anything. I'd like to be with you when I can, sure, but there won't be any hold on you."

"You're crazy!" she said. "Crazy, but sweet.

"But it couldn't work the way you want," she said, her voice soft. "If I quit the business, I have to leave."

"Boulevard?" he asked

"Yes, and no. Boulevard wouldn't stop me. There're a lot of girls who'll work for Boulevard. But he would stop protecting me. Just business. Without his protection there are people ...people like Billy T. who would love to hurt me."

"I'll protect you!"

"One cop takes on the streets? You know how long you'd last? And me...

"No, if I quit, I have to leave. You won't see much of me. What would your money be buying?"

"Stock in your freedom?" he answered.

She touched his cheek.

"You're crazy but nice..."

"Look at it as an investment, in both our futures, " he said.

She grinned.

"Speaking of money, " she said. "I've really got to go. Got to see Boulevard this morning before he turns out the troops looking."

"I put the money in your purse earlier, when you were showering, " he said.

She picked up her bag and started to open it, then looked up at Slats, patted the outside of the black felt, and started for the door.

Slats followed.

"Think about my offer, Maria. I mean it."

"All right, crazy cop! I'll call you."

She kissed him and pulled the door closed behind her.

As she walked away Slats felt her energy draining from him. Was he really crazy? Would he really part with his savings for an ex-hooker? And if he couldn't have her...?

Then the rush he had felt in the midst of their lovemaking the night before warmed his chest, and he knew he would do anything he could to help her.

Three days later she called. She would accept his offer.

He picked her up and they spent the day ...a soft late spring day driving the old River Road, walking the levee, and making love among the willow shoots on the banks of the river. They spent the night in his apartment, and before he left for his early morning shift, he wrote her a check for eight-thousand dollars, virtually all of his savings from three years as a patrolman.

She kissed him, held his hand tenderly against her breast, then watched him walk from the apartment.

He hadn't seen her since.

She seemed to vanish from the face of the Earth. Slats didn't try to find her for several months, expecting to hear from her.

When he didn't, finally he went looking, but his efforts dead-ended at Boulevard.

Two years later a series of envelopes appeared under his door. They contained cash and a couple of brief notes expressing her appreciation for his assistance. Over a period of three months, she repaid the debt but left him no clue to her whereabouts. Slats cornered Boulevard, but the big pimp consistently denied any knowledge of Maria.

That was when his dreams...his Maria fantasies...began. They grabbed his mind when he least expected it, embellishing and enlarging memories of her, replaying in color and wide screen their lovemaking, and creating multiple variations on the theme. He had relieved their moments beside the Mississippi thousands of times, yet each time the fantasy, the dream, was new enough that waking before its conclusion frustrated him.

Something's wrong!

"Hey, wake up guy. It's my last stop. "

Slats struggled to shake off the vestiges of his dream.

He realized he had overshot his destination. Another bus was pulling up at the corner across the street. He vaulted off the bus and hurried across the street, jumping aboard the inbound as its doors hissed shut.

Midafternoon.

It was hot when he got off the bus, and he welcomed the air conditioning in the federal building. It was cooler still in Falgout's office. His reception as he introduced himself was a blank stare.

"Courant said we should talk," he said.

Falgout gestured toward a chair. Slats pulled it to the corner of the workaday steel desk and sat. Falgout pulled out of the desk's top drawer a sheaf of papers that Slats recognized as a copy of his "white paper" to Courant.

"What do you think?" Slats asked

"Quite a theory, L-t," Falgout said, his face still expressionless.

He leaned back in the swivel chair, flipped the first page of the sheaf, and stared at the page for a moment.

"Yes, quite a theory. Is everything here accurate? Y'know, dates, times, places?"

"Of course," Slats said, rankled. "Sure, check it out."

"We've had dealings with Boulevard before, you know," Falgout said. He tapped a file on the corner of his desk. "He used to import a lot of his women.

"But, to the best of my knowledge, Boulevard has never belonged to any organization. He has no syndicate connections, and frankly I don't think he's smart enough to be a part of anything like this," and he waved the report.

Falgout headed off Slats protestations.

"But I am going to help. If there is an international drug conspiracy, it is in my bailiwick. I've assigned three agents to recover your ground, " Falgout waved Slats report again.

Slats knew his face was reddening.

Adrian Falgout had been transferred in to head the unit last year. A native of South Louisiana, he should have fit right in.

He did. He fit the model beautifully. Trim and dark, tall for a man of Louisiana French ancestry, he dressed in tailored suits and drove a Porsche.

And while most of the agents in his office did their jobs quietly and efficiently, Falgout loved headlines. Shortly after arriving in the city, he took an ongoing chop-shop investigation public, capturing a local Mafia don's son in a daylight Ninth Ward raid. Falgout was big on the six o'clock news for three months.

Slats knew that Falgout would take credit for any success with which he was even vaguely involved. And conversely, he would blame anyone he could for even minor embarrassments.

"Adrian, I'll do whatever is necessary to bring this case to a successful conclusion."

"Good." Falgout's face remained impassive.

"But what if I'm right, Adrian? Shouldn't we bring in the secret service."

The agent's face changed for the first time since Slats had sat down. The corners of his mouth took on a cruel slant.

"Hell no!" Falgout snapped. That might mean sharing the limelight, Slats thought.

"It's a drug thing, man," the agent said, relaxing and tilting back in his chair. "That's all. Courant agrees with me. It's just a drug operation, a big drug operation, and we're going to get to the man... don't go spouting your theories where the wrong people might hear them."

Slats felt his face flush again.

"Adrian, " he said, feeling his anger rising, " it's still my case. And who don't you want to hear my theories!"

The poker face returned.

"I can make it mine if I have to," Falgout said.

Slats understood. He was saying, "let me make a couple of headlines and I'll give Courant the good word."

Anger puckered Slats face. He stood and walked out of the office, using all his restraint to keep from slamming the door as he left. Instead, he slammed his office door when he walked in. He paced for a few moments, then sat down at his desk. He pulled open the file drawer, dug until he found a form titled "Request for leave time" and cranked it into the old Underwood on which he still wrote reports in this day of megabytes and microchips.

Vacation!

Better than watching Falgout dig for headlines.

Time off. The department owed him at least a month.

Slats knew Falgout would retrace his every step, and review every word in both his original report and his subsequent white paper. But he wouldn't find anything in either report about the strangely marked charts found in Boulevard's home. Or about an island called Grand Turk.

Vacation! Paid vacation!

And Slats knew just where he wanted to go.

Chapter Fifteen

Jusquevera's impatience showed.

He paced the small airport lobby, avoiding a knot of black youths drinking beer and playing the slot machines. The group, boys, and girls were loud. It was Saturday, and they would party until early Sunday. Tomorrow the church would be full, but many parishioners would drowse through their priests' admonitions.

On his sixth trip to the window overlooking the runway, Jusquevera saw the Lear. He watched the small plane glint in the late afternoon sun as it turned lazily onto its final approach. Then he pushed through the terminal's swinging doors.

"Hey! You can't go out there!"

He turned.

"Oh! Mr. Jusquevera. Uh, how are you today, Sir?"

The voice belonged to the fat man who had charge of the customs desk. He had moonlighted in his off-hours as a laborer on the construction of Jusquevera's hangar-warehouse, which now added the sparkle of new metal to the overall old look of the airport. It sat on a small apron near the western end of the runway, well removed from terminal traffic.

Jusquevera's forehead wrinkled as he watched the plane touchdown and roll to a stop. As he strode toward it, the door popped open and steps extended. A small, darkly beautiful woman emerged. Tight fitting jeans and a denim jacket accentuated her lithe curves as she stepped to the pavement.

She looked up at him.

She appeared younger than he expected. She turned to accept a briefcase-sized handbag from the man following her. The man was Raul, Jusquevera's pilot. She moved away from the plane toward him, moving with an easy grace, her head held high. Jusquevera saw her as a thoroughbred ready for the race, and sure to finish in the money.

She stopped before him, the top of her head barely reaching the height of his shoulders. She said his name softy.

"Yes," he replied. "And you are Maria."

"Yes," she acknowledged.

"You are..." he began, slowly, watching her face "younger than I expected..."

"I trust that does not create a problem."

"...and exquisite," he continued, smiling now.

She returned his smile and briefly bowed her head as if to acknowledge the compliment. She stood with her feet apart, both hands on the briefcase handle with it resting on the front of her thighs. She shook her head slightly as the wind whisked strands of her dark hair across her eyes.

"Now that we have the ceremonies out of the way, what next?" she asked.

"We walk." Jusquevera gestured toward the terminal. "Raul will bring your luggage. I'll carry your bag."

He reached for her briefcase, but she made no move to relinquish it.

"Thanks, but this is all there is, and I don't mind carrying it."

But when Jusquevera did not retract his outstretched arm, Maria handed the case to him.

He hefted the bag.

"You travel very light, " he said.

"I don't need much," she replied. They took several steps in silence. Distant seagull chatter punctuated the whisper of the trade wind, finding a rhythm with the tap of their feet on the tarmac.

"I thought you knew my age. In fact, I assumed you would know everything there is to know about me, " Maria said.

Jusquevera replied without hesitation.

"I know enough. I know you are from Bogota. I know that you were...exiled...as was I. Your father expressed differences with the administration and that cost your family its livelihood."

"It cost much more than that." she said, emotionless.

"I know you went to The United States, that you lived in New Orleans for a time, and that you are close to the flyer."

"Charlie!"

She broke stride momentarily and look up at Jusquevera.

"Have you heard from him?" she asked.

"Indirectly," he replied. They resumed their trek toward the terminal.

"I had a message from the captain of the boat with whom he was to rendezvous. They are underway, and should be here in a few days."

"They are coming by boat?"

"We arranged things to make it look like Captain Adkins crashed. If he is as skillful a pilot as you believe, the ruse should have worked. We will know before the plane gets here. "

They reached the terminal, and at the customs desk, the chubby black man slapped a sticker on Maria's bag without even taking it from Jusquevera's grasp. Maria felt his almost palpable gaze on her body as she followed Jusquevera across the lobby. She was silent during the brief taxi ride, in a beat-up ten-year-old Chevy Malibu, to the Kittina Hotel. They skipped the lobby, where an early fall influx of divers was checking in, and Jusquevera ushered her into a second-floor room overlooking the ocean.

"Couldn't get you a room at the Saltraker," he said. "Too many divers here right now. But this is the nicest hotel on the island. You'll be comfortable, just don't drink the water. And... "

He reached into his jacket pocket and extracted a small can of baby powder.

"...the showers are saltwater. Use this liberally after your shower and you'll never know it wasn't fresh water."

Maria took the talc and looked up into Jusquevera's face.

"I enjoy new experiences," she said.

"Well, perhaps we shall find a few more for you around this little island," he said. "I'll give you an hour to settle in and freshen up, then meet me in the dining room for supper. There is much about you I should like to know. "

"You're spies weren't very efficient, were they," she asked as she deposited her case on the bed and clicked open the hasps.

"They weren't my spies," he said. "And other people's spies are always inept."

When Jusquevera left Maria walked onto the balcony and studied her surroundings.

The hotel facade was newly whitewashed stucco, arches behind a knee-high limestone fence overlooking the broken asphalt road. Across the road, a beach of coarse sand and limestone fell away toward a quiet surf. Above the arches, fresh cedar siding set the building apart from the surrounding limestone, stucco, and painted wooden cottages.

Her room was modern, clean, and the rival of any at any Holiday Inn stateside. Maria locked herself in, pulled the drapes against the afternoon sun's glare, stripped and stretched out on the bed. She allowed herself ten luxurious moments motionless on the bed, then headed for the shower.

The hot salt water reddened her skin, and she remembered dancing as a child under a shower so hot she thought she would boil, watching her mother laugh at her antics. The memory stirred an ache deep in her chest, and she hugged herself as she stepped out into the chill of the bathroom. The memory faded with the shower's steam. She touched her face sparingly with makeup, then selected a pale green cotton-acrylic tee-shirt dress. Before slipping into it, she doused herself liberally with the baby powder Jusquevera had given her, savoring its soft aroma.

She found Jusquevera at one of the courtyard tables. He was sipping from a tall glass. He stood as she approached, his lean frame casually elegant in black slacks and a smooth white shirt open to mid-chest. He pulled a chair away from the table, and she sat.

"Lovely, " he said, studying her for a moment before returning to his seat. "May I order you a drink?"

"A pina colada?"

A waiter standing nearby raised one finger, nodded to Jusquevera and disappeared into the bar.

"You seem well known," Maria commented.

"It's a small island."

"Been here long?"

"Six months. Grand Turk was my second choice."

"Oh..."

"Yes. I had planned to set up in the Caicos. More ..." he hesitated..."creature comforts. But the locals proved too inquisitive."

"Inquisitive?"

"Inquisitive," he repeated.

"Inquisitive. Nice word. May I be inquisitive?" Maria asked.

"Of course, and you will find me that as well," he answered.

"Why do you know so little about me?" she asked.

"As I told you earlier, the people who recommended you to me weren't my people. They were working for an acquaintance. A man named Maarten."

"Maarten, " she repeated. "Will I meet him?"

"I'm afraid not. He died quite recently, in New Orleans."

"In New Orleans?" Maria asked, as her drink was placed before her. She picked it up, more to have something to do with her hands than to raise it to her mouth.

"Yes, in New Orleans. It was a gun battle, with police. I believe you knew one of the men who died."

"Oh," she said and took a sip.

"A strange name, " Jusquevera said. "Boulevard..."

"Boulevard?" Maria stuttered.

"Yes, Maria. You did know him then."

"Boulevard's dead," she made it a statement, not a question.

Jusquevera studied her intently.

"There's no sorrow, " she said. "I ...worked for the man, once upon a time. But that was a long time ago. Except for the call that put me in touch with you, I haven't had any contact with Boulevard for years. There's no sorrow."

"Boulevard was a procurer, wasn't he?" Jusquevera's voice had a hard edge to it.

Maria hesitated, and when she replied, her voice rasped.

"Yes. He was. And I was one of the things he procured."

Jusquevera didn't speak. The lines in his face seemed deeper; his face chipped from the limestone that tiled the courtyard.

"I was a call girl in New Orleans for several years. I worked for Boulevard. If that makes a difference to you, I can leave." she said, pushing her chair away from the table.

Jusquevera pushed back from the table, crossed his legs, and studied Maria.

"I was startled, that's all," he said. "Please. Sit down! The only aspect of your past that's important is your heritage.

"You would like to go back to Colombia, wouldn't you?"

"Yes, " she said, her voice thick. "Very much."

"I thought so. That's one reason I wanted you to acquire the flyer. Boulevard had convinced Maarten. But it was my decision. It was unbelievable luck finding you in Pensacola!"

Maria sat down.

"I wish you had known my past more intimately, " she said. "It might have made this evening more pleasant."

"I regret that your past disturbs me," he replied. "I have two sisters, and I worked very hard to keep them from doing just what you did."

"People have to eat."

Jusquevera did not reply. They sat in silence for several minutes before he renewed the conversation.

"I dream of going home, Maria."

She smiled.

"So do I, " she said.

The waiter appeared at Jusquevera's shoulder.

"Permit me," Jusquevera said and ordered conch salad, small filets, and a Mouton Cadet.

"Have you eaten conch?" he inquired as the salads were placed before them. "You'll find it somewhat tough."

It was. But it was pleasantly chewable, tart with the dressing, setting off crisp vegetables. Maria nibbled while Jusquevera consumed his rapidly.

"My apologies if the conch offended you," he said, noticing her almost full plate.

The waiter opened and poured the wine, proffering the glass to Jusquevera. But he held up his hand.

"It will do, I'm sure."

Momentarily both had full glasses in their hands. Jusquevera held his up.

"To Colombia, and to going home!"

Maria touched her glass to his, feeling lightheaded. The expectancy in her heart very real at this moment, here in the courtyard of a Caribbean hotel. But was it truly a harbinger?

"Can it happen?" she asked.

"Maria. We will make it happen!"

He tipped his glass up and drained it. Maria sipped at hers.

"Ever since Boulevard's message, I have been hopeful. It's the first time I've ever thought I might go home. "

She hesitated.

"It won't be the same without my family, of course. They can never return. But if I can repay in kind those who fashioned my father's death, I will risk anything."

Jusquevera did not reply. She watched him consume his steak, eating with obvious enjoyment, but slowly, meticulously. Each bite that passed his lips was a small, neatly sliced cube.

Watching him she felt her expectancy quaver, the weight of doubts pulling it into the pit of her stomach, changing it into fear.

"But how can you hope to succeed?" she asked.

"Do you have an army that can oppose the government's forces? From what I have heard, they are sizable, well trained and supplied. "

Jusquevera put a finger to his lips. Maria stopped.

"Please, " he said. "We will speak more of this later, alone."

Maria looked around. There were other guests within earshot, but they seemed deep in their conversations. She heard references to diving tables, to decompression, scuba tanks, and re-breathers. No one paid them any attention.

She looked across at Jusquevera.

"Are you a diver?" she asked.

"No, " he replied. "But it does sound enticing."

Their conversation turned to diving, and Maria, who had earned a certificate from Martin's School of Diving in New

Orleans, agreed to teach Jusquevera the basics. He expressed surprise at her knowledge.

"Even hookers have hobbies," she said, grinning, wondering at her lightheartedness.

By the time they finished their meal and the bottle of Mouton, the evening had grown warm. Jusquevera lit a cigar and asked Maria to walk along the beach.

As they left the courtyard, Jusquevera remained quiet until they reached the waters' edge.

"I wasn't concerned about the tourists overhearing, " he said. "They never speak of anything but diving and drinking, and sex. But there may be other ears about, ears more attuned to politics and the upheavals of the world.

"And I did not want any of the locals, many of whom have come to know me, to hear me talk about politics. I do not want them becoming aware that I have interests other than Computer Dynamics. I have stretched my plausibility near its limits already...but the cover must hold up for another few weeks."

"I understand," Maria replied.

"We must have time to train."

"Train?"

"A pilot."

"A pilot? Just one?"

"Just one. We have one plane. And we have one pilot for that plane. We need one more, a back-up. I trust the plane. But as they say, the flesh may prove weak."

"One plane." Maria felt the disappointment in her voice. One plane, one little fighter would be of little use against the Colombian government forces.

"I know what you're thinking," Jusquevera said. "One plane will be enough! But if that pilot should be disabled, ill, unable for whatever reason to fly. That's why we need a back-up. "

"A back-up, " she repeated.

"A student pilot," he said.

"Where is he?" she asked.

"I'm talking to her," he said.

"What?" she asked, trying to look into Jusquevera's eyes. The water washed the beach inches from their feet, hazily visible in the moonless night. She turned away and walked toward the road.

"You're making fun of me," she said.

"I'm not making fun of you," he said, following. "I'm absolutely serious. You must be my back-up pilot."

"I've never flown anything but a kite!" she heard a stammer in her voice. She paused and took a deep, slow breath. "What you're asking is impossible."

"Maria, you have the motivation. The motivation and the intelligence. You can learn. You will learn! Because you want so much, because you need so much.

"Maria, you are a godsend. The Holy Mother herself interceded on our behalf, and our Father sent you to us. Such good fortune as we have had in the past few months has been directed. You are the answer to a prayer...an answer that cannot fail."

Maria felt a power in his voice, an aura that seemed to emanate from his hands as he put them on her shoulders, turned her to face him. Now she could see his eyes reflecting the myriad stars cascading across the sky.

"Maria, will you fly for me?"

He could feel the fear in her. She stared are him, her eyes seeking something in his face. He couldn't tell if she found whatever it was she sought.

"I'll try," she said and shivered.

"Good, good."

"It frightens me!"

"You can start tomorrow."

"What? But...the plane. You said it would be days yet."

Jusquevera kissed her. No passion. His lips touched hers lightly, pressed momentarily. It was more that of a general saluting an officer.

He stepped away from her.

"You will start in the Lear," he said. "Raul will teach you. I want you flying the Lear before the Harrier arrives. The sooner you are ready, the sooner we return to Colombia," he said.

"And don't worry! I'm sure your Charlie Adkins will fly the mission. But you must be ready."

Maria was trembling, perhaps not so much from worry as from fright.

She touched Jusquevera's arm.

"What good will becoming a flyer do, anyway?" she asked. "You have but one plane. The men who control Colombia have an air force at their disposal."

"Many say it is hopeless," Jusquevera answered. "But I have been fighting this 'war' now for more than two decades. And I have learned that winning takes more than armies. We have scored many small victories, and, small or not; they were important. Sometimes few can wield power in such a way that strong men are swept away.

"That is what we shall do.

"The specifics are for later. For now, learn to fly, Maria. Begin tomorrow."

He stepped away, a note of finality in his voice, in his posture.

"And what of you?" she asked. "While I am frightening myself to death to acquire this new skill, what will you be doing?"

"A meeting of El Carib," he said. "I meet on our farm with the ...the organization. The timing of the events must be meticulous, and all depends heavily on having the appropriate information. There are many things to be done before our dreams can gain material form."

Jusquevera grasped her shoulders, and Maria thought for a moment that he would kiss her in earnest. She didn't know if she wanted that or not. He was an attractive man, tall, and with a command tempered by world-weariness. He reminded her of Charlie, a Latin autocratic Charlie Adkins.

But he didn't kiss her. He merely held her at arm's length, regarding her in the faint glow from the hotel courtyard, bade her a good night's sleep, then trudged away into the darkness.

Despite his entreaties, Maria slept poorly. She dreamed of airplane cockpits, and visions of the earth rushing at her, pictures of the world captured from space shuttle cameras, her mind's private visions of a pilot's window to the world.

The phone in Maria's room rang as she showered; Jusquevera informing her that a taxi, one of the island's rattletrap Chevrolets, would take her to the airport as soon as she could be ready. There Raul would take over her world, while he, Jusquevera, would be departing on a morning flight to Puerto Rico.

Maria was afraid to eat breakfast. She feared losing it in the cockpit of the airplane and knew that Raul would not appreciate such a faux pas. She liked the grizzled little Colombia and had felt totally at ease on the flight from Miami. But how would it be having him as a flight instructor?

She remembered his attempts to entertain her with his stories about growing up in the mountainside slums of Bogota, of fighting his way out and joining the army, of fighting to fly as part of an infant air corps, of fighting for, and then against a new government when the National Front arose. For most of his fifty plus years, Raul had fought every authority figure he had served, until he met Jusquevera.

He made his loyalty to Jusquevera evident. Maria sensed that he would put his life on the line gladly.

He knew the Lear by heart, could describe each system and its redundancy, and virtually single-handedly maintained the little jet. Maria wondered out loud why he was not to be Charlie's back-up pilot.

"Oh, I shall be flying, señorita," he said. Despite the fact that they were standing on the apron almost a quarter mile from the terminal and any prying ears, he kept his voice low.

"When the operation begins, señor Jusquevera will supervise from the air. I will be flying for him."

"Operation?" she questioned. "There's more of the intrigue! I'd like to know what is going to happen."

"Señorita, I know only that it means flying. "

"But flying to where? " she asked, not expecting an answer. "We cannot attack Bogota with one fighter and a Lear jet!"

Raul pulled the bill of his New York Yankees baseball cap lower on his forehead.

"Señorita, I am sure señor Jusquevera will tell us what we need to know when the time comes."

"I hope so," she replied, wondering if she was dragging out the conversation just to avoid climbing into the cockpit of the plane.

"Are you ready?" he asked.

She looked up at a doorway that from the hot tarmac looked like a tunnel into another dimension.

"I suppose," she replied, finding no conviction in her voice.

"Good. First, we inspect the plane."

Raul walked her through the exterior checklist, moving control surfaces, feeling for slack in aileron and elevator movements, pulling the red-flagged sock from the pitot tube, and looking closely at the engine fan blades.

While they walked through the pre-flight, Raul rattled off bits of flight theory and concept, bits that simply rattled around in her head. She knew she wouldn't remember them.

"I don't need to know what keeps it up," she said. "I just want to know how to get it down!"

"That, señorita, is the easy part. What goes up..." Raul let his voice trail off, then turned to her with his face masked in seriousness.

"Most students, señorita, do not learn to fly in a jet."

"I've always been fast, " she quipped, but Raul's expression didn't change.

"Okay!" she said. "I understand why a plane flies. Okay?"

Raul stared at her a moment, and his smile returned. He led her into the cockpit, which was stifling hot from sitting on the dark apron in the full Caribbean sun. Raul quickly started the engines, then taxied the plane into the hanger. Maria imagined what the Harrier would look like in space now occupied by the Lear. It was a much bigger plane. It would be a tight squeeze.

The temperature in the cockpit dropped 15 degrees the moment the nose of the plane rolled from the stark sunshine into the shadowed interior.

Raul throttled the plane back and killed the engines. Listening to dying turbo whine, Maria inspected the clustered instruments and remembered how the various controls had moved so precisely under Raul's hands on the flight from Miami.

"Although the controls in the Harrier will be quite different, the principles of control will be the same. To turn the plane to the left, you turn the yoke to the left and step on the left rudder pedal."

"To go up, you pull back on the yoke, and to go down, you push forward.

"Simple, si?"

Maria said nothing, and Raul took that as an affirmation to proceed.

"Señorita," Raul puffed himself up in the seat. "You have one of the best instructors ever to fly a stolen airplane out of Colombia. You will be flying this airplane this afternoon."

Maria felt the center of her being turning to ice water.

"Señor. You are insane!"

"Wait and see."

"Raul! I have worked with US Navy pilots for several years. It takes months before they even get into a jet. And you're telling me that with less than a day's training I'm going to fly this airplane?"

Raul launched into an explanation of the plane's instrumentation, from the artificial horizon to the turn and bank indicator to the gyro-compass. By noon, Maria had reviewed the controls and instruments more than a dozen times. Even in the hanger, the cockpit was close and warm, and she felt soaked with perspiration when they finally took a break. The cold Coke from the refrigerator whirring in the open bay flowed like nectar down her throat. The pause that refreshes. Even in this out of the way Caribbean backwater lacking in drinking water, Cokes were abundant.

Then they were back in the plane.

Raul ran the startup checklist a half dozen times, making Maria repeat it, then pointing out to her the printed copy affixed to the dashboard.

"But you may have no such thing in the other plane, so you had best sharpen your memory," he said.

Raul had the plane in motion and was clearing for take-off with Grand Turk's tower before Maria became aware that he was talking to her.

"We'll review start-up and shut-down procedures separately," he said. "I think that now I had best get you up, eh, señorita?"

Maria's tension bubbled into her throat as a giggle.

"That sounds like a proposition!" she said.

"Eh?"

"Never mind. Sorry."

"Okay. Now, take hold of the yoke and put your feet on the pedals. One hand on the throttle. Now, do what I do. I 've got the plane. Just let my hands fly and you follow."

Maria felt the throttle and the yoke move, and her stomach wrenched violently.

"First, you'll learn the hardest thing in flying, taking off!"

"I thought landing was the hardest part," she said.

"Señorita, what goes up..."

Raul's expression didn't make her feel any better.

Her hands and feet followed the controls as Raul rolled the plane onto the runway and lined up on the centerline. He pushed the throttle to full, and Maria heard the engine's whine slide up the scale. The little plane edged forward and quickly gained momentum.

"This is nothing compared to what you will feel in the Harrier. It will crush you into the seat, " Raul said.

The yoke slid back almost to her breasts, and she watched fascinated as the nose of the plane lifted above the horizon. She watched the altimeter as Raul took the little plane up and in moments he had leveled off at 11,000 feet. She watched as he trimmed for level flight.

"Now," he said, "the easy part."
"Oh, what is that?"

Chapter Sixteen

Maria looked down at nothing but water.

"Where's the island?" she asked.

"We are moving quite fast, señorita." He pointed out the airspeed indicator which showed just over 250 knots.

"Okay, " Raul said, "she's yours. You fly for awhile."

"What?"

"You have the controls."

Raul made the last statement with Latin emphasis, waving his hands before her.

Maria swallowed the panic that leaped into her throat.

She looked at her hands. She did indeed hold the yoke. And her feet were on the pedals. But she applied no pressure. She knew, she just knew that if she moved, she would fall unceremoniously into the ocean. Quite a sight that would be, huh! Hell of a splash!

But the plane kept flying.

"Raul, please, " she begged. "Hold onto the controls!"

"No need, señorita."

And to emphasize the point, he leaned back, his hands clasped behind his head.

"She is trimmed," he continued. "She almost flies herself.

"But make no sudden movements with the controls. You are in control. Do what I tell you but do it slowly and precisely. Okay?"

Maria became increasingly aware of the plane. She could feel the engine vibration, a mild buzz that seemed to flow from the skin of the plane through the controls into her feet and arms. The sensation raised the hackles on her neck.

Her mind ranged through her memories. Had she ever been so scared?

Of course she had!

The night her father had been taken flashed into mind. She saw him sitting at the kitchen table, dressed in shirt and tie, as if ready for work. He was waiting, for something or someone. And when she asked him what he was waiting for, he patted her head and said 'for visitors.' She had been how old, ten, or perhaps eleven? The years were aggravating some portions of her memory, but not the picture of her father waiting. And when the visitors came, they came with guns drawn. The greatest fear she had ever felt erupted in her belly when the men with the guns dragged her father through the door of their home, her mother crying behind them.

She had spent years trying to conquer that fear. Perhaps she never would.

But she would conquer this one!

"Okay. What do I do?"

"First we make a slow left turn."

For three hours Maria flew under Raul's patient tutelage. She made left turns, right turns, ascending turns, descending turns, banking maneuvers, figure "s" turns.

Raul watched her closely. He could see the fear easing from her, but he could also see the result of that fear, of the tension engendered by working hard at something unfamiliar.

"That's enough for today, señorita. You are tired, and that is not appropriate for so lovely a lady as yourself."

"Thank you, " Maria said, "for the compliment as well."

She released the controls to Raul, and he eased the plane into a slow turn. She glanced at the sheet of ocean spread below, and wondered how he could know where they were. Surely she had zagged them across three oceans. But moments later she saw the long, narrow shape of Grand Turk blotting the ocean below. Raul made a long sweep around the island, talking to the tower, then eased the little jet back onto Mother Earth.

He taxied to the hangar and stopped just outside.

When Maria stepped down from the jet, she was so tired and so relieved to have ground beneath her feet, that she failed to see Jusquevera until he spoke to her.

"God!" she exclaimed. "You scared me more than this damned plane."

"I'm sorry," he said. He looked past Maria as Raul emerged from the plane.

"And what of your pupil?" he asked, addressing the diminutive pilot.

Raul smiled broadly.

"She is quick, and I am not very patient."

Maria raised her eyebrows. "By the time you return, she will be flying the Lear. Alone."

Maria tossed her head.

"You give me too much credit."

Jusquevera turned and took her by the shoulders as he had the evening before.

"Maria, you are strong and competent, " he said, looking deep into her eyes. She watched the breeze fluttering the curls, dark but tinged with gray, along his hairline and over his temples. She noticed the reflection of her face in his dark pupils. When he spoke, his voice was so mellow she had to struggle to understand his words.

"You are also beautiful...more beautiful that I had imagined. Were the situation different..."

His voice trailed off, and he began again.

"What I mean is, we shall be going home. That is the one thing we must concentrate on! We shall go back not as guerrillas, hiding in the jungles and slums. When we return home, we shall walk the streets with out heads held high and proud. We can restore our families..." he paused and squeezed her shoulders "and our families' honor to the land where they toiled so hard.

"So I shall commend your beauty and my desires to that day. I look to you now as a sister in El Carib. Be strong, work hard. Learn to fly. And one day we shall go home together."

He looked deep into her eyes, and she imagined herself standing on a balcony overlooking Bogota itself and felt a strange splendor rising beneath her breasts.

Raul stood back from the scene and wondered what he was witnessing. There seemed magic in Jusquevera's short but dramatic speech and Maria's reverie. He would not destroy the aura.

But the scene dissolved quickly. Jusquevera relaxed. Tension drained from his arms. He let his hands fall from Maria's shoulders. She smiled up at him, and he stepped away, turning to Raul.

"Teach her well, " he said. "She must make a good soldier."

He turned toward the terminal, stopped, and addressed them both.

"I'm leaving on the evening flight. My task should take about ten days. If your Lt. Col. Adkins arrives before I return, set him to teaching you to fly the Harrier. But it must not be done here. The plane will fly in and out of here only under cover of darkness, and it will be using false identification. I left a packet in the office with complete instructions. Please follow them exactly.

"Wish me luck, " he said, "Hasta luego."

"Via con Dios! " Raul said.

Jusquevera acknowledged with a small salute, then walked deliberately into the terminal.

In the office after Raul finished a quick servicing of the little plane's engines, they found Jusquevera's instructions, three neatly typed pages on how to handle the arrival of the Harrier and code words for communications that might arrive from Jusquevera or from the vessel transporting the plane.

The plan was for the barge carrying the Harrier to anchor in the Caicos Bank. The Harrier would fly from there into Grand Turk under cover of darkness and taxi into the hanger. Before the plane's arrival, three men would arrive as employees of Computer Dynamics. Under Raul's supervision, they would repaint the plane and give it civilian numbers, although it was obvious such subterfuge could not hide the craft's identify from anyone with even a meager knowledge of warbirds.

For most of the time required for Maria to learn to handle it, the plane would operate from one of the small, normally deserted cays surrounding the Caicos Bank. With luck, no one would suspect that a military aircraft was flying nightly missions about the Southern Bahamas. Refueling would take place aboard the anchored barge, and maintenance would take place inside the Grand Turk hangar.

Jusquevera's instructions appeared simple and clear-cut. Maria wondered how many of Jusquevera's operations went as planned.

For her, the next several days sped by in a haze of takeoffs, landings, right turns, left turns, altimeters, artificial horizons, transponders, and the endless minutia of flying.

She was learning faster that she had thought possible, and by the fourth day, she was wondering aloud why the US Navy took so long to teach students to fly.

"They have to learn much more than the mechanics of flying, señorita, " Raul responded, sounding slightly annoyed at her new-found self-assurance.

"I was foolish to be afraid, wasn't I?" she asked.

"A little fear can be a good thing."

Raul was fond of truisms.

Some of her fear rebounded when they started on touch-and-go landings. Not wanting to arouse curiosity, they avoided the airport. Raul picked a small cay and spent all of her sixth day teaching her landing techniques. She watched him line up an imaginary runway, set up the descent, then apply power and lift away moments before the plane's wheels would have touched the sand.

Maria's stomach knotted when he handed the controls over to her with the admonition "now, for your turn."

Following Raul's lead, she made a long, slow turn over the water, reduced her power and adjusted to keep the nose of the plane above the horizon. The plane slipped easily toward the speck of sand that was growing rapidly below and ahead of her. She smiled.

"Piece of cake," she muttered to herself.

Then a thermal blown off the cay caught the plane and lifted the right wing sharply.

"Damn!"

"Level it!" Raul commanded.

The plane slid to the left, and instinctively she pulled back on the yoke.

"No!" Raul yelled.

Raul's hand closed over hers on the throttle, and the yoke moved forward against her will. Raul's hand shoved the throttle forward, and the little plane dipped its nose and shot forward, the cay rushing up at them. Maria's heart jumped into her throat, and she felt she couldn't get her breath.

The pitch of the engine whine climbed rapidly, and the nose of the plane began to come up. Seconds before the wheels would have touched the sand, Maria realized the Lear was level and beginning to pitch up. Water and sand gave way to blue sky and puffy clouds.

It took several moments for her heart to slow down. When she looked at Raul, concentration lines etched his face, but if he had felt any fear, it was invisible.

"Thank you..." she said and leaned back in her seat.

"De nada, señorita. But remember, even good pilots are often a little scared. Be ready to be a little scared and you will not panic. A little fear sharpens your reflexes. But...panic kills.

"Are you ready to try again?"

She wanted to say no. Not just no, but "hell no, Never Again!"

But she couldn't. She knew she had to try again.

This time, she was ready. When the thermal grabbed the plane, she made slight adjustments to the ailerons and rudder and was pleased to feel the Lear respond as she expected. Moments before touchdown she added power and put back pressure on the yoke and almost laughed as the nose came up and she climbed smoothly away.

"Very good, señorita. Now, again! And again! And again."

For hours, she flew touch-and-gos, never actually touching the sand, and always in control. Raul explained several times to her that if she were flying into an actual airport, she would have several devices, lights and electronic marker beacons, to help establish proper glide paths and pinpoint touchdowns. But these were of relatively little value to her since most of the flying she would be expected to do would be from small airports and hidden strips planned more for subterfuge than landing ease.

Back on the ground at Grand Turk an hour before sunset she found herself so exhausted she could barely walk. Raul noticed her plight, and as they were locking the hangar doors, he invited her into the office, where he produced from a file cabinet a bottle of Glenlivet.

"You have expensive tastes," she said.

"In whiskey, and in women," he replied.

Maria's "Salud" caught in her throat.

She might enjoy his company. Although small, he wasn't a bad looking man. He was obviously intelligent, and he had shown great patience. But...

Instead of a reply, she lifted the plastic cup and tossed off the whiskey, wishing for ice as it burned it way into her gullet.

Raul held his cup aloft.

"To my prettiest and smartest pupil," he said.

She held her cup out, and he poured more of the single malt. She lifted the cup and sipped, welcoming the flush that spread from the fiery patch it carved down her throat. It burned away some of the fatigue that weighed down her extremities. It melted the haze from the backs of her eyelids and for the first time since her morning shower, she felt herself relaxing.

Someone knocked on the outside door.

Raul dropped his cup, walked to the door, and opened it. Three men stood there, lean and dark.

The man in the center spoke.

"This Computer Dynamics?"

It was meant as a question, but unaccented. The English was precise and clipped, obviously spoken by someone not native to the tongue.

"Quienesson ustedes?" Raul asked.

"We are technicians, señor," the reply again in accented English. "We arrived a short time ago and have been waiting in the terminal. We saw you land, so."

Raul stepped back, gesturing the trio into the office.;

"You have arrived sooner than we expected. I will show you to your quarters. "

He turned back to Maria.

"I shall get these gentlemen settled in, then I think you and I should look for some supper."

Raul and Maria had made sandwiches together in the office on several occasions, but he had never before invited her to join him for a meal. She studied him as he led the three through the inner door into the hangar and down wall toward the small suite that had been prepared especially for their use. Raul had seemed big-brotherish to her. His happy countenance, salt and pepper hair, slight potbelly. She couldn't believe he would try to seduce her.

But his offhand remark a few moments earlier put an uneasy edge on his supper invitation.

The phone on the desk, a satellite cellular phone installed only days earlier, erupted into a chirruping bleat, startling her. It was the first noise it had made. Its clamor so surprised her that it rang three times before she answered it.

"Hello, " she said, hesitantly. "This is Computer Dynamics."

She felt like a secretary, and the mannerisms of her civil service days returned quickly and effectively. She reached for a pad and a pen as she awaited a greeting.

"Ah, someone of the feminine persuasion."

The voice boomed through the phone, sounding as though it originated in the same room.

"This is Computer Dynamics," Maria repeated.

"I'm looking for Jusquevera de Arrellano!" the voice boomed back.

"Mr. de Arrellano is off the island now. This is Maria...his...secretary, " she lied. "Can I help you?"

"Ah, Maria," the voice returned, with a brogue as phony as it was thick.

"Sure and it's good to hear your voice lassie. It must be summer in Dublin since last I laid eyes on you."

As she started to reply, the words struck a chord in her mind. She yanked open the desk drawer and pulled out Jusquevera's sheaf of instructions. There was something in them about code words, identifications. Dublin?

She found it.

Dublin was the code word for the vessel transporting the Harrier.

"Captain Greely?" she asked.

He didn't answer.

"Captain, are you forgetting about last Christmas in San Francisco?"

There was a chuckle at the other end of the call.

"No, no Lassie," Greely shot back. "Christmas was great, wasn't it? Must do it again sometime. But now, no time to reminisce. There's some weather getting up. Nothing we can't handle, but we don't want to risk damage to our cargo. I suggest we make our first delivery today. "

Raul stepped through the door, and Maria motioned him over.

He listened for a moment.

"But we weren't expecting the cargo for several days yet," she replied.

Raul guessed the source of the call.

"The plane?" he asked.

"The weather, " Maria said. "They want to deliver today."

"Not in daylight!" Raul protested.

"Captain, the delivery is much earlier than expected," Maria said into the phone.

"Aye, Lassie," Maria hated the phony brogue.

"But if we wait much longer, we may have naught left to deliver."

She hesitated. There had been nothing in Jusquevera's instructions for such a contingency. But they couldn't risk losing the Harrier.

"Then make the delivery!" she said.

"Thanks, lassie. Tell Jusquevera that Greely will speak to him soon about his next shipment."

Maria hung up the phone without speaking. She looked up at Raul, who stroked his chin and glared off into space.

"Well, " he said, spinning on his heels. "I'll alert our technicians. They certainly arrived none too soon."

Maria was alone with her thoughts.

The prospect of seeing Charlie again pleased her.

When she had first set out to seduce him into stealing the plane, she had expected an unpleasant task. She had gone into the assignment knowing that she would hate the man. She had based her feelings on Charlie's military record, and on the gossip that pegged him as a supreme egotist.

In Maria's experience, macho egos belong to stupid, often cruel men.

But somehow Charlie hadn't fit the mold. Despite his macho flair, he had proven intelligent and sensitive and seemed to care about her feelings. Of the thousands of men Maria had known, few had touched her as had the handsome, graying Lt. Col. Most of the men she had known, many of whom had used her and many she had used, had faded totally from memory. She knew only a handful would remain with her for a lifetime.

Charlie, Jusquevera, Raul, Boulevard, Slats.

Slats.

Lichester Jones. Slats to those who worked with and knew him.

Her mentor in days now long past.

Slats had made it possible for her to leave the streets, providing not only motivation but the money to make it possible. It hadn't been a lot of money. But it got her through a secretarial course and paid for food while she sought a civil service job.

She still nursed a little heartache when she thought about Slats. He had been in love with her. She had known it then, and she knew it now. She had repaid his money. She had paid her debt ...her financial debt. But she could not repay the emotional debt. She would never have been able to love Slats as he would have had her love. He had been...still was in her memory...a very special man.

She glanced out the window. Dusk was settling on the island. Perhaps the Harrier's early arrival would not be noticed.

She wondered if Slats was still a cop.

The roar of a jet engine creased the early evening Bahamian stillness.

Chapter Seventeen

His name was Juan Valdez.

Most of his friends called him Johnny.

And those who didn't call him Johnny, teased him about his name.

Had he picked any good coffee beans lately? Was it real Colombian coffee?

The only thing any of Johnny's friends knew about Colombia was what they had seen on television. That was where they learned about Juan Valdez and Colombia. They grew coffee there. And Juan Valdez picked that coffee, by hand. Because it was the richest coffee in the world.

But despite making fun of him, most of Johnny's friends envied him.

Johnny's friends lived their lives on the streets with little hope for any future. They ran those streets without purpose. Twenty years from now they would still be running the streets, pimping or running numbers.

Or just standing on the corner "hey baby-ing" any attractive woman who had the unfortunate circumstance to walk the sidewalk.

Johnny's friends envied him. They knew he would get out. They knew he would get out because his uncle Renaldo had gotten out.

Johnny's uncle Renaldo had driven himself hard to escape the prison of the 'hood.' Twenty years Johnny's senior, his name had been a watchword in his mother's house as Johnny grew.

Uncle Renaldo had started driving cabs as a teen. By the time he reached twenty, he had his high school degree. Then for six years he moonlighted to put himself through New York City College.

In school, he became an avid politician and landed a student body presidency his junior year. He involved himself in street politics and before he finished school he was credited with swinging seven precincts in the city's mayoralty election.

His reward was a job in the city clerk's office. He held the job for four years while continuing his education and an active political life. He earned a degree in international law and through sheer persistence got a job in the foreign service.

Thus, it was that when Johnny turned eighteen, his uncle Renaldo invited him to join him for a month at the US Embassy in Bogota, Colombia, where Renaldo had now worked on the consular staff for almost ten years.

Johnny's friends thought that cause for a celebration.

They bought a jug of Gallo Piasano ("Only the best for you, man.") and they consumed it sitting on the steps of the tenement that Johnny had called home for most of his life. Five guys pretending to get drunk on one bottle of wine while they whiled away the afternoon acting drunker than they were, talking about girls and money, and money and girls.

That had been two weeks ago.

Now, Monday, October 20th, Johnny had lived in Bogota for seven days. Here he was called Juan, and no one asked him about coffee beans. Never in his life had he lived so well. Renaldo had taken him straight from the airport to a mall where he had purchased two suits, and several-shirt-and-slacks combinations appropriate to the internship post. Not so comfortable as the jeans and T-shirts to which he was accustomed, but they were sharply cut and well tailored.

He had never eaten so well as he did in the embassy dining room. And, perhaps most important, he had never before felt the sense of pride he felt at seeing someone in his family in a position of real responsibility.

Never before had he been called "Sir."

Monday had started as had most days during his week at the embassy. He woke early, bathed, shaved, and dressed, then selected a copy of Time from the small sitting room and wandered into the courtyard that separated the main building from the quarters and recreation areas.

The air was light and fragrant, a bright Andean morning, and it invigorated him. He watched the hubbub of activity about the kitchen where the aromas of bacon frying and bread baking mixed with the mountain fragrances.

Johnny thought how lucky he was to have an uncle like Renaldo, a man who could drag himself from the streets of Puerto Rican New York into the embassy halls, and who could take his nephew with him. Sitting in the courtyard on this bright, chilly fall morning, so far from the streets of New York, Johnny felt a strong affection for his mentor.

After only a week of his uncle's company, he felt a part of something. It wasn't like membership in the gang. That did provide a sense of identity, but little else. Work in the embassy had a purpose. Johnny could see that Renaldo had reason to live. He had obvious, real expectations of bettering the relationships among governments, of improving economic ties, of facilitating communications across Anglo-Hispanic boundaries.

Despite the fact that Renaldo spent much of the time with his nose between the pages of rather dreary looking books and legal documents, Johnny could feel his enthusiasm for his work. Johnny had never realized that people could enjoy work. The code of the street had made work something to be despised. Labor, be it physical or mental, degraded, or as his friends were want to say, "sucked." Only old men worked, and old women kept house. Guys in the know had other ways of providing for themselves.

A familiar voice shattered his daydream.

"Buenas Dias, Johnny. The morning is beautiful, is it not?"

Renaldo was the only one in the embassy to call him by his nickname.

"Good morning, Uncle. It is ... and the smell of the cooking makes me ravenous. I could eat Mama Nunarri's whole place in one bite."

It was at Mama Nunarri's little Manhattan eatery that Renaldo had for years parked his taxi, and where he had told Johnny what he planned for his future. The reference sparked a smile that lit Renaldo's face. It was while sitting on the curb in front of Mama Nunarri's that eight-year-old Johnny had kidded Renaldo about his plans to leave the streets.

He had called his uncle's plans dreams.

"Perhaps to you, little boy. But the dream is mine, not yours. And it is a dream that I shall make come true."

And he had.

Johnny had watched while Renaldo built his dream into a life. And that observance had created within Johnny a dream of his own. Johnny could imagine himself in tie and tails hosting an official reception for a newly appointed officer, dancing at the ball with the most beautiful woman on the floor.

"C'mon Johnny. Let's get some breakfast. "

As they entered the dining room, Johnny noticed a blond girl about his age, sitting alone at one of the half-dozen tables. Renaldo followed his gaze to Teresa Vincencia, the ambassador's daughter. Teresa was as fair as her father was dark. Ambassador Diego Vincencia's European wife was one of the most beautiful and intelligent women Renaldo had ever known, and her daughter was wrought from her mother's mold. Her green eyes caught droplets of light from the dining room's crystal chandelier, and her smile dazzled Johnny as they stopped at her table.

"Ah, Tia!" Renaldo said, extending a hand to grasp hers briefly. "How grand that one of Colombia's precious emeralds deigns to cast her fire upon so humble a servant as I."

"Señor. Such poetry. And so early in the morning. Do you practice all night?"

"One need not practice paying so appropriate a compliment. Only truth is required."

"I am without words! Thank you."

She grinned broadly and indicated the other chairs at the table.

"Please, join me. I should appreciate the company. "

Before her on the table a white linen cloth left bare the four corners of the dark mahogany table. Settings for three had been removed, leaving only the tableware before the girl. Renaldo beckoned across the room, and a white-jacketed youth sprang into action.

"Before we join you, permit me to introduce to you my nephew, Juan Valdez."

Johnny felt as though his brain had frozen and he stammered several times before managing a soft "hello."

He wanted one of the smiles she had bestowed on her uncle.

He extended his hand and folded his fingers about her delicate grasp. Her green eyes looked steadily into his. He wanted to speak, but his tongue remained frozen.

"Johnny. This is Miss Teresa Vincencia, daughter of the Ambassador, better known here as Tia. But...you may call her Miss Vincencia."

He glanced up at Johnny and smiled.

"Uh..." Johnny was still grasping her hand, and vocabulary still eluded him.

"Sit down, Johnny," Renaldo said.

The busboy slipped plates and utensils onto the cloth as they adjusted themselves in the high-backed mahogany chairs.

The early morning sun slanted in the high windows on the east wall, painting the wainscoting a golden brown and sending slivers of rainbow sparkle glinting off the crystal chandelier.

The busboy turned waiter sat a steaming pitcher of coffee on the table and Renaldo poured servings into each cup.

"Tell me, Tia, " Renaldo said, stirring cream into his coffee, "How is the ambassador? I'm told the doctor had him confined to his bed yesterday."

Tia glanced at Johnny, and he felt a warm blush rising in his chest.

"Oh, señor Renaldo, it was nothing," she said. "A little virus. You know my father. Keeping him in bed for even one day was a formidable task. He kept my mother running all day fetching papers and documents and conveying messages of one sort or another. My mother is a saint to put up with that man."

Despite her words, Tia's affection for her father was obvious. Johnny could feel in her manner the love she had for the man he had not yet met.

"You shall see him today, won't you, Renaldo? He was breakfasting with Mother. I think the two of them were feeling amorous, so I wanted to leave them alone. And that's why you gentlemen have the pleasure of my company this morning."

Johnny could feel the radiance of her smile.

"Father leaves for Europe next week, you know," she added.

Johnny could not explain the feeling that threatened his composure. He wasn't a virgin, and his experiences while relatively few had been varied and complex. But none of the women he had known had made him catch his breath, physically or emotionally.

"Si, Tia. I know, " Renaldo replied.

He knew Vincencia was to travel in the company of his counselar officers to Spain, France, Germany, and Italy. Renaldo had helped to plan the series of discussions, aimed at the establishment of an energy cartel that would compete with the long established OPEC organization. All preparations for the trip had been completed yesterday, and a mid-morning meeting would review all arrangements.

"I had hoped to see your father this morning Tia," Renaldo said. "We have a meeting scheduled for 10:30. Do you know when I can expect him to arrive.?"

"Shortly, I hope," she said, absently. She was studying Johnny, who in turn, stared into his coffee cup.

"Tia," Renaldo said. "I think you are embarrassing my nephew. He is a bit shy."

Johnny looked up, a forced smile bending his cheeks.

He turned to Tia. And finally found his tongue.

"Pay no attention to my uncle. He's ...uh...he's just...getting old."

"Old! Am I getting old? At 37, I'm in my dotage?"

"Uncle Renaldo...."

"More comments like that and soon you'll be back on the streets in New York."

The remark brought a smile to Tia's face.

"You are from New York?" she asked.

"Yes, señorita, " Johnny replied, drinking in her smile.

She slid her hand across the table and touched his arm.

"Mother has an apartment not far from the UN," she said. "What part of the city are you from?"

In his mind's eye, Johnny saw the ancient brick tenement rising seven stories above the paper and trash blowing down the street.

"Not from your part, señorita, " Johnny said, looking down into his coffee cup.

Teresa felt his sudden withdrawal and tried to cover his embarrassment.

"Have you seen much of Bogota?" she asked.

Renaldo jumped in.

"I fear, Tia, that my nephew knows only about as much of Colombia as is featured in American television programs..drug cartels and hand-picked coffee beans."

"Uncle Renaldo!" Johnny objected, loudly, then realizing that several other people had filed into the room, he again felt the flush of embarrassment creep up his throat.

Tia squeezed his arm.

"I should be pleased to have you as an escort, Johnny, " she said, looking directly into his face, her eyes piercingly bright.

"Bogota is a fascinating city, and if your uncle allows it, I can think of many things to show you," she said.

She glanced at Renaldo, adding "Cultural things."

"Ah, Tia..." Renaldo began. "I have been trying to convince Juan...Johnny...that the foreign service would provide him an exciting life. I welcome your offer of assistance...particularly since I know there is no stronger motivation for a young man that a young woman.

"But don't let my nephew fool you. Those innocent eyes and that shy smile have charmed many. Don't think just because you are the boss' daughter he won't try to use his charms on you."

"Uncle!" Johnny protested. "I am not the Casanova you make me out to be, " he said, turning to address Theresa. "I would very much like to go with you, and you have nothing to fear from me. It would be my fist date here."

Teresa drew back, but the smile stayed in place.

"It will not be a date, " she said. "We will each pay our way. And I must be home before midnight.I shall be glad for your company.

"Seven?" she asked.

Johnny glanced at his uncle, who winked his approval, then nodded.

"Good, " Teresa said, "Now that that's settled, let's have some breakfast."

A small buffet had been set up at the far end of the room. With Teresa leading the way, they filled their plates, trooped back to the table, and fell silent with the brief pathos of consumption.

When the conversation resumed, it was limited to Johnny and Teresa planning their evening. Renaldo's attention shifted to the upcoming meeting, and the European mission. The diplomatic details of developing the proposed cartel were tricky. His plans had to be detailed, and they had to be good.

He finished breakfast, excused himself, and left the dining room, glancing back as he went. Johnny and Teresa were in quietly animated conversation; he slim and dark while she as blond and sleek as her mother; the epitome of what her northern European bloodline could produce.

"Handsome couple, " he muttered to himself.

Johnny found himself wondering how he would impress a woman so worldly as Teresa.

Back on the streets, Johnny had been part of a gang called El Padre de Morte. As a lieutenant in the gang, his bearing was sufficiently macho that the girls he sought to impress usually tumbled quickly. But somehow Johnny doubted that his leather jacket or his proficiency with his seven-inch switchblade would impress Tia.

"Excuse me, Johnny, " she said, breaking into his thought train.

"I promised Mama that I'd meet her at nine to go shopping. Papa will be here soon. You must ask Renaldo to introduce you. He's big, and sometimes a bit gruff. But he's awfully nice. "

She rose to go and turned back to Johnny.

"I'm going to buy something to look good in tonight. And some things for school next fall."

She paused.

"I'll meet you in the courtyard tonight at seven, all right?" she asked.

"Sure, " he said, standing and taking her hand.

"I'm very glad to have met you."

She let her hand linger momentarily in his, then stepped away.

"Hasta luegito, Johnny, " she said over her shoulder as she hurried down the mahogany paneled corridor toward the front foyer. Johnny stared after her, the memory of her dark green eyes and flashing smile painting his morning with an infinitely sweet sunshine.

Chapter Eighteen

He picked up his coffee cup, refilled it, and headed for the courtyard. There he sipped at his coffee while studying the Time magazine. He was surprised to find that he found the magazine's views on international issues interesting. Only weeks ago he would have addressed any question about international energy policies with his standard rebuke.

"It's all bullshit, man!"

He couldn't count the number of times he had used that phrase. His previous world had been several square blocks of cement, brick and asphalt, and he had cared more about how El Padre de Morte would fare in a face-off with the Urban Guerrillas than he cared about Middle East oil. But here, in a quiet courtyard in the Andes, surrounded by the trapping of diplomacy, his viewpoint shifted. Should someone now ask him about El Padre de Morte and his future: well, he had a ready answer.

Johnny didn't think the program his uncle and the ambassador were preparing would free the world from the current oil conglomerate's grip, but they were trying.

Just to be in the middle of something that could potentially change the world, that alone made all of Renaldo's self-imposed austerity and labor worthwhile.

His uncle's voice snapped him back to the courtyard.

Johnny looked up to see Renaldo standing alongside a big, gaunt, silver-haired man. He towered over Renaldo, imposing, yet distinguished in both features and bearing. His face was sharply cut, high cheekbones and a jutting, hawkish nose. He was big, but no belly hung over his belt. No bulges protruded from the lines of the Versace suit, a gray and silver pinstripe that accentuated the man's height. Johnny found it hard to believe such size came from Colombian blood.

"Johnny, I'd like you to meet the Ambassador."

Johnny stood.

"Ambassador Vincencia, my nephew, Juan Valdez."

The big man shook Johnny's hand firmly but made no attempt to impress the younger man with his strength.

"I met my daughter on the front stoop," Vincencia said. "She told me I should like you since you are to accompany her about town tonight. And, since you are Renaldo's nephew, I can hardly do otherwise. "

"I am trying to convince Johnny to finish school and college. He is here on a student visa. Would it be possible, sir, for him to sit in on our meeting? I will guarantee his behavior."

The Ambassador studied Johnny for several moments.

"For a budding diplomat, I believe we can oblige. I cannot, however, offer him passage to the European meeting, " he said, his gray eyes twinkling.

Renaldo chuckled.

"Accepted Sir! Come along Johnny, and I'll get you seated before the others arrive. Remember please that you are here as an observer, only. And what you are about to witness is in no way international intrigue.

"In fact, it isn't secret. There will be a couple of members of the press present although at this point I doubt that they will comprehend the enormity of the project.

"The surest way to tip off OPEC would be to hold these meetings in secret. The oil cartels have eyes everywhere. The middle eastern blocs will understand soon enough. So please, keep a low profile. I will explain everything after the meeting ends. Agreed?"

"Sure, Uncle Renaldo."

Renaldo paused, studying his nephew with a knowing eye.

"So, how did you and Tia make out?"

Johnny shrugged. But his eyes gleamed. Renaldo read the hope in his nephew's face.

The meeting room was large, with wainscoted walls, and an impressive oak table occupying much of the space. A small gallery of chairs filled one end of the room, separated from the table by a low mahogany rail. It was there, on the front row, that Renaldo seated Johnny. Already several Hispanic faces were in evidence, small groups of two and three people in quiet but animated conversation.

Renaldo pointed out several people he knew, representatives from Mexico and Venezuela, both nations essential to an energy management program. He also pointed out several Americans, midwestern in dress and in their whispered conversation.

"They are from the Department of the Interior, here to discuss reserves, both in oil and in coal. "

"Coal?" Johnny asked.

"The United States has vast reserves of coal, some of which we believe can be converted with modern technology to fill some of the energy demand now filled by refined oil."

"Oh," Johnny said. Renaldo could tell his mind was more attuned to Tia Vincencia than to the diplomats around the table.

"Most of today's discussions will center on resource availability and management. We won't start talking about a cartel until we get to Europe next month."

Renaldo left Johnny, strode over to the Hispanic entourage and in a moment was embroiled in a round of handshaking, back slapping and conversation in muted undertones.

At the far end of the room, near a large many-paned window, Johnny could see the Ambassador glancing at his watch. Then his voice boomed above the conversational rumble.

"Ladies and gentlemen, please take your seats. "

He paused for a moment while people shuffled about the table, seating themselves and pulling out notepads and pens, and sheaves of files.

"We have much to accomplish today," the Ambassador continued. "And of course, a little time in which to accomplish it. I would like to assure you from the onset that we have prepared an elegant luncheon that will be served at the appropriate hour in the dining room across the hall.

"But before you can partake, there are several speakers to be heard.

"There, now that the bribery is out of the way, we can proceed."

A couple of polite chuckles arose from the seated delegates. And there was a little murmuring in the gallery, which, Johnny noted with surprise, seemed to be filling to overflow.

Ambassador Vincencia assumed the moderator's position at the head of the table and described what he felt was the mutual interest of the conferees. He expressed a need for political integrity for the Earth's western hemisphere, where each nation chose its government and prospered according to its efforts.

"And while such individuality can work well in most endeavors, we are reaching an age ...a new epoch...that will not allow each of us to operate solely for our benefit in the matter of energy.

"In the Middle East, OPEC for all of its public unity is a divided cartel... an organization that stands ready to fall should a truly dominate force arise, perhaps in the guise of a new Soviet Union."

Murmured agreements arose along one side of the table.

"To make short that which might be a long dissertation, I will say that part of our purpose is to analyze what effects potential pressures on the Mid-East might have on us all, and how we can respond to those effects. And, " he added almost sotto voce, " yes, I am aware that there are OPEC representatives here with us today.

"Thus, with those comments, I shall ask the representative of Venezuela to react, and present an overview from that noble neighbor's perspective."

The Ambassador settled into his seat.

Renaldo studied the faces at the table. It was too early in the conference to read anything in the expressions of the twenty-two representatives. Their expressions were, for the most part, stoic. Renaldo wondered if he were viewing a political conference or the beginning of a professional poker tournament. Of course, much more was a stake here than at a gaming table. Perhaps as much as the fate of the Western World.

A smaller man, across the table from Vincencia, almost directly in front of Johnny, arose. He looked around the table, preparing to speak.

But he never got the chance.

At that moment, the double doors at the rear of the gallery slammed open, crashing back against their stops, and every head at the table turned toward the sound.

Johnny watched as two men in neat khaki uniforms strode purposefully into the room. Both carried automatic weapons, guns that even Johnny recognized as AK-47s. For a moment, Johnny thought they were part of the US Marine contingent that provided security for the embassy. But the uniforms carried no insignia, and the clothing fit tightly, without the pleats and creases the guard's dress uniforms displayed.

Vincencia was on his feet instantly.

"What is this?" he bellowed, then paused.

"Are you Colombian?" he asked, puzzling at the uniforms.

One man pushed his way through the low gate in the rail surrounding the conference table.

"Sit down, señor," he replied to Vincencia's question. "Yes, we are Colombian, but no part of this country's corrupt administration. "

A low mumbling filled the room, rising in pitch.

The khaki-clad figure turned to the gallery.

"Everyone be quiet and remain seated. If everyone remains calm, no one will be hurt. You shall shortly know what is happening."

But Vincencia would not stay put. In a half-dozen great strides, he stood confronting the man.

"You are on United States soil, " he said. "I demand that you lower those weapons and leave immediately. You are committing a crime and shall be dealt with accordingly.."

His approach halted when the barrel of the AK-47 touched his chest.

"Señor, you will force me to harm you. I have no wish to do so."

"Then leave!"

"That we will not do," the uniformed man replied. He pressed the rifle barrel against the Ambassador's chest.

"Sit down!"

One of the Bolivian representatives yanked a chair from his side and shoved it at Vincencia. The Ambassador sat slowly, facing the khaki-clad soldier and the gallery almost in front of Johnny.

He drew a deep breath, then slowly, almost resignedly, asked again.

"Who are you, and what do you want?"

"We are soldiers of El Carib!"

Johnny saw several of the people seated at the table flinch and heard the reaction in the gallery behind him. Fifty people drew breaths slowly, deliberately, lest their most basic need be misinterpreted. The aggressive good will displayed by the diplomats before the meeting was now replaced by expressions of fear. Johnny felt the dread about him. He felt it inside. A cold hand massaged his heart, and the 'hood streets came back to him. The musty taste of fear coated his tongue, and his mind snapped back to an alley and a dozen black-shirted members of El Padre de Morte following him into the dirty darkness.

His left hand slid into his pocket and found the hard outline of the old switchblade. He drew a strange comfort from its presence. He relaxed emotionally and physically. He knew he could take out one of the soldiers; the one who stood less than six feet away next to the small rail separating the gallery from the conference area. Six feet farther sat the Ambassador, glaring at the soldier. The second man stood a dozen feet back up the aisle, his weapon held high, turning slowly from side to side.

The unmistakable sound of an SLR shutter broke the silence.

The soldier nearest Johnny reached across the rail and snatched the camera from the Associated Press correspondent two steps to Johnny's right.

"No pictures, señor!"

The soldier swung the camera by the strap, bringing it down hard on the rail. The lens shattered, and the body sprang open.

"In here!" a voice called from the doorway. A tall, slim, dark figure appeared, also clad in khaki. Johnny studied him as he walked up to the soldier at the front of the gallery. He was several years older, handsome in a way that reminded Johnny of Antonio Banderas, and obviously in charge.

A commotion at the door caused Vincencia to jump from his chair.

Looking back, Johnny could see why the Ambassador leaped to his feet. Another khaki-clad figure was dragging Tia by her bound wrists.

"Tia!" Vincencia yelled.

"Papa!" she screamed, then broke free and ran toward her father.

But the soldier nearest Johnny stepped in front of her and slipping his arm about her neck stopped her flight. Vincencia started toward her, but the soldier tightened his grip.

"Don't move!" he yelled, "or I'll break her neck."

"Papa, Papa, they grabbed me outside the gate. They told the Marines they would kill me if they didn't put down their weapons."

As she struggled, the soldier's arm slid roughly down her body, crushing her breasts, and she cried out in pain.

Johnny heard his own voice as he yelled.

"NO!"

No conscious thought prompted him, but he was intensely aware of his reaction as he vaulted the rail. He not only saw, but felt, heard, and smelled the soldier and sensed Tia's pain. He felt his left hand slip the switchblade from his pocket, the blade locking open as he moved. His right hand grasped the soldier's collar and yanked backward while his left slammed the point of the knife in under the soldier's ribcage slashing upward toward the heart. He heard his gasp, smelled the blood, and felt the body tense, tremble, and fall.

And he saw Tia's beautiful face turning toward him, her eyes catching his.

She was so beautiful! So beautiful.

That picture became his eternity.

For at that moment, a bullet from the second soldier's weapon crashed through his skull, crushing his brain before the sound of the shot or pain from the wound could register.

He never knew he died.

Tia knew!

She saw the bullet tear away the left side of his head.

He fell atop the soldier he had just killed.

Tia screamed.

Vincencia grabbed her as she fainted.

"Stop!"

Renaldo heard the tall man shouting. He did not know the order was meant for the man who had just shot Johnny, and he wondered as he rushed to his nephew's side if he also was about to die. He knew Johnny was dead, but he had to look again! He had to be sure. Maybe he hadn't really seen his head explode. Maybe it had been just a trick of angle. Maybe he could be saved.

He fell on his knees beside Johnny. He turned him over and looked quickly away. He could not bear to see what had become of the once handsome young face.

"You knew him?"

Renaldo looked up at the tall, uniformed figure standing over him.

"He... he is..." he paused, and slowly drew his breath.

"He is my nephew," he said, breaking into racking sobs and burying his face in his hands.

"It is no consolation señor, but I regret his death. No one was supposed to die. The young man was brash."

Renaldo looked up at him.

"And for that you killed him?"

"My men too can be brash," he said, taking a step back. "It will do no good for me to apologize further."

The Ambassador, his arm about his daughter's waist, spoke softly.

"Señor. "

The tall man looked at Vincencia.

"Señor. We still do not know you, or the reason behind this. Did you come to my embassy to murder and loot?"

The tall man looked at Vincencia for a moment, then out over the fifty plus people in the gallery.

"Mr. Ambassador, I will say again I regret the death of this young man. But in war, death in inevitable. And we are at war.

"We are fighting an administration that under the guise of republican government has virtually enslaved a population, and destroyed some of Colombia's finest people.

"But" he turned to address the gallery "more to the point, I am here today to demand the release of nearly 100 people whom the present bastard administration has imprisoned on various charges.

"The names are here." He pulled a sheet of typescript from his jacket pocket and held it aloft. Then he turned back to Vincencia and handed him the paper.

"Until these people are released from prison, everyone in this embassy will remain prisoners of El Carib."

Vincencia looked at the paper, and after studying it for a moment, looked back to the soldier.

"And for this you have killed a man?" he asked

"There are other objectives as well. But there is no point in discussing anything further until the first conditions are met."

The tall soldier looked down at Renaldo.

"Give the list to the grief-stricken one. A job of importance may ease his suffering. He may leave and take with him my message. He may also take the body of his nephew, and see to my lieutenant's body as well."

Vincencia knelt beside Renaldo, supporting Tia with one arm as though she weighed nothing.

"You can do these things?" he asked.

Renaldo nodded slowly.

The tall man stepped away.

"Good," he said. "By now the police are on their way. I am needed elsewhere, and I must depart before they arrive at the gate. Lieutenant Reyes will handle all negotiations."

He put his hand on the shoulder of the soldier standing in the gallery aisle, then started for the door, pausing in the opening.

"My men do not like to kill. But they can and they will. As you have seen, they are good at it. Please do not force upon yourselves more violence. If you behave well, and the bastard administration acts with any intelligence, your suffering will be brief."

He strode from the room, and silence engulfed it. Renaldo stood slowly, staring at the body at his feet. It would fall to him to tell Johnny's parents. Despair tumbled in his breast. A life that had borne such promise.

Renaldo looked at the paper he held; four neatly typed paragraphs, a list of names, and a signature block.

For The Council of El Carib:

Jusquevera de Arrellano.

Chapter Nineteen

The television newsman didn't get it quite right.

"...witnesses said the gunman identified himself as Justin de Arrellano (he pronounced it Ah-rel-a-no)...

A fuzzy picture of a darkly handsome, slim man in khaki appeared over the newsman's shoulder.

"...the young man was killed before the man pressed his demands for release of a group of people he called political prisoners. The photo you see was taken by a Colombian newspaper man with a pocket camera and smuggled from the embassy by the uncle of the dead youth. He said the terrorists indicated that the demand for the release of the so-called political prisoners would be followed by other conditions. There was no indication what those additional conditions would be."

"A Colombian delegation is scheduled to begin negotiations later today. The terrorists call themselves soldiers of El Carib. Authorities identify El Carib as one of several underground organizations seeking the overthrow of Colombian President Garcia Fuentes.

"The body of the dead youth is being returned tonight to New York."

"Damn!" Slats said.

Olivia's voice responded from the kitchen.

"You say something Slats?"

Slats keyed the power button on the remote, pushed himself off the sofa and followed the sound of Olivia's voice.

"More damn terrorists. This time in South American," he replied as he pulled open the refrigerator door. "Is there any beer?"

Olivia looked up. Her granny glasses were perched on the end of her nose. She had been copying a recipe from "Southern Living" onto her laptop computer.

"Hostages?" she asked.

Slats found the long-necked Amstels on the refrigerator door and twisted off the cap as he replied.

"Colombia," he said. "They killed a kid when they took over the US embassy."

"They killed somebody?"

"A kid from New York. I didn't get it all...there was a picture of the guy they said did the shooting; kind of a fuzzy picture. The guy's intelligent looking. Name sounds kinda familiar. Can't be too smart though to take over the embassy. And to kill a kid. Damn!"

"Don't get so worked up, hon."

"But killing the kid babe. Jeez..."

Olivia watched Slats over the top of her glasses for a moment.

"Don't you have enough to worry about here... Colombia's a long way off.?"

She went back to her writing, then paused.

"Have you heard anything from personnel."

"No, but Courant's on my side. That should count for something."

Slats was hoping Courant's weight would push his request for leave through quickly, but he also knew that the department was short on manpower. Courant, of course, thought Slats was seeking respite from the emotional upheavals surrounding the Boulevard shooting. Slats had even convinced Olivia that his motives were primarily rest and recreation. It hadn't been difficult to convince her to make the trip. She loved to travel, and especially liked remote locations.

And diving at Grand Turk sounded very distant. In fact, until Slats brought it up, she had never heard of the island tucked in at the southern tip of the Bahamas. But she liked the sound of it.

Olivia's mother had readily agreed to babysit.

Personnel was the only holdup.

"Olivia, we're going. Courant will come through. And if personnel gets in the way, I'll threaten to resign."

Olivia's head popped up.

"Don't worry! I wouldn't really. I'm sure they won't let me go. Not that I'm irreplaceable, but Courant likes my work."

"Does he really?" she asked, studying her husband.

"Yes, he does. And he knows that the trip will get Falgout's tails off me. He's had me followed, you know."

Slats had been quite upset when he discovered the FBI surveillance.

He might never have noticed the tails. He found out about them when he dropped in to visit Johnny. The big man was out of bed, and sitting by the lone window in his room when Slats entered.

"Hey, boss, " Johnny said, "Who are your friends?"

"What are you talking about?" Slats asked.

Johnny motioned him over and nodded toward the window.

"Two guys about five parking spaces this side of the bus stop."

Slats studied the scene for only a moment.

"They pulled up just as you got off the bus, " Johnny said. "They had to fight some little old lady for that parking spot. They were pretty obvious."

For the next three days, Slats saw his tails everywhere. When he confronted Falgout, the FBI bureau chief admitted assigning them and refused to pull them off. In fact, he told Slats, "they'll be with you for the rest of your natural life."

Slats laughed and went to Courant, who grew livid with rage. He had the agent on the phone within moments.

"What do you mean, holding something back?

"Look, Falgout, this thing's as open as the Gospel according to St. Matthew. Pull your guys off, or I'll be talking to Washington, understand?" Courant slammed the phone down.

That's when Slats hit him up for help getting leave.

"I understand, Slats. It'll leave me shorthanded, but yes, I do think you need some time away. I'll see what I can do."

So the trip was on. Personnel would come through. Surely. And maybe he and Olivia actually would get a few days of R&R.

He had a little trouble convincing Olivia that he wanted to go diving. It would be a perfect cover. The brochures furnished by the travel agent promised magnificent SCUBA waters. He and Olivia had taken SCUBA courses while still in their courting days and had enjoyed rare trips to the Cayman Islands and the Florida Keys.

Slats remembered several dives beneath oilfield platforms in the Gulf, where Olivia had taken numerous photos of barracuda. The beautiful, streamlined fish with the nasty grins were normal habitants of the platform ecosystems. And their habit of hanging suspended a few feet from a diver to all intents studying a potential meal, gave them an ominous reputation, although Slats knew no one who had been attacked.

Slats had already booked flights, on Eastern to Miami and a Caribbean carrier, Southeastern, to Grand Turk. He had booked a room at the Hotel Kittina as well, a hotel the travel agent called the nicest one on the island.

Despite looking forward to the diving, and to making love to Olivia on a tropical isle, a long-shared romantic fantasy, Slats knew he wouldn't be going there but for the trail that led from Boulevard's shooting to Grand Turk.

He wasn't sure what he sought. But it had something to do with that remote Bahamian cay. Why had a course to Grand Turk been plotted on a nautical chart in the dead pimp's apartment?

There were lots of potential dead ends. If he came up empty after several days on the island, he would forget the case. He'd let Falgout and his federal buddies worry about it. He'd just enjoy the rest of his vacation, get some "quality" time with his wife, and come home rested and refreshed.

"Slats?"

Olivia shut the computer lid, and the snap brought him back to the table. Olivia walked to the counter, opened the cabinet over the sink and slipped her laptop into its cubby. Slats watched her turn, pick up the magazines she had been clipping, walk across the kitchen to toss them into the recycling hamper. He felt a warm tingle slide from his chest to his lower abdomen.

"Yes, Ollie," he replied.

It was a nickname that had followed her from elementary school to college, and she had threatened him with a sexless marriage if he persisted in using it.

She walked up to him, stepped behind his chair, and put both hands around his throat. She bent forward and whispered in his ear.

"I ought to strangle you."

Slats took a sip of his beer.

"No, on second thought" she loosed her grip and stepped around her husband. She bent and kissed him lightly on the nose.

"...on second thought, you don't get any for two weeks."

"What?! No... don't do that to me! We're going to the Bahamas."

He grabbed her hands and pulled them back to his throat.

"Strangle me, but don't put me on time-out."

"You're as bad as the kids."

He pulled her further forward and buried his face between her breasts.

"I'll be a good boy. I promise."

"Well..." she said slowly, "you'd better be very, very good. "

She pushed herself away.

"But you'll have to wait awhile. Before you so rudely interrupted me, I was going to ask if we need to carry our diving gear."

He pulled her down onto his lap.

"No. I'm sure there will be plenty to rent down there. Just carry your Rolex, and the cameras."

"I've already packed those. I think I've got everything, except last minute stuff like deodorant and make-up. I'm ready.'

He slid his hand up her thigh.

"You're always ready," he said.

"Careful, smart guy! You don't want to start something you can't finish."

Chapter Twenty

When Slats walked into his office the next morning, the envelope from personnel was on his desk, atop the morning pile of mail. He ripped it open. Courant's phone call had been effective. He had twenty days of leave, and he could take it immediately if he wished. And he wished.

Seconds later he was on the phone with Olivia.

He picked up his big Ruger .44 Magnum and his hip pocket .22, slipped both in his briefcase, and locked his office on the way out, knowing that there were probably a dozen other keys to the door. He stopped at Courant's door, knocked and on Courant's gruff "enter" pushed his way in.

"Just wanted to say thanks, Captain. We're on our way."

"Good, Lieutenant. Hope you have a good time. Just where are you going again?"

"Grand Turk, sir."

"Never heard of it."

"It's an island, in the Bahamas. Great place for diving, they say. And for sitting in the sun."

"Well, as I said, hope you enjoy it. It's apt to be tight around here."

"C'mon Captain. Ivey'll cover for me just fine. You won't even know I'm gone."

"Not if you keep hanging around."

"Uh, Captain Courant, if anything new turns up on the case, please call me."

Courant stared at him for several seconds.

"Sure, Slats. Now get out of here."

The next twenty-four hours was a haze of last-minute packing, goodbyes to the kids and Olivia's mother, taxies, airports, restaurants, and crowds. They spent an uneventful and restless night at the Miami Airport Hilton and were at the airport at nine the next morning for their flight to Grand Turk.

They were ready.

But Southeastern Air wasn't.

There was no one at the counter when they walked up to the ticket area.

The spaghetti board behind the counter showed two flights, one scheduled to leave Miami for Grand Turk at 10:02 a.m.

Slats rapped on the table.

"I've been waiting for them for half an hour."

The voice was a resonant baritone from the seating area to their right. Slats turned as a tall, darkly handsome man stood. The face seemed familiar. Slats wondered if he had met the man before. His 'cop sense' tingled. Is that anything like "Spidey sense?" Now where did that thought come from? And where did he know the man from?

He walked up to him, his right hand extended. Slats shrugged off his uneasiness and grasped the proffered hand.

"Half an hour, huh? Not the world's most efficient airline," Slats said.

"One of the least efficient, I would say," the man replied. "You and your lovely wife are headed for T-and-C?"

"T-and-C?"

"The Turks and Caicos."

"Grand Turk. Yes. That's where we're headed. "

Slats pulled a brochure from his jacket pocket.

"They say its some of the best diving in the hemisphere. "

"So I have been told," he said. "I am not accomplished as a diver, personally."

"But...Grand Turk is your destination as well?"

"Oh, yes. Yes...but my trip is for business, not pleasure. My company is Computer Dynamics. We have just built a distribution center on Grand Turk."

Slats voiced his surprise.

"On Grand Turk?"

"Really," Olivia said. "That seems a rather out-of-the-way place for a computer company."

De Arrellano shook his head.

"Not really," he replied. "It gives us a good jumping off place for South America and is central to the Bahamas and Caribbean. And we anticipate Cuba opening up to such enterprise shortly."

"You must know something we don't," Slats said.

There was a momentary silence, blurred by the din of the terminal, and Slats felt the unease creep back into his gut. He began searching for a way out of the increasingly awkward conversation when two young men appeared behind the Southeastern counter.

Both were dressed in flight attendant's uniforms, dark blue, with white shirts and blue ties. One unlocked a cabinet and set up two signs. One said "Ticketed" and the other "Unticketed."

"Excuse me, Mr..." Slats said.

A momentary pause preceded the response.

" De Arrellano," the man replied. "I know it sounds unusual, but not so in much of South America. It's a relatively common name in Latin countries."

Slats thought the explanation drawn out, but he didn't reply as he stepped to the "Ticketed" area, with Olivia beside him. De Arrellano moved to the other area.

"Strange," Slats muttered.

"What?" Olivia asked.

Slats looked at her.

"Isn't it odd that someone traveling on business, the way our new friend is, doesn't have a ticket?"

Olivia looked at him a moment.

"Tell me, detective lieutenant husband, what does that signify?"

"Search me," Slats said, shrugging. "But... well...he bothers me. I'd swear I've seen him before, but I don't know where, or when."

Olivia began to hum.

"Gosh that's an old song," she said.

"I'm serious, Hon!"

"Oh! Well...sorry. Sometimes its hard to tell, you know. Why don't you ask him?"

He paused, glancing over at Arrellano.

"Not yet. Maybe on the plane."

"Slats?"

"Yes, babe?"

"No mysteries, huh?" she asked. "Let's just enjoy the trip."

"Okay...okay. I'm just curious; that's all."

"Sure."

The attendant finished processing their tickets, and they walked into the waiting area, where over the course of the next thirty minutes they were joined by a dozen more people, including de Arrellano.

"Generally," he said, after shaking hands a second time, "the company provides me with a private plane for these trips. Unfortunately, it has been detained for other purposes. You know how it is with big companies. We peons must fend for ourselves."

He turned to the window overlooking the planes parked on the ramp below.

"Are you in business señor Jones:"

"No."

"Oh, are you civil service?"

"Not exactly," Slat replied. "I'm a cop, in New Orleans."

Slats thought he saw de Arrellano's eyes narrow.

"A police officer," the dark man said softly. "I have often thought that would be an interesting profession."

He looked back to the window as a small airliner rolled to a stop.

"Well, do you think that is our plane?"

"Gosh, I hope not. It looks very small," Olivia responded.

"My wife has an aversion to flying," Slats explained. "Particularly in little airplanes."

"I see, " de Arrellano said. "That señora is an Abrea-145. I'm afraid that is our flight. But the Abrea is a fine little plane with an excellent safety record. "

The three watched from the window as the same two flight attendants who had earlier ticketed them rode up to the plane on a baggage wagon and began filling the plane's cargo compartment. A moment later, one of the two appeared at the boarding door and began ushering passengers aboard. Slats felt some relief when he realized there were already two other faces behind the cockpit windows.

"Good grief," Olivia commented as they boarded, "it's so small."

The tight fuselage held seats for nineteen passengers, two per row left of the aisle and single seats on the right. Slats followed Olivia to a double seat near the rear of the cabin. He watched de Arrellano take the first single seat.

The plane began its taxi almost immediately, prompting Slats to wonder if their luggage would accompany them. Mild turbulence buffeted them on takeoff, and Slats spent several minutes reassuring Olivia, whose complexion paled visibly with the first few bumps.

Once the plane gained cruising altitude the turbulence vanished, and Olivia soon appeared to be enjoying the view from the tiny window, commenting on the abundance of islands on the horizon. The previous night's restiveness caught up with Slats. The muffled drone of the engines and the stale coolness of the pressurized cabin dulled his senses, and he soon found himself slipping into another world.

The blanket was wool, and scratchy, but neither of them cared. They lay in each other's arms, still coupled, the breeze blowing cool across their bare bodies. Their grass and cocklebur enclosed sanctuary on the riverbank left something to be desired, for they lay exposed to the river.

"We're probably giving some tugboat skipper an eyeful," Slats commented.

"Yes," she replied. "Wasn't it fun?"

"Babe, if you're as good with your customers as you are with me, you should be a rich lady."

She drew back.

"Don't say that!" she said, sitting up.

"Hey, I'm sorry! I did it again, didn't I?"

"You're not the same as my 'customers' as you call them. You are someone special, you know."

She hesitated, then continued. "Don't expect me to say 'I love you' because I can't. But you are 'special.'"

"Maria, I ..."

"Let's just be quiet and hold each other for a few minutes, can't we?" she asked, pulling herself down, flattening her breasts against his chest and nuzzling her face into the hollow between his neck and shoulder.

He held her.

"I love you, Maria, " Slats murmured.

She was silent.

A thunderous noise roared across them. Fire erupted in his chest, and Maria began to scream. He looked up at a tall, gaunt figure towering above them. The fire in his chest burned outward.

Who was the man standing over them? Surely it wasn't Boulevard. The big, black pimp was dead wasn't he? Or was he? Maria kept calling Slats name...shaking his shoulder. His right shoulder.

He looked into Maria's face.

But it wasn't Maria.

It was Olivia.

"Wake up, Slats! C'mon, now. You've got to move, Hon, so we can get this mess cleaned up."

She dabbed at his chest with a towel.

He looked down. His chest was wet, sticky, and painful.

"Oh my god!" he exclaimed.

"C'mon Slats!" Olivia said, "It's just coffee."

"Coffee?"

Slats looked up. There was a tall man standing over him. But he had no gun, and there was no river and no Maria. The figure standing over him was de Arrellano.

"I am terribly sorry señor. This steward, " he gestured to the uniformed attendant next to him, one of the two who had begun the journey with the passengers at the ticket counter, "is a most clumsy oaf. As you see, you are not the only one to suffer."

He held out a dripping sleeve.

"This man should not be allowed to walk about with coffee."

The attendant hung his head.

"I am so very sorry gentlemen," he said, addressing both Slats and de Arrellano.

"It isn't enough to be sorry," de Arrellano's voice hissed. Slats looked up into his face. De Arrellano's mouth was open and his brow knitted. The image from a newspaper photo flashed in his mind.

But it couldn't be.

The man who had engineered the takeover of the American embassy in Bogota must still be in Colombia, surely, locked behind the embassy gates, making demands in exchange for the release of his comrades.

And even if he weren't there, what were the odds that he would end up on the flight Slats and Olivia were on, flying of all places, to Grand Turk?

"I'm dreaming," he muttered.

"You're awake now, Hon. Sorry, it had to be such a rude awakening." Olivia glanced up at the steward, then turned her attention back to Slats.

"It must have been quite a dream, " she said. "Too bad you couldn't finish it."

"What are you talking about?" Slats asked, puzzled.

"Well, about the time he," she pointed at the steward, who cowered, "poured coffee on you, you were all smiles, and muttering something I couldn't make out."

Slats turned his face away as bits of the dream came flowing back.

"Oh," he said.

"What were you dreaming, anyway?"

Olivia stooped mopping at his chest and handed the towel back to the steward, who immediately disappeared into a small compartment at the rear of the cabin.

"I...I don't remember," Slats said, pulling his wet shirt away from his chest. "I'm going to freeze in this."

"Surehands there," she gestured toward the rear of the plane, "says he thinks he can reach your bag. If so, we will have you a clean shirt in no time."

"I hope señor, that you were not badly burned."

Slats looked up at de Arrellano.

Damn, he looks like the guy in that photo!

Slats shook his head.

"Oh, I'll be fine. If I can just get into a fresh shirt. But...thanks for your concern.

"Well, good. I'll speak to you later then."

De Arrellano returned to his seat. Slats watched him, then leaned close to Olivia's ear.

"I think he may be one of the terrorists!" he whispered.

Olivia pulled away and looked at Slats.

"What are you talking about?"

"I told you about the hostage thing in Colombia, remember?"

The skin on Olivia's nose wrinkled in what Slats called her 'puzzled panda' expression.

"Night before last, " she said, "but it seems like months ago."

"Well, it wasn't months. Just two days. And he ... " Slats nodded toward the front of the plane "looks just like the guy they said killed the kid."

Olivia shook her head.

"That's crazy! "

"I know, I know! But...he looks just like the guy in that picture!"

"That's crazy," Olivia repeated. "Look. If he were the man in the picture, do you think he would let himself be seen in public."

Olivia's argument stopped Slats cold. But he couldn't get the image from the photo out of his mind.

And the name.

It seemed very similar, although Slats had only heard it pronounced by a television news announcer.

Carrying the argument that extra step also meant opening up other possibilities that Slats could not accept. It was possible that de Arrellano simply looked like the man in the picture.

"Is this your bag sir?" The steward stood beside him in the aisle with his flight case.

"Yes, thanks."

Slats accepted the case and walked to the small cabin's rear compartment, which, he found, converted partially from a galley to a bathroom.

He wasn't impressed with the airline's sanitary arrangements.

Later, when lunch arrived, he was thankful it was sandwiches, each individually wrapped and sealed in plastic. Drinks were from sealed bottles, mixed at the seat. He looked for something he might read, but the plane seemed to lack the usual compliment of magazines. Noticing that de Arrellano had folded and put aside his newspaper, Slats went forward and asked to borrow it.

"With my compliments." The man's reply was courteous but cool.

On the lower half of the front page of the Miami News was a follow-up story on the take-over of the embassy in Bogota. It included a one-column picture similar to the one Slats had seen two days previously. He wondered if the names were spelled the same. The entire thing seemed too coincidental to be more than coincidence.

The newspaper account was more detailed, and it corrected one inaccuracy. The man pictured had not been the one who killed the youth. In fact, the young man from New York had been slain only after he had killed one of the terrorists.

At least, the loss was balanced, one for the good guys and one for the bad.

Slats never had any difficulty picking out the bad guys. At least, if this de Arrellano was the same person who had led the terrorists, he was not personally a murderer.

Surely de Arrellano was not the man pictured.

But...

A nagging uneasiness lingered. He felt he would have to take a look at de Arrellano's Grand Turk operations. It might cut into his investigation, but since he did not know where to begin that investigation anyway, Computer Dynamics seemed as logical a place to start as any.

He folded the newspaper and again went forward.

"Thanks again for the reading material," he said, standing in the aisle alongside de Arrellano.

"You are welcome," de Arrellano replied, tucking the paper into space beside his seat.

"I gather you know Grand Turk well." Slats said.

De Arrellano returned Slats' gaze coolly, but pleasantly.

"Yes. There isn't that much to know. It isn't a resort, by any means."

"So I hear. How bad is it?"

"Well, there are few of the things that you North Americans take for granted, such as cheap beer. Although most of the beer is from the US, it sells for imported prices."

"It's not like the Virgin Islands where you can get rum for five dollars a bottle and less. A good bottle of whiskey on Grand Turk could cost you forty bucks. Virtually everything is expensive.

"Fresh water is scarce. There is very little entertainment. The dogs and donkeys howl all night."

"Dogs and donkeys?"

"Yes. Dogs and donkeys. The island is overrun with both. And at night, they make a lot of noise."

"What kind of a place are we going to?"

"Some people consider it very pleasant. Particularly divers. I think you will enjoy the diving."

"Perhaps you would be good enough one day to show us about?"

De Arrellano examined Slats' face.

"It would be my pleasure." he said, hesitantly.

"However, my business there is just moving into a most active phase. I fear that I shall be occupied totally for the next several days. There are some people who work with me who won't be so occupied. Perhaps I can persuade one of them to assist you."

"Why so busy? I appreciate your offer by the way."

"You are most inquisitive. Have you interest in the computer business?"

Slats shook his head, maintaining his best poker face, and de Arrellano went on.

"We are, as that say, 'gearing up.' We have just finished our construction phase, and are now stocking the equipment and parts necessary to service our Bahamian customers and prepare for future expansion."

Slats began to feel uncomfortable standing in the aisle.

"It sounds like your company has quite an operation. I should like very much to see it. Would I, uh, be intruding if I stopped in?"

De Arrellano cocked his head.

Slats expected him to say no.

"We would be delighted." de Arrellano replied, meeting Slats' gaze.

"There is little to show, yet, save for our new building. Stocks are scheduled to begin arriving very soon. But please do come by, and your lovely wife. Perhaps I could even interest you in purchasing some stock in the company. I believe you will find that we have an excellent earning potential."

"Thank you. I shall certainly accept your tour offer. I doubt, however, that we would be interested in stock purchases."

"Of course. I realize that police officers seldom have much to invest."

Slats felt the hair on his neck bristle. He could not tell from de Arrellano's expression if the insult were intentional. But it irritated nonetheless.

"I like to keep my assets liquid, you see," Slats said, fighting the temptation to return insult for insult.

A chiming lifted Slat's attention to the seatbelts sign.

"We must be nearing our destination," de Arrellano commented.

"Excuse me," Slats said and returned to his seat. As he buckled himself in, the PA system hissed, and the pilot announced their descent into the Grand Turk airport.

"You missed it, Slats," Olivia said. "You should have seen the Caicos Islands. The water was so clear; I felt like I could reach down and touch the coral. It's all so beautiful."

"Nice, huh?"

"Oh, yes. I think this is one vacation I shall really remember."

"I'm sure we will remember this one for a long time," Slats said.

They lost a little time in customs when Slats declared his weapons. The handguns would not have been noticed, otherwise. The search consisted primarily of shaking the bags. They had been asked to open only one until the inspector glanced at the declaration card Slats had signed.

"Oh! I'm sorry, but we cannot allow you to bring weapons onto the island."

"But I'm a police officer, and I am lost without them!"

"I'm sorry sir, but the rule is no weapons."

"Look, here's my identification," Slats said, slipping a folded twenty-dollar bill under the Id wallet and handing it to the inspector. "Can't you contact the attorney general or someone and get me permission to have my pieces along?"

"I'll see what I can do. Just a moment please." The man disappeared into a small cubical that said "Customs" on the door. Two minutes later he was back.

"The attorney general's office is most understanding, Lieutenant Jones. I must obtain the registration numbers from your weapons, and you may keep them with you. You will, of course, be held liable for any damages that they might inflict while on the island. You understand."

"Certainly."

The formalities were taken care of quickly, and Slats and Olivia were on their way to the Kittina Inn, where they were ushered into a second-floor ocean-side room with a balcony overlooking the island's major thoroughfare, a broken two-lane slice of cement that bordered the beach.

When Slats inquired about the adjacent rooms, he learned that a woman had the end room past theirs, although she occupied it very little, and the room on the other side was to be taken by a physician and his wife from New York, also down for the diving.

Chapter Twenty One

Their settling-in included meeting one of the two local diving masters, Alex Kuttner.

Kuttner scheduled them for their first trip the following day, and they set out for a late afternoon walk on the beach. As the day wore on, the blistering sun, several degrees hotter than the south Louisiana version, dropped low in the west, and Slats felt his appetites building. Olivia's graceful figure and the dimples that showed beneath her swimsuit excited him. And somewhere around the edges of his psyche, his libido, engaged earlier by the interrupted fantasy, stirred. He snuck up behind his wife as she examined a conch shell, turning it with her toe, and kissed her gently on the nape of her neck, his hands running down over her shoulders to stroke her breasts.

"Slats, don't. Someone will see."

"So?"

"So...do not!"

"So...okay. But you'll get yours later, Babe."

"I hope that's a promise and not a threat," she whispered, hugging his arm.

He slapped her buttock lightly. A mutual warmth spread from their shared grasp.

"Shall we go back to the hotel and have some supper? We probably should get to bed early," Slats said, "since we have a big day of diving coming up."

Olivia looked into his face. His mouth curved into a rather broad grin.

"All right, Hon. I suspect you're right."

By the time they reached the hotel, it was almost dark. They changed, Slats into casual slacks and a pullover shirt, Olivia into one of the lightweight summer dresses her husband appreciated.

"Have I told you lately that you've got a great bod," he said as they descended the stairs toward the dining room.

"No. And I would appreciate it if you would. Frankly, the effects of aging are getting to me."

"Aging? You sound like a grandmother."

Slats willingly played Olivia's ego game, and he soon convinced her that she shared the physical attributes of Salma Hyack, Scarlett Johansson, and Natalie Portman.

They were on their way back to their room, buoyed by the aphrodisiac of shared sexual awareness when Kuttner stopped them at the top of the stairway.

"The meeting's about to start. C'mon."

"What meeting?" Slats asked.

"The diving meeting. You do want to go tomorrow, don't you?"

"Well, sure. But you never said anything about a meeting."

"Sorry. Must have slipped my mind earlier. But with so many divers on these trips, it is essential that everyone understand the rules. I don't mean just the rules of diving, but how we organize this, who goes down first, how long we stay, what area we will cover. If you're going diving with me, you've got to go to the meeting."

Slats and Olivia looked at each other. She shrugged.

"Well..."

For the second time in four hours, Slats made a conscious effort to turn down the flame of his sexual fire.

"Where's the meeting?" he shrugged.

"In the upstairs bar. Go on in. I have to pick up some visual aids and I'll be right there."

They found the bar, a large, open room with two glass walls, packed with people.

"Where have they all come from?" Slats asked Olivia. "There aren't enough rooms in the hotel for that many people."

They sat down at a table near the door and immediately fell into conversation with another couple. It turned out they were at the Saltraker Inn just minutes up the beach. Many of the participants evidently didn't stay at the Kittina.

"Shucks," said the man, in a Texas drawl Slats thought he must have purchased at Neiman-Marcus, "there're not enough rooms on this island for all the divers who want to come here. Why I could keep this place running for fifty years just with divers in Houston."

Kuttner arrived, clanking through the sliding glass door with a large aluminum tripod and illustrated flip charts. A slim, dark woman slipped into the room behind him, and although he could see little of her face as she edged past Kuttner to the bar, a chord of recognition hummed in his brain.

"Damn!"

"Something wrong, Hon?"

"Not really, but... You see that girl at the bar?" He nodded toward the slim figure in a white cotton dress, half-hidden behind Kuttner.

"Just barely. Why?"

"I think I know her."

Olivia raised her eyebrows.

"Another one?"

"Huh?"

"First the guy on the plane, and now the girl in the bar."

Slats paused, taken aback.

"Yeah, well. I guess it does seem a bit far-fetched. But I wish I could just see her better."

"Not tonight, Sherlock. Not even if she walks up and says, 'Hi.'"

Slats tried throughout Kuttner's dry, lengthy lecture to obtain a better view of the girl, but the crowded room and his lack of mobility prevented it. When the talk ended, with instructions for assembling the following morning, the milling crowd let the girl disappear before Slats could reach her.

That night Slats made love to Olivia until they were both exhausted, finally falling asleep in each other's arms, only to waken an hour later drenched in perspiration. They shared a quick, salty shower, and then slept deeply and soundly until Olivia's little travel alarm shrilled them awake.

They threw on swimsuits and rolled up extra clothing to protect them later from the blistering sun. Olivia packed the Nikons, and they headed for the dining room for a quick breakfast. When the truck arrived to take them to the boat, it was already loaded with equipment and several passengers on wooden benches. The ride was noisy with the clanking of diving tanks and weight belts, and smelly as the truck exhaust leaked into the cargo-passenger area.

But the boat made up for their discomfort. The forty-foot-long catamaran was spacious and comfortable even with thirty people aboard. A couple dozen more were assigned to a smaller boat that would track their craft to the diving area.

The ocean was calm, the air salty-sweet, and a light breeze cooled skins that even at 8:00 a.m. could feel the intensity of the Bahamas sun. Cruising across the unbelievably clear water, absorbing the nuances of sound, color, and the odor of the sea, sky, boat, and people, Slats managed to forget that he was on Grand Turk for reasons other than personal pleasure.

He led Olivia to a spot near the bow and sat, holding her hand, reveling in his feelings, and psyching himself for the dive.

Kuttner, meanwhile, circulated among the divers, assigning groups of people to his diving assistants, most of the groups having no more than five people. Slats and Olivia drew the couple with whom they had shared a table the previous evening. They sat near them on the bow as the boat rounded up into the breeze and its anchor splashed down. Slats noticed their partners whispering to each other. He also noticed that the young woman was ashen, and the man seemed to be taking her pulse.

"Bill, I'm not going to dive today. I just can't," the young woman said.

"All right, baby. I'll stay with you."

"I don't want to spoil your fun. You go ahead."

"You sure?"

"Yes, You go ahead."

Bill became aware that the conversation was open to Slats and Olivia. He glanced at them.

"Sorry, folks. She's just having a bad period."

The girl turned white.

"Bill!"

Chagrined, Bill smiled uneasily.

"Sorry, Baby!"

He looked at Olivia.

"You see, I'm a gynecologist, and sometimes I forget the difference between clinical and polite conversation. I hope I haven't offended anyone."

Olivia said nothing.

"Don't worry about it," Slats said. "But if your wife isn't going to dive, hadn't we better tell Kuttner?"

"I'll take care of that," Bill said. "Soon as I get Mary below."

The two of them rose, Bill supporting his wife, and walked around the cabin toward the stern of the boat, where the sound of diving preparations had turned the quiet sea scene into a metallic cacophony.

Moments later Bill returned.

"My wife's bunked down in the cabin, and Kuttner assigned a single girl who had been with a larger group to dive with us. We'd better get back there. We're due over the side soon."

When they reached the stern, the diving platform was already in place, and the first group had splashed overboard. A blond, deeply tanned youth pointed out to them the racks of equipment and helped them assemble what they needed near the diving platform.

"Where's our fourth person?" Slats asked the youth.

"Below, getting some of her gear. She'll be here in a minute."

"Slats. Can you help me here, Hon?"

It took Slats only a minute to help Olivia lift the single tank onto her back, and when he turned around, he noticed the girl, their new diving partner, her back to him, attempting to lift her tank into place. The straps were twisting badly, and she needed help. Bill was down on one knee, intent on zipping on a pair of wetsuit boots, and didn't see her predicament.

"Here, let me help you," Slats said, walking up behind the girl and lifting the tank. She gave a bit of a grunt and a twist, and the straps settled over her shoulders. Slats let the tank's pack ease down against her back.

"Thank you, kind sir," the girl said, turning around slowly toward him. Her voice had a familiar hazy resonance. "I don't think..." she began and stopped as she looked up into his eyes, a head above hers. She drew a sharp, quick breath and stepped back, almost toppling over the side of the boat.

For a moment, Slats could not accept what his senses told him.

"Maria?" he asked.

Chapter Twenty Two

When Lt. Col. Charlie Adkins prepared to fly the Harrier from the pitching barge, he hadn't been sure he would get airborne. Luckily, the tug captain was a man of skill and knowledge, and luckily also there had been a small cay handy. There was still a sea running in the lee of the cay, but the windbreak tamed the wicked chop that ran across it. Charlie ran through the starting procedures and listened with a critical ear to the throaty whine. When he was satisfied with that sound, he tried to attune himself to the sea.

He had the wing tiedowns removed before start-up, but had kept on the fore and aft cables and wheel blocks to assure that the plane did not slide off the barge on the lift of an unusually large sea.

The rolling motion of the barge had slowed in the lee of the cay. He hoped the little pile of limestone and sand was sufficient to provide him some lee above the water as well. He knew that an impromptu gust from an unexpected direction would set the little plane on its ear. Charlie wanted desperately now to complete his mission. Not only did he wish to live through the day, the prospects for which were questionable, but he wanted his place in the sun with the Colombians, and he wanted to feel Maria's body again close to his own.

The captain was bringing the tug up to weather, and the barge was swinging into the wind. Charlie felt the plane's wings vibrate as the wind rushed over him. A small tropical low was building a hundred miles southwest of them, and cumulus were beginning to grow along pressure gradients running hundreds of miles. The system could graduate overnight from depression to tropical storm.

Charlie and the captain had watched the system through the day. He had decided a couple of hours before dusk that if he wasn't airborne by nightfall, he might never be.

Charlie felt the pressure on the plane easing as they slipped deeper into the lee of the island. He saw the barge stabilize as the seas stripped their mantles of foam and smoothed out, running slightly ahead of the vessel's starboard beam.

He held up one clenched fist, and the crewman who had stayed with him on the barge ran forward and kicked loose the pins that secured the cables to the plane. Charlie waited a moment longer while the crewman let himself down through a rusty hatch into the barge's interior.

Charlie clutched the throttle.

He wanted full power, and it was there. He gloried in the change of pitch as thrust built, and he prayed for lee enough to get altitude.

"Just a little," he muttered under his breath.

The plane almost jumped skyward, and he had to fight for control, afraid that he would topple off the fountain of fire that lifted him. It was the wind, the force five wind increasing across the wings as he lifted above the island.

Then he was above it.

He had the altitude. But the plane was beginning to rock wildly. With a couple of quick moves, he knocked it out of the hover. Momentarily the plane looked as though it were about to nose into the water. Then it was flying.

The wash of the jet bathed the tug in the odor of kerosene as it roared away into the graying sky.

Charlie made a pass over the tug and flew off into the clouds. He had pored over charts throughout the day, but it took him a moment to right his bearings. He flew out of the band of cumulus and noticed another looming ahead, fiery in the evening sun's reflected light.

The excitement of again beating the odds coursed through his body. He snap-rolled the plane, and, as he brought it back to a cruise, he saw the semi-circle of the Caicos.

By now they knew on Grand Turk that he was on his way. He would be earlier than expected. But he was eager to see Maria, and to meet Jusquevera.

Charlie didn't understand why Jusquevera had taken over the US Embassy in Bogota, but he had no doubts that the man mentioned on the radio reports was the same one Maria had described to him. He must have plans for the hostages, something that would help him gain control.

Otherwise, it was a senseless act, and while Charlie did not disdain violence, he wanted it to serve a purpose. His purpose. Well, he would have his curiosity assuaged shortly.

Charlie called Grand Turk approach control and raised the airport on the first try. He identified himself as a light transport, leased by Computer Dynamics Corp., and requested landing instructions.

He made a high pass, telling control he wanted to see the lay of the runways before landing. It was sufficiently dark on the ground that personnel in the tower would not identify the plane.

"CD jet, this is the tower. I have a commercial flight closing that will be on final in about ten minutes. If you do not put down now, you will have a thirty-minute wait. Understood?"

"Understood, tower. On my way."

Charlie put a wing down and swept in, long and clean. He could make out lights in two distinct airport buildings. In the tower, they would see him land, but while they might wonder about the strangely shaped plane, they would not be able to make out the distinguishing characteristics; unless they were warplane buffs. He hoped none were.

He dropped smoothly onto the runway and taxied immediately to the hangar, where he found three men holding open the doors. He nudged the plane in past the Lear that had been pushed outside onto the apron. The Harrier fit snugly in the small building.

As the hangar doors rolled shut Charlie shut down. He opened the cockpit and saw Maria standing near a door into a glass-boxed office.

The three men who had opened and then closed the hangar came forward and chocked the plane's wheels, and before Charlie was clear of the plane they were examining its fittings and finish. One had a small file with which he cut a crease across the leading edge of the port wing.

"Hi, Charlie," Maria said as he walked up to her, shedding his flight suit as he went. "Have a bad time getting here?"

"It was a little rough, sweetheart," Charlie said in his best Bogart imitation. Maria winced.

"So I heard. Charlie, this is Raul. He's Jusquevera's pilot, and he's been teaching me to fly."

"Oh?"

Raul extended a small but, Charlie found, strong hand.

"Teaching you to fly?"

"Yes," she said, a grin digging wrinkles into her smooth face. "And now you have to take over!"

"What are you talking about, beautiful?"

"I'm supposed to be your backup pilot, Charlie. You have to teach me to fly the Harrier."

"What?" Charlie's mouth fell open. "That'll take months!"

Maria's smile disappeared.

"The hell it will. I've learned to fly the Lear in just over a week, haven't I Raul."

"That is true, señor. The lady learns very fast. You will see."

"Well look, I've had a rough few minutes. I'm tired, and I could use a drink."

Maria's smile returned. She reached out and hugged the flyer.

"I'm sorry, Charlie. I've just been bursting to tell you. I wanted to see how Mr. Macho would react to having me as a pupil."

Charlie shrugged.

"I'm not Mr. Macho. As far as having you for a pupil, it could prove a pleasant task."

"Unless she kills you, señor."

Charlie thought he detected a note of jealousy in the man's voice.

"And with the drink, I should like very much to meet Jusquevera. I've heard a lot about him, particularly recently."

"Recently?" Maria questioned.

Charlie studied for a moment the puzzled expression on her face.

"You haven't heard?"

"Heard what, Charlie? I guess we have been rather out of touch. I've been concentrating so on the flying. What have I missed?"

"A man who identified himself as Jusquevera de Arrellano led a group of guerrillas who took over the American Embassy in Bogota three days ago. Every radio station in the hemisphere has been talking about it. He killed a man in the take-over."

Maria looked stunned. She was momentarily motionless and silent. Then she looked at Raul as though seeking confirmation.

"Señorita, I'm sure if a man was killed, it was necessary," Raul said, spreading his hands in a gesture of helplessness.

"But, why?"

"I'm sure we shall know soon, señorita."

"Then Jusquevera isn't here?" Charlie squinted.

"Si."

"I had thought it was probably a diversion to keep attention away from whatever he is doing. I figured it was just somebody using his name."

"It was Jusquevera, señor. He left several days ago."

"Well," Charlie tossed his flying gear at a nearby tool-rack, watching it land askew.

"What about that drink?"

He felt a vague disquiet at the absence of the man he had hoped to meet. But the prospect of good whiskey and the companionship of a beautiful woman compensated for it.

Maria led him back to the small crew lounge, with Raul following. There she dug from a cabinet Raul's bottle of scotch and a bottle of soda.

"I'll have mine straight up, señorita," Raul said.

"As you wish, my dear friend. After all, it is your bottle."

They had soon toasted the success of Charlie's trip, the prospects for the mission, and, at Charlie's instigation, Maria's beauty. Not that any of them understood the purpose. All they knew was that the next step was teaching Maria to fly the Harrier.

Suddenly a thought crossed Maria's mind.

"Charlie! Does that plane have room for the both of us?"

"Huh? Oh, yes. The Harrier is a single place fighter, but this version was built for training. It has an extra seat. Don't worry, lovely lady. You and I shall have plenty of time together."

Charlie cast a quick glance at Raul, but if the little Colombian had understood the entendre, it didn't show. Maybe he had imagined the earlier flicker of jealousy he had seen flash across Raul's face.

It didn't matter. While he was on the island, Maria was his. He tossed off the remainder of his drink.

"Well! That's better. Now I think some food would be in order. And I'll need a place to stay."

"For the time being, señor, it is best that you sleep here with the crew."

"Here?"

Charlie glanced around.

"Think I'd rather get a room in town. Surely they do have some hotels on the island."

"Very few, Charlie," Maria said. "And they are chock full of divers right now. There probably isn't a room available anywhere."

"What is this, a conspiracy?"

He shifted his gaze between Raul and Maria. "I'm getting the short end of the stick. I mean, after all, did I or did I not steal a multi-million dollar airplane for you? And I just risked my neck getting it here. Now you're telling me I can't even sleep in a bed tonight? I have to bunk in a metal cubbyhole?"

Maria walked up to him, draped an arm over his shoulder, and kissed him lightly on the cheek.

"Charlie, take it easy. I know what you've done, and believe me, we appreciate it. There is a lot for you in this, wait and see. I'm sorry the hotels are full, but why don't we go to my hotel for supper and you can tell me all about your trip."

Charlie liked the idea but was disappointed when he heard Maria ask Raul to join them. His disappointment vanished when the Colombian refused, saying he should supervise the crew that already was preparing to alter the appearance of the Harrier. Charlie thought it stupid to try to make a fighter unrecognizable.

"Can't be done," he muttered to himself as he and Maria crossed the hangar. Already, he noticed, the plane's numbers were obliterated by a nondescript paint. Surely they wouldn't leave her that color!

A few moments later Charlie cleared customs (he had nothing to declare, bringing with him only his jeans and the western cut shirt he wore to accentuate his powerful chest) and they caught a cab to the Hotel Kittina.

To Charlie's mind, the meal was sumptuous, and the wine passable. By the time they had finished, Charlie felt mellow indeed. He reached under the table and clasped Maria's Jean-clad knee. The denim was soft and yielding, and Charlie remembered caressing the thigh beneath the cloth.

"You're staying here?"

"Yes, she replied, deftly spearing bits of a fruit compote. "Jusquevera didn't want me staying in the crew's quarters. Said I might distract the men." She winked at him over a forkful of pineapple.

"He was right," he said.

"Would you like to see my room?"

"I would."

"Let's have coffee, first."

Charlie ordered two coffees and, as an afterthought, cognacs. If Maria's coolness was anything but feigned, he wanted to melt it early.

"Feeling better, Charlie?" she asked.

"Much. And perhaps, even better, later?"

He studied her expressions as she nibbled at the last bite of fruit, then poured the cognac into her coffee and sipped. She seemed to be studying him over her cup, and he caught himself sitting a bit taller. He too sipped at his coffee, trying to appear relaxed and unhurried.

"What's going on, Maria?" he asked.

She continued to study him.

"I know little more than you," she said.

"Can you fill in some blanks for me."

She put her cup down and leaned in, her voice little more than a whisper.

"Jusquevera runs an organization ... a Colombian underground...called El Carib."

"That name! That's the terrorists who took over the embassy in Bogota."

Maria paused, a puzzled look tilting her countenance, then continued.

"What Jusquevera is planning is a coup. El Carib will take over from people who have been running Colombia for the past 30 years."

"And then?"

"And then we go home!"

"We?"

"Jusquevera and I... we return to our homeland ...and you get a new home, a home with great promise, where you can be all you can be!"

She looked at Charlie, realizing she had just been quoting marketing gibberish from the Marine Corps and momentarily avoided his eyes.

"Sorry about the word games Charlie. But I am serious. That's what this is all about, going home. Jusquevera can reinstate his family into its rightful place, and I can cleanse my father's name. And you can build a career such as you've only dreamed of."

Charlie leaned back, absorbing her commentary.

"It sounds too simple, Maria."

She paused, leaned away, and stared at him, lost in her word pictures.

"Maria, does Jusquevera have an army? And why did he take over the American embassy?"

Maria was slow to answer, and the words came with a shrug.

"I know," she said. "I've asked the same questions. Jusquevera said we should be patient. When we need to know, we will. Right now, he fears leaks. I believe him..." her voice trailed off, and Charlie saw the pointlessness in pursuing the subject.

He placed his hands on the table.

"What's next?" he asked.

Maria leaned in, took another sip of her coffee, then looked Charlie in the eye.

"How about my place?" she asked.

Charlie barked at the waitress, and moments later they were on their way to Maria's room, leaving the waitress muttering under her breath about spendthrift patrons. Charlie followed Maria into the room, spun her around and lifted her easily and kissed her deeply.

"I hope you missed me," he said.

She stroked his hair.

"Of course, I missed you, " she replied. "Now put me down and open the door to the balcony, please. "

When he had done her bidding, Maria pushed the drapes aside and walked out, pulling Charlie with her. A half moon just past the zenith glistened on the limestone sand. A breeze, neither cool nor warm, brushed past and the swish of the surf on the beach formed a background for the tinkle and clatter, and the mumble of conversation from the dining room below.

She leaned on the balcony rail and slipped her right arm into the crook of Charlie's elbow, drawing him to her side.

"What do you want most in this world, Charlie?"

Without hesitation, he replied.

"You."

She looked up at him, the studious gaze that had now become to Charlie as familiar as her face leveled at his eyes.

"I want everything that was taken away from me as a child," she said. "I want servants, and breakfast in bed. I want fine wine and handsome lovers."

Charlie stiffened but did not pull away.

"I want to be able to walk down a street, a street with my name on it, and look down my nose on the peasants. I want to the be the most 'crat' of all aristocrats."

As she spoke, she slipped her left hand around his neck, pulling him away from the rail, and snuggled her body up against his. His right hand, trapped between them, pushed her away and began unbuttoning her blouse. By the time he had it open his mouth had moved to her breast and he tongued her left nipple. She let her head hang back, sighing.

"Let's go inside, " he whispered.

She allowed him to lead her back through the open doorway and guide her to the bed. There, with deft hands, he slipped her jeans down her thighs, and tried to tug them over her feet, but they caught on her shoes.

"Damn!" he muttered.

"Charlie... don't be in such a hurry. We have all night. Be slow, Charlie...slow and good!"

Charlie eased back and looked at Maria.

The moonlight that cascaded through the skylight above the bed painted her lithe, small-breasted figure in silver. The same moon washed white the sheer drapes that moved in the breeze. He smelled her, alive with potent sexuality. He fought the urge to spring onto the bed and ravish her savagely. Instead, he removed her shoes, slowly, kissed her feet, pulled the jeans off, then stood her up and kissed her while he hooked his thumbs into her panties and slid them down her legs. She kicked them away into the darkness.

"Now undress," she said.

Charlie complied, quickly, and Maria led him to the shower where they spent ten minutes luxuriating under the steaming salt water and exploring one another. They toweled each other dry; Charlie taking extra pains to fluff the dark triangle across her mons. As he stood up, his erection betrayed his increasing excitement, and Maria snapped to attention and saluted.

Charlie was puzzled.

"This is funny?" he asked

Maria was startled. She had expected a laugh!

Not wanting to lose the ardor of the moment earlier, she reached out, clasped his erection, and kissed him.

"Fun, yes!" she said. "Funny, no! I was just returning the compliment your body paid mine. If I offended you, I apologize. All right?"

Charlie hesitated. Was she making fun of him?

But the heat of his desire burned away his peckishness.

"I get it now, " he said. "You want to play games, huh?"

"Only if they're fun games, Charlie."

And they were fun games. And they played hard until Charlie tried to tie her to the bed.

"No bondage! No, too many bad memories. You don't know how kinky some people's pleasures can be when they think they own you, even for an hour."

Under Maria's coaching, Charlie provided her with several high-intensity orgasms before she allowed him his own. She wanted him exhausted, and she got what she wanted. Five minutes after his release, she heard his breath slip into the rhythmic pattern of deepening sleep. Letting one hand rest on his chest, she drifted off as well.

The next day was hectic. Charlie accompanied Maria and Raul on an early morning flight in the Lear, and Maria displayed what she had learned in her training. Charlie was impressed. They flew several times over a cay Raul had picked out for the Harrier training, and for storage of the plane when it was off island. Charlie approved. Although small, probably less than two square miles in area, the island had a semi-circular limestone spine forming its western face, and wind-built dunes along the eastern shore created a valley shielded on all sides from the water. A simple net would hide the plane from pilots who might cross the cay while island hopping. After several low passes, with Raul at the controls and Charlie observing, they picked out a landing site for the Harrier, then headed back to Grand Turk.

"Can you find it in the dark, Captain Adkins?" Raul asked.

Charlie glanced over his shoulder at Maria. He winked.

"I always have," he said. Maria grimaced, then smiled.

When they returned to the office, they found a telex message waiting. Jusquevera was returning on the afternoon flight from Miami.

They also found that the technicians had fitted the Harrier with a phony nosepiece and wingtip tanks, as well as repainting the entire airplane. Charlie had to admit it looked different. More so that he would have thought possible.

"How much, " he asked, tapping the nacelle,"will this change her performance?"

"It's lightweight carbon and epoxy," the tech replied. "She should fly virtually the same as ever."

"But," Raul interjected, "these gadgets might not take sustained high speeds."

Charlie thought a moment and felt his face flush.

"Dammit! How am I supposed to teach somebody to fly this if I can't be sure of its performance?"

Raul studied the red-faced Charlie for a moment before replying.

"I'm sorry señor. You can fly her fast enough for your purposes, and should a part become damaged; we have replacements."

Charlie felt his anger draining and wondered where it had come from. Was it jealously? After all, it was his plane being defaced. She didn't look like the same craft anymore.

"Test fly her, señor. As soon as it gets dark. You need to take her to the other island as soon as possible. Tomorrow night perhaps. And tomorrow we shall have a boat meet you there. You and Maria will live on the boat for the next few days."

"Suits me," Charlie said, all of his anger now vanished.

Chapter Twenty Three

The Miami flight with Jusquevera arrived.

When he walked into the hangar office bay, Maria was startled by his haggard appearance. But he smiled when he saw the Harrier, and he strode immediately to where Charlie, Maria, and Raul waited. He and Charlie sized each other up, the tall, thin, darkly aristocratic Jusquevera looking down on the broad and powerfully built German. Finally, Charlie stuck out a hand.

"Glad to meet you, Jusquevera! "

Jusquevera accepted the handshake.

"And I, you," he said. "Especially so if you can fly as well as I have been led to believe."

"Oh, I can fly," Charlie said, "but I'd like to know what kind of mission I'll be flying."

Jusquevera sighed.

"In good time," he said. "I will explain everything to everyone in time. But for now, I feel the need for food and rest. Would you," he asked, gesturing to include the three of them, "care to join me at the Kittina?"

Thirty minutes later they were seated around a table at the hotel. Jusquevera ordered a round of drinks, and when they arrived, he lifted his glass and with a "Salud" tossed off the contents.

Charlie thought he could see some of the strain in the handsome Hispanic face melt away. He knew Jusquevera would be a powerful friend or a dangerous adversary. He had the bearing of one who made decisions easily and well. Charlie pictured him leading his group of guerrilla soldiers into the embassy, wondering how he had gotten past the Marine guards.

He lifted his glass and returned Jusquevera's "Salud!"

After they placed orders, Jusquevera, glancing about the room, said in a too-loud voice, "Well, now, my friends! No talk of business this evening. Only pleasantries, all right."

Charlie couldn't miss the message. Too many ears about.

Jusquevera looked at Maria and raised his refilled glass to her.

"To you, lovely lady. Have you plans for tomorrow."

She smiled and leaned across the table to touch Jusquevera's hand. Charlie felt an odd burning in his gut as he watched her return Jusquevera's smile.

"Let's dive tomorrow!" she said.

Jusquevera hesitated.

"That's a splendid idea," he said. "But being a novice, will they allow me along with the group?"

"Let me ask Alex," she said, almost purring the name. "I think I can convince him."

"Yes," Jusquevera said. "Ask... Yes, I think we all need some recreation. Will you go with us?"

He addressed the question to both the other men.

Charlie bit back the hint of fire in his voice.

"Oh, no!" he said, too quickly. "No. I love to sail on the sea, and I'll do anything in the air. But underwater is for fish. Thanks anyway, but I'll do my recreating on top of the water."

"I also, señor!" Raul said, dipping his grizzled head. "I too prefer to stay above water. I can get all the recreation I desire exploring the new airplane...so I shall stay behind."

Jusquevera glanced about.

"Shhhhh! Raul...as you wish."

"But the plane won't be here!" Charlie said sharply, "I'm taking her out tonight."

"But you'll be here tomorrow," Raul rejoined. "You have to be."

Jusquevera cleared his throat brusquely.

"Gentlemen, please... " he looked from one man to the other. "Save this conversation for later."

Charlie glanced about, then settled his gaze on Maria.

"You sure you want to go diving?" he asked. "I was hoping we could find a sailboat to charter for the day."

She returned his gaze levelly.

"But it's been so long since I've been diving," she replied. "And Jusquevera promised he would go with me."

Charlie felt the strange sensation in his gullet again. Perhaps he didn't like the tall Colombian after all.

A momentary black hole swallowed the conversation, and might have pulled the participants into the void had not the food arrived. When the conversation resumed between mouthfuls of lobster and scamp, it was talk of diving. Jusquevera demonstrated a knowledge of the technology which surprised Maria. She had taken up the sport during her early days in Pensacola. She had learned well, and her knowledge stood her in good stead when she went to work for Bulgy Tichner, who had in those days been an avid diver. But increasing responsibilities, and waistline, had slowed Bulgy and in the past decade, there had been little of the sport in his...or Maria's life.

While Maria and Jusquevera talked, Charlie and Raul ate silently. For his part, Charlie pouted. He had expected Maria to jump at the chance to sail with him, and he had entertained visions of recreating the evening with Maria aboard his boat, an evening that now receded into the distant past.

But she had turned him off as though what they had shared last night was meaningless. She had shut him out so that she could go diving with Jusquevera. What was he to her anyway? Charlie watched them in animated conversation, something about decompression tables and anchor lines.

Yes, there was something between them. But he sensed none of the electricity that he and Maria had shared. Was it just hidden? Or was there something else there, something he could not comprehend.

At that moment, Maria rose, patted Jusquevera's hand, and said she was going to find Kuttner. She turned to Charlie and blew him a kiss.

"Bye..." she said, "See you, Raul."

And she was gone.

The three men looked at each other, then completed their meal in silence. Finally, Charlie looked at his watch, remarked that he had to fly, and asked Raul to take him back to the airport.

After they had left, Jusquevera carried a coffee and brandy onto the terrace and settled down to watch the stars. Tension from the week's events vanished into the night sky. He ignored the small pain in the pit of his stomach.

He thought about the day to come.

Sunny skies, blue water, and the company of a lovely lady. Should be a relaxing day.

He questioned his feelings toward Maria. He found himself admiring her more each time he saw her. Not only was she beautiful, but her strength, her character, and her zest for life fascinated him. Perhaps tomorrow, on the boat, they would talk.

Maria, meanwhile, had stopped at the little outdoor bar, ordered a pina colada, and started toward her room, planning to call Kuttner at his shop. But as she passed the meeting room she noticed the throng of people. So she waited.

Sure enough moments later Kuttner appeared, stumbling up the stairs with a flip chart and easel. He almost fell trying to edge through the sliding door into the conference room, so she took one end of the easel and walking a step behind, directed him through the door.

Before she could ask Kuttner about Jusquevera, he greeted the assembled group and launched into his prepared pre-dive presentation. So she edged her way into a relatively open spot near the door, Kuttner and his flip-charts between her and most of the guests.

She sipped her drink.

Kuttner's presentation would win no medals for enthusiasm. He reminded her of the ancient nun who had taught her sums at St. Joseph's in Bogota so many years before. His Adam's apple slid up and down, and she imagined it a prune shrunken by the dryness of the voice passing over it. She noticed a man in the audience who appeared to be watching her, but it was too dark to see him well. His attention disturbed her, so she turned and slipped through the door.

After what seemed an hour but was in reality no more than fifteen minutes Kuttner had summarized plans for the morning trip, and she trapped him as he exited the room, again dragging his flip-chart board. He agreed readily to allow Jusquevera on board but withheld judgment on his diving capability.

She hurried off to find Jusquevera, but he was no longer in the hotel. She intended to phone him but found a note slipped under her door.

"Dear Maria. The evening air has relaxed me after an arduous journey. I must retire, but I shall call you early. Your servant, Jusquevera."

Damn!

She still had a thousand questions for her Colombian benefactor. But they would have to wait.

As she prepared for bed, she thought briefly about Charlie. She remembered the previous evening and their lovemaking. It had left her with a pleasant glow, and she found herself wishing for more. If nothing else, she would like him there to curl simply up beside.

Not that she was lonely.

She had felt real loneliness only twice in her life: when her father had been spirited away, and when her mother had died. She had thought then the loneliness would kill her. But it hadn't. She had lived, and felt that she must have lived for a purpose.

And now she had found that purpose... or it had found her.

She was part of something special, a new movement, an organization that would bring a corrupt government to its knees, an initiative of social change that would be felt around the world.

She slept well.

When she awoke the day was bright and warm, the trade wind softly billowing the curtains where she had left the balcony door ajar. She slipped into her bikini and pulled on a tee-shirt and khaki shorts. Stepping onto the balcony, she could see Kuttner at the dive shop next door loading the travel-all with tanks and gear. Red frangi-pangi flowers shook lightly in the breeze, and the scent of other tropicals rode the air.

She inhaled deeply, thoroughly enjoying the freshness of the morning.

Blue sky, blue water, a warm breeze; the day held much promise.

The phone by her bed beeped, and she walked back into the room, pulling the door shut behind. She knew it would be Jusquevera's voice on the phone.

"It's a beautiful morning," she said into the receiver without waiting for a greeting.

"For you perhaps," came the reply. It was Jusquevera's voice, but it was soft and tinny.

"Is something wrong?" she asked.

"Perhaps I am getting soft, or I'm getting too old for my endeavors. Whatever the cause I seem to have contracted one of these intestinal viruses. I'm afraid I must excuse myself from our diving expedition."

Maria didn't try to hide her disappointment.

"Oh no! And I was so looking forward to it."

"Well, " Jusquevera began, and Maria had to strain to hear his voice it was so soft on the phone. "You should go anyway. You've earned it. I know you've worked hard. Go! Enjoy the diving. And I'll visit the island's dispensary and see what remedy they might have for my discomfort."

"I wouldn't feel right going without you," she said. "Besides, we're not supposed to dive without a partner."

"Nonsense. If my infirmity prevents you from going, it will make me feel worse. And I'm sure there will be one or more young men willing to accompany a lovely woman to the depths of the sea."

She hesitated.

"Yes," she replied. "Yes, I'll go. And I'll tell you all about it this evening. I hope you're feeling better by then."

"Good! Yes, this evening I expect to be much improved. And we do have things to discuss, don't we? But for now, enjoy your holiday. And watch out for the sharks, especially the ones not in the water."

She hung up, disappointed but still finding an eagerness within for the day ahead. She grabbed a foam cup of coffee and two donuts from the breakfast buffet set on the terrace and was first in line at the dive van. But Kuttner appeared driving his car and offered her a lift to the boat. He sympathized when she told him of Jusquevera's problem, and assured her they would find her a dive partner or Kuttner himself would make the sacrifice and go with her.

Maria smiled to herself. It never hurt to have nice legs.

Being the first to arrive at the boat, Maria took one of the flybridge seats near the helm and relaxed. She doffed the shorts and tee-shirt and let the warmth of the early morning sun soak into her skin.

The moment was pleasant.

She noticed peering out from beneath the cushion on the helmsman's seat the dog-eared pages of a paperback book. She pulled it out and leafed through it. It was The Story of O, now ancient '60s pornography. The words flowed with a rhythm that caught her attention and, strangely, aroused her. She had reached page twenty-four when someone in cutoff jeans stepped in front of her and coughed. She looked up into the face of a tall, golden-tanned, blond youth.

"This yours?" she asked.

"Yes."

She tossed him the book, which he stuffed into his back pocket before seating himself at the controls. He turned keys, and Maria watched as the big diesels belched black smoke from the stern. She noticed that while she had read, the boat had filled. At least a dozen people stood on the back deck, and she knew there were probably as many more in the cabin.

The blond helmsman shouted a couple of commands and the docking lines fell away. The boat slipped away from the pier, picking its way among a dozen vessels moored to buoys in the small harbor, and a smaller boat fell in behind. The helmsman brought to boat up to speed, and it slapped across the small seas with scarcely a tremor. Maria tried unsuccessfully to engage him in conversation. He seemed totally involved in driving the vessel, watching his global positioning system display, and checking his watch.

She noticed though that his eyes wandered over her body when he thought her attention was elsewhere.

Still it was a beautiful morning, the water an unbelievable blue in the depths, and crystal green where it washed onto the sandy beaches of the nearby cays. On the western horizon, a few fluffy white clouds marched hazily away, remnants of a tropical system now moving rapidly toward Mexico.

She was half drowsing by the time the young helmsman pulled the throttles back and yelled to another youth on the foredeck. The anchor splashed in, and Maria was fascinated with its descent through the darkening depths.

A long, low sea rolled the boat slowly at anchor, sleepily, encouraging lassitude.

Kuttner meanwhile bustled about, checking assignments that had initially been arranged the evening before. He placed Maria with a group of five New Yorkers, all women, and apologized for not offering more personal attention. She assured him that on such a day, she would enjoy the dive regardless of companions.

She went below and pulled a tank suit on over her bikini, and as she emerged from the cabin, Kuttner stopped her.

"A young lady with a group of four has become ill and cannot make the dive. I think they would appreciate it if you would join them."

"I'd be happy to," she responded. "Are they all women?"

"No. You'll be partnered with the lady's husband. He's a doctor. The other couple is from New Orleans."

"Fine."

"You'll be number two over the side. The first group is about to go over now."

He indicated a group of four struggling into their gear near the stern.

"I'd better hurry, then," she said and ducked back into the cabin. She emerged a moment later belting a flat-black dive knife to her right calf. Glancing up, she watched the first group of divers splash over, and saw the other three moving out onto the platform. She didn't want to hold them up. She stepped over to the racks, grabbed the smallest fins and mask she could find along with a new Mae West and a small weight belt.

She carried the gear to the transom door, where the three other members of her party were busy with their equipment, and returned to the tank rack. She picked out the newest looking tank, checked the fill indicator, and hauled it to the platform

It took her a moment to arrange her equipment, minus the tank. Then, setting the tank upright, she knelt with her back to it and slipped the straps over her shoulder. But when she stood, the straps developed a life of their own, twisting across her back and bulging painfully across her shoulder blade. She tugged at the straps, but the twist wouldn't relinquish its back-numbing bulge. She was about to sit and start the process anew when she felt the weight of the tank lifted.

A masculine voice accompanied the lift.

"Here. Let me help."

In a moment, the strap was straight, and the tank settled comfortably in place. She turned, somewhat clumsily, to her benefactor.

"Thanks," she said, raising her eyes to look up at the lean face. " I was...."

Her voice failed! She stared at a face etched decades before into her memory.

The eyes looking down at her smiled then widened.

Shocked, she involuntarily stepped backward, her thigh coming up short against the combing. She might have circled over the rail into the sea had his hand not grasped her shoulder.

"Maria?" he asked.

"Slats?"

"Yes," he said.

"Oh God! " she said.

Slats looked back over his shoulder. Maria's glance followed his. The other two members of the party were obviously so involved in last minute preparation they had not noticed the exchange.

Maria read his mind.

"We can talk later Slats. For now, thanks for the help. You look good. And the lady, she's with you?"

"Uh, right." Slats continued to stare at her. "And you look good yourself."

He turned, and stepped over to Olivia and Bill, Maria following. Slats introduced her, by the first name only, as though they had just met. The blond helmsman stepped onto the dive platform, did a quick, routine check of their equipment, and motioned them over the side.

Maria went over last and swam up beside Bill as the four made their way to the anchor line and descended along it. Her mind was ablaze with questions. She knew Slats would have many for her. Where had she gone? Why had she never tried to contact him? Most she would counter best with the truth.

But what could she tell him of her purpose on Grand Turk?

And why was he here?

Chapter Twenty Four

Fifteen minutes into the dive, Olivia began to wonder about Slats. He was distracted, paying little attention to the massive coral formations and the myriad fish that darted about them. He had taken no pictures with the Nikonos that he carried. In the past, he had always been an eager, if not particularly skilled, underwater photographer. Olivia snapped picture after picture of ogling grouper and retiring lobster. The colors her strobe sparked in the coral formations fascinated her. But when she attempted to point them out to Slats, he simply shrugged. For Olivia, the dive ended much too quickly.

For Slats, the dive was a reverie, caught in the blue-green twilight world of the reef. What kind of wrinkle in the fabric of fate, he wondered, had reunited him in such circumstances with the woman who had been his fantasy for most of the past twenty years? He still felt the cold spear that had driven through his heart when he recognized her standing there in the glaring tropical sun. Her lithe body in the tank suit filled his mind. And pictures, half fantasy-half memory, from the past, jumbled in to compete with the new image. She was as slim and strong as he remembered. Her face still seemed chiseled from olive marble; skin darkly tanned and flawless. Perhaps a few lines about her eyes now, but a beauty as sharp and clear as it had been when the flaming sun had framed her in the squad room doorway more than two decades past.

Back on the boat, Olivia bubbled with enthusiasm over the dive, and for the hour required to return to Grand Turk, she could talk of little else.

"I can't wait to see my pictures," she said as they stopped at the hotel desk to deposit her spent film. "I wish I could develop them myself."

She paused and looked at Slats.

"Why didn't you take any pictures?" she asked.

He shrugged.

"It all seemed a bit dreary."

"Dreary?" Olivia's gaze searched his face. "Hon, that was some of the most spectacular scenery ever. Are you sure we were looking at the same things?"

He shrugged again.

"You just can't get away from it, can you?"

For a moment, Slats was lost. Get away from what?

Then he understood.

"You're right," he said. "And I apologize. I'll try harder to forget Boulevard and the whole mess, okay?"

"Do try, Babe!" Olivia responded. "I missed you down there."

From her vantage point on the flybridge, Maria had watched Slats and Olivia. She saw them get into the van to her hotel, and she edged into the vehicle behind them. She was even more surprised when she inquired at the desk and found they had the room next to hers.

Wanting to tell Jusquevera about the strange twist, she dialed his hotel.

A female voice responded to her query.

"I'm sorry Miss. Mr. Jusquevera is not here."

"Oh!"

It was still early in the day. He might have gone to the Computer Dynamics hanger.

"We had to take him to the hospital, Miss."

"What?"

"Yes. He was having great pains in his stomach."

Maria hung up abruptly and dialed the airport taxi stand. In five minutes, she was dressed and waiting when the cab pulled up in the street, halting in a cloud of limestone dust. Moments later it ground to a halt in another dust cloud, this time in front of a low, red-brick, dingy looking building with a large black and white sign proclaiming it the GT Hospital.

She pushed her way through double swinging screen doors and almost ran headlong into Raul, who was pacing the short entryway corridor.

"Raul! What is going on?"

He stopped his pacing and turned to face her. He took both her hands and clasped them in front of his chest.

"He will be all right, señorita."

"But what's wrong?"

"The doctor says he has an ulcer of the stomach, and it perforated. He said it happens to businessmen subject to great stress. They are operating now. The doctor says he will recover fully."

Raul crossed himself.

Chapter Twenty Five

Raul predicted well. By that evening, the doctors had completed their work, and the prognosis was good. Jusquevera would spend several days in discomfort, but he would make a complete recovery. With a proper diet and a regimen of reduced stresses, he should have no problems.

Raul chuckled when he heard the attending physician recommend less stress. Maria failed to see the humor. She sat by his bed until he awakened. Then she thought that her tale of meeting Slats, a cop who had befriended her two decades ago, would raise his spirits. But the first time she tried to tell the story, he obviously could not understand. His head lolled, and he kept drifting off to sleep, only to arouse with a moan as he tried to reach his stomach with hands which were strapped to the rails.

Raul went back to the airport to coordinate the transfer of the Harrier, and to make sure the boat that was to provide Charlie and Maria housing for portions of the next three weeks was in route. He returned early the following morning and told Maria to get some sleep.

"We've lost some time already. You have to learn the Harrier soon. So be ready to leave tonight."

Maria still had not been able to communicate with Jusquevera.

"I want to talk to him before I go."

"Perhaps this evening. But if you don't get some sleep, you will not be able to fly tonight."

The burning behind Maria's eyelids told her that Raul was right.

She took a taxi back to the hotel, and as she crossed the courtyard, she heard her name.

She turned to see Slats, sitting alone, the remains of a large breakfast spread across the courtyard table. She walked up to him.

"You're alone?' she said.

"Good Morning!" He smiled at her, then squinted as though he were having trouble seeing her face. "Can I offer you some coffee? You look tired."

"You're alone?"

"Sit down, please."

She pulled out the chair at his right and sat. Slats flipped an inverted cup upright on a saucer and poured coffee from a small vacuum pitcher.

"That does smell good." Marie sighed, stirred a half teaspoonful of sugar into the coffee, and sipped. Then she looked up at Slats.

"I am tired. I sat up most of the night with a sick friend. Where is the lady I saw you with yesterday?"

"My wife, Maria. She and a lady we met on the boat yesterday have gone into town to see if they can find anything to buy. I hope they won't be too successful."

"Your wife?"

"I've been married for years. We have twin boys who are probably driving their grandmother to distraction about now. I'm still a cop, a lieutenant heading a special narcotics unit. And I have a moderately good opportunity for advancement.

"Sounds very domestic."

"And you?"

"There's not a lot to tell Slats."

"Are you kidding? Why did you disappear in the first place?'

"I told you before I left. Staying around would have put both of us in danger."

"I could have handled that."

"No, I don't think so. And even if you could have, there was another reason."

"Oh?"

"I think I was beginning to fall in love with you then. I couldn't let that happen."

"Why not?" Slats leaned against the table, his eyes intense.

"I couldn't have explained it then. I can't now. If you're going to grill me, I'll have to leave."

Slats leaned back in his chair and forced himself to relax.

"Okay, Maria. I'm sorry. I guess I'm still in love with you. I catch myself dreaming about you all the time, or making up things about you."

"Well, in a way, I'm glad. I liked having you in love with me. And I guess I want you always to be in love with me, even if it is only in a dream."

Slats leaned forward and took her hand. It seemed small and very dark in his grip. The white tablecloth accentuated their colors.

"Then you got your wish, Maria. Tell me. Where did you go when you left new Orleans? And what are you doing here?"

The first question was easy. But Maria was uncertain how to answer the second part. Truth for the first. For the second?

Maria described for Slats her life as a civil servant in Pensacola, detailing for him how she had used the money he had provided to live while attending a business school. She poured herself more coffee and leaned sideways in her chair to escape the sun slanting over the bougainvillea. She talked about life working on a naval base, and about the abundance of men, most of whom she avoided. She described her relationship to Tichner and his generosity with gifts.

"Is that how you managed to repay me? I'll never forget how I felt when Boulevard showed up with the last of those envelopes with your notes and the money. I used to wish I had given you a lot more. Then, at least, your notes would have kept coming."

"How I got the money doesn't matter anymore. Strange how things change. Boulevard's dead, you know."

"Yes, I know." Slats hesitated. Should he tell her?

"I killed him."

Maria almost dropped the cup. "You?"

Perhaps he shouldn't have told her.

"It was self-defense. We thought he was involved in a big drug deal. When we went in, he tried to smash my skull. I had to shoot him. Crazy bastard. And as he was dying he ..." Slats paused. He shouldn't be telling Maria all this.

"Look, Maria. I'm sorry I killed him. But...it was necessary."

Someone else had said something recently about killing as a necessity.

"Maria?"

She was just sitting there, her mouth slightly agape, staring at Slats, her arms half folded over her chest, her right hand holding the coffee cup, its contents momentarily forgotten.

"So that's where you have been all these years. Well, what are you doing on Grand Turk? You and your boyfriend, what's his name, Tichner? Here to dive?"

Slats hoped his question would bring Maria back to reality. She seemed poised to bolt and run. He shouldn't have told her about Boulevard. Although she already knew he was dead. Strange that she should keep such close track after so many years. But why should it affect her so much now? He remembered her once saying that she didn't care about Boulevard, except on a "professional," as she called it, basis. Or was that just part of one of his fantasies?

"Oh," she mumbled, visibly gathering her emotions. "Oh, yes. The diving is great, isn't it?"

"Maria, I'm sorry."

"Oh, it'll be all right. I just, somehow, never pictured you killing anyone."

"I'm a cop, Maria. Sometimes it can't be helped."

"I suppose that's true."

"You say you're here to dive?"

"Yes, but not with Bulgy."

"Bulgy?"

"Colonel Tichner. That's his nickname. No, he... he couldn't come. I came by myself though I've met some friends here."

"They weren't with you yesterday?"

"No. One of them got sick. He wanted me to go anyway. And when I got back, they had taken him to the hospital. That's why I look this way. I sat with him all night."

"That's too bad. I am sorry, Maria."

"He'll be all right. It was an ulcer. He didn't even know he had it or if he did, he didn't let anyone else know. It perforated, but they repaired it and said he'll be all right. I want to go back to see him later."

She got up.

"Thanks for the coffee, Slats. I'm exhausted. I'd like to talk later."

"Sure. I guess our time is about up. Olivia will probably be back pretty quick."

"Olivia's your wife?"

"Yes, I introduced you yesterday, remember?"

"Thinks were a bit blurry yesterday. I was so startled at seeing you"

"Believe me, I understand. Well, 'bye."

"Bye, Slats." She bent quickly and pecked him on the cheek.

Then she was gone up the stairs and around the corner. Slats signed his check, then went to the telephone on the table half hidden among the bougainvillea. When he picked up the receiver the hotel operator answered.

"Will you connect me with the Computer Dynamics offices, please."

"Let's see, Computer Dynamics," the British-accented reply came. "Just a moment please." There was a pause, and Slats heard the distinct shuffling of pages.

"I'm sorry, sir, but I seem to have no listing."

"It'll be new. I understand they've been on the island only a few months."

"Oh, yes. That's the new concern at the airport, I believe. Hold a moment."

There was the sound of connections and reconnections, then a female voice asked, "May I help you?"

The hotel operator asked for the Computer Dynamics number and as soon as he had acquired it he dialed.

"This is Liechester Jones. I would like to speak with Mr. de Arrellano, please."

"I'm sorry sir, but Mr. de Arrellano is indisposed today. We do not, in fact, expect him for several days."

"Oh? We met on the flight down from Miami. He offered to show me around the operations."

"I see."

"When did you say you expect him?"

"It is difficult to say. He is in the hospital."

In the hospital? What a strange coincidence. Or was it possible Maria's friend was de Arrellano. Somehow it didn't seem likely.

"Well, would it be possible for me to come out in Mr. De Arrellano's absence? I'm sure from the tone of his invitation that he wouldn't mind."

"No, I'm sorry sir. Besides, there are only a few technicians about now and I don't think any of us are capable of explaining this operation. If señor de Arrellano invited you I suggest you wait for him. Good day, sir."

The connection died before Slats could reply. Now his curiosity was piqued. He would visit the Computer Dynamics operation soon and perhaps pay de Arrellano a visit at the hospital.

Olivia's voice broke his train of thought.

"Hi, hon. I hope you weren't too lonely while I was gone."

He looked up into his wife's smiling face. His tongue felt thick and slow.

"Oh, no. I...I ran into that girl who dove with us yesterday, remember? She's here at the hotel also. We had a conversation."

"All clean, I hope."

"Just over coffee, that's all. How was shopping?"

"Disastrous. Even those people who have money to spend wouldn't be able to spend much here. There's nothing to buy, nothing to see, nothing to do.

"Except dive and be lazy."

"Is that all you can think of?"

"This is a polite conversation."

"Oh, speaking of the diving, are we going tonight?"

"No. I think I'd like to do a little exploring of my own."

"What kind of exploring?"

"I think I'll go visit the company that our friend on the plane told us about."

Slats led the way up the stairs toward the room.

"But why tonight, Hon? Surely he could show you around better during the day."

"Ah, but he won't be there. As a matter of fact, he's in the hospital."

As he climbed the stairs following Olivia, Slats couldn't help but appreciate his wife's softly curvaceous body. But he couldn't totally rid himself of Maria's presence.

She had left in her wake an aura, and Slats found it odd that Olivia did not sense her recent presence. He shook his head as if the motion would clear his mind. Maria was his private fantasy. He owned the rights and no one, perhaps not even the flesh and blood Maria, could control his relationship to her. She would come and go from his mind as she pleased and no one would be wiser. But now his task had become complex. He now must separate the real Maria from the one in his libido.

Chapter Twenty Six

When he and Olivia arrived in their room they made love; a little too quickly and harshly for Olivia's liking. She preferred gentleness and caring to the strange lust Slats sometimes exhibited. Still she found herself feeling warm and, if not fulfilled, pleasant in the afterglow.

"That was nice, stud," she said. "But were you racing for the finish line?"

"What?" Slats whispered, his eyes closed. He lay on his back next to Olivia.

"You seemed to be in an awful hurry."

"Sorry, babe. Guess I'm just hornier than usual. Being on vacation's a bit like when I was in the army reserves. Every time I put on that green uniform I had an erection."

"I don't underhand."

Slats rolled up on his elbow and kissed her lightly on the lips. "It's nothing to worry about. I'll make it up to you next time."

She sat up, grasping her knees, and studied him. Then reached out with her left hand to pull his head toward her.

Momentarily he wondered if she could feel another presence.

"That's a deal. And I'll hold you to it," she said.

"I hope so."

They napped briefly then donned swimsuits and headed for the beach.

Slats spent much of the afternoon mapping an approach to Computer Dynamics. He had no idea what, if anything, he would find in the warehouse set by itself in the airport field. But it, and de Arrellano were certainly more than they appeared.

Half dozing in the beach chair he watched his wife walk the beach where small wavelets bubbled sand about her feet. Occasionally she bent and picked up a shell, which she would hold up to examine, glancing at Slats now and then, noticing that he was deep in thought..

Certainly, walking up to the door at Computer Dynamics and saying, "Hi, de Arrellano sent me," would accomplish no more than had his earlier telephone conversation.

So.

He could sneak in after dark.

He felt an odd thrill in his gut, a feeling very unlike the tension that shadowed everyday police work. It was something he had felt first as a teen reading Ian Fleming's Dr. No. The mystique of Fleming's hero, one of Slats' teenage idols, still fascinated him. He had always liked the tongue-in-cheek way the undercover work turned out whenever Bond packed up his Walther PPK, or his little skeleton grip .25, and set out into the darkness.

Slats assumed there would be a night watchman of some sort. And the technicians mentioned in the brief telephone conversation might be on duty. But, while he was not Bond, Slats was certain he could gain entrance to the building and get a look around. He didn't know what he expected to find, but if de Arrellano was who he suspected, then the Computer Dynamics building must be a front, a front elaborate enough to warrant detailed study.

It would be a simple matter to sneak onto the airport property. He could follow the beach until he reached a point that lined up with the runway marker lights, then track the taxiway to the Computer Dynamic's building. He would handle the watchman situation if it became necessary. With any luck, he would be in and out before anyone could detect him.

Olivia plopped down in the beach chair next to him.

"You seem to be somewhere else," she said.

Slats thought a minute, then told her of his plans.

"For God's sake why?" she asked.

"Call it cop's intuition. De Arrellano is more than he appears, I'm sure of it. And it might tie in with..." he couldn't finish his thought.

She stared hard, wondering who is this man sitting next to me? Where did I leave my husband? What happened to our holiday?

He couldn't tell her about Maria. But didn't he feel a growing need to free the long-imprisoned secret?

"Well if you're going, then I'm going too," she said.

Slats wouldn't allow it.

She had proven herself physically capable of keeping up with him except in hand-to-hand combat. But she didn't share the special sense that cops develop for finding the missing part of the puzzle, or for seeing the wrong lines in the picture. Her presence would distract him.

"No. You'll have to back me up at the hotel. If I'm not back by eleven, you call in the local gendarmes."

Maria awoke slowly, watching without moving as her sight returned hazily in the evening light trickling through the balcony doors. For the first few seconds, she didn't know even her own name. She ached, but the sensation seemed to emanate from deep within. Reaching out mentally she felt the various parts of her body and pronounced herself whole at about the same time that she remembered that she was Maria. And that there was a man in the hospital she needed to see, and that she wanted to talk to a cop she hadn't seen in twenty years, until two days ago. The confusion ebbed and with it went the pain.

She was to fly out tonight with Charlie and spend the next several days learning to fly a military airplane. First, however, she had to talk to de Arrellano. And she wanted also to see Slats, but for reasons less definable. She had been surprised earlier in the day that the link with Slats seemed far stronger than should have existed. She had thought of him often in the past years and her memories had been more than gratuitous images. She often recalled their physical relationship and had been surprised that he had been able to draw from her pleasures she had assumed were lost.

After her first year spent earning a living sexually, surviving by virtue of youth and beauty, she had assumed that the act could never again thrill her. But when Slats had touched her she had enjoyed it immensely. She didn't know from whence came the water of ecstasy that flowed under his touch, but she blessed the well from which it sprang. That knowledge, taken with her when she had run from the city, had helped her as much in the ensuing years as had Slats' money. It had been the basis for new relationships, although no touch had inspired her quite as Slat's had.

Maybe that is what she wanted to tell him. Maybe she just wanted to say thanks for giving her back part of herself she had thought she had lost.

And if she could find him again away from his wife she wouldn't mind expressing herself with more than words.

But that would prove difficult. Even if she found them together she could still say a few things that only Slats would understand.

So first she would try to see Slats. Then she would return to the hospital and de Arrellano.

She dressed carefully, and after examining her image in the mirror, white cotton t-shirt dress over her dark skin, she pronounced herself fit for a rendezvous. Then she hurried downstairs fully expecting to find Slats and Olivia in the courtyard or the dining room. As she walked she tried to come up with an excuse that would appropriately separate a man from his wife for the several crucial minutes.

But they were in neither location.

On an impulse, Maria went to Slats' room. Olivia answered the door and recognizing they young woman with whom they had dived the previous day, invited her in.

"And your husband?"

"He had to go out."

"Oh? But I thought you were here on vacation."

"We are."

"I see." Maria felt uncomfortable in the larger woman's presence. She felt no intimidation, but she wanted a plausible excuse for approaching her.

"I wanted to check and see if you were going to dive again soon. I should like to accompany you."

"Oh, I'm surc wc shall be diving again. But I don't know just when. We expect to be here several more days, you see." Olivia had emphasized the several, but Maria failed to understand the implications.

While Maria didn't understand whatever it was that Olivia was trying to get across, it was obvious that Olivia wasn't expecting Slats soon. She said she would talk with them about diving again shortly and excused herself.

She ate a quick sandwich in the dining room. Darkness hardened the soft tropical twilight as she reached the hospital. She found Raul already there and de Arrellano awake and in reasonably good spirits.

Raul confirmed what she already knew. Charlie was anxious to leave. The plane was ready and the boat that was to be her home for several weeks was en route. She said she was ready, but she knew that she would be leaving something incomplete.

She told de Arrellano her story about diving and Slats and, without details, about her past relationship with Slats. De Arrellano gave her some odd glances as she related her tale of a poor cop's generosity.

"You like this man?" he questioned.

"Yes," she admitted, "he was a great help to me."

"I met him on the plane coming down from Miami. I think he suspects who I am."

"How can that be?"

"He spent much of the flight studying me. He had seen the newspaper photo. It was that damned newsman at the embassy. I had not expected any press and I thought the pictures had all been destroyed. It was a lousy photograph, but your 'Slats' seems to have a keen eye."

"But even if he does suspect, so what. He and his wife are here on vacation. They are diving. What would, what could they do?"

De Arrellano shook his head and winced as the movement reached his belly.

"I do not know. But it seems almost too coincidental that the New Orleans cop who killed your Boulevard is here on a diving vacation. I believe he bears watching." de Arrellano looked at Raul who nodded.

"Now, they will chase you away from here in a moment. Please try to keep things on schedule. Maria, you must learn the plane quickly. I should be out of here in a week, and I should like a report on your progress in person at that time. Raul, tell Captain Adkins that I will want to see all of you in a week, and then I will outline for you the final days of the mission.

"Now I must sleep."

Maria kissed him lightly on the cheek, and she and Raul left the room. Looking at him as she pulled the door closed behind her, she thought how frail he looked; totally unlike the commanding being she had met when first she had stepped from the plane onto Grand Turk. Strange the power of physical misery.

Chapter Twenty Seven

Maria still found her thoughts drawn unwillingly to Slats, but she could think of no way to delay the night's inevitable flight. She knew de Arrellano was right. Although she was not privy to the plan she knew instinctively that the schedule was suffering.

So on the drive to the airport she forced her mind into the necessary bent. She would accept not seeing Slats and prepare for a hard week's work. Such decisions might not be easy, but Maria's mind carried within it a penchant for self-discipline characteristic of particular aristocracies. It had served her well.

Charlie was anxious to get away.

The hanger was too small. The plane looked ridiculous with its recently grown protuberances and off-white paint job.

The constant babble of Spanish while the technicians worked. The enforced inactivity, sitting around for two days while everyone else either worked or played. He felt like a pawn in some kind of a South American chess game and he hadn't signed on to be used. So to work off the frustrations that inactivity built up within him, he puttered about the plane, getting in the way of the technicians putting the finishing touches on their alterations.

They had finally given up, a bit peeved at his unending interruptions of their tasks and headed for town and whatever amusement they could find. They didn't invite Charlie.

The light falling through the overhead had dimmed considerably making it difficult for Charlie to see the instruments as he sat in the cockpit of the plane meticulously cleaning each bit of metal and plastic. When he had difficulty seeing the level indicators on the artificial horizon he gave up, pulled himself out of the cockpit and headed for the kitchen. In the refrigerator, he found sufficient bread, cheese and ham to build a satiating if not satisfying sandwich which he washed down with a totally unsatisfying Red Label beer.

By the time he had finished his makeshift supper and leafed through a well-creased copy of Penthouse he found on the lounge floor, darkness was intruding through the undraped windows. He glanced at his watch and muttered to himself. Why the hell did de Arrellano have to get sick now? He hoped the man would not let his illness set their timetable back too far.

Charlie was anxious. He was skeptical about teaching Maria to fly the Harrier. But the more time he could spend with her the more likely she would be to learn successfully.

Charlie was anxious also about Maria's feelings toward him. She had seemed cool, somehow, in the motel. The fire that he had felt that night aboard Dawn Trader, now a thousand miles and weeks away, had flickered. It smoldered now, still warm, but no longer bright.

Could it be that Maria was having second thoughts about their relationship? Charlie wondered if he would have agreed to the scheme in which he was now involved, even with a promise of a position in the rebel government, had Maria not thrown herself in as well.

The office telephone rang.

Charlie left the kitchen/lounge and stumbled against a tool rack in the dim hangar on his way to the office. He clicked on the office light and saw it throw a bright pattern on the dark hangar floor.

On the telephone was Raul, telling him that he and Maria would arrive soon. Maria had to stop at the hotel and pick up some clothes.

Good, Charlie thought. Now we can really get this show on the road.

He hung up the phone and pulled out a chart from a group of charts in the pigeonhole arrangement against the office wall. He spread it on the desk and began memorizing various headings and land masses to use as references. Teaching a woman to fly the Harrier would be difficult enough under ordinary circumstances. Doing so here, in the middle of an ocean, flying mostly at night seemed impossible. Charlie wanted to be sure he knew their location every moment. If he was going to wind up in the water he would be able to tell potential rescuers where he was.

Something moved in the hangar.

So absorbed was Charlie in his task that although he noticed the movement it was several seconds before he realized he had seen anything. He looked up from the charts and stared through the office window into the dark hangar. The plane took up most of the space and the shadows where the office light passed the plane etched its silhouette against the far wall.

But except for the light from the office window the hangar was dark and no amount of staring through the window would improve his vision.

What he had seen, and he was certain he had seen something, could not have been the technicians. They would have turned on the lights.

The lights!

The hangar was lighted by three rows of florescent lamps, but the switches were on the end wall near the doors. Charlie left the window and opened the door into the hangar. It was a good sixty feet from where he stood to the light switches. He wanted to call out, to warn off any intruder, to tell him to get the hell away or else, but he could think of no viable "or else."

Charlie stepped into the hangar and pulled the door shut behind him. He studied the pattern of light from the office window where it threw a paneled glare on the floor, and left the plane silhouetted against the far wall. He held his breath and listened but heard nothing. He hated shadows and dark, hidden corners. Charlie would sooner have faced the open barrels of a Mig's cannons at fifty thousand feet than walk across the sixty feet of dark floor between himself and the light panel.

There was someone else in the hangar! He sensed it. He knew it!

He ducked beneath the office window to avoid backlighting. Waiting for his eyes to adjust to the darkness, he tried to tune his ears to people sounds and headed for the light switches. He bumped the same tool rack he had hit a few minutes earlier but caught it before it tumbled to the floor, cursing under his breath and rubbing his shin where he knew a large purple bruise would soon blossom.

At one point he thought he heard footsteps, but he could see nothing but the outline of the plane. Then he was at the wall, and his groping hand found the hangar door. As he reached to his right for the row of switches he knew were but inches away, something thumped against the wall to his left. Charlie swept his hand upward across the switches and turned to face the noise.

The fluorescent clicked and flashed and in staccato lightning, Charlie saw a tall, muscular man in a dark swimsuit and sneakers hurtling at him. He threw up an arm to protect his face and took a sharp blow to the stomach. It doubled him over. He grabbed his knees in pain and rolled backward to avoid another blow. His assailant rushed past him. Charlie saw his hard, chiseled features clearly as the man grabbed at the door handle and wrestled with it, finally wrenching free the lock bar. He slid open the heavy door just enough to slip through, exclaiming loudly, almost screaming, as he stumbled.

By the time Charlie had regained use of his feet the man was gone. Charlie walked carefully around the plane but could find no signs of damage. As he completed his inspection, Raul and Maria arrived, Maria carrying a small duffle.

Charlie told them about the intruder, embellishing only slightly his struggle. Maria was disturbed at his description of the assailant. Raul immediately went out and returned ten minutes later with the crew of technicians who in short order pronounced the Harrier untouched. Raul pointed out a patch of blood on the cement where the roller guide for the hanger door was bolted to the floor.

Raul had noticed Maria's confused expression when Charlie described his assailant. He asked her about it directly.

"You think, señorita, it was your policeman friend?"

"No," she replied. "I mean, why would he break in here? It was probably just some islander trying to heist a few pennies. Charlie's description could fit lots of men."

"Very few of the islanders are white," Raul said.

"But... I mean, why would Slats come here? And even if he did, so what?"

"If he did, señorita, he saw the plane."

Thirty minutes later she and Charlie departed in the Harrier apparently arousing no suspicion as it rolled to the end of the runway and disappeared into the night sky.

As the Harrier roared away into the darkness, Raul sat down at the desk and reconstructed Charlie's tale on paper. Raul wanted to neither embellish nor denigrate the flyer's story.

He would repeat it to de Arrellano as accurately as possible. He would let de Arrellano weigh the probabilities. His job was to carry out orders, not make decisions.

Then he shoved the paper aside, dug a cigarette from his shirt pocket, lit it and leaned back in the desk chair. It was too large, and Raul felt as though he were about to be swallowed by a wooden whale. He got up, wandered down to the lounge where he engaged one of the technicians in a game of chess.

He won in short order.

Chapter Twenty Eight

Sixteen hundred miles to the north, light glowed behind several windows in the best-known house in the world. Seated behind a glaring desk lamp in his White House cubbyhole, Jim Cavanaugh, the President's Chief of Staff, was halfway through a ream-thick stack of paper.

Cavanaugh was a detail man, planning the President's upcoming trip to Miami, where he was scheduled to address delegates to the American Federation of Labor convention.

Everything was there. Counted, stacked, and re-stacked. The pages of the itinerary contained every possible stop, every speech, every pause for water, name and address of each member of the traveling party, the rank and serial number of each serviceman in the entourage, as well as particulars on the pilots and crew of the chartered jet that would carry them.

The President had insisted on chartering instead of using Air Force One.

Cavanaugh was the President's most trusted political advisor. They had known each other forever. Cavanaugh had grown up in a middle-class family and as a child lived not far from the family of the man who was to become President of The United States. Jim Cavanaugh and Robert "Bob" Carnahan were boyhood chums, grade school buddies, and high school athletes together.

After high school they had gone separate ways; one into a family business that was to serve as a political springboard; first a Missouri state senate's seat, then the Governor's mansion, before seeking the highest post in the land. The other had gone into the military, then to college and into a journalistic career, a career which soon disappointed him with its mendacity and self-servitude.

It had taken Jim only a few years to discover that journalism, in all of its increasingly technologically diverse media, suffered from the same compromises as business, industry, and government. Everything was suborned to "making it." Whatever "it" was.

Not that Jim hadn't been "making it." Jim's syndicated column "Cavanaugh's Corner" appeared daily in more than one-hundred-fifty newspapers nationwide. He had moved from a small, conservative daily in a Missouri backwater to an editor's desk in Washington DC.

He was "making it" better than most of his contemporaries. It was his vantage point from atop an important endeavor that a dozen years after entering the field made him quit.

Making it, he found, had held little real reward, either financial or psychological. He had become middle-aged, bald, and slightly chubby, and had neither accumulated his fortune nor rendered America socially perfect.

That was when his boyhood chum looked him up, saying he wanted to become President of The United States.

Jim thought about it for a moment.

"Now, dammit, there's a challenge," Jim thought.

That was six years ago.

Jim had labored tirelessly. But he had been more surprised that anyone when the election went just as he expected. He had single-handedly manipulated the American voting public with the power of his words, his unsophisticated "Superman" logic, his perception of human nature; it had all worked together to shape an electorate first to nominate and then elect a President.

Now that was satisfaction.

And now he had to do it again.

The nomination, this time, had been simple. Even a severe moral failing wouldn't keep a modern President from the nomination. But the election would not be as simple. Jim's boyhood chum had made some stupid mistakes in the last few years; political errors and moral misjudgments. It was one thing to run a campaign for "Mr. Smith" but another to plan for the elevation of would-be "Mr. Casanova-Smith."

So a man who should have been a shoe-in for another term now had problems, particularly among the blue-collar, majority interests of the party.

When the opportunity to speak to the American Federation of Labor convention had presented itself, Jim had jumped. It was to be in Miami, in the summer, a time of hot nights and ethnic unrest. But also, a time when the right words to the right people could hit with the force of a hurricane.

Staring at the words as Jim flipped through them for the third time this night, his eyes red, his stomach sour, Jim wished for something more than words.

An event.

He needed an event. He needed something to focus the eyes of the entire nation on the President, to make everyone hear, really hear, the words. Oh, the words were good, but how many would be listening?

Issues were of little real importance, except in retrospect. Promises were meaningless unless they were broken. What was called for was rhetoric that aroused, that made men feel something deep down inside; words that flowed from the soul, not from the brain.

And he had those.

But.

Public Apathy.

Audiences are like the proverbial mule. The speaker needs a two-by-four to hit them with. Especially a political speaker. A big two-by-four.

Everything was in order for the Miami speech. The President and his wife, five members of their staffs, undersecretaries of defense and the interior, secretaries' secretaries, a security contingent, and Jim, would breakfast together aboard the chartered jet at seven a.m. en route to Miami International. There they would be met by Florida's Governor and members of the Florida Democratic Party. They would spend the afternoon in three suites on the top floor of the Miami Hilton, and would host that evening, Thursday, a reception for the union hierarchy.

On Friday, the President would tour the city, from the neighborhoods, often lit by the passions of expatriate Cubans, to the posh South Beach. Then an evening of rest, in preparation for the Saturday morning convention speech.

Jim pinched the bridge of his nose and rubbed softly at sore eyes, then flicked out the desk lamp. The years of desk jockeying had left Jim slightly bulky, and he felt blob-ish as he leaned the chair back and sighed. He glanced at his watch. Five a.m. Little rest for the weary.

There was a knock at the door, sharp and distinct.

Jim ignored it, hoping whoever was outside his office would simply vanish.

But they didn't.

When the knock sounded again, he pushed himself from the chair. As he opened the door, he tried halfheartedly to adjust his tie.

What am I doing? It's five a.m.

A White House security agent and a marine corps captain stood across the threshold. The guard, although neat and unrumpled, seemed slouchy next to the ramrod straight marine.

"I'm sorry sir," the guard said, "but I thought the President was with you."

"He went to bed several hours ago," Jim replied. "Something I can do for you?"

"He has a message for the President," the guard said, gesturing off-handedly toward the marine.

"I'll take it, Captain," Jim said.

"Sorry sir," the Marine replied, only his jaw moving. "I'm directed to hand it to the President."

"I have presidential clearance, Captain," Jim said, reaching toward his jacket pocket for the green tag that he was entitled to wear, one of the privileged few.

It wasn't there.

He turned impatiently and walked back to the desk. There it was atop the cluttered stack of papers he had just put aside. He walked back to the doorway and shoved it under the nose of the marine, who was forced to break his stance to scrutinize the badge.

"All right sir. Please sign to indicate acceptance," he said, holding out a small, hardback notepad with several notations across the surface and space for a signature. Jim signed and took the proffered yellow envelope.

"Thank you. Now excuse me, gentlemen."

Jim turned, pushing the door so that it clicked shut as he reached the chair. He sat, clicked on and adjusted the desk lamp, scowled tiredly at the envelope, and at the receipt.

The notations indicated that the message had been received less that half an hour ago at the State Department's Foreign Service Office message center via telex from Bogota, Colombia.

Bogota?

Jim stared at the envelope a moment more, then picked up an ornate letter opener from the corner of the desk, slit the envelope and withdrew the contents. He began to read.

"Well I'll be damned!" he whispered.

Chapter Twenty Nine

Jim Cavanaugh couldn't believe his eyes. It was too good to be true. You work your ass off planning, detailing, writing, and never know if it'll be good enough. Then suddenly fate drops it in the bag!

I couldn't have planned anything this good!

The words on the yellow paper fuzzed a bit before Jim's bloodshot eyes. He had already read them three times. Now he had committed them to memory. Had he music he would have sung them.

"The Colombian Government has proven it cannot be trusted. We will negotiate the release of our hostages only with the President of The United States.

"Jusquevera de Arrellano, for the Council of El Carib."

The situation was perfect.

The President could delay his tour, fly to Colombia, negotiate the release of the hostages (let's see... happened last week. Several international bigwigs among the hostages.) and return to Miami in time to make his speech before the convention.

If the negotiations were successful, the whole world would thank him. And if the negotiations aren't successful, the world will know the President tried. Either outcome will enhance the President's image. Either will be just what the spin doctor ordered.

The speech will need a few revisions, but nothing drastic.

Yep, this is it. From here on out, it's downhill to the White House, all the way.

Unless Erik snuffs it.

Erik Grosvenor, director of the Central Intelligence Agency, was, like Jim, a long-time confidante of the President. His viewpoints were often counterpoint to Jim's, and he would object to the President flying off to Bogota. The decision would be the President's, and Jim would have his ear first, and have it exclusively until the plane lands in Miami.

Jim assembled his papers, straightened his tie, and hurried from the office. Already there were the early morning sounds of staff readying the traditional home of American presidents for the hundreds of trespassing feet that would tramp the marble floors through the day.

Jim had barely made it through his shower, shave, and shine before the limo appeared outside his Georgetown apartment. The drive out to John Foster Dulles was tedious, although they were a good hour ahead of the morning drive-time. The chartered 777 stood alone on the tarmac. The President was already aboard and greeted Jim with his usual hearty tone.

"Good morning, ole buddy. Glad you could make it. Thought I might have to send security to find you. Did you get lost?"

Jim waved off the comment, glancing at his vintage Mariner. The time was 7:05. He wasn't late. He was never late.

Jim followed the President to the first class section. Already the plane's engines were whining their way up through the power bands. With a slight shudder, the plane rolled away from the mini-terminal and, with priority clearance, was airborne moments later. The "Fasten Seatbelts" lamps winked out as Virginia's green hillsides vanished into the morning haze.

As soon as the plane's climb had stabilized, Jim heaved himself from his seat, stepped across the aisle, and perched on the arm of the seat across from the President. He pulled the yellow envelope from the pinstripe suit coat's lapel pocket and held it out toward the President.

"This came a couple of hours ago, Bill. I think it might be crucial."

The President looked from the envelope to Jim, studying his face. Even Jim found the level gaze of the hazel eyes disconcerting. They seemed to be plumbing depths hidden to most. Jim knew the President's gaze was one of his more marketable characteristics. Jim had seen that ice-pick gaze pin an adversary's attack in his throat on several occasions. When a cabinet meeting drifted toward chaos, the power of the President's eye contact often restored order.

"Well, Jim, ole chum. Been opening my mail again, I see."

The eyes sparkled. Pity there isn't more real understanding behind them, Jim thought. Familiarity breeds...

"I felt it might require an immediate response, but after reading it decided it would wait for a moment more propitious than five a.m."

"Right, right," the President said, pulling the message from the envelope.

It took but a moment for him to read it, and a frown creased his brow. His eyes scanned the page a second time as he read the message aloud, then met Jim's gaze.

"Jim, ole buddy, are you thinking what I think you're thinking?"

No one in the cabin spoke. The only sound was the muted whine of the engines and the whoosh of pressurized air. The President's eyes were steely under the shock of silver hair that slipped down his forehead.

"Well, Jim, what do you think?" he asked.

"I think you should go."

"It would help, wouldn't it?"

Jim crossed his arms over his chest, stood up in the aisle, and turned to face the silver haired man and the woman seated beside him squarely.

He hesitated for a moment, unable to launch the speech he thought he should make, and said instead, "You've seen the polls. What do you think

"Remember who you're going to be talking to in Miami. A lot of the blue collar types still think of you as the man behind one of the biggest tax increases in history. Are they going to listen to you, even if you promise tax cuts and cheap gasoline? They won't hear a word you're saying."

"I hear you, Jim. You think if I do what these bastards in the embassy demand, I can get them to listen to me in Miami?"

"Yes! Yes, I do. And when you talk to them, you're not going to talk about foreign policy or economics. You're going to talk down-home, good-old-boy, mom and apple pie. I know it's trite. You've got something to tell them...but first you've got to get their attention."

The President waved the sheet of paper.

"And this will get their attention."

"Yes!"

Chapter Thirty

Olivia tempered her relief at Slats' return with concern for his injured foot. As he limped through the door, she jumped from the bed and hurried to his side, slipping herself beneath his right arm, to take part of his weight as he made his way to the bed.

"What happened, hon?"

She picked up his foot, hesitant about removing the wad of material he had jammed into the sandal, wrapped about his toes.

"Kicked the edge of a door. It's not cut badly but it does hurt," Slats said, grimacing.

Olivia pulled away the bloodstained handkerchief, slipped the sandal strap down his heel and removed the open-toed thong. She examined the ball of his foot where the sharp metal had torn an inch-long gash.

"Got to clean it, hon. There's some peroxide in the bath."

While she was searching for the medication Slats examined the cut. It didn't look serious, but any pressure brought the intense pain. He told himself he didn't care. The pain was a small price to pay.

He had seen the plane! An odd sense of elation masked his pain.

They had tried to disguise the Harrier but even in the almost lightness hangar, he'd recognized the warbird.

And there was no doubt that the broad-shouldered, blond man he'd body-blocked to make good his escape was Lt. Col. Charles Adkins. The U.S. Navy and the Coast Guard had written him off as dead; his plane destroyed. Yet here they were, plane and pilot, thousands of miles from New Orleans and both in excellent shape!

Except for Adkins's solar plexus, which would undoubtedly be sore for a few days.

Olivia returned, spread a towel on her knee as she knelt before Slats and lifted his foot onto the towel. She had difficulty opening the peroxide and handed the bottle to Slats.

He flicked the cap off with a twist, then steeled himself. He felt little-boyish looking at his wounded foot. He couldn't believe the tension that welled in his chest as he watched Olivia tilt the peroxide bottle over his toes. The liquid splashed across the cut and began to bubble furiously. A tingle spread through his foot, changing to fire as it reached his ankle, then searing back to the wound. Slats hissed through clenched teeth.

"You find anything, hon.?"

Her question was meant to take his mind from his injury.

It worked.

Slats told her how he had worked his way up the beach to the end of the runway and from there to the hangar.

He had set out just before sunset, clambering up and down the peculiar limestone breakwaters (every few hundred yards great quantities of the native limestone had been packed into wire mesh cubes and the cubes stacked six feet high from the high water mark well out into the surf). The short dusk of the islands engulfed him as he neared the airport property and he could see the runway marker lights stretching to intersect the beach several yards ahead.

He glanced toward the terminal. If he were going to be seen, this was the moment. The sea and the sky reflected just enough light to outline him against the sea. Slats stood still, minimizing the likelihood that a human eye would pick him out from the surrounding shadows. He watched the light fading, first from the water's surface, then from the sky, the darkness marching seaward at the setting sun's invitation.

When he barely could see the terrain near the runway's end and the marker lights glowed brightly, Slats set out toward the terminal. Floodlights marked the eaves on one side of the Computer Dynamics building. He stumbled twice before reaching the side of the runway, and he swore at himself for not changing from the open toe sandals to sneakers.

He remembered a trip into the desert near Las Vegas where his parent's had taken him on vacation. It had been twenty-five years ago, but he would never forget the snakebite. It had been a pencil-length, dun-colored creature and it had bitten him on the toe. His father had acted quickly, and the knife blade had hurt more than the snake as he opened the tiny wound and sucked out the poison. Slats had watched fascinated, alert and not truly frightened. But then the poison that had made its way into his system began its work. The world went fuzzy, and the pain became sharp and omnipresent. His stomach writhed. His father had assured him he would recover, and he did, but he carried with him now a dread of terrain such as that he now had to traverse.

By the time he reached the end of the runway, Slats felt clammy. Perspiration trickled down his face. Stepping onto the tarmac brought a flood of relief. Slats thought he remembered reading, probably in a Caribbean vacation brochure, that there were no snakes on the island. But that did little to quash his intense dread of the low-lying brush and limestone. He would walk the hard surface and hope that in the few minutes it would require reaching his destination no plane would have a need for the runway.

He was still a hundred yards from the Computer Dynamics building when he saw the main door slide open a couple of feet and four men exit. They were conversing, but Slats was too far away to hear their words. They were halfway to the terminal moving rapidly away from Slats when a car screeched to a halt on the apron near them. All four piled into the vehicle which made a squealing circle and headed back toward the terminal.

Would they leave the place empty?

Slats walked up to the building avoiding the wing lit by the flood lamps. On the dark side of the building ran the massive sliding door that the four men had just closed behind them. Under the flood lamp at the far corner of the building were a man-sized door and several multi-paned windows. Although new, brightly-painted metal, the building reminded Slats of a World War II Quonset. He wouldn't have been surprised to see the hangar slide open to reveal a cavalcade of P-41's, props spinning before painted shark jaws, ready to leap into the night sky.

Slats walked the perimeter of the dark side of the building, listening intently. He wondered how much noise the big door would make if he pulled it open. If, that is, the men who had exited had not locked it behind them. Examining the door, Slats could find no handle nor any indication of a lock. He pushed tentatively at the door in the direction he had seen it move, but it refused to budge.

He stepped back to evaluate. The window that was lighted fronted several small rooms. The other windows were dark, including the window alongside the small door.

Feeling exposed, Slats looked up at the terminal. It was several hundred yards distant. And what if someone there did see him try the door? Who was to know that the figure wasn't the watchman or a GD technician.? Slats walked slowly around the building and slipped beneath the lit window. It was cracked open at the sill and Slats could hear someone inside. The sounds resolved themselves. Someone was eating and shuffling papers. Careful not to let his sandals slap the pavement Slats crept back to the door and tried it.

Locked!

He slipped a penknife from the chain around his neck and slid its flexible blade into the crack between the door and the jamb. A deft movement, a faint scraping sound, and the door pulled silently open.

Slats stepped into the room, closed the door behind him and listened.

He heard the sound of someone whistling under his breath very faintly. He recognized the tune. It was the Marine Corps Hymn.

A bright patch of light fell into the room through the exterior window. He was obviously in an office. On one wall was a large map on which he could make out the southern tip of Florida, the Caribbean and much of South America. The wall opposite the door held another door and a window that looked out onto the hangar floor. From his vantage point near the exterior door, Slats couldn't see through the interior window.

He stood perfectly still for another sixty seconds, but nothing changed. The whistling came and went, and the only other sounds were creaks and groans of metal cooling unevenly.

Slats walked around the desk and looked through the interior window. He saw, dim in the light entering the hangar from another window and door fifty feet away, the plane. It ain't no Gulfstream, he thought. It looked like no commercial aircraft he'd ever seen.

Its nose was too long and sharp, its body to bulbous and it carried wing-tip tanks.

The "brinnnn" of the telephone struck Slats like an electric shock. He leaped toward the desk, thinking to silence the instrument. But the single ring might still bring the lone occupant of the building to the office. Before the phone rang a second time, Slats slipped through the door into the dim hangar.

As he closed the door, a shadow flashed across the building, and he saw the silhouette of a man exit the lighted door to his left. Slats took three steps into the darkness to his right and froze. The shadow moving toward the office bumped something and cursed softly. Then he heard the office door open as the phone rang again and a light flipped on.

The exit blocked, and unsure of his ability to open the hangar door, Slats slipped behind the plane.

The aircraft's long nose was comical, a mechanical personification of Pinocchio, with wings. Glancing under the plane Slats saw a broad back and blond head in the window. He worked his way forward and examined the plane's strange proboscis. In the darkness, the skin of the plane appeared seamless until, from about ten inches away, Slats could see the joint between the body of the fuselage and the nosepiece. Using his penknife, he scraped at the paint. It fell away easily.

Behind the nosepiece joint, he could see another paint beneath that which scraped away. But he could distinguish no color in the dim light.

He stepped back trying to see all of the plane at once but in the dimness all he could manage was a silhouette. Mentally he stripped away the nose cone and the wing tanks and slimmed the fuselage. He overlaid the mental picture atop the image of a Harrier that he had dug up following the disappearance of Captain Adkins.

It was the Harrier!

Suddenly the office door opened, and the man in it stood perfectly framed in the light from the overhead panel. He was alert, and his head panned back and forth, his eyes scanning the darkened hangar bay. Slats still had some advantage. He could see the man in the door clearly. But the darkness prevented the blond-headed man from seeing him.

The man's action bore out his conjecture. Slats estimated that he was forty feet away from the man. He could not break past the figure and exit the way he had entered. He would have to stay out of sight and wait his chance.

Then suddenly the man (it was Charles Adkins!) turned to his right, bumped something and cursed, then started toward the end of the hangar.

The angle would keep him within a few feet of Slats. If Slats could get behind him and tumble him, he could break for the office and be gone before the guy could regain his senses. He tried to match his tread to the figure's, dimly visible in the glow from the office window. Where was he going anyway?

He crept down on the figure, straining to keep his eyes on him, knowing that if he lost him, he would never find him again in the darkness. Lost in concentration, he failed to see the wall looming ahead of him. His feet hit one of the massive sliding door's braces, and a bolt head slipped between his sandal and the ball of his foot. He felt the sharp steel gash his foot.

The fierce pain surprised him, and he straightened suddenly. Overhead fluorescent lights flickered to life. Less than a dozen feet away Slats saw Adkins; his hand still poised over a bank of switches. He also saw that the massive hanger door was moving. So that was why he had been unable to find a handle outside. It was electrically operated. Adkins stood between him and the opening door. Slats suppressed his pain and with one step toward Adkins, he feinted a blow at the bigger man's head. Adkins threw an arm up to protect himself and Slats buried his left hand, fingers compressed into a rigid rod, in Adkins' solar plexus.

Then he was running through the door and toward the terminal. He would take his chances on being seen rather than return along the tarmac to the beach. The pain in his foot was biting. He slowed as he entered the terminal's lighted area and tried to look as nonchalant as possible, which was difficult for a man with a bloody foot wearing sandals and a bathing suit.

He peered in through the terminal's swinging rear doors and saw no one in the waiting area, True to the code of janitors worldwide the crew was now gathered in the office of the terminal manager, consuming several Mr. Pibbs and discussing the potential of beating the new slot machines that adorned the lobby.

Slats ducked inside, heard loud voices emanating from the room with the open door in the back and slipped into the men's room. He examined his foot. It was bleeding profusely. Using paper towels from a dispenser above the laboratory he dabbed at the blood, and then applied a solid pressure for several minutes. The bleeding eased. He remembered that his trunks had a hip pocket and that he had earlier crammed a handkerchief into that pocket. He wrapped the cloth about his toes and slipped the sandal on over the bundle. It fit, barely. The he slipped out of the terminal and limped back to the hotel.

"Sounds like a rough time, hon," Olivia said as he concluded. "Now what are you going to do?"

"I suppose I could go to the police. But Adkins saw me, and I'll lay odds that that plane won't be there another hour."

Slats had hardly finished speaking when the roar of a jet taking off shook the windows.

"That'll be it now," he said.

Olivia applied a pad of gauze to Slats' foot and tied it expertly.

"You could call Courant," she said.

"What good would that do? Even if he believed me, he actually couldn't do anything."

"He could call Washington."

"And tell them what? That one of his men is vacationing in Grand Turk where he saw a disguised jet plane that he thinks poses a threat to national security? Hell, we'd hear them laugh all the way down here."

“But what are you going to do then?"

"The only thing I can do. Confront de Arrellano."

"It sounds..." she hesitated..."dangerous."

He stood up, testing his bandaged foot.

"Not bad, not bad at all." He looked down at his wife and kissed her on the forehead. "It may be a bit. I wish you'd go home.”

"The hell you say," she replied. "I'll not sit at home wondering what's happening to you here. Besides, there's still a lot of diving I don't want to miss."

"Oh, yeah. Well. This is awfully important you know."

"What else can you do, Slats? You still don't know what is going on. You just going to sit around the hotel and figure it out?"

Olivia made a good point. He had no plans other than to let de Arrellano know that he knew that he was up to something. And that he had no idea which way to go and no timetable.

"You think you should talk to that man?" Olivia asked.

"If he knows that someone is on to him, ..." Slats let the sentence hang unfinished.

"You think all this is tied to what happened in New Orleans?"

"I'm sure of it."

"And to the hostages?"

"I don't know how it all ties together, but I believe it's a plot against the life of the President of The United States. And since no one else will believe that, I've got to do this alone." Slats was almost shouting.

"Not quite, hon. Not quite."

"Oh, uh, yeah. Sorry Ollie."

He wrapped his arms about his wife and squeezed. Olivia moaned.

"Take it easy, Lone Ranger. You wouldn't want to crush your faithful sidekick and Indian companion, now would you?"

"Only with passion, Ollie, only with passion." He bent and kissed her right breast.

"Good grief, Slats," she said, pulling away and walking to the bed. "What am I going to do with you."

Chapter Thirty One

Raul awoke early the next morning and made himself a quick breakfast of leftover ham and cheese from the lounge refrigerator. Then he called the hospital.

De Arrellano was groggy but sensed Raul's discomfort. He directed him to come at eight a.m. when the hospital officially opened its doors and asked him to bring the most recent copy of the Miami Herald available.

A small sundries store next to the island's major grocery had several racks of newspapers, and there Raul located a two-day-old Herald.

The headlines dealt with the U.S. presidential campaign, the World Hunger Conference in Venice, Miami area crime and a small single column head over a story about Colombian government attempt to negotiate with the terrorist holding the U.S. Embassy in Bogota. The terrorists had reduced the number of political prisoners they said the government had to release. For its part, the government was promising safe conduct out of the country for any terrorists who would surrender, except for the man responsible for the murder of the New York youth. He would have to surrender.

When Raul arrived at the hospital, he found de Arrellano sitting up, minus the octopus-like tangle of plastic tubing that had yesterday been connected to his arms. He held in his hand a glassful of something that looked like a frothy white milkshake, complete with a straw. He was still the lone occupant of the room, the bed closer to the door unoccupied. The worn tiles around the bed were damp from an early morning scrubbing and the room reeked of disinfectant.

Chintz curtains billowed in the morning breeze from the open window through which de Arrellano could see the one and only green and grassy lawn on Grand Turk. Had he been able to change his angle a bit he might have been able to see up the alley-like core of the island where miles of salt ponds glinted in the early morning sun.

It was evident that de Arrellano would not long remain on the disabled list. Already, some forty-eight hours after the operation to repair the hole in his stomach, his coloring again seemed natural, his eyes clear and his voice strong.

"Ho, my friend," he said as Raul pushed the door shut behind him. "I told you they could not keep an old jaguar down for long. And how are the rest of our charges?"

Raul hesitated.

"I'm pleased to see you improved. I hope what I have to report will not spoil your day."

De Arrellano looked steadily into Raul's eyes for a moment and sighed deeply. His eyes shut and he closed himself off from the sunny world outside the hospital window; a world where hundreds of people were preparing for a day of diving; a world where Slats and Olivia were starting down to breakfast at the Kittina, while Slats tried to decide what he would say to de Arrellano when he saw him and where Olivia concentrated on not thinking about her husband's problems.

De Arrellano opened his eyes.

"All right, my friend. What news have you for me?"

Raul took the handwritten pages he had folded carefully into the newspaper and opened them. He spread them across the folded paper and handed the entire package to de Arrellano, who looked first at the date.

"Ah... only two days ago. Good."

Then he turned his attention to Raul's handwritten notes. Once he had to ask Raul to clarify a garbled word. He finished the two pages quickly, laid his head back on the pillow and drew a deep breath through clenched teeth.

"It must have been the New Orleans policeman. And now he has seen the plane and Adkins. I do not like this. Not at all."

"But what can he know?" Raul asked.

De Arrellano shrugged.

"Anything he does know could hurt us. We are so very close, and things are becoming delicate." He turned toward Raul.

"Did the plane leave?"

Raul nodded.

"Col. Adkins and the señorita are now aboard the boat."

"Good. Then even what he does know is not provable. The police here would laugh at him." He hesitated, "He is not stupid. He will tell no one, not yet. So we have some time to plan."

"I will leave that to you, señor," Raul said.

De Arrellano smiled at the small Colombian.

"Thank you, my friend. Your faith means much to me."

He winced.

"I am tiring and feeling some pain. I'm afraid your news has disquieted me. If you don't mind, I shall rest now and think about how best to deal with Maria's friend. I shall call you."

He let his head sink on his pillow and closed his eyes. Raul stood quietly a moment, watching the lean face, then brought himself up stiffly to his full height, snapped off a salute, and let himself out.

For some time de Arrellano lay without moving, calming the pain that coursed through his bowels. Then he opened his eyes, pushed himself up to a semi-sitting position, and picked up the newspaper. He began to read the story about the presidential campaign carefully. Down in one corner of the page a bold-faced box detailed the itineraries of the candidates.

As he read down the list, his brow knotted. He muttered soft unpleasant sounds under his breath.

"Too soon," he heard himself saying. "Too soon."

There was a knock at his door.

De Arrellano winced.

Neither the doctors nor the nurses knocked.

Who the hell could it be?

He spread the newspaper across his lap and called, "Come in."

His heart rate increased two-fold when Slats walked through the door, pushing it closed as he entered.

"Good morning, señor de Arrellano. I heard you were ill, and I thought I would drop in and pay my respects."

De Arrellano forced a pained smile.

"Señor Jones. It was good of you to stop by. I trust you and your lovely wife are having an enjoyable time on the island."

"More enjoyable than are you I would say." Slats looked about the room.

"Oh, this. Yes, I am confined for a few days. But I shall be up and in action again quite soon I can assure you. But what have you done to your leg? You seem to be limping."

"Nothing much. Just stubbed a toe. It won't stop me from doing the things I came here to do."

"Oh?"

"Yes. As a matter of fact, my wife has scheduled us for another diving trip already; the day after tomorrow I believe."

"I see. And you have been doing some sightseeing too?"

"As a matter of fact, I have. By the way, I want to thank you for your invitation to visit Computer Dynamics. Fascinating place you have there."

De Arrellano knew his expression betrayed him.

"Oh? Were you able to convince one of my people to show you about in my absence?"

"Something like that. Some interesting equipment you have there. When you are on your feet again, I should appreciate it if you would show me how it is used."

"I see." de Arrellano's grimace dissolved into vacuousness. He looked past Slats, staring out of the window. In the distance, Slats heard the roar of a big jet's braking thrust. The morning Air Florida flight had arrived. The expression on de Arrellano's face shifted. He had made a decision.

"Our schedules are quite hectic, señor Jones. But perhaps we can work you in next week. If all goes well, I should be out of this wretched place by the weekend. Please call me then and I shall personally make arrangements for you."

"You are most kind. Tell me, does your company have a branch in New Orleans?"

Slats thought de Arrellano looked surprised.

"Why do you ask?"

"I think I met one of the your...confederates there."

"I suppose it is possible. We once had an office there, but it's closed now."

It sure is and guess who closed it.

Well, he's certainly gotten the message by now. And the next move or lack thereof, is his. Now that someone is wise, and he knows it maybe he'll just fold up his tent and steal away.

"Well, señor. Best wishes for a speedy recovery. I hope to see you next week."

"If we are both lucky, señor. Adios."

Slats left heading back to the hotel.

Within thirty seconds de Arrellano was on the phone, summoning Raul back to the hospital. The little Latin arrived fifteen minutes later. De Arrellano outlined what had transpired.

"But why is he doing this?" Raul asked.

"I do not pretend to understand his thinking. He has become an open adversary and a dangerous one. He must be dealt with and quickly."

There was a new note of urgency in de Arrellano's voice.

"Is there something else wrong, señor?"

"Yes." De Arrellano gestured at the newspaper and the itineraries he had torn roughly from the corner of the page.

"The President's schedule has changed again. And it is not as I was told it would be. He will be in Miami too soon."

"I don't understand, señor."

De Arrellano took a deep breath and relaxed, resting both hands on his stomach.

"Yes. Yes, I know. Only I and the other four members of the council know the mission. I will explain it to everyone but only all together. It must be soon for we will have to move next week. It becomes imperative."

"But the señorita will not be able to fly the plane by then."

"That is true. But she can fly the Lear, can she not?"

"Si."

"Can you fly the Harrier, Raul?"

"Señor, I can fly anything."

The Colombian drew himself up to his full stature.

"Well, then, my friend. I hate not to have you by my side, but Maria will be my pilot for the mission, and you will stand ready to fly the Harrier in case something happens to Lt. Col Adkins. You understand?"

"Señor, if those are your orders, they will be obeyed."

"Thank you, Raul." He reached out and rested his hand on Raul's shoulder. "Without your help, this entire program would have been infinitely more difficult. You are a true friend and patriot."

Raul seemed to swell with pride.

De Arrellano continued, "and as much as I hate to ask it of you there is one more task that must be completed."

Raul knew what he was being asked to do.

"The American?" he asked.

"Yes. I understand that he and his wife are to dive again shortly. I believe that you should make the trip also and see to it that señor Jones does not return."

Raul shuddered.

"I despise the water, señor. Can not I do it another way?"

"Raul, hundreds of people come to this island every year to dive. Occasionally something happens, and some fool injures or kills himself. If a tourist makes a stupid error ten fathoms under the sea, and that kills him, who is to blame? There will probably not even be an investigation.

"But if something happens to him on the island, anything violent, then the police will surely investigate. And if there is anything to tie him to us in any way, as there well may be, the investigation will hamper us. We do not now have the time for delays. We must act next week, and we must do it without the attention of the police."

"I understand, señor. Very well, then. I shall dive with señor Jones."

Raul paused, thoughtful.

"What about his wife?'

"I think she is simply a woman vacationing with her husband. She is little or no threat to us and while one diver dying in an accident may be explainable, two would not. No. Do not harm the señora."

The conversation ended on an up note with de Arrellano assuring Raul that he would leave the hospital within two days so that he could return to the office at Computer Dynamics and make final preparations for the mission. He asked Raul to acquire several charts from the office files to enable him to begin preparation while still bedridden. He would explain to curious nurses that he planned to make a cruise upon leaving the hospital and that he was studying the charts to determine good passages and anchorages.

Raul was nervous. He knew the rudiments of diving. He had descended three times into the crystal water of Campeche where, while he found the views spectacular, he had discovered the claustrophobia that affects some divers. The feeling of being crushed in an airless container reminded him of the butterflies that as a youth he had imprisoned in small jars. He fought the nightmarish feeling for several minutes each time and each time it had gotten worse. The ocean became a living creature, tightening an invisible hand across his chest, squeezing life itself from his lungs.

But if de Arrellano said he had to dive, he would dive.

Chapter Thirty Two

After he left the hospital Raul visited one of the island's diving emporiums and purchased a brand new set of U.S. Divers equipment. The youth who attended him asked for his certificate and was hesitant to sell the gear despite its $800 plus cumulative price without the certificate. But when Raul insisted that the equipment was to be a gift for a friend and a new resident of Grand Turk, who would be taking lessons from the proprietor of the establishment, he relented.

Raul asked to have the equipment delivered to Computer Dynamics, then set off to the anchorage at the south end of the island where he acquired the day use of a Mako open fisherman for the remainder of the week.

His final stop was at the Kittina, where he checked the posted diving schedule for Kuttner's Diving Expeditions and Lessons. He found trips listed each of the three successive days including, if the weather held, two deep water dives. He would simply watch Slats and follow them.

Raul hadn't seen Slats previously. He needed first to identify him. It was nearing the supper hour, so he and his wife might well be in the dining room. A bit of judicious listening convinced him that the room Slats shared with his wife was unoccupied. He then called Computer Dynamics and instructed Jules McCain, the technician pulling office duty in Raul's absence, to call the hotel and have Slats paged.

A quick check revealed only one telephone convenient to the patio and dining areas. It was on a sandstone faced kiosk near the outdoor bar. Raul sat, ordered a drink and waited. The page was moments in coming. Raul's drink arrived just as a tall, muscular man with dark, wavy hair walked up to the phone and picked it up. He spoke into the mouthpiece a couple of times, looked puzzled, hung up the receiver and walked back to a table across the courtyard to where a pretty round-faced woman sat musing.

So that's the policeman de Arrellano wants dead. He has a pretty wife.

Raul finished his drink studying the couple as they conversed quietly, somewhat animatedly, across the courtyard.

For the next twelve hours, Raul battled with his subconscious, trying to steel himself for the dive he knew he had to make. He slept little that night, the bunk room at Computer Dynamics closing in on him each time he shut his eyes. At six-thirty the next morning he was again seated in the Kittina courtyard and he was rewarded by seeing Slats and Olivia descend the stair to the patio where they sat at the table they had shared the night before. Slats ordered a grits and grunts breakfast which they consumed quickly.

Raul downed his coffee, wishing for a brew with more body, remembering some of those he had drunk as a youth in his native land. He left money for the coffee on the table, grabbed the arm of a cabbie seated at a nearby table and urged him to his vehicle.

A quick stop at the CD hanger for his newly purchased equipment and ten minutes later he was loading the Mako. He noted that Kuttner's diving vessels were still locked up and estimated that thirty minutes, at least, would be required to ready them for the morning's expedition. Raul sat down at the Mako's stern, in the single fighting chair and began stripping twenty-pound test monofilament from one of the boat's several large spinning rigs kept aboard for those anglers who made the run occasionally to the banks to stalk the huge silver bonefish that roamed the flats.

Chapter Thirty Three

Slats worked hard at putting de Arrellano, the Harrier, and Maria out of his mind for the day. He wanted Olivia to enjoy the dive, and he hoped to get some pleasure out of it himself. There was nothing further that he could do about de Arrellano. The plane was certainly no longer on the island. And conjecture could not produce hard evidence.

He thought that his visit to de Arrellano might provoke some action. A thought that he would not express to Olivia.

Maria.

He couldn't keep her face from his mind. And he wondered why he had not seen her in the past two days. Would she dive today?

Olivia's face, across the table, was washed in the slanting early sun.

"Beautiful day, lover," he said across a slice of buttered toast.

Olivia agreed.

"Hope we can get some good pictures today. You will shoot some, this time, won't you?"

"Sure will."

The temperature increased rapidly as the sun climbed over the bougainvilleas. Their route was similar to that of three days earlier, but this time, they were in line early and rode in the van instead of the clanking truck with the equipment. At the boat, they went up to the flying bridge and sat on the port berth. From their vantage point, they looked out over the entire marina, its rickety piers and the dozen-odd boats tied up to them. Olivia watched absently as the occupant of one of the nearby boats struggled with fishing gear. He seemed to be working intensely and every so often he scanned the diving boats. Once she caught him looking directly at her.

She told Slats.

"Which guy?"

"The one in that open boat working on the fishing tackle."

"Doesn't appear to be having much fun does he?"

"No. But I would have sworn he was looking right at me a moment ago."

Slats slid down the berth, leaned out over the edge of the cabin and gave Olivia a long stare.

"Can't say that I blame him. You're well worth looking at."

Olivia screwed up one corner of her mouth and sighed deeply.

"Oh pshaw," she said. "I guess all of your intrigue is wearing off on me. I'll be a good girl, I promise."

Slats looked at her and reached up to brush a lock of hair from her forehead.

"There was a little girl,

"Who had a little curl,

"Right in the middle of her forehead.

"And when she was good, she was very, very good,

"But when she was bad, she was better."

He grinned broadly and slid his right hand up her thigh to nestle in her crotch. She picked up his hand and folded it between her breasts.

A blond head popped up over the cabin coming.

"Hi, folks," the youth said, and he clambered onto the bridge. "Ready to go?"

Thirty minutes later they were anchored, the water beneath them cobalt blue and crystalline. And although Olivia noticed that the fisherman she had seen at the marina, anchored only a few hundred yards away, she said nothing to Slats.

She wasn't going to give him another chance to make fun of her.

They were in the third group over, again only four people and again with the blond helmsman as their guide. They were in over ninety feet of water, and they planned on working for approximately twenty minutes then taking approximately twice that long to ascend and decompress.

The seascape intrigued Slats.

This time he saw it without Maria's presence to blind him to the blue-green beauty about him. Massive coral and limestone canyons ranged about them while great schools of open water fish swarmed above them. Reef fishes and crustaceans were everywhere and every time his or Olivia's flash lit the bottom he was amazed at the colors.

For several minutes he followed a brilliantly colored butterfly angelfish, unaware that he was drifting away from his group.

When the fish swam through a crevice too small for him to enter, he looked up for Olivia. He had rounded a bend in the coral canyon up which he had followed the fish, and neither she nor the rest of the group was in sight. He glanced up and noted that the boats seemed several yards farther east than he expected. His watch told him that it was approaching time to begin the ascent.

Suddenly he saw a figure twenty yards up the canyon. It wasn't Olivia although it was small. And it seemed to be beckoning to him. Curious, Slats started toward the figure glancing at his watch as he went. He had to allow himself sufficient time to decompress. He had seen the bends once, and he did not relish the idea of joints bloated and contorted or the resulting pain and the possibility of a cardiac embolism. Looking back toward the figure he saw that it had started swimming away from him still beckoning. The man (at least it appeared to be male) clad in a black wetsuit, swam with small rapid movements apparently in discomfort. He was working hard to maintain his distance ahead.

What had begun as curious encounter was becoming a pursuit and Slats didn't have time to waste. He began to push harder, and he brought his arms into play. He timed his breathing and revolved his body in tempo with his arms. The small man ahead kicked frantically, and his breathing left a constant stream of bubbles. He swam deep into the canyon virtually grazing the bottom but was losing ground rapidly.

Slats calculated that he would reach the figure in less than a minute.

Then Slats felt his reaching right arm pushed back against his shoulder. Something unseen gripped his throat, and as he brought his left arm up toward his face, it was stopped and held. The pain in his throat was sharp, cutting and tightening. Slats kicked upward and more unseen fingers wrapped around his body and his legs.

The black edge of panic jumped up his throat, but Slats beat it back. He looked up toward the surface and saw flush against his face mask a thin hard line. Then he saw another, and another, crisscrossing his mask and his body, wrapping more tightly the more he struggled against them.

Monofilament.

Lightweight monofilament fishing line. It had been strung back and forth across the canyon, an all but invisible web. The force of swimming into it had wrapped it about him so that he was effectively netted, jammed headfirst into the tough web like a mullet in a gill seine. And while the line was light enough to be virtually invisible in the depths Slats knew how tough it would be to break. He remembered the times fishing as a youth when his hooks had snagged obstacles on the bottom.

That twelve pound Stren had taken a monumental pull before it broke.

But he had a knife and with a little patience he would soon be able to retrieve it from its calf scabbard and cut himself free. He looked up and saw the diminutive figure he had been following a few yards ahead. The man had stopped and appeared to be toying with a small silver container that he held at waist level. From the box protruded a rod.

My God, it's a detonator!

Even before Slats could react, the figure shoved the plunger home.

The explosion was not loud, and the concussion did little more than rock Slats. He looked for the source of the sound and saw coral mushroom on the side of the canyon fifty feet above. He saw too that the wall of the canyon above the bloated area was in motion, falling ponderously; a dozen pieces of coral and limestone that would quietly and unhurriedly bury him forever.

A rush of bubbles erupted around him, and something grabbed at his left hand, the hand he had been trying to free. He twisted and saw Olivia. She had his arm and was hacking at the entrapping line with her knife. He wanted to tell her to run, to get away, that there wasn't time. He could only gurgle against the monofilament that circled his throat. He watched as his wife slashed at the mesh and tried to gauge the speed of the falling rock.

Then his arm was free. He grabbed for his knife and slashed at his throat and the right side of his neck. The line was parting, and he was moving now, but the rushing rock pile was almost upon them.

He grabbed Olivia and kicked at the nearby coral. Some of the monofilament tore through his wetsuit and into the flesh of his right shoulder and left thigh, the cuts burning like fire in the salt water. He pushed with all of his strength and the bonds broke. He shot up the canyon as the first of the massive stones rumbled into the cleft. He was looking ahead, literally dragging Olivia when she suddenly arched from his grip, screaming, her regulator mouthpiece blown from her mouth.

Slats turned, grabbing her under the arms as pieces of the rubble, one a small boulder of limestone, crushed her left leg into the floor of the canyon. It jammed tightly into a small crevice. Olivia recovered her mouthpiece and refitted it. Slats could see the pain in her eyes behind the mask, but at least, she had not lost consciousness. She pointed upwards.

Slats followed her gaze and saw the small figure that he had followed into the trap churning frantically toward the surface. He wanted to go after him, feel his throat in his hands and crush the life from him.

But he couldn't.

Olivia needed help.

She had to be freed, and they had to begin their ascent soon, or they would run out of air. As it was, they would risk the bends since neither had sufficient air for decompression.

A movement up the canyon caught Slats' eye. It was the blond diving instructor who, having lost two of his group, was now looking for them. He wondered why people couldn't learn to follow instructions. As soon as he saw Olivia's plight, he pulled a Plexiglas board from his belt tether and a grease pen.

"Extra tank," he wrote. "At anchor line. Be back."

And without waiting for an acknowledgment he swept smoothly up out of the canyon toward the boat. Slats remembered the instruction session and the fact that two extra tanks complete with regulators were attached to the anchor line for use in case of emergencies. Certainly no one had anticipated such an emergency as this, but Slats was thankful for the divers' preparedness.

Slats went to work on the rock that had trapped Olivia's foot.

Two small shards of coral sticking out from the canyon sides seemed to hold it in place. He began chipping away at the coral with his knife and hoards of small reef fishes appeared to feed on the minute fauna displaced by the blade. Olivia winced as the blade struck the rock, thrusting it against her leg. She lay almost flat on her back, floating above the narrow canyon floor, her eyes barely visible in the blue-green twilight, all that remained of the brilliant noon sun ninety feet above.

She gestured upward again, and Slats looked. The small figure had reached the surface but was now thrashing widely, beating the surface to foam. Other swimmers were moving toward him from the big boat, and as they reached him, he ceased struggling.

The three figures, two swimming and one motionless, began moving back toward the boat.

The blond helmsman reappeared over the rim of the canyon with the extra tank and immediately set to work helping Slats free Olivia. The task was quickly accomplished. The wetsuit and the near darkness made it impossible to determine how badly her leg was injured, so they began the accent, carrying the extra tank between them.

Slats and the youth hoisted Olivia under each arm. The rise to the surface seemed painfully slow, and twice the blond youth had to hold them back, emphatically signaling Slats to slow down. Their tanks all ran dry before they were halfway to the surface, but the single extra had sufficient air to sustain them.

Olivia was all but unconscious when they reached the surface and the pain evident on her face as they handed her up from the sea to the boat.

"What the hell happened down there?" Kuttner asked as Slats pulled himself up onto the platform.

He turned to two other young men who had Olivia in a basket carry between them.

"Get her below," he ordered. "Crazy bastard tried to kill me." Slats muttered as he shed his tanks and fins and followed his wife.

"Who?" Kuttner asked.

"Little guy you pulled in a few minutes ago. I want that bastard."

Kuttner stopped as Slats ducked into the cabin behind Olivia. The two attendants put her on the port berth and stood back. Slats looked at her leg. He couldn't tell how bad it was through the suit but when he touched the leg Olivia screamed. She remained conscious, however, and asked for something to ease the pain.

"All I have is aspirin," Kuttner said from the doorway.

"Well, get her some," Slats said. "Then get us back to the island. Call ahead and have a doctor standing by."

"That's already been done," Kuttner said, shaking several aspirins from a large bottle.

"Here." He handed them to Slats, who handed them to Olivia.

"Can I have some water?" she asked.

A few moments later when they had made Olivia as comfortable as possible and placed a seaboard on the edge of the bunk to ensure that she could not roll out, Slats cornered Kuttner on the after deck.

"Where is that little bastard you pulled out of the water? I want him."

Kuttner looked him straight in the eye.

"It's too late."

"What do you mean?"

"Follow me."

Kuttner led him through the cabin and the galley and down into the forepeak. The peak was small, nothing but four bunks, two port, and two starboard. There was scarcely room for the two men to stand between the berths. Kuttner cracked the overhead hatch to let in some light and gestured at the lower port berth. What was obviously a body lay on the berth covered by a blue woolen navy blanket.

Slats looked at the body, then at Kuttner. Kuttner turned back the top of the blanket. A small Latin face stared blankly at the bunk above, darkly grizzled hair matted about the ears, and trickles of blood in one corner of the mouth.

"What happened?'

"He didn't decompress."

Slats remembered the small man kicking frantically for the surface.

"Bends?"

Kuttner shook his head.

"Spontaneous pneumo-thorax. His lungs collapsed."

Slats stared at the body. He knew the theory behind pneumo-thorax. An air bubble forms in the chest cavity outside the lungs, generally caused by a diver holding his breath as he ascends. The pressure change forces the air in the lungs to expand driving it into the pleural cavity. Slats had never heard of it killing before.

Kuttner read his mind.

"He didn't know beans about diving. He shouldn't have been down there in the first place."

Kuttner covered the body. He turned in the cramped space to face Slats.

"Did you know him?" he asked.

Chapter Thirty Four

The tibia and fibula, the bones of the lower leg, had broken in three places. The imprisoning rock had also caused a lot of soft tissue damage. Surgery was indicated, and soon.

The diagnosis had been at the hands of the island hospital's chief surgeon, a gray-haired, big black man named Kenneth Gobody. The prognosis was good if, and only if, he emphasized several times as he spoke to Slats and Olivia at the latter's bedside if an orthopedic surgeon could get to the leg soon. Otherwise, he said in his most guarded tones, the tissue destruction might be permanent.

Gobody convinced Slats.

He wanted to ship Olivia home immediately. She could be on an operating table at Oschner's in suburban New Orleans, one of the nation's finest surgical hospitals, in twelve hours. Her mother would attend to her after surgery, and she would be walking again in a couple of months.

"And what are you going to do?" she asked, her words slurred by the painkillers dripping into the network of tubing attached to her left arm.

"I wish I could come home with you, Ollie, but I can't."

"That man tried to kill you."

Gobody shifted his gaze from Slats to Olivia and back.

"Yes, I know. And he would have succeeded if you hadn't been there."

"You can't stay alone, hon."

Slats didn't reply. He looked coolly down at the doctor and coughed.

Gobody nodded.

"I'm leaving," he said. "But I advise you to get your wife to a surgeon as quickly as possible." He turned on his heels and walked away.

Olivia was one of only two patients in a dozen bed ward. The other bed occupied was at the opposite end of the pale green drab room. Dark curtains, dingy with age, hung pulled back and strapped to the wall between the beds. Only the late afternoon sun, blazing through the chintz curtain, added a touch of cheer to the scene.

Gobody stopped at the bed at the opposite end of the room where he lifted the wrist of an elderly black man who lay staring at the fly-specked ceiling.

Slats sat carefully on his wife's bed, picking up her left hand and kissing her fingertips.

"I love you, Ollie," he whispered. "I love you, but I can't go back with you now. Arrellano's behind this and I don't know what he's up to. You understand, don't you?"

Olivia's eyes were glazed but her voice strong.

"Slats, it's drugs. You know that! They're smuggling dope, and they'll not let one little cop stand in their way."

"It's not drugs, Ollie. It's something more. But I've been warned now. And I'll be ready. I've been in tighter scrapes."

"But you've always had Ivey, and Johnny. now you're by yourself. You, you ..." she stuttered. She couldn't remember exactly what she was trying to say.

"I love you," she mumbled.

Her eyelids drifted down. She heard herself trying to talk, to warn Slats. She felt him squeeze her hand, then place it on the sheet, cool beside her body. His voice came from somewhere miles away.

"Sleep well, Ollie," he said. "I've some phone calls to make. Be back later."

When he was sure Olivia was sleeping, he cornered Gobody. The doctor agreed to keep to himself the conversation that he had overheard.

"I suppose it could be called privileged information," the chubby face grinned. "Although my curiosity is, I admit, piqued."

Slats left the doctor grinning, walked out of the ward and the hospital and back to the hotel. The thirty-minute trek through the warm dark cleared his mind. His shoulder hurt where the monofilament had cut through his suit. But the pain was manageable, certainly nothing like what Olivia would feel any time her medication wore off. He wished he could exact vengeance on the man who had caused his wife such suffering, but the man's stupidity had robbed him of the opportunity. He remembered the look of terror and pain on the dead face when Kuttner turned back the blanket.

He also remembered Kuttner's puzzled expression when Slats had replied to his query "Do you know him?" with a simple "No."

He had later told the Grand Turk police the same.

Although sure the dead man had attempted to kill him, Slats did not want island police launching an investigation that might interfere with his. So, for the record, the death of an unidentified, inexperienced diver, and the accident that badly crushed the left leg of a female diver in Kuttner's party were unrelated. The only witnesses to the incident had been Slats, Olivia, and the dead man. He would get Olivia off the island as quickly as possible.

When he reached the hotel, he called Olivia's mother and spent ten minutes talking to the boys, telling them about diving on the reef, the wild donkeys, the dogs that barked all night and the flight to Grand Turk. Then he told Olivia's mother about the accident. She was shaken, and when Slats said he wouldn't be returning with Olivia, her voice rose a full octave.

The accident, Slats told his mother-in-law, might have been perpetrated by another diving operator, a competitor of Kuttner's. Therefore, to prevent a potentially fatal confrontation, he had agreed to stay on and assist in the investigation. Olivia, he said, felt his participation in the program necessary since he had been the only eyewitness to the accident. Slats was uncertain his mother-in-law bought his story, but she agreed to meet Olivia at the airport and to care for her needs until he returned. She also would arrange for the surgeon and direct him to contact Dr. Gobody at the Grand Turk Hospital.

Slats then called Florida Flying Service, Inc., in Miami and made arrangements for a charter ambulance flight from Grand Turk to New Orleans. God, he thought, Blue Cross and Blue Shield will have a Blue fit.

Those tasks completed, Slats showered, stretched out on the bed, and fell quietly asleep only to awaken in the grip of a nightmare. It was a vivid dream in which he saw himself and Olivia in the bottom of a coral canyon surrounded by sharks, monstrous mako sharks, all howling like wolves beneath a full moon.

He opened his eyes, staring at the moon through the balcony's sliding glass doors. The howling continued. Perspiration poured from his body as he worked to convince himself that he heard not some demon sea creature but the island's dog packs in soulful communication.

For the rest of the night, sleep was difficult. Every time he felt himself drifting, a specter grabbed his feet and pulled him down into a morass of coral and monofilament, toward beckoning, grinning dead eyes.

He said a small prayer of thanks when the dark sky beyond the balcony began to gray, and the stars vanished slowly into the dawn. He pulled on his swimsuit and walked down to the beach where he watched the near flat sea sweep the coarse sand. But he could not bring himself to dive into the brightening water. Revulsion washed over him, and he retched dryly on the sand. His stomach and intestines ground together and for five minutes he heaved in agony. Then it was over and he was a last able to stand straight again. The sleeplessness left him fatigued, but his mind was clearing.

He could face Olivia rationally and convince her, if she still needed convincing, that she had to return to New Orleans, and he had to remain.

Slats returned to the hotel, showered again, scrubbing away at his skin, trying to attune his body to his mind. He dressed quickly, called a cab and fifteen minutes later he was knocking on the front door of the hospital. Through the door windows, he could see a white-clad figure at a small desk. It dominated the tiny lobby. The nurse walked up to the inside of the door and looked at Slats. She pointed at the little sign to the right of the doors that indicated visiting hours. But Slats was persistent.

She opened the door a crack, and after listening for a moment agreed to let him enter. She did so, she assured him, only because there were so few people in the hospital and he could not likely disturb anyone. Slats thanked her, and as she returned to her desk, he set off down the hall toward the ward where he hoped Olivia would still be sleeping. He stopped in the hall outside de Arrellano's room, waited a moment, listening, then stepped inside.

Chapter Thirty Five

The tall Latin slept.

Slats watched him for a moment, unsure what he was feeling, then slipped out of the room and walked on to the ward.

Olivia was asleep when he walked up to the bed. He pulled a cane-backed chair to her bedside and sat down. She slept peacefully, although small lines cut into the normally smooth cheeks as her mouth pulled down at the corners, evidence that even in her sleep she felt pain.

When she began to moan softly, Slats took her hand and squeezed it, hoping that his presence would buffer her suffering. It didn't and rather than listen to her pained muttering, Slats pulled the cord at the head of the bed. The nurse appeared in seconds, took a quick pulse and studied a clipboard that she had carried into the room.

"I can give her another injection for the pain if you wish," she said.

"Please."

"Very well. Kindly step away for a few moments."

She put her clipboard on an ancient white cupboard and picked up a syringe. She selected a small bottle from several arranged neatly atop the cupboard and filled the syringe. When she was satisfied that she had the right amount of liquid and no bubbles in the plastic shaft below the gleaming needle, she placed it on a white towel on the side of the bed, unsnapped the curtains from the wall and motioned Slats away. Then with a swish and a rattle, she and Olivia disappeared behind the dingy cloth. Slats paced up the ward. The other bed occupied last night now stood empty. He wondered if the black face that he had seen the evening before still bore the spark of life.

The nurse finished, returning the curtain to the wall. Olivia was awake now, and the nurse cranked her bed to elevate her head, then left.

"Hi, Ollie!"

Slats kissed her on the forehead. She smiled and grimaced at the same time, caught his face between her hands and kissed him hard on the lips.

"If you're going to play James Bond, you could, at least, kiss like him," she said.

Slats laughed.

"And how do you know how James Bond kisses?"

"A memory from my wilder days," she replied.

She patted the bed next to her and winced as he sat down.

"How is it, Ollie?"

"It hurts, hon."

"She just gave you a shot. It'll take effect soon."

"Yes, I know. And then I won't be able to talk straight."

She squeezed his hand and looked up into his face.

"What are you going to do, hon?"

"You're going home. I've already called your mother. She's making the hospital arrangements right now."

Olivia was silent.

"Ollie, you must go. You heard what that funny looking doctor said about your leg."

"Yes, I know. And I'll go. But I'm going to worry terribly about you."

"Of course, you will. And I'm sorry. But I assure you I shall be all right."

"You better be, you big Irish coon-ass." She squeezed his hand tighter. "or else..."

"Or else what?"

"That's a mystery. You'll have to come home to find out. See, if a mystery got you here, a mystery should get you back home. Right?"

"Well, it had better be a good one."

"It will be. Now, when do I get out of here?"

"I've made arrangements for a plane to pick you up this afternoon. All we have to do is find Gobody and check you out."

While he talked, Olivia's eyes glazed, and she dozed.

He sat with Olivia awhile then went in search of Gobody. The nurse at the front desk had been joined by two others. The three sat drinking coffee as he approached and explained his intentions.

Nothing to worry about said one of the new arrivals. Dr. Gobody would arrive well before noon or perhaps as early as nine o'clock. Slats glanced at his watch. Eight a.m. A wait of from one to four hours. Island time! One hour, three hours, who cares, mon.

One of the nurses offered Slats coffee which he accepted. Then he walked back to Olivia's bedside. She slept soundly. Her breathing, the only sound in the ward, was deep and regular. The pain furrows in her cheeks and forehead were smoother, less noticeable.

If Olivia couldn't be aware of his presence, Slats decided he would return to de Arrellano, even if visiting hours hadn't begun. Looking up the hall Slats could see two of the nurses still engaged in conversation at the desk. The third would be across the desk, out of his field of vision. Slats wandered slowly up the hall, then as he passed the door into de Arrellano's room he slipped quickly inside.

De Arrellano was sitting on his bed; a newspaper spread across his lap.

"What is it?" he asked, looking up as Slats entered. When he recognized him, he straightened and drew a sharp breath, but his composure remained.

"Señor Jones. I had not expected to see you again... so soon. It is rather early. However, good morning."

He leaned back, still apparently weary.

"Hello, señor de Arrellano. I expected seeing me would surprise you."

Slats was certain now. There had been just enough fear in de Arrellano's reaction. He had expected never to see Slats again. He had assumed that his grizzled little henchman had accomplished his task.

"I mean, it is early, and you're right. I didn't come here just to see you. My wife is here. We had an... an accident while diving yesterday. My wife's left leg is crushed badly."

De Arrellano seemed to be weighing Slats comments searching for some missing piece of a verbal puzzle.

"And you, señor? You were not injured?"

"No, thanks to my wife's intervention. She saved my life."

"And no one else was hurt?"

"Oh, I'm afraid that's not true. You see, one man died."

De Arrellano sat forward.

"Oh? Who? What happened?"

"No one seems to know, quite. He was a rather small Hispanic man."

De Arrellano blanched but remained motionless.

Slats skipped the part about the monofilament trap and the rock fall. Such details were for the moment, meaningless. If the man who had made the attempt on his life was, as Slats conjectured, in de Arrellano's employ, then Slats' recitation was hurting de Arrellano. It was calculated pain and Slats wanted it sharp.

"The man didn't know what he was doing," Slats continued. "He panicked and swam to the surface holding his breath. When divers do that, they leave themselves open for something called spontaneous pneumothorax. The air he was breathing almost 100 feet down was under great pressure. As he rose, he was holding his breath. Air forced its way out of his lungs into the chest cavity. Then, when he attempted to breathe at the surface, the bubble of air in his chest cavity crushed his lungs."

"Madre Dios!" De Arrellano muttered.

He was staring into space. What he saw, Slats could only surmise. He was not so hardened that he could wave off such a death as if it were cigarette smoke. Slats could see the tiny movements beneath the skin surface as muscles tensed and relaxed. Outwardly he seemed to accept the news calmly, almost disinterestedly.

He looked back at Slats.

"It is a shame, señor," he began, "that your vacation had to be marred by such tragedy. I assume that you will be cutting your stay on Grand Turk short."

"That was my intention, but my wife will not hear of it. She insists that I remain and take in all the diving I can. You see, a policeman needs all the leisure he can get, and I have had very little lately.

"So, although I am sending my wife home today, I shall be around for a while longer."

"I see." De Arrellano spoke slowly, a heaviness in his voice. "I hope then that you have no more accidents."

"I intend to be very careful."

"Yes, I'm sure. Well, if you'll excuse me, señor, I am feeling rather tired."

He leaned back in the elevated bed and closed his eyes. Slats regarded the slim, dark figure on the rumpled white linens. He didn't know if he hated the man for his treachery or feared him for his cunning. Fear, he thought. Fear, respect, and hatred share common bounds. Only degree separates one from the other.

Chapter Thirty Six

It was to be another training day for Maria. They had spent most of the prior evening sitting in the Harrier, where Charlie had reviewed the aircraft's operating systems for what Maria believed was the twenty-first time. She had rapidly tired of the repetition.

"I understand, Charlie," she had said, exasperation in her voice. "Isn't it time for me to fly?"

"When I'm satisfied that you understand her; the controls, the differences in the operational modes, then you can double on the stick. But not until I think you're ready."

Maria was seeing a side of Charlie she didn't appreciate. And it wasn't just in the cockpit of the plane.

Their temporary quarters was an old Tahiti ketch, comfortable enough for sleeping, but cramped below, and cluttered. It lacked refrigeration and air conditioning.

The first night aboard she had fallen asleep in the spacious cockpit. Charlie awakened her the next morning, caressing her arms and letting his hands stray to her breasts. She responded and they enjoyed making love, the early morning sun warming their bodies to match their ardor. Then over the side they splashed into the cool, silver-green water, the bottom fifteen feet down a clearly drawn forest of feathery coral.

Back aboard Charlie asked her to make a brunch, which she accomplished after several minutes of frustration getting the ancient alcohol stove to respond. They ate in the cockpit, relishing the taste of eggs and bacon, enriched by salty air and sunshine.

Her frustration returned as Charlie watched her clean up the meal remains, instead of offering to help. And when she went back on deck he grabbed her, roughly, his intentions obvious. Infuriated, she slapped him and dove overboard. When she surfaced, he stood in the cockpit, right hand to his still reddened cheek, fury in his eyes.

At first, she wanted to laugh but, studying his expression, apologized instead. It was important to keep the peace.

Charlie accepted the apology, but the lines in his face remained, and Maria sensed a shift in their relationship. It became more evident as they progressed in her training. Charlie pushed her, physically and emotionally. He would belittle her each time she failed to recite correctly the function of an instrument or control, or remember a "V" speed or power setting. Several times she had been on the verge of confrontation.

But she maintained her composure until the morning she awoke to find the boat's sideband radio switched off. She had planned to ask for more ice and request some additional foodstuffs.

"Charlie! The radio's off! What if they'd tried to reach us?"

Her voice in the tiny cabin raked across his eardrums like fingernails on a blackboard.

"Hey, calm down!" he barked in response. "It's noisy as hell, and I got tired of all that static."

And as Maria punched the power switch, the radio came to life.

"CD two, this is CD base, respond please," a clipped voice urged over the background buzz.

"I'll be damned," Charlie said. He pushed toward the radio, but Maria plucked the microphone from its clip.

"CD two, base. Go ahead," she said. "Been trying to reach you for hours," the voice, apparently de Arrellano's, replied. Maria glared at Charlie. De Arrellano's voice, blurred by the radio static, continued.

"Imperative you return this evening. Do you understand? You must return this P.M."

Maria continued to stare at Charlie, who could only shrug in reply.

"Base, this is two," Maria replied. "Understand that we are to return to base this evening. Is that correct?"

Again the static-edged voice. It confirmed the instructions.

Maria's puzzlement was evident on her face. She thumbed the mike again.

"Why?"

There was no response.

Maria stared at the radio for a moment, then returned the mike to its clip.

She and Charlie stared at each other for a moment, then she squeezed past him and climbed into the cockpit. Charley followed. There was no bimini cover to shade the cockpit, and the sun, nearing azimuth, seared the off-white paint. Maria stood near the mizzen, shading her eyes with her hand, looking toward the beach fifty yards from the stern of the boat. In a small hollow beyond the ridge of green above the sandy beach sat the Harrier, invisible from the water.

Maria dropped her hand and turned to Charlie.

"Wonder why Jusquevera wants us back so soon," she said.

"Sometimes I think de Arrellano is a mite touched," Charlie replied.

"You know," she began, speaking softly but clearly, "I've heard people say the same thing about you."

"Ouch!" Charlie said, seating himself on the cockpit rail in the shadow of the mast. "You got me with that shot. What's wrong with you these days, anyway?"

"What's wrong with me? Me?" Maria paused, staring at him. "You're what's wrong! Pushing me around, acting like I'm chattel."

Charlie paused, then mimed lighting a cigarette.

"I'm just trying to give you what you want, sweetheart," he said, his voice deep in his chest.

"And stop that stupid Bogey imitation. I can't stand it."

"All right. All right."

Charlie held up both hands in resignation, then hoisted himself over the bridge deck and slipped below. He emerged a moment later with three bottles of Guinness in his hand and gave one to Maria.

"Peace?"

She accepted the amber bottle, icy cold in the noon heat, and, watching him smile, felt herself almost unwillingly return the smile.

"Anyone ever tell you you're impossible?" she asked.

He tilted one of the bottles up and poured the dark liquid down his throat, then tossed the bottle overboard.

"Only other men," he replied, starting on the second Guinness.

Maria stared at the bottle bobbing behind the boat.

"Go easy, big guy. I can't fly that thing back to Grand Turk," she said, deciding against chastising him for littering.

"Don't worry, lover. I can drink six beers and still fly, fiddle, and fuck all at the same time."

"Okay. But you don't have to prove it to me."

A cooling breeze was rising. They made their way below and stretched out on separate berths to nap the afternoon away, thankful for the ketch's numerous ports and hatches.

Shortly before sunset, they swam to the beach. A walk two hundred yards inland took them across the ridge and into the limestone and sand-walled basin where the Harrier sat. It took them several minutes to dispose of the white camouflage net and to change into flying clothes.

Darkness was slowly filling the draw as they made their inspection of the plane. The were clearing the chocks when Charlie trapped Maria between his arms, pinning her against the fuselage.

"If I've hurt your feelings these last few days, I apologize," he said. "Teaching a woman to fly wasn't something I expected and it makes me nervous."

"I'm not looking for apologies, Charlie. But you have been hard to live with."

Charlie tilted his head back and sighed.

"Me? Hard to live with? Look who's talking." he paused. "You've been a real bitch, except in bed, of course. I guess you're sufficiently well practiced to separate lovemaking from the rest of your life?"

Maria felt the flush suffuse her face. She knew it would be crimson had enough light remained to see it. She felt the anger deep in her chest. Her hand lashed up and caught Charlie flat-palmed across his left ear.

As the echo of the slap died away, leaving only the wash of water on sand, Maria knew she had made a mistake. Charlie stepped away, his hand going to his face.

"That's two..." he said, more than a trace of menace in his voice.

"You were ......using my past against me, Charlie," Maria's voice was shrill and harsh, softening as she continued.

"My days in New Orleans taught me a lot, but not to separate sex from anything. Sex is part of a relationship Charlie, even if that relationship is bought and paid for.

"With... friends, sex is an enterprise shared, with affection the medium of exchange. I didn't have sex with you just for the sake of an orgasm. That I can manage alone. I shared myself with you because we had something good...something that sex would only improve.

"Do you understand?"

Maria watched Charlie's face, dimly lit in the sunset's afterglow. He didn't move during her speech, and only a slight frown molded the corners of his mouth. Then he turned and strode toward the cockpit ladder.

"Let's go," he said.

He spoke not another word during the flight to Grand Turk. Only after they were on the ground taxiing toward the Computer Dynamics hangar did he speak. His voiced was very formal in the headset, and she could not see his face.

"Maria," he muttered, "I apologize."

As they left the aircraft, she reached out to him, and he took her hand, only to give it a quick, firm squeeze, and release it. She lifted her gaze to his, but the might-have-been communication was interrupted by one of the young technicians

"Señor de Arrellano is waiting for you in the office," he said.

They hurried to the lounge and quickly changed out of the flight gear. Jusquevera sat behind the desk in the office, and the techs were seated on folding chairs as though they were students in grade school.

Maria glanced around.

"Where's Raul?" she asked.

Jusquevera's gaze remained downcast. He studied what appeared to be a newspaper clipping as he replied, quietly.

"Raul is dead."

"What?"

"He died yesterday...in a diving accident."

He looked up at Maria, his dark eyes moist and glinting, but no tears stained his cheeks. He gestured toward the folding chairs.

"Sit, please!" He paused, cleared his throat, and continued, his voice weak but clear.

"Raul had an assignment. He was following your policeman friend, Lt. Jones."

For a moment, Maria was silent. Then she exploded.

"Damn you!...You sent Raul after Slats!"

"Maria! It was necessary. The Lieutenant is too close. But...Raul made an error, a mistake that proved fatal. Perhaps I pushed him beyond his capabilities...and if that is true then I am responsible..."

He paused again and this time when he resumed speaking, his power and force returned.

"But Maria, I have no time to grieve. Nor have you!"

"Damn it, Jusquevera! Raul..." her voice trailed off. "And Slats hasn't done anything. He doesn't know..."

"He's too close, Maria. But if you're concerned about his well-being, don't be. He's fine. His wife, however, was injured. The lieutenant sent her home today."

Maria's anger paled, and was replaced by a great sense of loss. Perhaps she didn't have time to grieve, but she intensely missed the grizzled Colombian. His patience with her in the cockpit of the Lear, teaching her the fundamentals of flight, had been so human, so different from the authoritarian instructor she had put up with for the last four days.

Jusquevera interrupted her stream of thought.

"The Lieutenant visited me in the hospital, Maria. He made it plain that he is aware of my identity."

"Can that hurt us?" she asked.

"Yes. Yes, it can. And I fear only you can stop him."

Maria jumped from her chair.

"What are you asking of me?!"

Jusquevera pushed himself away from the desk, one hand over his belly, pain contorting his face.

"Maria! Wait! I'm not asking you to become an assassin. I believe, in the wake of Raul's death, that it will be better to mislead him. If he trusts you, then perhaps you can convince him that all of this is nothing more than an elaborate heroin smuggling operation.

"I believe that's what he expected to find when he came here. So, confirm it for him. These islands are full of dope, most of it looking for a way to the States.

"So just blow smoke in his face. Make him think I'm running the biggest drug operation in the Caribbean.

"Can you do that?"

After a moment's silence, she replied.

"If I must."

"You must!

"We go this weekend, on Saturday. And with Raul's death, I no longer have the luxury of a backup pilot for the Harrier. You will fly for me, Maria, in the Lear."

Charlie coughed.

De Arrellano shifted his attention from Maria.

"Señor de Arrellano," Charlie began slowly, tilting his chair backward until it balanced precariously on two legs. "I still do not know what kind of mission you expect me to fly. And before I commit further I want assurance that there will be a place for me in your organization when this ...is finished."

De Arrellano glanced at Maria, then back at Charlie, his eyebrows high and his face strained.

"Captain Adkins, I assure you a position of grave responsibility and appropriate reward will await you. I give you my word."

Charlie laced his fingers and slipped his hands behind his head.

"Your word..." he said and smiled. "It's quite enough. But I would like to know what I have to do to earn the position of which you speak."

De Arrellano paused, cleared his throat, and stood up, slowly. He looked at a map on the wall behind him. Maria sat down, the electricity of anticipation evident in her breast, in Charlie, and to a lesser degree in the technicians. De Arrellano's breath came in short spurts as he leaned across the desk.

"I wish we had more time," he said. "But we don't. On Saturday, we shall take..."

He paused and drew a slow, deep breath.

"We shall take hostage the President of The United States of America!"

Chapter Thirty Seven

De Arrellano's voice was firm, his baritone strong and resonant. She heard his words, but they bounced about her brain like popcorn kernels in a hot skillet.

The President of The United States?

She had spent months preparing for an attack against the Colombian government. She had been using her skills, her intellect, and yes, her body, to establish a power base for her mission.

She wanted a revolution in Colombia.

But they were going to kidnap the President of The United States?

Why?

She heard her voice give vent to her question. It sounded like someone else speaking, someone distant, and hollow.

Jusquevera stared at her. He hadn't expected her outburst. He had assumed she would understand. His eyes panned the faces before him.

Surely they could see.

He looked back at Maria, a spark of anger now coloring his cheeks.

Maria's "Why?" echoed in his mind.

"Maria! Can't you see? We will hold in our hands the single most powerful man in the world."

"But...but..." she stammered.

"I thought we were going home," she said. "To...to fight for our birthright. What good can it do, as you say, to 'take' the President of The United States?"

Jusquevera didn't answer. He turned and walked to the window. He stood for a moment, his back to them. When he turned to face them again, his face was a resolute mask, a bas-relief of certainty.

"Look at our country, Maria. Even now it is torn apart. A penniless and powerless government, a left-wing guerrilla organization that kills civilians and serves no one but its generals. And the drug cartels, purveyors of misery. They seek American dollars, and they have a product greatly in demand. But in one way they are correct.

"The American dollar is the key.

"In Colombia now the government begs for American dollars. The cartels sell heroin and cocaine for American dollars. And the guerrilla's, well, they take what dollars they can.

"Soon El Carib will have all the dollars, enough to virtually buy Colombia. What we will get in ransom for the President will buy us our country...we won't need an armed revolution. Soon we will have a product even more in demand than the cartels' drugs.

"Think Maria! We speak not of millions, but billions of American dollars. We will fund, not a war, but a revolution of another kind, one that will give us back our Colombia.

"And yes, the U.S. will pay. The life of the world's most powerful man will be worth whatever we ask. All we want is money, and The United States has more than enough.

"That, Maria, is how we will win!"

And somehow it made sense, a disheveled, unruly sense.

Greed was the key, and certainly that was one trait shared by all who now held power in Colombia.

A clique of businessmen and farmers suddenly with the wealth of a nation could certainly purchase politicians and generals, and hold sway over a bankrupt military. And later they could field their own army to deal with the left wing, should such prove necessary.

It could work!

Jusquevera saw the color rise in Maria's cheeks.

"I understand," she said, her voice scarcely more than a whisper.

Charlie's face remained stony.

Was he not going to fly in battle after all? His thoughts flashed back to the images burned into his mind so long ago; his plane falling from the sun, shrieking over the tree-tops, those below looking up in awe and fear.

"Why my plane, then, if we're not on a mission of war?"

"You, Captain Adkins, are the tool that will pry the President from his environs. The President will be flying to Colombia Saturday morning. We will intercept him en route. The details are here."

He handed Charlie a manila folder. As he opened it, Maria could see aeronautical charts and typed itineraries.

"And Captain," Jusquevera continued, "If necessary afterward if some enclaves prove stubborn beyond the reach of money, your abilities will help further our cause."

Charlie looked up from the sheets on his lap and nodded.

He was smiling.

He would fly in combat. There would be at least two escorts for the President's plane. And the pilots would be excellent. But they wouldn't be good enough. Maybe no tree-tops yet, but the sun would be handy.

The meeting drew to a firm conclusion. Charlie went off to study the charts and agenda prepared for him. Maria returned to her room and spent much of Wednesday afternoon preparing herself for another seduction. Her mind flashed back to past times with Slats. She remembered his warmth and his prowess. And now he was alone on the island. Perhaps this assignment might be more pleasant than the last.

Chapter Thirty Eight

After seeing Olivia safely aboard Florida Flying Service's Piper Aztec ambulance, Slats returned to the Kittina. He walked to the bar, ordered a Johnny Walker and pulled himself onto a stool.

He glanced at his watch.

After four.

Wednesday afternoon.

He wanted to see de Arrellano again, to goad him further, maybe force him to react. Could he trick him into returning to the U.S.? In Miami, he might convince someone that De Arrellano was the man behind the takeover of the embassy in Bogota. Or if he could get him to New Orleans, he could, what? Parade him front of Courant?

Damn!

Tired! Not thinking. Need some rest.

De Arrellano can wait until morning.

Slats tossed off the whiskey, made his way to his room, shucked his clothes and fell onto the bed. He crunched the pillow beneath his head, mumbled "Goodnight Ollie," and fell instantly asleep.

A tapping awakened him.

The room was dark, except for the splash of moonlight falling through the balcony doors.

He listened for a moment.

The tapping repeated. Someone was knocking on his door. A glance at the bedside clock told him it was nine-fifteen. He had been asleep for several hours.

Tap-tap-tap!

More insistent this time.

Slats slipped his hand under the mattress and pulled out the big Ruger. Then with all the stealth his semi-asleep body could muster, he crept to the door and flattened himself against the wall.

"What is it?" he asked, his voice creeping into falsetto.

"Slats?"

It was a woman's voice.

"Yes?"

"Slats, it's Maria!"

Slats lowered the gun he had been holding in both hands before his face. He clicked on the light, grabbed his jeans from the floor and pulled them on, pressed the big blue gun back into space beneath the mattress, then pulled open the door with his left hand, pulling his shirt on with his right.

Maria looked at him across the threshold. She was wearing a loose fitting dress so dark she blended into the shadows of the foliage.

They stood without speaking, momentarily examining one another.

"May I come in?"

Slats stepped back into the room.

Maria watched him move and exclaimed, "You're injured!"

He glanced down at the bandaged foot and shrugged.

"I thought you'd left," he said. "Haven't seen you in the past couple of days."

Maria sat down in one of the ladder back chairs near the balcony door.

"Had to do some island hopping. How did you hurt your foot?"

"Long story."

"Did it happen when your wife got hurt?"

"How did you know about that?"

"A friend told me. Did it?"

Slats sat and propped his foot on the table. Talking about it had made him aware that it still hurt.

"No. Olivia was injured in a diving accident. I just stepped on something."

"Oh? And how about your shoulder?"

The right sleeve of his shirt had rolled when he pulled it on and exposed the wound where the Monofilament had sliced through his wetsuit.

"I got tangled in some fishing line. Nothing to worry about."

"And your wife?"

The questioning began to irritate. His answer was more brusque than he intended.

"She'll be okay. I've sent her home to her mother. She'll get first class care."

"And why are you still here?"

Maria could feel the exasperation in his reply.

"God knows, Maria! It's a long story. Not worth going into at this time of night."

Maria stared at him, and he returned the gaze, coolly at first. He smiled slowly.

"You look awfully good, lady. I swear you haven't changed in twenty years.

She tilted her head back and laughed.

"Oh yes, I have, and more than you could know."

She studied him, her gaze sweeping him from head to toe.

"And I wish I could say the same about you. But you look like you've just showered in home-made sin. Why don't you clean up a bit? They're still serving in the dining room."

Slats realized he was, indeed, hungry. He also realized that the lovely, dark woman sitting across from him still intrigued him. Something in her eyes reminded him of times past, times when that spark had been for him. He remembered her face framed by the narrow iron pickets surrounding the Greco-styled seal house at the old Audubon Park Zoo; the sparkle in her eyes as she laughed at the antics of the great bellowing bull herding his harem about at feeding time.

"He looks just like Boulevard," she said, grinning. "Big, black, and very ugly. But he'd just die without his women."

Slats heaved himself from the chair to stand before the mirror. He saw a bedraggled, unshaven man, still lean and well muscled, but slouched with exhaustion.

He stuck a furred tongue at the apparition in the mirror.

"All right. Give me a few minutes to get human again."

He dug into the dresser for clean clothes and headed for the bathroom. Minutes later he stood again before the mirror and admired the transformation. Looking back was a tall man in tan Duck Heads and white Polo tennis shirt stretched across a well-shaped chest. He splashed a bit of Tabac on his cheeks and winked at himself.

"Liar," he muttered, then turned to Maria.

"Well?"

She hesitated a moment.

"Not too shabby," she said, holding out her arm, elbow crooked.

As he hooked his arm over hers, she turned to him and raised up on her toes. She brushed her lips across his cheek, and they came to rest on his mouth.

Her aroma and her warmth flashed through him. Feelings for two decades confined to fantasy flooded his chest and sparked like white light behind his eyes. She was suddenly an ache deep in his belly, an ache he knew no meal would ease.

"I've missed you, you know, for a very long time!" he said.

"And I've missed you," she whispered.

But!

There were other things to consider now; chief among them Olivia. He pictured his wife in the tiny cabin of a little airplane streaking across the Gulf of Mexico. There was also his vastly improved career and his current involvement in a seemingly bizarre plot that might endanger the President of The United States.

He wondered how Olivia was faring. She should be touching down at New Orleans International airport very soon, where she would be whisked across 15 miles of Jefferson Parish to Oschner Hospital. Slats felt a twinge of guilt that he would not be by her side. But, her mother would be. It had been right to send her home, and he had to be here. He had not questioned his decision to remain. He had to be on Grand Turk.

But with Maria?

Slats never questioned his love for his wife, or for his children.

But Maria?

The surge that pounded in his breast threatened to sweep him from the shallows, to trap him in the rip tide and pull him under.

Maria had been a part of his life for so long, and his feelings were so different from the love he felt for Olivia. The fantasies had taught him that. It was as if the women lived in separate rooms in the attic of his soul. And one was real while the other was but a dream. She was a dream even when her flesh warmed his belly, and her scent filled his throat.

The old James Bond movie theme blared through his mind.

"You only life twice, one life for yourself...one for your dreams..."

The Kittina dining room was virtually empty. They seated themselves near the courtyard archway. A waitress in a bright green blouse and dark slacks hustled to the table, informing them that only prepared entries were still available.

When Slats ordered lobster for two, she stared at him for several seconds.

"I'll see," she said, impatience etching her voice, and vanished into the kitchen. She returned only moments later.

"Okay," she said.

Slats wanted to reply with a quote from Bart Simpson, but choked on his silliness, and instead ordered a New York state Chablis from the short wine list.

Maria lifted an eyebrow and when the waitress left, asked, "Are we having a party?"

Light from the large candle, garish in its green glass container tucked off on the side of the table against the stucco wall, flickered in Maria's dark eyes as he leaned forward to touch her hand.

"Yes, it's a party, a reunion party. We didn't have much of a chance to ...to communicate the other day."

"On the boat?"

She squeezed his hand.

"How will this evening end? I think I know," she whispered.

"Maybe yes, maybe no," he said, pulling his hand back.

"But, whatever happens, it's the one evening we've had in twenty years, and it may be the only evening we'll ever have."

Slats felt the words tumbling from his throat and thought how strangely prophetic they felt.

Maria didn't reply. She sat quietly, looking into Slats' eyes, and squeezed his hand again. She held it that way for several moments, until the waitress returned, a chilled bottle in a wicker cradle.

Slats went perfunctorily through the routine of sampling and approving the wine, and the waitress filled both glasses brimful, then departed.

Slats sat with his tanned arms folded across one another, the skin dark in the dim light of the candlelit tabletop.

He searched Maria's eyes.

"Are you looking for something?" she asked.

"You. Just you. Will you spend this one night with me, Maria?"

She replied without hesitation.

"Of course."

He continued to study her face.

"I wish I could say it will be like the old days, but we both know that we've changed in the years since you left. What will it be like to make love to you?"

"It sounds like you're planning a scientific experiment. Will you make love to me out of curiosity?"

He shook his head.

"I carry no computers to bed," he said, then smiled. "Unless they're black leather and lace."

"Aha. A kinky cop? You wouldn't be the first one you know," Maria leaned back in her chair, giggling quietly.

Slats remembered the brazenness of Maria's humor, and the vision jarred him. He shivered, his laughter gone.

"Maria," his tone now quiet, serious, "what are you doing here?"

Maria's smile faded as well

"You mean here with you, or here in the islands?"

"Both. I'm having difficulty believing that you're here on vacation. What gargantuan twist of fate has thrown you back into my life after all these years, and at a time like this."

"A time like this?" she asked, the question hanging unanswered momentarily before she continued. "Didn't buy my story of sun, sand, and solitude, huh?" she asked.

"Not you, Maria. You're not a loner. Never were, never will be. You're here...here on Grand Turk because of a person, and not to get away from a person. Am I right?"

Maria sighed.

"Of course," she said, "You know I'm a sucker for a good looking man."

Slats knew she meant to tease, but he didn't return her smile.

The darkness in the dining room seemed to close in on them. It was swallowing Maria as she leaned back in her chair. Slats thrust his face forward into the candlelight.

"And the good-looking guy on Grand Turk? Could his name be de Arrellano?"

Maria started as though someone had slapped her face. Her body tightened across her frame like a rubber band. How could Slats associate her with de Arrellano?

Slats watched her composure return, a jigsaw puzzle of emotions testing the muscles of her cheeks and chin. She leaned forward, her face no more than inches from Slats', candlelight shadows hiding her eyes.

"I...I'm working for him," she said. "I didn't know you knew him."

"I don't, not really. He flew down on the plane with us." Should he tell her of his suspicions? "You're working for him?"

"Yes," she said, slowly, studying Slats' face.

Would her own eyes betray her?

"General Dynamics...de Arrellano hired me to manage the office here. But..."

"But?" he echoed

"But..." she repeated.

"What?" he asked, insistent.

She hesitated again. Will he see the act?

"I don't know exactly what's going on, but General Dynamics isn't what it seems," she said.

Bingo, Slats thought.

"There's a load of equipment to be shipped to the states soon," she said. "But it's going by barge."

"So?" he asked.

"It's supposed to be computer stuff. Would you deliver computer equipment by barge? It should be going by air. Computer equipment shouldn't spend weeks on a barge traveling across miles of salt water, should it?

"But they're loading a barge, and it's over in the Caicos," she said.

Slats said nothing. He wondered at her admission. Did she really not know what de Arrellano was doing or was this all an act?

She took his hand.

"I think they're smuggling drugs into the States," she said, "A lot of drugs!"

"Damn!"

Slats muttered under his breath. He didn't know what he had expected from Maria, but it wasn't an admission of complicity, albeit unconscious complicity.

"The first major shipment of equipment is supposed to arrive this weekend," she said. "It's part of a towboat cargo from Miami. But before the barge gets here it's stopping at Provo in South

Caicos. I heard one of the men say the barge would be loaded with 'blow' before it gets here."

"But how does that fit in with de Arrellano, with Computer Dynamics?"

"When the equipment arrives some of it will be found 'damaged.' But when the crates are put back on the barge, they won't contain equipment."

"How did you learn all this, Maria?"

Maria smiled.

"One of the supervisors drinks too much. He's just a small hood, but he thinks his exploits impress me. And he wants to get into my pants."

Slats sat with his chin in his hands.

It made a strange kind of sense. Drugs were the most logical explanation. It could all be just some convoluted Caribbean connection. There was no plot against the country, no terrorist bent on killing the President.

It's just a new, elaborate cocaine pipeline.

Most illicit drugs making their way into the southern U.S. crossed the Gulf on ships, rusty tubs carrying timber or bagged cargo routinely from Mobile, Tampa, New Orleans to South America, returning with holds packed with coke or heroin, cargoes that were off-loaded on calm, dark nights onto cigarette boats too fast for Coast Guard or police patrols to catch.

Here was a new vehicle. Blue-water tows were carrying more and more diverse cargo, delivering goods quicker, cheaper, and into more shallow water ports than could the massive container ships. The tows often received little more than a cursory inspection from customs officers.

A smart smuggler could indeed find ways to transport tons of stuff in seagoing barges.

So he had been wrong.

There was no national security threat. Old Boulevard's ramblings were meaningless; code words perhaps keyed to some particular phase of the operation. But some switch deep in Slats' cerebellum refused to close. Doubt continued to flow down an emotional stream that logic refused to dam.

"Can you help?" Maria asked.

It took a moment for Maria's question to register.

"Oh...Maria..."

His gaze sought her eyes.

"I'll try. I'm not sure what I can do."

"You're not here on vacation either, are you Slats?"

The waitress's arrival halted their conversation and changed their mindsets. She placed the lobster tray between them, the two spiny crustaceans steaming on a bed of greens, surrounded by small white condiment dishes.

Slats broke open one of the shellfish, slid a steaming tail onto a small plate and offered it to Maria while the waitress filled their wine glasses and quietly departed.

Slats felt ravenous. He savored the first bite, but when he looked up, Maria was staring at him.

"You're right, Maria," he said, washing down the lobster with half his glass of wine. "I came looking for ...well...a smuggling operation. It was something that started back home...when Boulevard died, as a matter of fact.

Slats felt he was choking on the words, but the words were logical. And what Maria had told him supported the logic. His theories didn't.

"What will you do?" she asked.

Slats took another bite of lobster and chewed thoughtfully.

"I'll go to South Caicos. I need to see the barge being loaded. Then when it heads for the states, I'll contact the FBI. The agency can get the Coast Guard to shadow it. They might even be able to find it with a satellite. It is amazing some of the things the feds can do these days.

"When it makes port the Bureau can move on it."

He thought for a moment.

"I guess that's about all I can do," he said. And certainly not what I had expected to do, he thought.

"What ?" Maria asked

He realized he must have voiced the last thought.

"Nothing...just mumbling in my lobster."

Her gaze made him wonder how he looked chewing on a mouthful of lobster. Were his cheeks bulging? Was he a little bug-eyed?

Maria was speaking to him.

"Why, do you think, has fate brought us together again?" she asked.

Slats stopped his attack on the lobster and stared at the face, so darkly beautiful in they half-light across the table. He knew the face even now as well as he knew his own. But did he know the creature whose emotions manipulated that face? Did he ever know her?

"Is it fate, Maria? I don't know."

Hesitantly, he added. "But I'm still in love with you."

"You're married," she said, a simple statement of fact.

"Yes," he replied, feeling the heaviness in his voice.

"And I love my wife and children very much. I even love my mother-in-law. But ...it seems...nothing can change the way I feel about you. What I felt in the past...I still feel."

They sat, staring at each other, trance-like. The very air about them seemed to reverberate with the unsaid. The poignancy of the question was acrid on her tongue as Maria searched for words.

"Would you...?" she began and paused.

"What?" Slats asked.

A taste like chicory crimped her lips. Why ask? She knew the answer. And she didn't want to hear him say it. It made little difference. Her future held no place for him.

"Never mind," she replied. "It's not important." She pushed away from the table.

"I've had enough lobster."

She picked up and drained her glass. "And wine."

She looked at Slats and stretched her hand toward him.

"But I am still hungry."

Slats felt his heart accelerate, and he tried for a moment, unsuccessfully, to find a reason for the flush he felt spreading across his face. Why should this woman still excite him so? He was no longer a callow young cop awash in hormones. He had enjoyed the sexual favors of several women, beautiful and intelligent girls with whom he had shared some intense pleasures. And he had found great satisfaction in his marriage, physical and emotional.

But....

He could not deny the hurricane of need and desire that Maria's presence unleashed in him.

He forced himself to be methodical, to pick up the check, compute and add an appropriate tip, inscribe his room number, and sign it. He stood slowly, took Maria's still outstretched hand, and walked with her from the dining hall. Neither spoke as they crossed the courtyard, mounted the stairs, and followed the sweep of the mezzanine to his room.

He led her across the darkened room and switched on the bed lamps. She stepped out of her shoes, nuzzled her face against his chest through his open shirt, and said she wanted to shower.

"I'd like to join you," he responded.

Moments later they were standing, her naked back to his belly, under the warm spray. He picked up the miniature bar of Camay and began lathering her body, remembering the smooth, taut flow of her muscles across hips and thighs, the soft roundness of her breasts. She accepted his ministrations for a few moments; they stepped away into the force of the shower. She took the soap and began to lather his body, her hands playing across his nipples and working their way together to his penis.

He was erect now, and she toyed with him, her soapy fingers quick and gentle.

He signed deeply, then slipped his arms beneath hers and lifted. He pushed his body forward, pinioning her against the plastic wall, his face next to hers, his penis probing her thighs. She lifted her legs, wrapping them around his waist. Then she reached down and helped him enter. She cried softly and bit at his neck as he thrust. He slapped her buttocks against the wall with each stroke, oblivious to the water that poured across their faces and to the raucous thumping of the shower stall.

Orgasmic electricity coursed through his body, and his pulsing deep inside her triggered her climax.

The fire burned slowly away, and Slats felt his body begin to relax. The water rushing over him seemed to carry his essence gurgling down the drain.

"Stand up, Maria, please. Before I fall on you."

They became again separate people, toweling dry on the cold tile, looking at one another, sharing a clear sense of wonder.

Chapter Thirty Nine

Thursday dawned warm and golden.

It reminded Slats of the days he had loved as a teen in New Orleans, a hazy summer morning on its way to a steamy noon, the sky a bowl full of sunshine, the earth hot enough to bake your feet.

He and Maria lazed in bed well past the breakfast hour, making love again while the sounds of the hotel came to life around them. The diving vans packed with equipment and people clattered up the street below their window, and voices rose and faded.

It had taken three tries before he was able to get a telephone connection to Oschner Hospital. The hospital's patient advocate told him Olivia was out of surgery, and doing well, but was sleeping.

Slats wondered how he would have responded had Olivia been able to speak to him. Could he lie next to Maria and tell Olivia that he loved her?

He knew he did, of course. He loved his wife and knew his love was returned. But would Olivia's love remain should she discover that Maria was more than a fantasy?

He turned over and stared at Maria, who returned his gaze, her eyes soft and inviting.

Slats shoved aside the cloud that threatened to shade his golden summer day and asked Maria to spend the rest of it with him. She agreed.

"But tomorrow I must work," she said.

When they dressed, Maria ducking next door for a change of clothes, and went down, the dining room had closed. They breakfasted in the courtyard on hot tea and toast.

They borrowed snorkeling gear, rented the hotel's last bicycles, decrepit cruisers with rusty chains and rims, and headed across the island. They stopped for sandwich makings at the island supermarket, a single-aisle, block building cooled by an overhead fan that clanked noisily as it stirred the salty dust. The place smelled of limes, fresh fish, and old meat.

Pedaling across the spine of the island, they stopped briefly to examine the panorama of Grand Turk. The town ambled along the western shoreline, square block buildings in white, shell pink and mango skin green, bordered inland by the salt ponds. Square impoundments that looked like they should be growing crops, they filled with the sea with each high tide. The only break in the visual monotony was a small church, its steeple an exclamation mark against the etched gray salt pond quilt.

"Not much to see, is there?" Slats asked, kicking his bike into squeaking motion.

They found a sheltered half-moon cove near the south end of the island with water sufficiently shallow to snorkel comfortably. A smooth limestone boulder provided them a picnic spot, where they spread their bread and sausage and warm strawberry soda.

They spoke little, watching one another closely, always on the verge of speaking, but finding no words. After they had eaten, they snorkeled, poking about the shallows, Maria excitedly pointing out an octopus devouring a large crab. Myriad tiny striped fish hovered, waiting for scraps from the cephalopod's meal.

They tried, clumsily, to make love in the water. But fins and masks and snorkels rattled their passion, and they gave up, laughing. They settled for a bit of petting and the promise of a more appropriate setting back at the Kittina.

They clambered atop their limestone perch, spent several minutes massaging sunblock on their backs, legs, and arms, enjoying the tactile ambiance of fingers and sea breeze, sun and oil. The sun gleamed on Maria's dark skin. She stretched across the rock and closed her eyes.

Slats sat next to her, one leg folded against his body, the other parallel to hers.

"Slats?"

"Yes."

"What are you going to do?"

"What?"

"What are you going to do...after?"

"After?"

"When you...when you finish here?"

Slats paused a moment.

"I'll go home."

Slats listened to the water washing the beach, a few gulls mewing in the background. He smelled the ocean, vaguely acrid and salty, and the aroma of sunblock, sun, and flesh.

"Slats?"

She lifted her head and looked at him.

"Would you leave your wife for me?"

Slats stared at her for a moment, then leaned down on his right elbow to touch her cheek with his left hand.

"Would you want me to...really?"

She thought for a moment, then draped her arms across her eyes.

"No," she replied, softly. "No, I would not."

She giggled.

"Imagine me and some ancient cop. No. You're not bad as a lover, but you could never be a good husband."

"Why don't you come back to the city?" Slats asked. "We could see each other ..."

She lifted her arm from her eyes and slipped her hand behind his neck.

"The City that Care Forgot?" she said. "Be your mistress. Thank you, but no. I've been a mistress. Professionally ..." she hesitated, "I couldn't be your mistress and have you always running back to your pretty wife.

"Funny...but I thought that was supposed to be the wife's line. No, I can't go back to New Orleans, even for you. I've cut my ties with my past. I don't want to dig up any more than what you've already unearthed. You...you're one of the few good things from my past. So, I'll keep you as you were then, and as you are now, but...but not as you would be back there.

"Besides...I have a purpose now. A good... job, and, I think, a unique future."

"Unless I close down Computer Dynamics." Slats said.

"Oh, I don't think it will work out that way," she replied.

"What do you mean?" Slats asked.

She pulled his face to hers and kissed him.

"Tell you next week," she said. She released his neck and sat up.

"It's getting late. Hadn't we better get back?"

Chapter Forty

"Fantastic fucking Friday," Slats muttered to himself. He sat on the edge of his bed, trying to apply a band-aid to the ball of his right foot. The wound was healing, but it still hurt when he walked. And he felt as though he had tramped the length of the island, although he had walked only through what passes for Grand Turk's business district. It had been his first task of the morning.

He had sought police assistance to, he told the elderly bureaucrat at the Bureau of Justice and Security, to quash one of the largest smuggling operations ever to run dope into The United States.

The venerable black man in the spotless uniform hadn't been impressed. He accepted Slats' identification and listened to his story. But when Slats finished, the man shook his white-crested head.

"I'm sorry, sir. What you say is fascinating, but of little consequence. I am aware of the rumors that say our islands are havens for smugglers, but I have no evidence.

"And if I had evidence, I could do little. I have but a dozen men to cover as many islands, to maintain security for some precious real estate."

"Director," Slats asked, "If I can provide hard evidence, will you furnish men?"

The old man smiled and shrugged.

"I would discuss it with my superiors."

He turned to gaze out the window overlooking the dusty sandstone street and the blue water beyond, and Slats knew the interview was over. Of course, you'll discuss it with your superiors, Slats thought, wondering which governmental pocket had the silver lining.

Slats knew that photos of barges loaded with potential contraband were the only evidence he might reasonably expect to acquire. So he needed a camera, something other than his Nikonis, which took fine underwater images but would be useless for his current clandestine needs. So he had gone in search of a camera, hoping to find a 35mm with a telephoto lens.

But the only thing he found on the island, besides another Nikonis, was a cheap off-brand. The price was ridiculous, but he bought it anyway. He'd put it on his expense account when he got home. He was using it to protect taxpayers, wasn't he?

Slats took his new camera and had tried to make a Saturday morning reservation on the island service flight to South Caicos.

"I'll take your name sir, but the plane has engine trouble, and I can't promise it will fly tomorrow," the clipped but feminine voice on the phone had said. "Please check with the airport in the morning."

So as the afternoon slipped away, Slats sat on the edge of his bed, muttering obscenities and doctoring his sore foot. He finished applying the band-aid. It still hurt.

He sat, hoping the phone would ring. Maria had promised to call if she heard that the shipment was to be delayed. And Olivia's mother should be calling soon to report on Olivia's status. But the telephone was silent, and there had been no message in his box on his return from the morning trek.

He picked up the phone to call New Orleans. Even his mother-in-law's voice would provide some comfort.

"Sorry sir," the operator said. "The microwave is down, and we are temporarily without service to the states. Please try later."

"Damn! Damn! Damn!" Slats slammed the receiver down.

He rocked himself up, ignoring the pain in his foot.

It was time to go to the bar.

Chapter Forty One

While Slats ambled to the bar intending to relieve his frustration with a scotch and water, Jim Cavanaugh found himself in the midst of a meeting he had hoped to avoid.

The President sat in the center of a large divan, his back to a vast expanse of plate glass, twenty-one stories above suburban Miami, in the Hilton's appropriately designated Presidential suite. In a chair at his right sat Erik Grosvenor. The President had reached him from the plane, and he had followed them down on an afternoon flight. The President had followed Jim's itinerary through the evening reception while Jim set up the meeting, bringing in Secretary of State Frederick Brown, and Colombian attaché, Enrique Cervantes.

Cervantes was assessing for the President the militants holding the embassy.

"We know little about the organization, Mr. President," he said. "El Carib has been more of a rumor than a reality. It is said to have been responsible for the deaths of some highly placed individuals in our government over the last 20 years, although most have attributed those assassinations to the leftists guerrillas we have battled for so long. There has, in fact, been little proof that El Carib exists, until now that is. And no, El Carib does not appear to be connected to the guerrillas.

"And we don't know what their objective is in holding the hostages. Our government cannot give in to their blackmail and release prisoners, criminals who have been convicted in the courts of nefarious crimes."

The President nodded, then asked, "Could you agree to any of their demands?"

Cervantes shrugged.

"I have no instructions. We were not aware of their demand to negotiate with you until now."

"I know. The message came directly from the embassy in Bogota."

The President paused. "One more question. Would your government afford me protection in Bogotá if I choose to meet with these...people?"

Cervantes passed his hands across his temples, sweeping his long, black hair back.

"Well, of course," he replied. "There are more than just your people inside that building. We will cooperate in every way possible."

"Well Fred, Erik...what do you think?"

The burly Fred Browne pulled an empty pipe from the corner of his mouth. He spoke as though he were putting the words on paper, carefully, distinctly.

"Aside from concerns for your personal safety, sir, if you succeed it might open a few doors into Latin America that now seem locked, or unreasonably expensive."

The President was aware of Colombia's request for three billion dollars in aid money, ostensibly to fight the increasing drug traffic.

"And if your efforts bear no fruit, well... " Browne continued, "we are none the worse for the effort. Just your presence in the hemisphere could bolster our image as a neighbor."

He sat back. He had said his final word on the subject.

The President looked to his right.

Dammit, Erik, don't blow this one for us. Jim Cavanaugh almost voiced the thought and smothered it in a long sigh. The President glanced at him, then back to Erik. The dour face was expressionless. But the words flowed easily from his lips, so easily they could have been prepared text.

"Mr. President. We have had only a few operatives in Colombia in recent years. The country has been relatively stable, politically. Since the National Front parties were established in the fifties, and their successors followed in the seventies and eighties, the governments have been solid, although not particularly solvent. Only the left wing rebels have caused any major problems, and even that insurgency is contained. A few splinter organizations have tried through ineffectual movements to convince the populace that the parties were fronts for some underground Junta, rich military men who run the country.

"But...most Colombians are as politically blasé as most Americans if you'll pardon the analogy in the midst of an election campaign."

"What you're saying, Erik, the President interjected, "is that you don't know any more about it than we do, right?"

Grosvenor drew himself up to his full five-feet-six-inches. "We think El Carib is one of those splinter organizations and that this is their way of gaining notoriety. It would be an, excuse me for putting it this way, a coup for them to get the President of The United States to bargain with them."

"Erik, I don't believe they would harm the President," Jim said, intervening.

"I do not want him in that embassy," Grosvenor said. "Close quarters! We can't cover him."

Cervantes offered a solution.

"We can set up an arena in the street in front of the embassy. The El Carib people can meet the President there, in front of television cameras, where the whole world can watch."

"But would they agree to that?" Jim asked. He liked the idea of the whole world watching.

"I believe they would see it to their advantage. They still have all of their hostages in the embassy, and no one would try to harm their people with the President on the spot as well," Cervantes replied.

Grosvenor said nothing, but nodded, his jowls bouncing.

"Then I shall go to Colombia. Fred, get the plane." the President said. The plane, of course, was Air Force One. The trip was not part of the campaign. This trip was business.

Chapter Forty Two

Slats was on the corner stool in the Kittina's inside bar when the "CBS News Special" announcement logo popped onto the screen of the small television behind the bar. It interrupted "All My Children" and the hard-faced girl halfheartedly drying glasses in the semi-darkness uttered an expletive not intended to describe bedclothes.

Slats slid from his stool and walked around the end of the bar. Just as he turned the volume up, a man who looked like a young Roger Mudd filled the screen.

"...and the President, in Miami for a speech before the American Federation of Labor, has asked for this news conference to discuss the hostage situation at the U.S. Embassy in Bogota, Colombia."

Slats returned to his stool. His drink empty, he tapped the glass against his front teeth and chewed the ice chips.

The hard-faced girl looked at Slats.

He held his glass out toward her. "It's the President," he said.

"Whose?" she asked.

"Mine," he replied, shaking his glass to emphasize its emptiness.

The President was on the screen now, looking his usual steely-gray self. He strode across the small room to the podium and was motioning for those in the audience to be seated. His face wore an expression of concern, and when he spoke, his voice rumbled even through the television's tiny speaker.

He outlined the hostage situation, reviewing the chronology.

More than two weeks of negotiations had produced no agreement. One person died in the take-over, and the lives of others remained in the balance.

"There was little hope for successful negotiation with this organization, this El Carib, until today," the President said, the pitch of his powerful voice rising.

The bartendress placed the tall glass before Slats. He couldn't help noticing the swell of her breasts above the bandeau top of her dress. Mahogany in the dim light, they looked as hard as her face. He wondered what would happen in he rapped them with his knuckles. Would they have the hollow ring of an old wooden door? Surely her face would.

The camera zoomed on the President's face. He looked cool and composed as he held up a small, yellow sheaf of paper.

"This morning I received through our foreign service office this message from the militants."

He recited the words that he had now committed to memory.

Slats watched more closely as the camera pulled to a medium shot and the President placed the paper on the podium. He looked back into the camera.

"After much consideration, and discussion with those closest to the situation, I have decided that I shall go to Colombia!"

Slats felt startled. Is the President going to Colombia? Surely that could be dangerous.

Could he accomplish anything by such a trip?

And why would a Colombian militant group ask to negotiate with the President of The United States?

He wondered about the security precautions that would be in place to protect the best-known man in the world.

Cop reflexes, Slats thought.

I should be thinking about covering my ass on South Caicos tomorrow. With the thought came an uneasy vibration, a qualm he could not identify.

If I even get to South Caicos, the way the damn planes work down here. Perhaps a boat would be better. Slats drained the glass, wanting another, but instead nurtured the slight buzz. He sucked an ice cube as he watched the youthful Mudd image reiterate the President's remarks.

"And," the image intoned in practiced timbre, "in a statement the White House indicates the President will leave Homestead Air Force Base at nine tomorrow morning on Air Force One. He expects to begin negotiations no later than Sunday morning."

Well. The President and I'll both be flying tomorrow. Slats couldn't keep the cynicism from his thoughts.

Maybe arranging for a boat would be prudent. Where would South Caicos lie from here? Slats remembered the chart he had stuffed in his luggage. It should still be in his flight bag. He could check the lay of the land when he went back to his room. But first, a little supper.

He had hoped Maria would appear. She had said she probably would not return until late, but he wanted company.

He picked a courtyard table near the entrance, watching the overgrown walk from the drive. He wouldn't miss Maria if she returned while he dined. He found the whiskey buzz still with him, and the President's speech kept repeating, in the form of television sound bites, in his head. The President's promise to fly to Bogotá bothered him. His unease was vague, indefinable, but definite.

It has to be de Arrellano.

Why is he here?

If Slats was right and de Arrellano was the man behind the embassy takeover in Bogotá, why was he on Grand Turk? Shouldn't he be in Colombia to negotiate with the President?

True, he isn't well, but he's not so ill that he couldn't have flown to Colombia.

Perhaps it isn't the same person.

Maria must be right. De Arrellano's a Colombian drug lord developing a new pipeline to the U.S.; nothing more, nothing less.

He would have proof of that tomorrow.

If the planes fly, or the boat floats. Or pigs sail.

He had to get to South Caicos and get some pictures. Then he could, perhaps, persuade the Turks and Caicos officialdom to detain de Arrellano.

And he could find out if all men named de Arrellano look alike.

When ten o'clock passed with no sign of Maria, and his meal beginning to digest pleasantly, Slats climbed the stairs to his room. He mustered a small reserve of energy and packed his aluminum-sided camera case, replacing the Nikonis and its array of lenses and attachments with the off-brand camera, his big blue Ruger forty-four magnum, and the tiny twenty-two.

He had hefted the big gun before he stored it beneath the foam packing in the case. Larger and clumsier than his nickel-plated Beretta, it was difficult for close work but awe inspiring against open field targets. And he didn't intend to get close enough to the barge to need the Beretta. He dug out his Bahamas chart and placed it on the case. He would study it in the morning while waiting to see if the island hopper would fly.

Shucking his clothes in a heap, he crawled into bed and fell into a restless, irritated sleep peopled by scuba diving caricatures of his wife in a body cast from toe to hip, and of a tall, thin Latin, who smoked dope inside his diving mask. Maria was there too, alongside the Latino, laughing with him as they pointed at Slats.

He awoke, metal-mouthed and thirsty, with the cusp of nightmare hanging on the edges of his vision. He stepped out onto the balcony, the warm night air caressing his shoulders and thighs. The waist-high railing assured his privacy, and he sat in one of the nylon mesh outdoor chairs.

The mesh bit into his skin.

Trying to think, to creatively sort the hundreds of logic bits that would, he hoped, produce a picture of international drug trafficking, he opened himself to the ambient world; the warmth of the breeze, the multitude of stars crowding the early morning sky, the whisper of the near calm surf.

But where he sought a picture of organized crime, there appeared a vision of his wife instead. Olivia lay warm and contented in his arms. It had been in Olivia's bed, in her apartment, after they first made love.

They had spent the day in the sun, sailing Hobie cats, and worn themselves out. Or so they had thought. It was their fifth day together, and they had spent it holding the tiny cat to a wet and flying streak across Lake Pontchartrain's muddy waves. Sometime during that day, sometime in the midst of salt spray and sunburn, they knew they would wind up in bed together.

And if that worked...the potential...

Slats drifted, and, this time, memory, sharp and savory, supplanted fantasy. And he slept.

Chapter Forty Three

In the hangar, Computer Dynamics fluorescents burned all night. Technicians checked and rechecked the Harrier's every system and instrument. They spent hours removing the phony nose and fuselage accouterments with which they had tried to disguise the craft. Charlie wanted nothing to detract from the plane's abilities. It had to be, as he drummed into Maria during her training, one with him when he flew into combat. His fingers had to feel what the ailerons felt, his toes what the rudder felt.

Jusquevera, walking but often with a grimace creasing his face, reviewed with Maria and Charlie details of plans for the next morning.

Jusquevera sensed Maria's uneasiness, and it disturbed him. It had to be the American, he thought. A former lover (why did he have to be a cop) to whom she had told the big lie. She had obviously been convincing. Slats had booked or tried to book passage on the island-hopper to South Caicos. It was going to be easier to fool the cop than to kill him. Too bad he hadn't realized that before sending Raul to a useless and painful death.

Jusquevera blinked back his remorse. There was no place for such sentiment now. The risks that lay immediately ahead were grave. But the reward, the potential, immeasurable.

He tried to assess the depth of Maria's discomfort. He wished, momentarily, he had made her his mistress when first she arrived on the island. It's always easier to read, if not to understand, the emotions of a lover. And he felt a distinct need to know what troubled her. Not for a moment did he doubt that she would have accepted his sexual overtures and the emotional bond they entailed.

He knew she shared his need for the country, and for revenge. Nor did he doubt her commitment to achieving that end. But she had balked at the means when first he announced the objective of their mission. She had questioned the reasons for kidnapping the President of The United States.

She had seemed to accept the reasoning; the strength of the bargaining chip El Carib would hold when it held the most recognized man in the world.

Maria acknowledged the power of the gambit.

Was her problem then just with the New Orleans cop?

"Slats isn't part of our war," she had said.

"Sometimes, in war, even children die," Jusquevera had replied. But he had not made a second attempt on the man's life.

And still Maria seemed uncomfortable. It wasn't fear. He had never sensed fear in her. It was disapproval. And Jusquevera remained worried. Even if she had to do nothing more than fly for him in the little Lear, she had to do that competently.

She sensed his foreboding.

"I don't want to die tomorrow," she said.

Only Charlie seemed comfortable. He exuded confidence.

The mission thrilled him. It gave him a sense of power he hadn't felt since flight training. Tomorrow he would be one of the most powerful people on Earth. He would hold in his hand the life of the President of The United States; to order his fate, and the fate of the world, with the press of a tiny button. Come Saturday morning, Charlie would fly as he had never flown before. He would be the eagle sweeping from the sun, the power of a god in his hands.

Charlie smiled as Jusquevera reviewed the Saturday schedule.

The President and his party would depart Homestead Air Force Base south of Miami at nine Saturday morning on board

Air Force One. The flight path would follow the archipelago giving substantial room to Cuban airspace, and make a stop in Puerto Rico.

An estimated five-hundred mile an hour cruise speed placed Air Force One and its escort (two F/A-18s) in the vicinity of Grand Turk at ten a.m. Charlie would take the Harrier aloft thirty minutes before, and hold near the plane's sixty-thousand foot maximum altitude. Jusquevera and Maria would depart at the same time, and fly a search pattern to the north. On both planes, newly installed radios would be scanning military and civilian frequencies. There was a slight possibility they could miss the President's flight in the restrictive corridor, but Jusquevera discounted that possibility.

The mission plan called for Jusquevera to order Air Force One to Salt Cay. His message would alert the escort fighters, and it was up to Charlie to disarm them ("you mean to shoot them down, right?") and then to assume the escort service.

The Air Force pilot would, at first, refuse to land Air Force One on Salt Cay, but Jusquevera believed that a burst across the big plane's nose would convince him. Jusquevera and Raul had painstakingly measured more than two miles of ten-inch deep salt ponds to be the President's runway, ponds that were now abandoned and stagnating.

Charlie was to put the Harrier down next to Air Force One, weapons trained on the President's plane. Jusquevera felt certain that knowledge of the Harrier's destructive capabilities would be sufficient to deter resistance by the President's Secret Service guards.

The plan called for the President to walk to the Harrier, take the front seat, and return with Charlie to Grand Turk. There Jusquevera would broadcast his initial demands for a fifty-billion-dollar ransom.

Shortly after that, Maria and Jusquevera would depart for Colombia in the Lear. Charlie and the President would follow.

Charlie was unconcerned about the possibility of the Air Force blowing the Lear to pieces under them.

"Even if the President were willing to martyr himself, the people who make such a decision would have to answer to the public. We could have grandchildren, Maria before they could make that decision."

"Charlie?"

Charlie smiled and nodded.

"Maria?"

"I'll be ready," she said, a bit too quickly, Jusquevera thought. He looked at her closely.

It had been a long time since he had shared a woman's love. Maria had impressed him the moment she had stepped from the Lear to the hot tarmac. The lithe muscles that carried her body so easily spoke to him of hips and thighs, of prowess that might drain a man's libido as quickly as it drained his testicles. In the small sterile metal office, seated now only inches from her on a folding chair, he couldn't avoid her scent.

He met her eyes. He thought he saw in the reflection of the overhead fluorescent lights above a mutual need. Her body would feel so good against his. He leaned back in the chair and closed his eyes. Pain welled up in his belly and overwhelmed the ache above it.

No, lovemaking was not for him. Not tonight. There would be better nights, later after tomorrow, after it was all over. There would be luxury then; golden bathrooms and soft beds, music, and wine. There would be time to heal, time to love, and time to laugh.

There would be a time.

But it was not now.

For tonight, rest. They must rise with the dawn, refreshed and alert.

So Jusquevera sighed a sigh that rose from belly and libido, and passed to Maria and Charlie each a small pill guaranteed, he said, to assure a night of sound sleep. Maria patted his shoulder as she followed Charlie from the room.

Chapter Forty Four

The mockingbird awakened Slats.

The sky was a chalky white, misty, with a bit of hazy blue directly overhead. The bird perched on the balcony rail, apparently watching Slats, singing strongly and melodically, summoning the sun. As if on cue the white sky flared golden as sunlight careened across the billions of minute droplets.

After a moment's confusion, Slats realized he had slept the rest of the night on the balcony. He cursed to himself as he rose and the mesh chair tried to hold him. He ran his hand across his back. It puckered liked alligator hide and had the sensitivity of a brush burn. Standing hurt. But so did sitting.

He made his way painfully inside, hoping his display of flesh had gone unnoticed by other patrons of the hotel and to the shower.

When the shower steamed in its plastic shell, he stepped under the pelting water. The hot water began erasing the pattern the chair had etched into his skin, and the mixture of pain and pleasure keyed a memory of the Hotel Kittina tee shirt when first he'd seen it spread across a shapely young chest on their arrival. "Hotel Kittina --D.W.T.G.D.W."

Olivia had noticed him looking at the shirt, and the woman wearing it.

"Cute shirt, huh?"

"Sure is. I wonder what it means."

"Do you?" she asked. "Or do you just want to get close to her?"

"Olivia!"

He grinned, sheepishly.

"Well, ask her. But, no body-English!"

They walked up to the well endowed young woman together, and Slats asked his question.

"Would you believe, " she replied. "This is the only tee shirt I could find on this whole island. You'd think somebody could run a decent concession here. It means 'Don't Waste The God Damned Water.' Not very inspired. Huh?"

Olivia had watched Slats watching the girl during their exchange. As the young woman departed, she looked up at Slats.

"I didn't know you were such a tit man, " she commented.

Mixed with the pleasure and pain of the scalding water pelting away the checkerboard on his back and buttocks was a terrible longing to see his wife again. Momentarily he considered foregoing the trip to South Caicos and grabbing the next plane for home.

God alone knew when that plane might fly.

But Slats knew he couldn't walk away from what must be the answer to the mystery that had begun in a firefight in an Irish Channel walkup.

He finished his shower and dressed, discovering as he put on his watch that it was already eight a.m. The South Caicos flight, if it flew, was scheduled for nine.

He grabbed his camera case and the map atop it, stopped in the dining room for juice, toast and coffee, and scanned the map.

It would be a long boat ride if the airline didn't fly. What he planned was possible, but much more challenging without the plane. In addition to speed, the plane's altitude would allow him to scan for the towing vessel he sought.

The waitress deposited his order and walked away.

Slats stared at the chart as he slathered jam on the toast, remembering the flight in from Miami; the long archipelago of islands, their beaches so white against the blue, sometime azure waters.

In an unbidden flash, Slats saw the President standing at his podium during his televised announcement yesterday.

"I shall go to Colombia!"

There had been a map on the dais providing background to the picture, a map similar to the chart he had before him. He could see the islands of the Bahamas and Caribbean looking like stepping stones from Miami to South America.

A bit of jelly dripped onto Slats' chart.

The President would be flying right by him. Air Force One would be following the archipelago and would probably be within a few miles of Grand Turk. And he and the President would be in the air at the same time. That is if Slats' flight got into the air.

Or would the fact that the President's plane was in the vicinity ground the island hopper?

Slats glanced at his watched. His flight was scheduled in only twenty minutes. He hurriedly signed his check and headed for the hotel entrance.

He slid into the back seat of one of two ancient Chevrolet taxis parked at the front entrance, and in ten minutes was at the airport.

But there was no one at the counter where the sign for the island hopper hung.

Slats wondered if there was a cosmic conspiracy to keep him from South Caicos.

A heavy-set black man, an occupant of the Customs Office, excused himself when Slats inquired about the plane. He vanished through an unlettered door into the rear of the building.

Several young people, the boys dark and lean, the girls angular and displaying, joked noisily about one of the half-dozen slot machines that dotted the tiny lobby. Except for the young lady hauling the machine's handle, each held a beer bottle in one hand, occasionally pausing in animated conversation to take long draws from the dark vessels.

The girl at the machine howled with laughter each time the whirring logos chimed home. Several times Slats heard the tinkle of coins into the machine's metal maw.

The big man reappeared.

"She'll be here." He went back to his cubbyhole office.

When SHE appeared she was a pretty but disheveled young woman, a light sheen glistening on her black skin. He noticed the huskiness in her voice when she asked how she could help him, and he thought he detected double entendre in the question.

"The plane," she said, "I'm told, will fly. But it will be 'bout thirty minutes late."

Her voice was losing some of its sultriness.

He asked about a ticket.

"See de pilot."

She exited through the door from which she had appeared, with what Slats thought an exaggerated shake of her hips. Several other voices emanated from the briefly opened door.

Slats wandered across the small lobby, avoiding the slot machines, and found a day-old Miami Herald on one of the hard plastic seats. He scanned it for coverage of the President's new conference, then realized the story had broken too late yesterday. He flipped through the scattered sections and stopped at the comics. He searched for, found, and savored his favorite, Andy Capp.

He chuckled at the bar room repartee involving Andy, his wife, and the comely barmaid.

He glanced at his watch, then to the window overlooking the tarmac.

Where's that damned plane?

As if on cue he heard the high pitched scream of turboprops and a small twin rolled into view. Slats watched it go past the Computer Dynamics building and wondered if Maria was there. He hadn't seen her at all last night. She had said she would be working late. Would she be back at work this early on a Saturday?

As he watched, the hanger doors slid slowly open.

The Lear was parked outside the building, clear of the doors, its wing tie downs lying on the tarmac. Must be putting it inside for some maintenance, Slats thought.

Then a plane rolled from the hangar and started down the taxiway toward the end of the runway. The unexpected appearance of the plane startled Slats. Then, suddenly, he realized what he was seeing.

It was the Harrier.

And it was stripped of the ornamentation that had adorned it the night he had seen it in the hangar, the night he had heard it leave the island. Why was it back?

Slats' mind was dancing. Suddenly the mental refuse of the past three weeks began sorting itself out. The Harrier rolling toward the runway was part of a new picture taking shape in his brain. The image was bright, some segments sharp and clearly drawn on the canvass of his mind.

De Arrellano was at the center. He could see him clearly. Computer Dynamics wasn't real. And drug smuggling was just one corner of the picture.

But what about Maria. Her part of the picture was smudged and hazy. Was she just a pawn in a political chess game, or was she a player?

But clearest of all was the fact that the President of The United States was flying into a trap. The Colombian hostage situation was a ruse, bait to draw the President to Grand Turk. De Arrellano wanted to shoot him down with a stolen fighter plane!

Why?

Slats grabbed his case and pushed through the door onto the airfield. The chubby Customs agent couldn't see him, and the kids at the slot machines didn't even know he existed.

It was too late to stop the Harrier.

It was at the end of the runway, turning, its strange, stubby nose pointed west. It's thundering take-off roll reached Slats as he darted up to the Lear, keeping the craft between himself and the windows along the side of the Computer Dynamics building. The door of the Lear stood open.

Slats had no plan beyond confounding de Arrellano, and he hoped the tall Latin hadn't been aboard the Harrier. He was relieved when he heard de Arrellano's distinct baritone barking orders inside the hangar.

Near the jet, a small tarpaulin had been thrown off a stack of fifty-gallon drums. As the voices grew louder, Slats pulled an end of the tarp over himself and a couple of the containers.

It was hot on the tarmac. A strong kerosene order almost overpowered Slats as he peeked through a hole in the canvas. He watched de Arrellano and two men approach the Lear. He drew a sharp and painful breath when Maria stepped from the shadowed hangar to follow de Arrellano to the plane.

After a moment of animated conversation in Spanish, too rapid for Slats to understand, the two men headed back into the hangar. Maria and de Arrellano disappeared into the Lear. Slats watched the two men walk into the stall, then sprinted up to the little jet, still carrying the case with the camera he had intended to use at South Caicos, and his weapons. As he pulled to a halt bent double under the tail, he heard its turbofan engines begin to wind up.

He listened at the door and heard voices from the front of the plane. He glanced quickly inside. A partially drawn curtain separated the passenger area, outfitted with two small tables and seating on each side, from the cockpit.

Slats stepped carefully into the plane, but as his weight came down, the craft bounced slightly.

"Carlos?"

The voice was de Arrellano's, muffled by the increasing pitch of the engine.

"Si?" Slats replied.

De Arrellano obviously had expected one of the men back, and the engine's increasing volume all but drowned his reply in harsh Spanish. Slats drew himself into the seat beside the door, hidden by the partially drawn curtain from the cockpit. He didn't attempt to reply to de Arrellano's brief tirade.

"Carlos?"

This time, there was anger in the voice.

"Si?" Slats replied, almost yelling.

This time de Arrellano responded in hard and angry English.

"Lock us up, dammit, Carlos! We've got to get up there."

Slats leaned back along the wall, slid aft and slammed the door down, securing the latch. The high whine had changed to a roar. A subtle shift in the air flow and pressure told Slats that they were now sealed from the outside, in a cabin capable of keeping them comfortable several miles high.

He was not reassured.

The plane was rolling now, and Slats was wondering what his next move should be. He had had no contingency plans. He thought he knew what the man in the cockpit was doing, but what about Maria? Why was she aboard? Perhaps he should leave the next move to de Arrellano. Was he armed?

As the plane gathered speed, the engine roar drowned all other ambient noise. Slats clicked open the camera case and withdrew his big Ruger magnum. He stuck the gun in his belt and shoved the camera case under the seat.

The plane was ascending rapidly now. The acceleration pressed Slats comfortably into his seat, but the plane lurched as it climbed. Slats thought that de Arrellano was not the most expert pilot.

He examined the cabin carefully. He noted its width, the availability of emergency exits.

Okay. I'm here. Now, what?

Slats glanced from the window. A few puffy clouds poked brilliant white heads up from fairy-tale blue waters. They were already quite high and still climbing. A white-hot sun flared through the lens of the window, stabbing the floor with a bright shaft.

Slats imagined Lt. Col. Charlie Adkins in the Harrier hanging somewhere above them, waiting.

The President of The United States was flying into a lethal trap. How could Slats warn him?

He must confront de Arrellano.

But that confrontation could only end badly. And even if Slats could get the best of de Arrellano, would that stop Adkins and the Harrier?

As if in answer Slats heard the radio crackle to life.

An excited voice, a voice that Slats knew must belong to Charlie Adkins, burst loudly through the plane.

"I've got them! I've got them! They're at three-zero thousand fifteen miles in front of you."

Slats pictured de Arrellano and Maria straining their eyes, searching ahead. Again the question, what was Maria doing here? She obviously had lied about her relationship to de Arrellano.

De Arrellano was speaking forcefully into the radio.

"Switching channels," he said, and repeated it. The radio repeated his words. Then de Arrellano was speaking again.

"Air Force One! Air Force One! This is El Carib. Acknowledge!"

Chapter Forty Five

El Carib!

Slats saw in his mind the news picture of de Arrellano. The name El Carib would be known on Air Force One. Perhaps not by the pilots, but certainly by the President's staff.

There was no immediate reply. De Arrellano repeated his message. Still the radio remained silent. The little jet's engine roar had diminished, and the "G" forces had vanished. Slats leaned forward and tried to peer past the curtain into the cockpit. But he couldn't see past the heavy drape.

"Air Force One! Acknowledge this transmission!"

A thin, reedy voice replied.

"This is Air Force One."

"Thank you, " de Arrellano replied. "To whom am I speaking?"

A reply was slow in coming, but when it did, it emanated from the plane's speaker in the same reedy voice.

"I am Erik Grosvenor of the Central Intelligence Agency."

"Do you speak for the President?" de Arrellano asked.

Again the pause.

"I do."

De Arrellano's voice took on a new quality, malevolent and commanding.

"Then you will direct your pilot to look to his left and slightly below. He will see a Lear jet. He will follow that plane to Salt Cay, where he will land."

De Arrellano knew that there were ears other than those aboard Air Force One listening. Two fighters, F/A-18s, were in position a half mile off both of the big plane's wings. Even as he finished issuing his instructions, he saw them altering course to intercept him.

Behind the cabin curtains, Slats grew more confused. He braced with his right hand on the cabin ceiling as the little plane wheeled into a tight turn.

Land Air Force One on a tiny island in the Bahamas?

The reedy voice took longer to reply this time, and de Arrellano cleared his throat just as the radio bleated.

"Ah," Grosvenor whined, "the pilot says he cannot land on Salt Cay."

Salt Cay? Salt Cay? Slats remembered the low sandstone slab glistening with shallow salt ponds. How could anyone land on Salt Cay?

Maria shoved the throttles open, and the Lear jumped ahead. The plane had swung through a tight one-eighty and de Arrellano could no longer see the fighter escort. But he knew they were behind him, and undoubtedly closing fast.

Now it was up to Charlie.

Chapter Forty Six

Brian Poston and Harve Negrel, both light colonels in the U.S. air force and pilots of the F/A-18 Hornet escort fighters, later said they would have fared much better had they been aware of the Harrier suspended in the sun above. Their planes were faster, more heavily armed, and almost as maneuverable as the little British fighter. True, they should have known he was there. They had seen the blip on their radars a few minutes earlier, a target crossing their paths east to west some fifteen thousand feet above them.

Negrel told those assembled at the press conference that he had assumed it to be a Cuban jet, out to check on their flight. And when the Lear had begun its broadcasts demanding that Air Force One follow the Lear, he and Poston had seen it, not the Harrier, an unknown radar blip, as the threat. Poston said he thought the Lear might be a terrorist intent on a kamikaze attack on the President. He was closing rapidly on the Lear when he felt his plane shudder as the Harrier's cannon fire tore through the tail and ripped apart the control surfaces.

Charlie had lived part of his fantasy, falling from the sun onto the F-18s like a falcon stooping on its prey. He fired one burst, a microsecond before flashing past the fighters.

Negrel hadn't had time to understand what had happened. He peeled off when he saw the tail of Poston's plane spew metal shards. He watched as Poston ejected, saw his chute open, then turned to find the threat. But by that time the Harrier had pulled out into a screaming loop that again lifted sunward of the F-18. And as Negrel make his first clearing turn, Charlie struck.

Negrel saw him coming and threw the fighter into a tight right turn.

But he was too slow, and the Harrier's puffing cannon blew away half of his right wing. With his plane tumbling out of control, Negrel chopped the throttle and ejected. In seconds, another chute billowed in the breeze.

And the Harrier was gone.

"I have never seen anybody fly like that," Poston concluded.

Slats had seen little of the fight, the planes flashing past the tiny starboard windows, but he had heard it. The strange, crunchy sound of mid-air fire, impact, and explosion in the distance.

The Harrier had destroyed the fighter escort. Air Force One could be forced to land.

The Harrier was a VTOL aircraft. It could land damn near anywhere.

The Lear's radio crackled.

"Got them both!" The voice sounded triumphant.

"Good!" de Arrellano replied. "Excellent." He sounded smug. "Air Force One, you will follow us."

After a moment, the voice that had identified itself as Erik Grosvenor replied.

"We will do as you instruct. But you must be aware of the consequences of your actions."

Slats thought the CIA chief an inept fool. How could the CIA let some half-baked terrorist group snatch its top man and the President of The United States?

"Your pilot will make a belly landing on Salt Cay," de Arrellano was saying. "The salt ponds are shallow and more than two miles long. If your pilot is skillful, no one will be hurt.

"When you are on the ground, the President will leave the plane, alone, and walk to the edge of the pond. He will be picked up there. Do you understand?"

The reply was slow in coming.

"I don't think we can let the President leave the plane."

De Arrellano sighed deeply.

"Then you must be aware of the consequences," he said. "I do not wish to take more lives, American lives, but if you force my hand..."

Slats wondered if Adkins would have the balls to shoot down Air Force One.

Yes, he would!

The Lear flew on. Slats pictured Air Force One tailing behind, the Harrier buzzing about the large plane like a fly teasing a dog. By now, assuming the conversation between de Arrellano and Air Force One had been monitored, a new flight of Hornets would be scrambled.

But from where? Homestead? At least six hundred miles away. At best their ETA would be thirty minutes.

By that time, the President would be ensconced in the Harrier, en route to God Knows Where.

Slats had to do something. And he had to do it now!

Unable to stand straight in the tiny cabin, he hunched forward, grabbed the curtain separating the cabin and the cockpit, and ripped it from its track with his left hand, bringing the big Ruger magnum up with his right. The curtain clattered away from its carrier.

"What the Hell!" de Arrellano shouted.

The tall Latin was in the right-hand seat. He craned his head back over his left shoulder to look disbelievingly at Slats and the big handgun.

"Sainte Maria..." he muttered.

It was then that Slats realized that Maria was flying the Lear. She half turned, not releasing the yoke.

"Slats!" she screamed.

Slats wanted to say something, but couldn't find the words. He forced his attention back to de Arrellano.

"It's time to call it off, de Arrellano," he said, as calmly and forcefully as he could. "Tell Adkins to take the Harrier back to Grand Turk."

When de Arrellano didn't move, Slats felt compelled to continue his monolog.

"There never was any drug conspiracy, was there? Was it all a plot to ...what? Kidnap the President? I've known egomaniacs before, but no one to match your insanity!"

De Arrellano was halfway out of his seat, perched on the cushion, one foot in the narrow space between the seats in the cramped cockpit. The eyes in the lean Hispanic face glistened. The face gleamed red, flushed with blood lust. Framed against the bright sky filling the windshield behind him, he was more apparition than real, a Latin demon conjuring Satan from within.

"You stupid cop!" the ghost screamed, his voice a shrill whine. "I'm going back to Colombia, you stupid cop! And we're taking your President with us! We have him, and we have the power. And we will have the money! More money that you can even dream of. You stupid cop. And you think you can stop us!"

Slats saw that de Arrellano was moving, very slowly, while he ranted. Slats saw too that Maria was watching, and listening, her expression incredulous, her eyes wide, as though she saw the same demon Slats saw.

"And you think you can stop us?" de Arrellano screamed. "What are you doing on my airplane? Kill him, Raul."

Slats almost turned to see if there really was someone else in the cabin. In that instant de Arrellano threw himself at Slats, his left fist driving into Slats' temple. Draping himself down Slats, de Arrellano reached with his right hand for the Ruger.

Slats knew he shouldn't fire the big handgun in the cabin of the tiny jet, but the smashing blow to his head roared through his consciousness and the response was automatic.

He pulled the trigger.

An explosion that in the tiny cabin roared like a ton of TNT tore de Arrellano from Slats and threw him against the small forward window. The heavy slug struck de Arrellano in the upper chest and ripped through his body before tearing the window panel from its frame. De Arrellano was dead before the explosive decompression crushed his body and spewed it from the side of the plane.

Slats fell across the cabin, behind the co-pilot's seat, wedged between the fastenings and the hanging closet. He felt the plane veer off and heard Maria scream. The plane howled as the rushing air tugged at his shirt and hair. His ears popped and screamed.

Then suddenly it was quieter.

Gravity returned.

He looked up and saw Maria, her face set, eyes wide, hauling slowly back on the yoke with her left hand, her right on the throttles.

God, she can fly this thing!

"I've got it Slats!" she yelled over the scream of the wind. "I've got it!"

Slats pulled himself into the co-pilot's seat and looked out. They were much lower now, surely only a couple hundred feet above the water. But they were climbing.

"I've got it, " Maria repeated.

Slats looked back at the hole where the window had been. There was no way to stop the screaming wind. Another sound overlay the howl. The radio! Its tinny voice was all but drowned in the cacophony of destruction.

"What the God Damn Hell is going on over there? De Arrellano? Maria? Answer me! Damn it, answer me! You're still flying. There must be somebody in there."

Slats looked at Maria.

"It's over, Maria," he yelled over the wind noise. "It's over!"

She nodded.

"Yes. I think I'm glad."

Her voice was barely audible over the wind shriek. "I almost backed out last week when he told us what we had to do."

She looked over at Slats, her concentration still locked on flying the plane.

"It was his ...dream Slats. It changed him."

A voice burst from the radio.

"...what the God Damn Hell is going on?"

Maria looked at Slats for a moment, then picked up the microphone.

"Charlie?"

"Maria! Damn... What happened? The big boy tried to make a break for it, but I herded him back. What now?"

"Charlie, de Arrellano's dead. It's all over. There's a man sitting here with a gun on me. He killed Jusquevera. It's all over, Charlie. It's over, understand?"

Chapter Forty Seven

Charlie didn't understand.

Never in his life had he felt a thrill as great as the moment that first F/A-18 sprouted shards and fell streaming smoke into the sea. Except perhaps for the second F/A-18. That had been some fantastic flying. There was nothing in the sky that could touch him.

Nothing!

He and the harrier. Together they could do anything.

Especially after this was over. Especially in Colombia.

Now he knew why he lived. Right now, in the cockpit of this airplane he could never die. In his plane, he was the dragon of Chinese mythology, ready to eat the sun.

No Maria, I don't understand!

So de Arrellano's dead. So who needs him. I've still got the Big Bird. El Carib still holds the embassy. Who better to lead them than me!

Charlie's voice crackled through the cockpit.

"Air Force One, this is the harrier. Proceed to Salt Key."

Maria looked at Slats, her eyes wide.

"Oh God, Slats!"

They saw the harrier at the same moment, dead ahead on a collision course, fire flashing from its stubby nose.

"He's shooting at us!" Maria screamed.

The harrier flashed above them, the roar of its engine and the stench of burned kerosene filling the cockpit.

"Get us down, Maria!" Slats yelled.

Maria pointed toward a small island several miles ahead.

Slats craned around in his seat, trying to find the harrier.

The radio crackled.

"Lear, if you copy...this is Air Force One...that Harrier is making a run at you from behind."

"Dive Maria!" Slats yelled.

But Maria was intent on the island ahead. Perhaps she hadn't heard the transmission.

"Lear ...the Harrier's slowed. He'll have a good bead on you."

Slats turned to his right. He was lifting the big Ruger, pointing it to the space where the window had been. He saw nothing but blue sky, but he leveled the weapon, turned at the waist, holding the .44 in both hands. This is insane, he thought. You can't fight a warplane with a handgun.

A banging tore through the plane. It sounded like someone pounding on the trunk of a car with a three-pound sledge, and with each crashing blow the plane shuddered.

But the Lear was still flying.

And then Slats saw the Harrier.

It had slowed to the point that its speed almost matched that of the Lear. Adkins meant to be certain of his kill. From behind, he had pumped several cannon shots into the Lear at point-blank range.

But the plane flew on. It's amazing we're still here, Slats thought. Maria's some fly girl.

The Harrier's wingtip almost touched the Lear. And Slats imagined he saw a puzzled expression on Adkins' face. Slats let his hands lead the Harrier, composing a sight picture over the barrel of the magnum, and pulled the trigger; once, twice, again and again, not waiting for a new sight picture, as the big gun jumped in his hand, just pulling instinctively as he had in ten-meter competitions.

There, less than a hundred feet away sat his target, a dim silhouette, dark in the backlighted cockpit.

On the range, Slats never saw the splash of the slugs into the targets. And he couldn't see the spray of bullets he fired at the Harrier. He didn't see the jacketed slug that cut through the fighter's fuselage immediately below the cockpit seal. The other slugs careened off the hardened canopy, but one sheared through the metal exactly at Slats' aiming point (the base of the silhouette) and smashed through Captain Charlie Adkins' pelvis.

Even after ripping through the tough metal and ricocheting from the seat the slug still carried enough kinetic energy to crush the bones in Charlie's right hip and tear his grip from the stick.

All Slats saw was the plane peel away and dive headlong into the water a split-second below. It was incomprehensible but...

"I got him! I got him, Maria!" Slats shouted, turning toward her.

"I got the bastard..."

He stopped, staring.

Maria wasn't there anymore.

Most of her body remained. It slumped forward, her beautiful face resting against the yoke, holding it motionless.

The seat belt held her in place, her arms limp. But much of her midsection was gone, ripped away by the huge projectile that had torn through the plane from aft forward to pass through the back of her seat. She sat there dead, shredded by lead and shrapnel, flying the plane.

Horrified more than by any police crime scene he'd ever witnessed, Slats looked away, forward, and there in the windshield was the island, rushing at him with incredible speed.

My God, I'm going to die!

The fear bloomed in his mind, but the words never formed. His brain shifted gear and the world, and his dash toward death slowed. He saw the throttles, still forward against the lock, and yanked them back. The engine roar vanished, leaving only the howl of the wind. The plane was tipping toward the island, and the salt ponds yawned like a gaping maw about to swallow the jet. He looked down at his waist and saw and meshed the dangling seatbelt ends.

"Maria!" he screamed.

God, how do you fly this thing?

He cried out loud as he grabbed the yoke and yanked back on it. Maria's body crumpled back into her seat. The nose of the plane moved up against the mounting earth, slowly, so slowly. He saw ahead the glint of sunlight on water, water and sand.

Then the plane hit.

He felt it coming apart about him. Something crashed against the back of his seat. The windshield sloughed away, and water cascaded over him, crushing him backward. His mind, still filming in slow motion, wondered if he would drown here, in inches of salt water instead of in the depths, a death from which a beautiful woman had saved him but days earlier.

His mind also recorded in slow motion the flailing in the seat next to him of Maria's body.

On Air Force One, the pilots watched as the Lear splashed and skipped across the salt pond, coming slowly to a sputtering halt.

They watched as it tore across the surface of Salt Cay, ripping apart, the tail and wings falling away as the fuselage splashed a mile across the shallow ponds before nosing over forward.

They watched and assumed no one could live through the crash. So they flew on, seeking a haven for their precious human cargo.

But when the US Army Reserve choppers (two from a squadron on maneuvers in the Bahamas), responding to the Lear's automated EPIRB (Emergency Position Indicating Radio Beacon) landed less than thirty minutes later, they found Slats not only alive but conscious. The pain of two broken arms left him less than rational, but he was alive.

The rescuers wondered at him, and the body of the woman in the left seat.

But they did their job, and slowly worked him free of what remained of the cockpit.

During the forty-five minutes it took to free him, they wondered at his babbling: nonsense about a plot to kidnap the President of The United States, about a Colombian drug lord masterminding the plot, about a beautiful woman diver with a broken leg.

They finally freed him, removed the other body, placed him on a stretcher, gave him a shot for his pain, and loaded him into the chopper.

They slid the stretcher in and secured it to the forward bulkhead, and Slats felt a terrible rushing fear. He craned his neck to see through the chopper's wide doorway. The remains of the Lear were bright under the noon sun, and so was the glistening black plastic in which they had wrapped Maria.

Maria, a dream never realized.

He would give Maria a funeral, in Bogota.

He owed her ...or her memory...that much.

And he would tell Olivia the whole story.

No!

Most of the story.

Not Quite All!

Some must remain his, alone.

"I love you, Ollie," he mumbled as the medication began its work, numbing both body and mind.

He drifted vaguely away from his pain.

You were right Johnny.

You sure were.

I'm never completely wrong.

End

If you enjoyed The Grand Turk File, look for another tale of terror and intrigue in The Dolphin Complex coming in paperback in Summer of 2016. Here you will meet Hickory Logan, a hard hitting woman in a detective's uniform, and Dr. James Crabtree, researcher and bio-engineering genius. Can dolphin pose a nuclear threat to the nation's Capitol?

The Dolphin Complex

Red Logan was hunkered down next to the Humvee's left front wheel.

He folded his lanky frame in several places to assure that the vehicle shielded him from rifle fire emanating from the house a hundred feet away.

A furious fusillade had greeted A-Company, first battalion, 407th Special Forces when their vehicles pulled to a halt in front of what was a rather strange building for northern Afghanistan. In the early morning darkness, it looked for all the world like a California ranch style home. But there was no Audi parked in the driveway.

The firefight lasted less than fifteen minutes. There was only an occasional round pinging off the slate-riddled soil and an occasional burst of automatic fire keeping the soldiers from charging the structure. Red wondered why the squads weren't using some of the heavier weapons. He knew the unit was armed with shoulder-fired missiles and a Carl Gustav 84mm recoilless rifle, but so far the big stuff had been silent.

The tip had placed Azam al-Zarahiri, who at the top of the Al-Qaeda planning council had overseen personnel organization of the 9/11 attacks, at the scene.

Numerous such tips over the past two years had come to nothing. Most of them originated in minds overly-motivated to garner the twenty million dollars American offered for the capture of several of the world's most wanted terrorists.

At least one Osama bin Laden look-alike had been found dead. And it took weeks before the body was identified. The man had been killed and left in a house to which an Afghan directed U.S. forces. Not only did he not get the reward he sought, but he was jailed by his countrymen for mutilating the corpse by cutting off its hands and feet.

Army intelligence, a title Red thought oxymoronic, had considered tonight's tip more credible than most since it had come in anonymously. The tipster hadn't mentioned the reward; only an emotional patriotism for his country. So the Special Forces unit had headed out in the predawn darkness for a two-hour drive north from Kabul into the mountainous terrain.

"Red?"The voice belonged to the figure squeezed into the wheel well behind him.

He could barely see Jessie's sinewy shape, strangely gawky where the video camera and its now-dark lights rested on her right thigh. "Yeah, what?" he whispered.

"Should I get some shots?" Jessie asked, cocking her left hand back over her shoulder.

"Hell No. Just keep your ass down! Besides, nothing to shoot."

Before he could finish his sentence an amplified Afghan voice rang out from the vicinity of the lead Humvee, imploring the occupants of the house to surrender. The answer was a three-shot rifle volley, the rounds pinging off the hard pack and whining away into the darkness.

"Now!" Jessie said, pushing past Red and swinging the camera onto her shoulder, leaning onto the Hummer's hood.

"No!" Red hollered, trying to pull Jessie to the ground. But it was too late. All but instantaneously the light on Jessie's camera flared brilliantly, then died in a crash of glass and the harsh double bark of a Kalashnikov. The rounds zinged away into the darkness, but Red heard in the report the crunch of bone.

"Jessie!" he screamed. She tumbled backward across him coiling over then coming to rest on her left side facing him. He grabbed the little clip-on LED flashlight from his belt and looked at her. She lay as though napping, her face on her left arm, eyes open, and a portion of the left side of her face missing, bleeding heavily from a gaping crease running from her cheekbone back through her left ear. He grabbed the bandanna she used to tie back her hair, and crammed it into the hollow beneath her eye, and started screaming for a medic.

More shots rang out from the house, and from farther up the line came a loud male voice.

"Put out that damned light, idiot!"

A tremendous explosion from behind him was followed by a brilliant flash and ear-splitting bang from the house.

The recoilless.

Then silence.

The troops were moving now. He heard them crunching across the rocky soil, heading toward the silent house.

A scrabbling behind him took Red's attention from the house. He turned to see a young man wearing medic bars leaning over Jessie's prone body. He watched as the medic fingered Jessie's throat, looking for a pulse.

"Got it," he muttered. "She's alive. Gotta keep her that way."

"You a doc?" Red asked.

"Close as you're gonna get out here. I'm going for a medivac." He vanished into the darkness.

Red watched Jessie. She didn't move. In the darkness, he couldn't tell if she were even breathing. But the medic had said she was alive.

"Well...fuck me," she groaned.

"God damn! Jessie!" Red said.

"Red? " Her voice trembled. "That you? Am I dead?"

were loading her into the chopper. Red walked alongside, scrunched beneath the rotor blades.

"Take off your cap!" the medic yelled.

"What?"

"Your cap! It could ruin the engine," the medic said. He pointed at the turbojet intake just above them. Red yanked the Cleveland Indian's baseball cap from his head and stuffed it in his fatigues pocket.

"I'll make it Red!" Jessie said, almost drowned out by the copter's engine noise.

"I know you will, Jess. I'll see you soon."

The medic jumped into the open door behind the stretcher, and the chopper lifted off immediately. Red stood motionless, the blowing dirt crusting his eyes and covering his hair. He watched the chopper spin sharply to the right, lower its nose and speed toward the horizon. "I know you will, Jess," he mumbled. He hoped he was right.

He turned and walked to the house, still lit by the headlamps of several jeeps and Humvees. Red walked up to the front entrance where the cannon shell had torn away much of the facade. A cold wind whipped over the remains of the exterior wall, a wind that smelled of grit, grime, and gunpowder. He stepped gingerly over fallen stone and into the cavern left by the explosion.

Two pole lamps powered by a little Honda generator filled the room with a glaring brilliance and a high-pitched thrum. Several file-sized boxes sat against a rear wall, and the paper was strewn everywhere. Two fatigue-clad soldiers were picking at the paper, squinting at the sheets in the harsh light, and stuffing the materials into empty boxes.

He saw Resume standing in the far corner of the room, near a stack of intact file boxes. He appeared to be deep concentration, staring at a folder that had obviously been a part of the paper stampede the troopers were trying to coral. His expression bordered on ludicrous, his face twisted as he tried to read the documents. When Red was close enough he saw the document wasn't in English. And there were several drawings on the page.

The figures were precise and the words were typeset, not hand-lettered.

Resume looked up.

"Hey, Red. She gone?" he asked, loudly over the roar of the tiny generator.

"She's on the bird. I think she'll make it. She's a tough kid."

"Good. Good. Hm...Don't know if I should show you this. How's your Arabic?"

"Poor, why?"

"Got some kind of a manual here. Interesting title page."

He pointed to a soldier trying to sort the mess. He was a slight, olive-skinned youngster with a three-day beard. "Jilly here says the title is Small Nuclear Devices"

"What?"

"Jilly's Iranian. He says this is a manual for assembling and handling small nukes, like warheads, or suitcase bombs. There's a bunch of handwritten stuff here too."

He hesitated, looking Red in the eye.

"He reads it like Al-Qaeda's got ... a bomb, a nuke."